# THE ROYAL WE

ALSO BY HEATHER COCKS AND JESSICA MORGAN

*Spoiled*

*Messy*

# THE ROYAL WE

HEATHER COCKS
AND
JESSICA MORGAN

New York Boston

This book is a work of fiction. All of the characters, incidents, and dialogue (except for incidental references to public figures, products, publications, and services) are imaginary and are not intended to refer to any living persons or to disparage any company's products or services.



Grand Central Publishing
Hachette Book Group
1290 Avenue of the Americas
New York, NY 10104

HachetteBookGroup.com

Printed in the United States of America

RRD-C

First Edition: April 2015
10 9 8 7 6 5 4 3 2 1

Grand Central Publishing is a division of Hachette Book Group, Inc.
The Grand Central Publishing name and logo is a trademark of Hachette Book Group, Inc.



Library of Congress Cataloging-in-Publication Data
Cocks, Heather.
The royal we / Heather Cocks, Jessica Morgan. — First edition.
pages ; cm
ISBN 978-1-4555-5710-3 (hardcover) — ISBN 978-1-4555-5712-7 (ebook) — ISBN 978-1-4789-0334-5 (audio download) 1. Princes—Fiction. 2. Royal weddings—Fiction. 3. Man-woman relationships—Fiction. I. Morgan, Jessica. II. Title.
PS3603.O294R69 2015
813'.6—dc23

2014049047

*To Brettne, a queen among women*

# THE HOUSE OF LYONS (c. 2007)

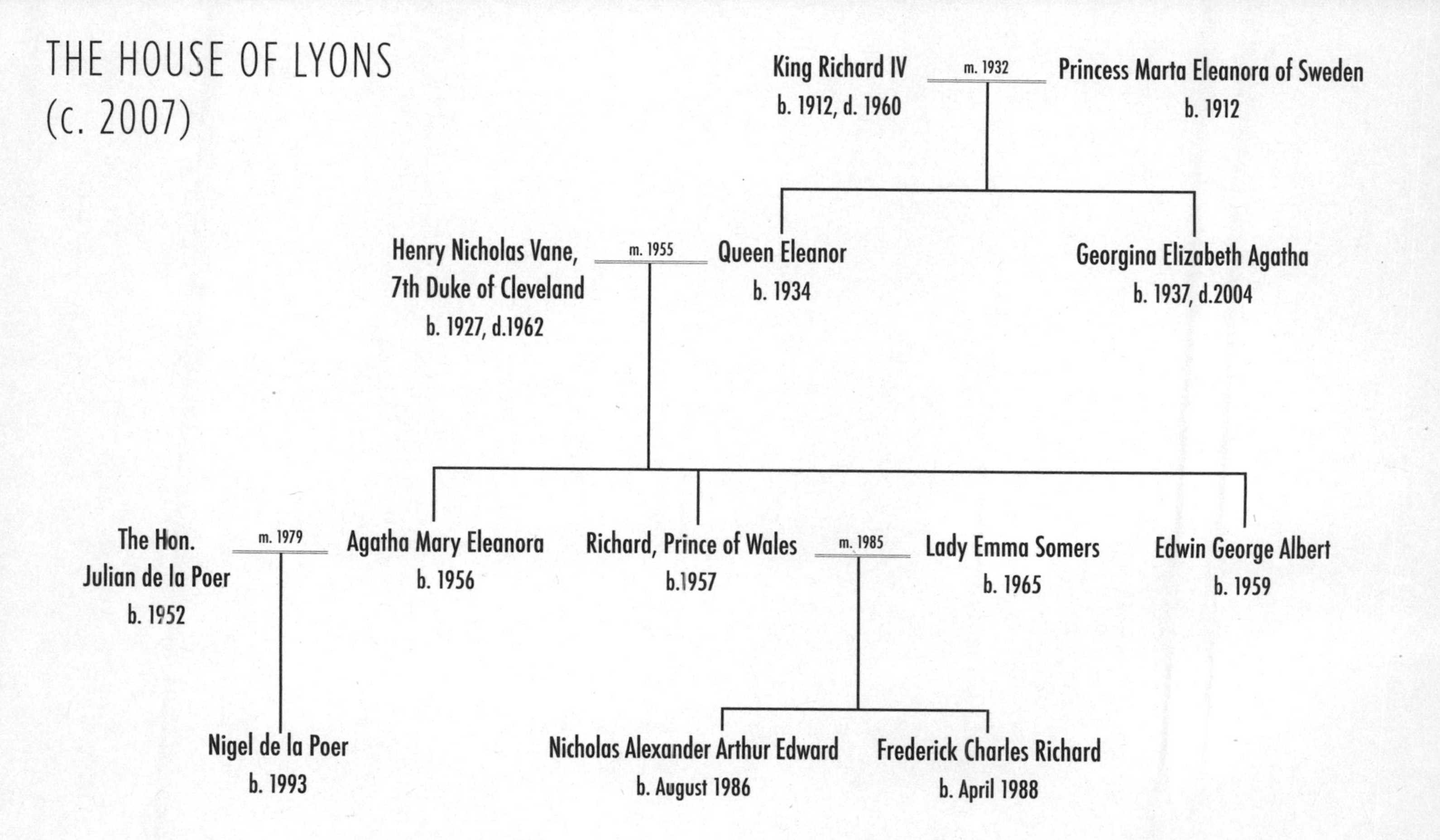

# THE ROYAL WE

# PROLOGUE

I don't know what to do.

The calls and texts are starting to pile up, relentless and suffocating. I'm afraid of what will happen if I don't give him what he wants, and I'm afraid of what will happen if I do. The TV isn't soothing my nerves, given that global hysteria over my impending wedding is the lead story on every channel. I can't lose myself in a book, because the only ones in my hotel room are dusty old historical tomes, and there are few things less reassuring right now than reading up on the spotty fidelity (and sobriety) of Nick's ancestors. And my sister is of no comfort to me. Not anymore. I'm officially in this alone. With every jolt of my cell phone, I feel more and more like the proverbial chaos theory butterfly from high school science—the one that flutters its wings in one place and causes a tsunami somewhere else. I always felt bad for that butterfly, being blamed for a meteorological mess just for doing what nature ingrains in it to do. Now I want to step on the damn thing for flapping around like a fool. Because I am that butterfly. That is, assuming I'm not the tsunami.

If only I were home, so I could freak out on familiar territory. But instead I'm stuck at The Goring in ritzy Belgravia, or Bexingham Palace, as the press calls it. Her Majesty has never met a space nor a situation on which she didn't impose her will, so Queen Eleanor's army of decorators dropped six figures to renovate the penthouse into bridal headquarters, evicting all The Goring's furnishings—although they thoughtfully left the life-size portrait of Queen Victoria I that sits, unnervingly, right inside the shower behind thick safety glass—and replacing them with priceless accent tables and figurines, ornate and uncomfortable sofas, landscape portraits pretending to be out for cleaning from the National Gallery, and a grand piano littered with portraits of the Lyons ancestors who will become my family tomorrow. It is a parade of mustache wax and sadness, only mildly mitigated by the official photo of Nick and me. I love that picture, which is lucky, because it's for sale the world over on thimbles, wastebaskets, tea towels, paper dolls, condom boxes, and—my favorite—actual condoms. If she were cheekier, Her Majesty would have put those items on the piano. As it stands, I've never heard any of the senior royals even say the word *condom*, although I suspect Eleanor would pronounce it like my own grandmother did: as if it's the nickname of the local cad who scandalizes all the gossips in the retirement village. ("Did you see Con Dom at the grocery store? He was buying six boxes of wine and a frozen burrito. What does it *mean*?")

Suddenly, from across the room, a red beaded frame in the collection catches my eye. I could swear it wasn't there yesterday, and when I move closer, the sight of the photo inside gives me the chills. The press would salivate over it, which is precisely why I thought it was locked away in Mom's wall safe, behind a yard-sale portrait of a rich-looking lady whom she pretends is a distant moneyed aunt from the continent. In the picture, which Dad took on a family trip to Disney World, Lacey and I are eight. She is clutching Cinderella's hand with the same urgent glee you see in people waiting to hear if they're about to come on down on *The Price Is Right*, and wears a poufy pink gown and a tiara on her golden ringlets. I am a careful half step away, in shorts and Tevas, attempting a smile that fails to conceal my boredom. My dreams back then were to swim the individual medley at the Olympics, or play Major League Baseball; the Disney version of happily ever after didn't impress me, and you can see that all over my face, as clear as the adoration in Lacey's eyes. It is the perfect photo of mismatched twins, but beyond that, it's deeply ironic given who Lacey and I have become, which is exactly why I asked Mom to hide it. I look like I hate Cinderella, yet now, to the world, I *am* Cinderella. The headline writes itself, and so does the karmic warning: Be careful what you pointedly don't wish for, because one day you might find yourself getting armpit Botox to avoid headlines like THE DUCHESS OF SWEATSHIRE. Dragging this photo out reeks of Lacey, and ordinarily, I'd have assumed she did it for a laugh. But today it feels like a threat. When my phone vibrates again, I half expect it to be her.

It's not.

YOU CAN'T PRETEND NOTHING HAPPENED.

That much is abundantly clear. I just wish I had more time to think. Tomorrow morning, I am supposed to walk Westminster Abbey's three-hundred-foot aisle, wearing the biggest skirt of my life—the gown has its own room at The Goring—and pledge myself for eternity to Prince Nicholas of Wales, a king-in-waiting. I cannot tremble. I cannot twitch, even if Gaz weeps that high-pitched wail of his. I cannot disappoint, I cannot bend, I cannot break, because two billion people will be watching (one of whom might even be that tired, retired Cinderella, who hopefully won't recognize the kid who once regarded her with so much skepticism). So, no, I can't pretend nothing happened. But if I acknowledge it out loud…

My phone lights up and I jump so violently that I almost drop it.

"Morning, love," my mother says, in the England-via-Iowa accent she's adopted. The press has nicknamed her Fancy Nancy. "I'm actually looking for Lacey. Is she there?"

I snort.

"Bex, no swining," Mom says, parroting a pun of Dad's.

"The *Daily Mail* says she got a spray tan for three hours yesterday. Wherever she is, I'm sure she's happy. And orange."

"Cut it out, Rebecca." That was a hundred percent American. My mother's faux accent always disappears when she's irritated. "You're getting married tomorrow. Do your twin thing and apologize and fix it."

Irritation strains my voice. "I can't apologize if I wasn't wrong."

And I wasn't, not about *that*. I'm squarely in the wrong now—Mom has no idea—but then again, so is Lacey, and I can't always be the one to lay down my sword to keep the peace. Especially not when I'm under attack.

I hear a fumbling at the suite's front door. "Mom, I have to go. The Bex Brigade is here."

Within seconds the room is swarmed by stylists, seamstresses, security officers, and all manner of other Lyons operatives. I shove the blackmail-worthy photo deep behind a seat cushion. Out of sight, out of mind.

"Cheers, Bex, you look like microwaved shite," chirps my personal secretary, Cilla.

"I'm just overtired." It's technically not a lie. "Actually, is it okay if I take a few more minutes?"

Cilla cocks an eyebrow, then nods briskly and hands me my usual stack of newspapers and tabloids. I excuse myself to my bedroom and fan them out on the paisley comforter. I'm everywhere. The *Guardian*'s front-page piece, GREAT BEXPECTATIONS, is about international wedding fever. WE'RE SO BEXCITED!, screeches *The Sun*, before handicapping what I'll wear down the aisle. HALF HUMAN HALF CHEESE WHEEL BORN TO LEICESTER COUPLE: *Mother Weeps, "I Always Knew We'd Brie Blessed,"* claims the *Daily Star*, dwarfing a blurb about whether I'd forced Nick to get hair plugs. The goofy photo they picked to illustrate this makes me smile. I haven't slept beside Nick all week, and I miss him—his bedhead, the snores that could dwarf a thunderstorm, the way he can't fall asleep unless we are touching. I even miss that he always burns the first waffle he toasts. I fell in love with a person, not a prince; the rest is just circumstance.

The problem is, it can be hard to remember that. Which is how I got myself into trouble.

A text comes through: TIME IS RUNNING OUT.

With a thump Lacey bursts into my room, atypically ashen considering how much money she spends never to be that color. I am so startled to see her that I can only blink as she slams the door and leans breathlessly against it. She feels so far away from me even though she's standing right here.

"I did something," Lacey begins, not quite making eye contact.

So did I, but of course she already knows that. Once upon a time, I would ask for her help, us against the world. Now, it's her against me, and the world probably will pick her side.

I might be Cinderella today, but I dread who they'll think I am tomorrow. I guess it depends on what I do next.

# PART ONE

# AUTUMN 2007

*"O then 'tis! O then, I think no joy's above*
*The pleasures, the pleasures of love."*
—King Charles II, "The Pleasures of Love"

# CHAPTER ONE

If you believe my unauthorized biography, *The Bexicon*, Nick fell in love with me at a pub on my first night at Oxford, and angels burst into song while rose petals fell from the sky:

> The King's Arms was packed with reveling youngsters hungry for one last bit of mischief before the new term. But Rebecca Porter radiated a halo of confidence and serenity, modestly leaning against the back wall, holding a ladylike half-pint she would only sip twice. "Bex was never a drinker," a friend says. "She knew how to have a laugh, but you'd never find her dancing on a table to impress people." Indeed, the more he watched the seraphic American student—diffident and humble in sweetly vintage clothes surely destined for the Victoria and Albert Museum—the more Nicholas knew he had to claim her. He had found someone special. He had found his queen.

Complete fiction. In fact, the whole book is so inaccurately gushy that I often wonder if the author is on Queen Eleanor's payroll. The week it was published, we were in Spain at what everyone refers to as "Prince Richard's cabin"—Nick's father's coastal spread with fourteen bedrooms and its own vanity winery—and Nick laughed so raucously when I read this section aloud that his aunt Agatha, a full fifty yards away, jumped and dropped her gin and tonic.

"Are you sure it doesn't say, 'You'd never *not* find her dancing on a table'?" he'd asked. "Isn't that more accurate?"

"I am not table dancing right now."

"Pity," he grinned, raising his scotch to me.

"There's still time," Nick's younger brother, Freddie, had said from his deck chair. "In fact, Agatha over there could use some pointers. I don't think she's had any fun since she married Awful Julian."

In reality, Agatha does occasionally have fun, though usually only when needling her boozy bounder of a husband about how his ancient father refuses to die (and thus hand down his viscountcy). Nick and I never went to The King's Arms, because pubs with royal nomenclature make him self-conscious. And when fate pushed a prince into my path, my hair was dirty, I smelled like the canned air of the Virgin Atlantic plane that had deposited me at Heathrow, and my jeans and sailor-striped T-shirt could only be classified as vintage because of their extreme age. Aurelia Maupassant, author of *The Bexicon*, would be crushed.

When we were small, Lacey and I would sneak flashlights under the covers to read aloud from books about plucky British kids, their boarding-school hijinks, and their ill-fated wartime love affairs. Lacey was obsessed with the swoony kissing parts, but what stuck with me was a different kind of romanticism—the sense of epic sprawl compressed onto a small island that positively burst with art, antiquities, and history hiding in plain sight. I itched to inhale it, to live it, to sketch it all. So when I found out Cornell could do an exchange with the University of Oxford, I applied about five minutes later. Oxford didn't sound as overwhelming as London, yet every photo I saw of its glorious collage of buildings—never quite new, so much as old, older, and oldest—promised it would be an artist's dream. The tour guides tell you to try every door you find because it just might open, and it feels true;

there are still quaintly cobbled streets with perfect, petite gardens behind wrought iron gates, and its picturesque nooks and crannies all but vibrate with centuries of secrets waiting to be unearthed. Its mystery, its age, its textures...Oxford is in all ways the opposite of Muscatine, my rural Iowa hometown (or even the bucolic North Atlantic beauty of Cornell), and for me it was perfect. I didn't come to England to fall in love with anything but England. I didn't come to get married. I came to draw. I came to be inspired. I came for adventure.

I suppose I got it.

Oxford's student body trickles in as many as two weeks before the beginning of the new term—the crew team needs to adjust its sleep cycle just as much as a jet-lagged American does—so I arrived late on a mid-September afternoon with about ten days to unpack, recalibrate, and explore. The academic colleges there function like mini-universities under the Oxford umbrella—as if my old Cornell dorm also had its own professors and classrooms—and I had been accepted to live and study in one called Pembroke. It was smaller than some of the other thirty-seven dotted around town, and its lack of notoriety may directly correlate to being right across the street from the imposing, absurdly famous Christ Church college. We lived in its shadows—literally, come late afternoon—and during my year there, when the omnipresent red tour bus stopped to point out the historic building that was in the Harry Potter movies and observes its own time zone, the guide wouldn't even so much as glance across the street. Now, Pembroke is the main stop on the Royal Romance tour, which leaves from the train station every forty-five minutes. According to Gaz, who took it six months ago on a lark, it's almost as fictional as *The Bexicon*. He cried anyway.

A light drizzle was falling that first day as I hauled two giant suitcases, a laptop bag, and my purse up the cobblestone road toward Pembroke's main entrance. My suitcase kept catching a wheel and flipping over, twisting my wrist and causing my shoulder bags to whack me in the leg; by the time I reached the door, I was panting and had slim rivulets of rain dribbling down my nose. I rang twice for the porter and cursed loudly when no one answered. It had been a plane, train, and automobile odyssey to get me from Des Moines to that front stoop. I was cold, wet, and exhausted, and, from what I could tell, my deodorant had not stood up to the journey.

I buzzed again. The door opened and a tall, sandy-haired guy poked out his head.

"Need a hand?"

"Oh, please. Yes. Thank you."

He held up a stern palm. "Wait, how do I know you're supposed to be here? I heard you swearing. Foul language doesn't befit an Oxford student."

I stammered an apology until I noticed he was grinning.

"I'm joking," he said. "You're Rebecca. I was told you'd be coming." He widened the door and came through to get my bags. "The porter is very protective of his tea break, so I said I'd sit in and look out for you."

"And you let me hang out here in the rain just for fun? Is *that* behavior befitting an Oxford student?" I said, stepping inside, cozy and warm after the rain.

"I may have been engaged in an in-depth study of REM sleep." He shrugged winningly. "I've had two pints already and they make me so tired. Besides, I couldn't have guessed you'd show up without an umbrella. That's like going to the Bahamas without a bathing suit." He hoisted up my bags. "Follow me."

We trudged up the winding dark wood stairs, past stately oil paintings that looked so rustic they had to be originals, and blank-eyed portraits of alumni and monarchs.

"Which one is he?" I pointed to a man with a square jaw and a beard as thin as he was fat.

"That's King Albert. Victoria the First's grandson. Early nineteen-hundreds."

"I feel like he's staring right through me," I said, shivering involuntarily as we wound our way up to the third floor. "He has kind of a homicidal face. Or is that just syphilis making him insane? British monarchs do love their syphilis."

"A prerequisite of the job," he agreed.

I snorted, at which he shot me a startled but amused glance before I followed him into a slender hallway, domed with carved beams and lit beguilingly with candle-shaped sconces. We passed six doors—three on each side—and stopped outside the last one on the left.

"Here you go," he said, digging in the pocket of his jeans and then handing me a key. "Stop by the porter later and he'll give you a full set. And come join us in the JCR, if you're so inclined." He gave me a crisp nod. "Welcome to Oxford."

He was gone before my numbed mind got off a thank-you, much less decoded that acronym. I fought a head-splitting yawn and fumbled with the key—right as the door opposite mine flew open and an auburn-haired girl shot out of it and grabbed my hand.

"I see you've met him, then," she said, in an accent I later learned was Yorkshire. "What d'you think? Rather nice for a guy whose face will be all over our money in fifty years." She smacked her forehead. "Oi, I'm a dolt. Sorry. I'm Cilla."

"Rebecca," I said, blinking hard. "And are you telling me that was...?"

"Nick, yes," she said. "Or rather, 'Prince Nicholas of Wales.'" She made the air quotes with four fingers whose nail polish was in various stages of peeling. "He's not insufferable about the title, thank *God*." She peered at my glazed eyes. "Didn't you recognize him?"

That I hadn't was laughable (he still teases me that it's treasonous not to tip your royal baggage handler). Lacey subscribed to every celebrity weekly in existence—she delighted in reading bits of them to me once she'd finished her homework, usually while I was still trying to do mine—and Nick had appeared in them all. But in person he lacked the macho sheen the media always tried to give him, and I don't care who you are or how many times your twin has told you to practice constant vigilance: You still don't expect the so-called Heartthrob Heir to be your glorified bellhop.

"So the future sovereign just heard me accuse his relative of having syphilis?" I asked faintly.

"Oh, that's a good one," Cilla said. "But don't worry. Gaz once threw up all over him and Nick didn't even bat an eyelash, and that's saying something because Gaz eats a *lot* and there were loads of chunks." She grabbed a bag and barged past me into my room.

I finagled my other suitcase through the doorway and took in my new home. There was an irony in coming all the way to Oxford to find that my room resembled the ones in every dorm in America: a twin bed with a metal bedframe, a radiator under the window, and a desk with a hutch that looked like it came from an office supply warehouse.

Cilla nodded at a heap in the corner. "I filched some of Ceres's things that she didn't take when she left," she said. "A rug, some throw pillows. Whatever might make it less awful in here. We can decorate later, though. First let's get you to the bar for a welcome drink."

"Shouldn't I change?" I asked, wondering if I smelled bad to people whose noses weren't as close to me as my own was.

Cilla waved at her torn jeans, creased boots, and woolly sweater. "Yes, we stand on formality here at Pembroke," she intoned. "Actually, Ceres would put on high heels and lipstick to go down and get the mail. If you're going to take *that* long, I'll just meet you downstairs."

I shook my head. "Can't walk in heels and never met a lipstick I didn't get on my teeth."

Cilla beamed broadly. "We'll get on splendidly, then, Rebecca."

"Bex. Please."

"Okay, *Bex*. Get on with it already. It's been ten whole minutes since my last pint."

It turned out the bar *was* the JCR—a dim undergraduate common area that looked cramped thanks to the jumble stuffed into it: mismatched chairs and chipped tables; a haphazardly hung flat-screen showing soccer highlights; and a substantial but inexpensive beer and booze collection, stocked by that year's Bar Tsar (his elaborately framed photo hung on the wall). Even with the haze of cigarette smoke hanging in the air, it was easy to spot Nick because at least half the room was ogling him, and I had only to follow the stares. He was perched on a stool in a snug corner, relaxed and quiet, with two guys and a punky girl who did not wear her pink hair with much authority. Cilla steered me through the crowd right in their direction. She may have been small, but she was solid, efficiently built, and clearly not to be trifled with, because people parted for her as if by magic.

"These are more of the people in our corridor," she said when she reached Nick's corner. "Everyone, this is Bex, just in from America."

One of them bounced to his feet so fast he almost knocked over the table. He had a kind face, bulbous nose, freckles, and a thick tuffet of orange-red hair—rather like Ron Weasley, but with scruff, and a round, compact belly that was either the product of a lot of lager, or his (ineffective) attempts to draw in enough air to appear taller than five foot six. Possibly both.

"Brilliant," he said. "I'm Gaz. I expect Cilla's told you all about me."

"Just the vomity bits," Cilla said.

Gaz grinned even wider. "That's about all of it."

A bespectacled dark-haired guy rose to his feet. "Please, sit. I'll get drinks," he said, gesturing to the threadbare, oversize chair he'd just vacated, and pulling out folded bills that were tucked into his back pocket with the same precision as the plaid collared shirt tucked into his jeans.

"That wonderful person with the fat wad of cash is Clive," Gaz said. "And this young lady with the shirt that looks like she made it out of tea towels is Joss."

"And I did make it out of tea towels," Joss said, appraising me as Cilla and I squeezed into Clive's empty seat. "Ceres was my fit model, but you'll do nicely. Built just like her. Tall, no boobs."

"Finally, being flat chested is an advantage," I said. "My twin sister will be astonished."

"Oooh, twins, eh?" Gaz said, wiggling his eyebrows.

"Get off it," Cilla scoffed. "Gaz thinks he's dead suave, but his father is a disgraced finance minister, so it's more like dead broke. He still owes me thirty quid from last term."

"I make up for it with piles of charm," Gaz said. "And this bloke here," he said, gesturing at Nick, "is . . . *Steve*."

He adopted a deep, dramatic intonation, lingering on the word like it was a rich dessert to be savored. Nick buried his face in his beer, but the telltale bubbles gave away his laughter.

"*Steve*," I echoed, trying on Gaz's tone for size. "Sure. I can roll with that, *Steve*."

Gaz slapped the table, which reverberated under his meaty hand. "You told her?"

"She'd have figured it out anyway," Cilla said. "So take it down about three point sizes, please, *Garamond*."

Clive was back and sliding the drinks onto the scarred coffee table. " 'Gaz' is short for 'Garamond,' of the Fonty Garamonds," he explained.

"As in, the *actual* font," Joss piped up. "His grandfather invented it."

"He's mad as pants. Won't even read anything in sans serif," Gaz said. "Couldn't he have invented something cooler to be named after? Like Garamond the Time-Traveling Motorbike, or Garamond the Lady-Killing Love Tonic?"

"I thought *you* were Garamond the Lady-Killing Love Tonic," Cilla cracked.

"Well, as long as we're talking stupid names," he said irritably, "somebody tell me why we bother with *Steve* if none of you uses it."

Nick rubbed the top of his head absently. "It's not really supposed to fool anyone," he said. "It's more for if I'm caught in trouble or doing anything embarrassing."

I met his eyes. "Embarrassing, like joking to a prince that all his relatives have an STD?"

"Exactly," he said. "Although no one in polite society would actually do that."

We smiled at each other.

Clive turned to me and pretended to study me deeply, as if my eyelashes were tea leaves he could read. "And you are...Rebecca Porter, almost twenty, from Iowa, father invented a sofa that employs a mini-fridge as a base—"

"Can you get us one?" Gaz interjected.

"...and you once got arrested for public indecency and trespassing because you accidentally tore off your trousers while climbing a barbed-wire fence," Clive finished.

"I maintain it tried to climb me," I quipped. "What else does my dossier say? Or do you just have ESP?"

"Of course there's a dossier," Gaz said, clapping a hand on Nick's shoulder. "The Firm has to know who's living twenty feet from the future of the bloodline."

Nick's discomfort was clear (one of his tells is that the tops of his ears start to vibrate—it's the strangest thing). He drained the last of his pint. "While you lot are busy frightening Bex, I need to go say hello to some people."

"Yes, right. Back to the grind." Clive grinned, nodding toward a giggling, coquettish cluster of blondes across the way.

"There are probably worse fates," Nick said. "I hear syphilis is a beast."

He slipped off into the room, but didn't make it far before he was waylaid by a cranky-looking patrician brunette in a high-collared blouse, who pulled him over to whisper in his ear.

Clive whacked Gaz on the arm. "You know he's sensitive about the king stuff."

"But it's exciting!" Gaz argued. "Big intrigue. I'm very respectful."

Cilla looked doubtful as Joss checked her cell phone. "I'm meeting Tank at the new punk bar over by the Ashmolean," she said. "Anybody want to come?"

I glanced around for guidance. Cilla shook her head.

"Suit yourselves," Joss said, leaving behind a quarter of a pint.

"Don't mind if I do," Gaz said brightly, reaching over and swigging it.

"Really, Gaz," Cilla nagged. "You'll be sweating lager next. My great-grandmother's great-uncle Algernon had that happen when he was courting the Spanish infanta and—"

"Ah, yes, here we go again," grunted Gaz.

"Cilla has more stories than Nick has stalkers," Clive told me. "I've no clue if any of it's true, but it's bloody entertaining."

"...and *then* of course she broke it off with him by trying to thrust a letter opener into his ear at her brother's coronation," Cilla was saying.

To better bark at him, Cilla clambered into the empty chair next to Gaz. Clive responded by settling into her old spot, smashed up next to me, our thighs touching. It wasn't unpleasant. He was the Hollywood archetype of a sensitive yet smoldering Brit—wavy jet-black hair, strong jaw, and a voice that was smooth and husky all at once.

"So, Bex, what are you reading?"

"Reading?"

"Studying," he clarified.

"It's not in my file?"

Clive smiled. "We only got the juicy bits," he said, sipping his drink and then licking the froth off his lip in a way that suggested he enjoyed my watching him do it.

"Well, theoretically I'm reading British history, toward my degree at home, but what I really want to do over here is draw," I said. "I mostly work in pencils, and so much of the architecture here lends itself to dramatic gray and black areas. The arches, the carvings, the gargoyles..."

"Did I hear you say *gargoyles*?" Gaz interrupted. "That reminds me." He pointed at the stern brunette. "That is our other floor-mate, Lady Beatrix Larchmont-Kent-Smythe. Otherwise known as Lady Bollocks, because of her initials, and also, she can be a bloody load of it."

Lacey later described Bea as looking and acting exactly the way you would expect a Lady Beatrix Larchmont-Kent-Smythe to look and act. Her posture is as impeccable as her tailoring, she never loses her keys nor her cool nor so much as a chip from her manicure, and I believe she intentionally waxes her eyebrows so that she always appears to be raising them at you with deepest skepticism. Clive explained that Lady Bollocks was a lifelong friend of Nick's family, and in fact, as we alternated pints and gin-filled highballs, he turned out to be full of tidbits: that Cilla's ancestors lost their money in a lusty *Downton Abbey*–style scandal; that the girl tending bar once had a pop hit called "Fish and Chips" about a memorable weekend with a famous boy band; that two hundred people had money on whether Cilla and Gaz would sleep together or murder each other (he had a hundred pounds on them doing both); and that Joss's continued enrollment was a mystery to everyone, because she rarely did anything except follow around her boyfriends and make clothes in her room, to the consternation of her pushy father—the Queen's gynecologist.

"She's a good enough sort, but we don't see her much," Clive said.

"Her father requested she be on Nick's floor, to light a fire under her or some such, and you don't run afoul of a man who has such, er, sensitive personal information."

"Keep your friends close, keep the secrets of the Royal Birth Canal closer," I said.

"Something like that." His hand brushed my leg again.

"And you're the person everyone wants to sit next to at a wedding," I said. "You'd have dirt on everyone in the room and at least two of their relatives."

"Only two?" Clive feigned shock. "I do want to be a reporter, actually. I like learning about people. My brothers think it's just an excuse for the fact that I'm afraid of having my ears torn off." At my quizzical expression, he added, "They play rugby. Professionally. The biggest, thickest clods you've ever seen. Cauliflower ears and broken noses and all."

"So how did *you* end up on Nick's floor?"

"My dad was mates with Nick's dad at St. Andrews," Clive said. "So we've known each other since we were born, same as Bea."

I glanced at Lady Bollocks. An immaculate blonde with a creamy tan was wresting Nick's arm from her, to the visible chagrin of nearly every woman in the room and a few hopeful men besides.

"India Bolingbroke," Clive said, with the precision of a spy. "The new girlfriend. Daughter of Prince Richard's second cousin twice removed."

"Good luck to her," I said. "I think the whole room is out for her blood."

"We tease him about it, but it's a bit unremitting," Clive said. "Last year Nick was with Ceres, the girl whose room you're taking, but she cheated on him with the polo captain. I think everyone hoped it'd be open season again."

Nick leaned into India as if she were the only one in the room. It was a technique he eventually told me he developed to freeze out the sensation of being devoured by hungry eyes, two of which, that day, belonged to Lady Beatrix Larchmont-Kent-Smythe.

"She's like a guard dog, that one," Clive said, tipping his beer at her.

And then her steely gaze found me. I saluted her comically with my gin.

"Well, nobody has anything to fear from me," I said, downing the dregs of my drink like a pro. "I'm not here for any of that bullshit. I just want to have fun."

"Bravo to that," Clive said. "And when poor old Nick is forced to marry one of these squealing aristocrats, promise you'll sit next to me, just like this"—he made a point of shifting so that I was half on his lap—"so I can whisper secrets to you."

"Deal," I said.

He held my gaze. An excited shiver ran up my spine. I wasn't there to get married, but I was definitely up for a good time.

And that's the true story of the day I met Nick: I left the bar with another guy.

# CHAPTER TWO

I am one minute older than my twin sister, and she seemed to view that accident of biology as some kind of challenge. If I got As, Lacey got A-pluses. When I hit five foot nine, she was already half an inch taller. She was school president and the head cheerleader, while I was just the softball team's least-effective relief pitcher (Lacey never understood playing for fun; to her, if you didn't dominate, it wasn't worth doing). When our dad had heart problems, we both studied medical textbooks, but she full-on memorized them and decided to go into cardiology—and then, I think, stuck with it mostly because *wants to be a doctor* looked so impressive next to *valedictorian* on our graduation program. So as I stared at the mountain of library books on my desk after just one day of term, I wondered what crossed wire had landed *me* at the very top university in the world when Lacey always had the edge in the Superstar Stakes (even if she was the only one who thought of it that way). My relatively brief settling-in period had ended when the calendar flipped to October, bringing with it the beginning of term—Oxford calls it First Week—and a raft of stern lectures from the academic fellows on the rigors of independent study, a stultifying pile of reading with which I had to be conversant in a hurry, and warnings from Nick's personal protection officers about acting completely normal yet maintaining constant vigilance. I needed moral support. But Lacey needed dish, and Lacey is good at getting what she wants.

"So how many times *have* you hooked up, exactly?" she pressed.

"It's barely even an interesting amount," I hedged.

"You're the artist," Lacey said. "Paint me a picture."

Bedsprings creaked through the phone line. I could picture Lacey the way she talks on the phone: on her stomach, legs bent, covering the receiver with a giggle to repeat what the person on the other end was saying. It was strange *being* that person. Especially because up to now, we'd always dissected our romantic lives over a messy plate of cheese and crackers, and that wasn't nearly as fun long-distance.

"I don't know," I said, pulling open a block of English cheddar. "Three. Ish. Okay, four. Anyway, you should *see* the beard on my history fellow—"

"Four times in like ten days? You must be into him!" Lacey squealed.

"No!" I said, perhaps a bit too loudly. "It's casual! We're young. Consequence-free making out is the entire point."

"You're such a guy sometimes."

I could practically hear Lacey roll her eyes. I *did* hear Lacey tapping away on her laptop.

"It's super frustrating that I can't find anything but grainy pictures of him on the Internet," she said. "The whole point of Google is stalking your sister's foreign hookups."

"He's dishy. You'd approve," I said, lifting up my cheese plate to pull my quilt over my toes. My radiator had one setting: inefficient. "Kind of a Clark Kent type."

"Ooh, I do approve," Lacey said. Then her tone turned wistful. "I can't believe I'm not there. Or that you're not here. It's so bizarre. I feel like half my inner monologue went silent."

Before Oxford, the longest Lacey and I had been apart was eight hours. We picked wildly divergent bedroom décor, yet ended up sleeping in the same room every night rather than retreating to our separate corners. Her school schedule never aligned with mine, but by dinnertime we'd snap back into place like a rubber band. We'd go to the same summer camps, and I'd bring home demerits for skipping sessions to skinny dip in the river, while she'd have an armload of excellence awards and sheaves of phone numbers from excited acolytes she'd immediately forget; it was enough to have secured them. We never deliberately froze anybody out, but it was challenging for other people to get very close. Scientists needed fifty years to split the atom. Our classmates didn't stand a chance.

Neither had boys. Lacey always dated whatever guy was currently the hottest commodity—our school's all-state point guard, or the kid who won a ton of cash on high-school *Jeopardy!*—and I'd drift along with whatever plus-one of his she fixed me up with, and inevitably our double dates would turn into them staring awkwardly off into space as Lacey and I monopolized each other's conversation. In fact, our classmates voted us Cutest Couple, and I don't think it was a joke. I even dumped my freshman-year boyfriend at Cornell when I overheard him referring to Lacey as The Trojan, because, as he disparagingly told his fraternity brother, she was around so much that she was the world's most effective birth control.

So I don't think Lacey quite believed it when I announced my England plans. History had borne out that our gravitational pull was simply too strong. Even as infants, Mom said that she'd set us down two feet apart in our crib, and an hour later we'd somehow be snuggled right up next to each other again, as if we were still in the womb. Nothing had ever come between us before, so it must have seemed highly unlikely that I'd willingly put an ocean there.

"It feels weird that you haven't met any of these people," I told her that night. "I keep turning to tell you things, expecting you to be here."

"How am I going to survive organic chemistry without you drawing obscene cartoon molecules on my flash cards?" she complained affectionately.

"Well, we can't be attached at the hip forever," I reasoned. "Nobody will let me hang out in the operating room sketching people's innards while you rebuild their aortas, or whatever."

"Why not? It'd be like a souvenir," Lacey said. "But *fine*, don't worry about me, up here with my face in a cadaver while you're living with a prince." She tsked. "I can't believe you don't even have any gossip on him. You are the worst."

"I rarely see him, Lace," I said. "Half the time he doesn't socialize with us. He hasn't even come into town."

By the sheer happenstance of Ceres Whitehall de Villency inexplicably (to me) opting for a year at Cornell, I'd landed smack in the middle of Nick's tight social cluster—everyone in our hall was a proven-loyal chum, or the offspring of one—and my own assimilation came largely thanks to Cilla, who didn't so much take me under her wing as wrestle me there. I think we were mutually grateful that we got along so well: me because Oxford was the first time I'd been without Lacey, my genetically built-in best friend, and Cilla because her proximity to Nick made her suspicious of outside girls' motivations, and her other choices on our floor were unsatisfying. Lady Bollocks was too aloof and consumed with horsy pursuits, Joss spent all her free time sewing and immersing herself in the essence of whatever oddball she was dating (which accounted for her current insincere punk look), and the mysterious eighth door in our hallway belonged not to a coed, but to Nick's personal protection officers. We were forbidden to buddy up with this taciturn quartet of ex-military men, so we never knew their names, instead christening them based on their various personal qualities (PPO Stout was as tall as he was wide; PPO Twiggy was svelte but could snap you like one; PPO Popeye occasionally had spinach in his teeth; PPO Furrow was a frowner). None was older than forty, all had wives and children at home, and yet to do their jobs they bunked two at a time in the most inelegant fashion—it must have felt like trying to shove a cat into a mouse hole—which surely put them on the fast track to sainthood.

Nobody said it directly, but I sensed that coming on strong with questions about Nick would raise the hackles of both my new friends and his trained killers, and it wasn't worth it just to find out if Nick wore boxers or briefs. So I couldn't tell Lacey much about him that she didn't already know from *People*. The day I got accepted to Oxford, she dragged her old Royal Family commemorative issue from the dusty archives under her bed, and showed me pictures of three-year old Nick roaming Balmoral's moors in buckle shoes and a tweedy plaid jacket, or waving from the Buckingham Palace balcony during a state occasion while Freddie waggled his tongue. None of it did much to create an image of an actual person; just a poster boy, a character in a far-off story.

"I did hear a rumor his room is totally bulletproof," I told Lacey. "But that's about it."

"Maybe he's just not that friendly."

"Well, but he's not *un*friendly," I explained. "He just socializes really sporadically."

"Shy, maybe?" she wondered. "Like his mom? She's basically a hermit. Or maybe he takes after Prince Richard. I read that he's super stiff." Lacey let out a puff of frustration. "It's killing me not to see for myself. Some people swear Nicholas has a wooden leg and that's why he never plays polo anymore."

"That's ridiculous. Are prosthetics even made of wood anymore?"

"You're missing the point," Lacey groused, but she was laughing. "I would kill to have a prince three doors down. Take pity on me and go make out with him, please."

"I can't, Lace. I already kissed his friend. And don't you remember? He will never—"

"Marry an American," we finished in unison.

Lacey let out a girlish giggle. "I still can't believe she actually said that to you."

I *had* seen Nick alone once more, on my third day, about thirty seconds before my inaugural conversation with Lady Beatrix Larchmont-Kent-Smythe. I'd forgotten my robe and towels in Iowa, so until I bought new ones—which was, naturally, exactly what I'd been planning to do on the day in question—I'd been wrapping myself in the tiny terrycloth loaner from the college and sprinting to my door. It had worked, until I bumped smack into Nick as he was coming into the bathroom. My bucket of toiletries went flying, including a box of tampons I'd left in there, raining feminine hygiene products all over him. It sounds like a quirky meet-awkward from act one of a romantic comedy, but it was mortifying, and I didn't have the advantage of being well-lit and cutely dressed. Or dressed, period.

"Sorry, sorry, I'm so sorry." I frantically tried to pick everything up without flashing him.

"No trouble," Nick said, gallantly gathering my scattered stuff. He was wearing ratty maroon gym shorts that proved definitively his legs were made of very nice muscle rather than wood. "Tricky business having to bring so much stuff to the shower."

"Thanks for helping," I said, feeling like an idiot. "Forecast for today did say 'sunny with a chance of Tampax.'"

*Syphilis and Tampax.* That's what I'll call it when I crack and write my own version of *The Bexicon.*

Nick kept his head down, but I saw his cheeks flush. He later told me that he'd never even *said* the word *tampon*, much less had to handle any, which of course made sense: Who sends the eventual leader of the Commonwealth out for lady supplies? Like the pro I would soon realize he is, though, Nick brushed it off, scooping up the last tampons and dropping them in their box before tossing it to me gently and continuing on his way.

As the bathroom door swung shut behind him, I heard a loud throat clearing and turned to face the one and only Lady Bollocks, polished and perfect in riding jodhpurs and a white button-down shirt.

"How trite," she said. "*Accidentally* running into him wearing a glorified hand towel."

"You're Bea, right?" I said, awkwardly rearranging myself so I could clasp closed my towel and still shake her hand. "I'm Bex."

"I know," Bea said, making no move to meet the gesture. "And let's be clear, *Rebecca*. Your little . . . whatever that was . . . is a waste of your time. He will never. Marry. An American."

She punctuated the last sentence with thrusts of a sharply filed nail. I was so flummoxed that, still dripping water onto the centuries-old Persian runner, I simply gaped as she vanished into her room.

If I had actually harbored fantasies of landing myself a prince, I might've been deterred by the intensity of the competition outside the cozy confines of Pembroke. Our college-mates, while clearly interested, were at least accustomed to the sight of Nick, and initially that was the only place I saw him. But off campus, so to speak, the curious eyeballs were more intense. Guys jockeyed to get him on weekend sports teams or present themselves as potential confidantes, the better to boost their own profiles; the ladies were eager for a shot at an heir they couldn't count on running into every day on their way out of the bathroom. They all tried to be subtle about it, and failed spectacularly. It was like dropping a steak into a rabid pack of horndogs.

The first time I witnessed this was about three hours after I'd hung up the phone with Lacey. I'd begun working my way through Oxford's pubs in my ten days there before school had started, thanks to the guiding hand of Cilla and the others, and that night I found myself outside on a bitingly chilly night, trudging past several warm and inviting ones.

"Where are we going again?" I asked Cilla, shivering as I tried to keep up. Her stride is all business.

"It's called The Bird," she tossed at me over her shoulder. "It's where C. S. Lewis and Tolkien and some other people got together and gave notes on each other's manuscripts and probably acted totally unbearable."

We pulled up our parka hoods against the mounting wind until we came to a plain yellow gabled building with its name in iron gothic letters across the front.

"The Eagle and Child," I read aloud. "I thought you said it was called The Bird."

"Same thing," Cilla said. "It got nicknamed The Bird and Baby because of the pictures on the pub sign, and that got shortened to The Bird."

"So its nickname has its own nickname?"

"If you think that's off, wait until Gaz busts out the old Cockney rhyming slang," Cilla said. "As if he's not indecipherable enough on his own."

She paused. "I also finally talked Nick into coming out to toast the start of term, so he'll be here. Just pretend he's normal." She stopped. "Not that he *isn't*, but... *you* know."

She pushed me inside the pub, where the boisterous, noisy vibe clashed with the unassuming exterior. Fresh paint butted up against original brick and stonework, the walls warped and bulging in some corners. Students sloshed beer over the edges of their pint glasses as they snacked on plates of thick-cut chips, and while the music was loud, the human din was louder. Later on I would flirt with the VIP club scene, but velvet ropes are more Lacey's speed than mine. I have always preferred a dive.

Cilla scanned the crowd, which wasn't easy, given that the pub was essentially a long chain of cramped rooms.

"I wish Gaz would invest in a stepstool," she groused. "His hair would be so easy to spot if he weren't so bloody short."

"I think we walked right past them," I said, gesturing toward the larger of the two front rooms. "Half of the girls in here are loitering over there."

We peered to our right, and eventually I recognized Nick's head, and saw that it was bent at an angle toward a group that included golden-blond India Bolingbroke. Standing to either side, like wardens, were Gaz and Joss, chatting up a gloomy guy with six rings in his nose.

"Oi!" Clive called out behind us, coming from the bar and carrying a large tray of shot glasses and Guinness pints. "You're just in time."

We let him pass through the crowded, uneven doorway—precious cargo, after all—then pushed through the crush until our hands found the shot glasses.

"Yikes," I said, pulling back a moment. "I wasn't expecting it to be warm."

Nick reached in and took a pint and a shot for India.

"You chase the warm with the cold," he instructed. "Right, all, this is Bex's first chaser. Let's have a toast."

"Three cheers to the lemons!" Gaz shouted, thrusting his hand in the air so hard that he spilled some whiskey on his cheek.

Cilla nudged me. "See what I mean?" she said. "Not a bloody lick of sense."

"How about a real toast?" Clive interjected. "One that uses words in a sensible order."

I held up my shot and thought for a second. "Thanks, everyone, for the warm welcome. Sorry about the Revolution."

Nick hoisted his pint glass. "We'll get you next time."

The warm whiskey went down like sweet, spicy fire. I gulped the

Guinness as quickly as I could, and put down my empty glass to see Nick watching approvingly.

"Joss," he said. "You're officially spared from The Glug this year. We've got a ringer."

Joss turned away from her date, who looked like Edward Scissorhands up close but without the roiling inner life. "I didn't want to do it anyway," she said. "College-sponsored drinking games are the tool of the patriarchy, right, Tank?" Then she nodded toward the door. "Heads up, Clive. Penelope Six-Names, your four o'clock."

"Not again," he said, gesturing at an eager-looking girl with straw-like bangs, a sunburn, and two large, full glasses. "Six-Names knows better than to bring him a drink we didn't see the bartender pour."

"I have no idea what anyone is talking about," I said to no one in particular as Clive slipped away to head off Six-Names at the pass.

"Never you mind about The Glug, you'll soon find out," Nick said. Then he went very still. "This song is brilliant," he said.

Everyone around Nick seemed to agree, and pretty soon, our entire room was screaming the chorus of "Wannabe." Nick smiled wide and shouted along, but—much like how he did not chug his Guinness, and wholly skipped the shot—he let his friends dance and rage around him, freely idiotic, like youthful, well-educated court jesters sans the belled hats. I sensed a reserve in his body language, suggesting he wasn't as comfortable outside the safety of Pembroke's walls, and I wasn't sure if that was natural shyness or the hesitation that comes from knowing you're not just in the spotlight, you *are* the spotlight. For me, partying next to Mr. July in the previous year's unsanctioned Hot Princes of the World calendar ended up being no weirder than walking into a Cornell house party and bumping into half the basketball team. Well-wishers, limelight seekers, curious fans—they're everywhere. The only difference was that this particular center of attention had a lot more self-control, and a bigger birthright.

And a more protective posse. That night, and many times since, I noticed how seamlessly Gaz and Clive, the PPOs, and a few other acquaintances from Nick's Eton days knew how to close ranks, no matter where we were (The Bird was a favorite because the small rooms made it easier to keep an eye on their quarry). Girls and guys alike sidled up wearing their ancestries or their social standings on their sleeves, and the lads gracefully deflected them—they were like a human condom, strategically positioned to keep everything treacherous out of the hot zone—which left Nick free to chat up girls who didn't seem like they wanted something from him beyond what any young thing might want from an attractive guy at a bar. The whole operation ran smoothly enough that it never got in the way unless you were one of the misguided missiles seeking royal heat. India Bolingbroke was on the inside circle; Penelope Six-Names, conversely, peered over Gaz's shoulder and protested, "I just want to say hi! I'm family! We're third cousins!"

"*Everyone's* a third cousin," Gaz said, twirling her and dipping her with surprising grace.

My edges were fuzzy, thanks to the alcohol. Everyone's edges were fuzzy a lot of the time at Oxford, which is probably why most of these details never leaked: People think they're telling the truth, but no one can remember for sure. Sometimes when we went out, I'd get a phone number written on my hand, and then forget and wake up with only half of it still there. Other times I'd stumble home on my own. But, more often than I ever intended, I'd end up with Clive. I had no interest in a relationship that would constrict my time in England—which makes me laugh out loud now, given that I ended up in the most constricting relationship *in* England—and it wasn't the shrewdest move to jump into bed with a guy living practically on top of me, but the whiskey wasn't always on my side. Fortunately, Clive was. He swore leaving Oxford with a steady girlfriend would make it too hard to build a serious journalism career, because he'd need freedom to chase a story (or presumably, an attractive source), making our friends-with-benefits arrangement mutually satisfying.

Mostly. Making out with Clive sometimes felt like sucking face with a math experiment. He fixated on a weird numerical pattern, nine turns of the tongue clockwise and nine turns the other way, like he'd memorized instructions from a magazine. It seemed odd at first, a guy with so much else going for him having so little game, but the longer I watched him with Nick the more I understood Clive did himself no favors. He took his role as Nick's wingman-in-chief almost as seriously as his journalistic aspirations. In fact, generations of men like Clive had spent their lives making sure their own Nicks didn't get snookered by opportunists or social climbers or enemies, nor poisoned, nor impulsively married to the peasant girl selling flowers on Tottenham Court Road. Whether Nick wanted to be or not, he was the sun, and everyone revolved around him. And anyone who resented this arrangement had the very fabric of the universe working against them: Like me and Lacey, like gravity itself, it simply was.

# CHAPTER THREE

When Nick and I got engaged, a newspaper column claimed I'd come to Oxford to sweep Nick off his feet as a way of legitimizing my father's fridge-furniture empire to the world—which is patently absurd, not least because the Coucherator was already the top-selling appliance in Luxembourg. The truth is, I rarely thought about Nick at first, and saw him even less. He'd been absent from communal meals in the Dining Hall, and wasn't particularly gregarious during passing encounters in the hallway. I got more information from the papers than from living with him: There was a story about him spending his reclusive mother's birthday with her at Prince Richard's country estate, Trewsbury House, complete with grainy photos of him exchanging a terse-looking handshake with his father (NICK AND DICK: NOT SO THICK? the headline wondered); and a gossipy tidbit claiming he'd gotten his teeth whitened after an heiress named Davinia snubbed his summer advances because she thought they were too yellow. Clive, who seemed to relish having the inside scoop, dissected these for me at length whenever we walked to lunch or the market (he swore Nick's teeth *were* lighter). I knew Lacey was dying of curiosity from her room at Cornell, so I dutifully listened for repeatable tidbits, but frankly, I had other priorities. The first of which involved giving Lady Bollocks no reason to poison my Weetabix.

And the second of which should have been school, but this was my first trip overseas, and everything outside academia felt so much more alluring to me: the identical array of gothic arches on the Bodleian Library; the Bridge of Sighs, an ornate, arcing enclosure gracefully connecting two parts of Hertford College; the snarky gargoyles atop the spire of the town's biggest church. They begged to be sketched, and I answered whenever I could, often in the peaceful, chilly morning hours when I could pick a spot and let the town wake up around me. Drawing has always taken me out of my own head. At Oxford, it helped me be in the moment completely, instead of wondering what Lacey was up to, or which baseball announcers were bugging Dad the most. Despite how welcoming most people had been, I missed my family. I missed knowing which way to look before crossing the street. I missed network TV and American football and the way Diet Coke tastes in the States. But with a sheet of paper and a pencil in front of me, I'm home.

On the last morning of First Week, I got up predawn and headed across the street to Christ Church. Ostensibly I wanted to draw the glow of sunrise over the college's meadow, all wild grass and pastured cows and squawking geese, but the Iowan in me also itched to stretch her legs, and my body demanded cardiovascular activity to offset the noble sport of drinking I'd undertaken. I started down the mud-and-gravel trail, under the canopy of tall, spiky trees whose leaves were preparing for their seasonal suicide leap, and snaked around the river—blissfully alone with my sketchbook and my thoughts, interrupted only by the occasional bark of the coxswain and the rhythmic splash of the crew team's oars reaching me through the mist. The road led me past a quaint folly bridge arching over the Isis that would fit perfectly into a series I was doing on the curves of Oxford. I hopped off the path and scrambled around the wooded edge in search of a flat rock to sit on, so lost in trying not to fall over a tree's root that instead I tripped over the outstretched legs of a man in a hooded sweatshirt. I let out a shrill yelp and he leapt to his feet, knocking over his light and landing in a weird defensive position.

"Shit!" he said.

I squinted at him. "*Nick?*"

In that instant, the hood on his sweatshirt slipped to reveal his face still frozen in a comical O of surprise. He had been sitting on a plaid blanket, surrounded by papers and books, as if he were on the quad at Pembroke in the afternoon and not a clammy field at dawn. Unsure what to do, I bent to pick up one of the papers strewn about the grass, which had flipped and scattered when he jumped.

"Are you doing a crossword?" I asked, bemused. "It's barely even light out."

Nick gave a shy *I'm busted* shake of the head, and pushed back his hood completely. He was pink-cheeked. "Yeah, the *Times* cryptic," he said.

"*Cryptic* is one word for this," I agreed.

"What are you doing here?" he asked.

It occurred to me, as his breath normalized, that he might've thought I'd followed him.

"I'm just on a run," I explained, gesturing feebly to my athletic clothes and earth-splattered shins. "Well, more of an, um, art jog. I came out to sketch." Then I froze. "Am I in someone's crosshairs right now?"

Nick relaxed. "You've not been shot yet, so that's a good sign," he said. "I'll have them drop their weapons if you can answer a clue or two. It's all tricks and wordplay and it's impossible." He handed me a printed sheet and pointed to one. "Like this. 'New pay cut with Post Office work is loony.' Gibberish."

"Don't look at me. I'm still trying to figure out why your salacious secret life outside Pembroke involves word puzzles," I said. "It's not very scandalous."

"It would be if anyone ever saw how blank these are." Nick sighed, taking back the crossword. "Freddie is brilliant at them, and he goads me about it. So I have to practice in private until I'm respectably competent. Someday I am going to finish one before he does."

"And this is your only way to do it in peace, because you don't ever really get to be alone," I said, not realizing until too late that I'd worked this out aloud.

Nick looked surprised, but pleasantly. "The PPOs and I have a pact—they let me lose them once a week, and I pretend not to know that they followed me here anyway," he said. "As long as I've no idea *where* they are, I mostly forget about them."

"Well, I should leave you to it, then," I said. "I don't want to step all over your one moment of privacy."

He dropped back down onto the blanket. "Oh, don't go racing away on my account. I've got loads of coffee to share and you look like you need it."

"What, no morning tea?"

"I am going to tell you something extremely dramatic that would rock the monarchy to the core," Nick said, opening the Thermos and pouring into the lid. "I am not a fan of tea. Gran keeps insisting that I'm simply not drinking it properly. After a while I gave in and told her she was right. It is not worth it to argue with the Queen about her PG Tips."

"So your secret perversions are crosswords and coffee," I said, settling in beside him and taking the steaming cup. "Truly depraved."

"My father would agree with you." But that time he wasn't smiling.

"My dad and I once had a fight because I refuse to put ketchup on my hot dogs," I said.

"That's possibly the most American sentence I've ever heard."

"I am possibly the most American person at Pembroke," I pointed out. "But rest easy. We made up. The hole in our relationship was patched with Cracker Jack."

Nick's face was blank.

"Candied popcorn, with peanuts," I clarified. "They sell it at baseball games. There's always a prize inside, like a ring or something. I keep all mine—one for every game Dad and I ever went to together. I must have fifty by now."

I felt Dad's absence right then. Against all odds, the Cubs had a shot at winning the division, and it was hard for us to have our traditional pregame panic attacks, thanks to the time difference and the fact that he kept accidentally hitting send on all his emails in mid-sentence.

As if reading my mind, Nick asked, "So you two are close, then?"

"Yeah, my dad's the best," I said, hugging my knees to my chest. "We like to road-trip to away games and eat the grossest snacks we can find along the way, just the two of us."

I picked at my shoe, swallowing a lump in my throat. Nick seemed to sense that my mood was shifting, and picked up the crossword again.

"'Decrepit and remote cathedral church,' two words, five and four letters," he read from the crossword sheet. He frowned. "It's an anagram, I think."

"Do you honestly enjoy doing those, or is this just a competition?"

"When you get one right, you feel like the most brilliant person alive, which I could do with a bit more often," he said. "But it mostly boils down to a competition with Freddie."

"I know how that feels," I said. "Lacey is really competitive, and she usually wins."

"I find it hard to believe that you're the loser, landing here at Oxford," Nick said.

"I'm totally lucky to be here," I said. "But she didn't even apply. She claims pre-med does not allow for a year abroad." It was a direct quote. "You know, when we applied to colleges, I didn't think it made a difference where I went if what I wanted was art, so I followed her to Cornell. But after a while, that felt like her experience, not mine. Sometimes I wonder..."

Nick let me trail off.

"I've never told anyone this, actually," I said. "But in eighth grade, Lacey cheated at algebra. Math was her one weakness, and I was pretty good at it. She spent the entire night before the test freaked out that she was going to fail, or worse, get a lower grade than I did for the first time ever. And then halfway through the test, I noticed her copying mine. Of course our grades came back identical, with all the same mistakes, but she told the teacher I'd copied *her*."

Nick's blue eyes got wide.

"Yeah. Pretty ballsy," I said. "But I knew she wasn't being malicious. She just didn't know how to handle the role reversal when she wasn't doing better than I was."

"So what did you do?"

"I took the fall," I said. "Told them I was afraid of being branded the stupid twin. They felt sorry for me, I got a month of detention, and after that, I threw a couple of tests so it'd look like I was making steady improvement."

"That's very stand-up of you," Nick said, pouring me more coffee.

"It was also cowardly of me," I said. "She was so grateful, she did all my chores for the month that I was grounded, and loaned me her favorite shirt, which... in Lacey currency, she might as well have given me gold bars." I smiled at the memory. "It stresses her out when things don't come easily, and I've always hated seeing her like that. But I probably didn't need to be *that* laid-back. The cheating thing was the first time I *volunteered* myself into the sacrificial role, and now it's almost like I'm stuck there."

"Is that why you came all the way to Oxford, do you think?" Nick asked.

"I'm not sure I ever thought of it that way," I said. "Maybe. I love being a twin, but people always want to define you in relation to each other, and I guess we slip into that trap, too."

"I certainly know that feeling," Nick said, tapping his crossword wryly.

"Not to get all philosophical on you before breakfast," I teased.

"Yes, I prefer my philosophy with a side of toast, but we can't have everything."

A light breeze ruffled Nick's crossword pages. He clamped a foot down on them and cocked his head contemplatively.

"I'm sorry it's taken this long for us to have an actual conversation," he said.

"It's all good. We're talking now. Even if it was mostly me yapping about my sister."

"I feel like I have to be so careful all the time," he said. "I have a non-hilarious conversation just once, and then the next day the papers write that I'm 'Nick the Prick,' because I wasn't grinning like a madman. But if I'm having too much fun, I'm a drunken lout."

Nick's bitter tone, it turns out, was because both of these had already happened.

"It gets exhausting. I forget how to be sometimes when I'm not *on*," Nick continued. "That's why I like coming out here at dawn. I have insomnia but I can't roam the halls like some medieval ghost when my room starts to feel constricting. I have to get *out*."

"Well. You never have to be *on* with me. I promise," I said, kicking out my legs and lying down on the blanket. "You can do your crosswords and drink your heathen coffee and chill. You're not *my* sovereign."

"Yes, your ancestors saw to that." He grinned, stretching out next to me, folding his arms under his head. Then he jerked upward.

"Notre Dame," he said. He felt around for the crossword and glanced at it. "Yes, 'decrepit' means it's an anagram of 'and remote,' and you get Notre Dame, in France."

"I'm taking credit for that," I said. "All this philosophizing unlocked your potential."

He scrawled the answer into the boxes in pen. "Nonsense. I'm just extremely clever."

"Not clever enough to do those in pencil," I said, tapping a portion of the page where several answers were angrily scribbled out.

"I have confidence in me," he said.

I blinked. "Is that a *Sound of Music* quote?"

"Er, what? Maybe. I don't know. Yes," he admitted. "They show it here every year on Christmas. But we watch in secret because Gran thinks Christmas Day should be reserved for prayer and reflection. She was steaming mad one year when she caught us, but Freddie got us off the hook by arguing any movie with nuns in it counts as a religious experience."

I laughed. "I like him already."

"Everyone does," Nick said. "You'll meet him soon enough."

Our eyes met. After a beat, I nodded. It was a casual statement, couching an assumption of friendship and permanence. It was also a subtle expression of trust. Nick likes to tell me that's the moment he knew, but he's as revisionist as *The Bexicon*. He didn't feel a lightning bolt as we sat on the cold ground passing around a Thermos, and neither did I. What I *did* feel was welcome. Sitting there, thousands of miles from my usual life, I'd been scooped into his.

# CHAPTER FOUR

Nick's serious blue eyes stared deeply into mine. "Does it hurt? Do you want to stop?"

He was worried about my comfort, even in the heat of the moment.

"I'm great," I panted, desperately trying not to stare directly up the Royal Nostrils. "Just another Sunday."

"That's what I like to hear," Nick said. "Your performance is extremely important to this country. No pressure."

I did feel pressure, but mostly in my brain. Gaz and Nick were undefeated at The Glug, and their streak rested on the newbie's shoulders. Which were upended in a handstand position, my palms flat on a table that kept me off the ground, while Cilla and Clive held my legs.

Nick straightened and nodded to the adjudicator, a brown-haired guy with a reedy beard and a giant stuffed lemon on his head.

"Right, the Gazholes are set," said the Lemonhead (which is actually the job's official name). "And the BeatNicks are ready. Let the finals begin in three, two, one... glug!"

A slim hose was shoved in my mouth, Nick tilted the Pimm's vat, and I started to drink.

The colleges at Oxford are creative and saucy in their social traditions. Worcester College used to do a Half-Naked Half Hour every Wednesday in the library. In late October, on the day British Summer Time changes to Greenwich Mean Time, Merton College holds a ceremony in which students claim to mend the space-time continuum by walking around backward in formal dress while drinking port. And legend has it that Lincoln College, physically linked to Brasenose College by a locked door, centuries ago barred entry to a Brasenose student who was fleeing a mob; as a faint apology for getting that person brutally killed, Lincoln opens the door to Brasenose for five minutes on Ascension Day during Easter week and serves any incoming students free beer... that has been lightly poisoned with ground-up ivy, because why *not*.

One could argue Pembroke's indulgence in insanity, The Glug, also constitutes attempted murder by alcohol. The legend goes that in 1878, a surprise two feet of snow began falling during Pembroke's traditional Second Sunday Party on the quad (at the beginning, accordingly, of Second Week—celebrating being that much closer to the *end* of term), and The Glug was invented as a way to get hammered quickly and stay warm enough to continue the outdoor party tradition. It involves teams of five competing elimination-style to see who can guzzle the most from their upended jug of Pimm's without breaking lip-lock with the straw, vomiting, or passing out cold—like the posh English cousin to a keg stand. Once you tap out, by choice or biology, you then have to pass The Reckoning: a full thirty seconds without falling. It is the kind of insane, irresponsible, potentially fatal activity that is catnip to college kids, and Joss—who'd thrown up three times last year—seemed glad to retire. Lady Bollocks refused to participate entirely.

"Pimm's is to be *sipped*. It's what separates us from the hooligans," she snapped when she caught Gaz coaching me in the hall. She'd aimed the last word at me.

"Don't worry about Bea," Gaz counseled. "She is allergic to fun."

She also had a point. The Glug was about as regal as a root canal. Fortunately, we sailed quickly through the early rounds, and now we were in the finals.

And really buzzed.

I was the leadoff hitter, so to speak. Despite never getting used to the discomfiting presence of a judge staring at my mouth at close range, I glugged for a solid thirty-one seconds—the record is a superhuman one minute and four seconds—and then passed The Reckoning with ease. I had out-chugged Penelope Six-Names by twenty seconds.

"Suck it, BeatNicks!" I whooped, as Cilla let out a howl of glee. We then performed a triumphant chest bump that ended with me belching involuntarily as we yelped in pain. *The Bexicon* nailed it again: There was no more delicate paragon of womanhood at Oxford that year than I.

"That was the sexiest thing I've ever seen," Gaz announced, as Clive and Nick about fell over laughing.

"Which part?" Cilla wheezed. "The bumping, the burping, or the mashed boobs?"

"Yes," Gaz replied serenely.

Nick and I attempted a high five. I swung wildly and missed.

"A classic case of Pimm's Blindness," he laughed. "So tragic in one so young."

"I think it's more that some of my brain cells just exploded."

"Try again," he said, raising up my arm. "If you watch the other person's elbow at the last second, you'll never miss."

We high-fived with a satisfying smack.

"Genius!" I said. "Lacey will love that."

"No, sorry, it's a state secret. Very sensitive government information," he said.

I felt arms wrap around me from behind. Clive lifted me up and whirled me around before setting me back on my feet.

"Clive!" Cilla shouted as I struggled to regain my balance. "Never spin a Glugger until half an hour after The Glug."

"Now you've done it," Gaz said. "She'll be too Brahms'd to stand up at the trophy ceremony."

"Sorry," Clive said, steadying me. "But that was ace. That record is going down today."

Unfortunately, Clive had barely gone up when he got penalized for breaking the lip-lock rule. Cilla and Gaz more than made up for it, though, and after the BeatNicks' best player fell twice during The Reckoning, we'd built an impenetrable lead of more than a minute.

"Go on, Nicky boy," Gaz said, rubbing together his hands. "Stick it to 'em."

A terrified-looking guy called Terrance, lean as a toothpick and just as pointy, approached the table. He was an alternate—his older brother had partied too hard the night before—and though Nick's turn was a formality at this point, Terrance's team clearly expected its last Glugger to make a massive fool of himself, and the poor kid knew it. He offered Nick a wobbly handshake, and somewhere, Popeye and Twiggy doubtless took deep, meditative breaths as Nick was hoisted upside down...and drank for a pathetic seven seconds.

"Must not have eaten enough," he said once he was upright again.

"After all your training?" moaned Gaz. "We could've made history! I bet thirty quid on you to crack a minute!"

I could swear Nick winked at me, but it was so slight, I may have imagined it. Terrance turned purple when he realized what happened, and when he was righted fifteen seconds later, he was roundly cheered by the entire crowd for this small individual victory against both Glug royalty and the real thing.

"Well done! You thumped me," Nick said, clapping Terrance on the back.

Terrance just nodded, looking as though he was trying very hard to keep an avalanche of Pimm's from decorating Nick's shoes.

"Bloody sportsmanship," Gaz grumbled, even as the Lemonhead declared us the winners.

Gaz was mollified by the fact that, as the Glugger with the best time, we gave him the Glug Mug trophy—a giant bottle entirely papered over with old Pimm's labels—to keep in his window facing the quad. By the time we folded our arms around each other for the team photo that would hang in the JCR, everyone's spirits and blood-alcohol levels were equally high. I remember Clive wriggling in and giving me a firm, overlong kiss on the cheek, and as the camera flashed, I had the distinct feeling that I'd been marked.

So when a knock came at my door much later that night, I was surprised that it was not Clive but Nick, holding the Glug Mug in one hand and a large carryall in the other. He still wore the traditional Glug uniform of microscopic shorts and a sweat headband.

"I talked to Gaz," he announced, "and we decided this should go to you. Consider it your Cy Young trophy."

"For baseball's best pitcher?"

"Unless the Internet lied to me," Nick said. "A pitcher can also be called a *jug*, which you chugged very nicely at your first Glug, so the Mug..." He paused. "I think I just wrote a poem."

"It was beautiful," I said. "I will take my Cy Young award and streak the quad with it."

"Precisely what Gaz had hoped, I'm sure," Nick said. "And Mr. Young, too."

The polite thing to do was to invite him in, but my brain boiled over on me—was there a protocol for this? Was it crass to encourage a royal to park his stately behind on an unmade bed, even when there was nowhere else to sit? Was Nick even allowed to be here, given that my room was not bulletproof? *Was* my room bulletproof? No one had given *me* a dossier.

I came up with a workaround.

"Where should I put it?" I asked, pushing the door wide and gesturing at the space, which was an avalanche of books and printed pages. Oxford prefers intimate, often one-on-one sessions with professors, rather than seminars. It sounds great, but there is nowhere to hide, and I was learning that the hard way. I'd promised myself I would return to the grind after The Glug, but naturally, I was too wasted to do anything but shuffle some papers around and then watch DVDs.

Nick strode confidently inside—etiquette problem solved—and put the trophy on my desk. "Are you actually studying after a Glug? That has to be a first."

"It's my special time with Hans Holbein," I said, flopping dramatically onto my bed. "Which is a problem, because I just realized our discussion is supposed to be about Hans Holbein the *Younger*, so now I have to start over."

"Just say this: 'Hans Holbein the Younger is the man whose portraits of Nicholas's corpulent great-great-great-something-or-other Henry the Eighth are routinely ignored by filmmakers who want him to be a chiseled Adonis,'" Nick offered. "And maybe these will help."

He handed me the bag he'd been holding. I peered inside and saw a mélange of weird-yet-delicious American junk food: Cracker Jack, Twinkies, Chiken in a Biskit, a slightly crushed box of strawberry Pop-Tarts, and a crumbled bag of Bugles. It looked like someone ransacked a 7-Eleven.

"This is perfect," I said. "This is *unbelievable.*"

Nick looked pleased. "It's to combat homesickness," he said. "When you talked about your sister, it was like your volume setting got turned down a bit. Not that it needed to be," he amended. "You just seemed blue. So I looked up America's most revolting-sounding snack food and had someone in my network of spies send me a package."

"Ceres?" I asked around the foil Pop-Tart wrapping I was opening with my teeth.

"I would never reveal my sources," Nick said. "More importantly, is that woman surfing on a coffin?"

He gestured toward my open laptop. I had forgotten to pause what I was watching on it.

"If that's Holbein research, then I seriously underestimated him," Nick said.

"Turns out you can't watch a DVD and type at the same time, so obviously I prioritized," I said. "And yes, she is. A coven buried her alive. Her vampire brothers blackmailed someone into breaking all magical bonds for five minutes, but *that* started a tsunami. She's making the best of it."

Nick stared at me. "Pause that," he said, walking over and quietly shutting the door.

I obeyed, thinking of how Lacey would react to me watching *Devour* with a prince dressed more like one of the Royal Tenenbaums while I wore ratty pajama bottoms and a Cubs T-shirt with no bra. She would stroke out.

"Right," Nick said, sinking onto my bed. "I need a complete account of what's going on here. And not a word to Gaz or Clive, or I'll never hear the end of it."

I scooted back on the bed to put a little social distance between us.

"Lacey promised to send me every new episode of our favorite show, which is this crazy-bad supernatural soap opera. I think the writers make all their decisions by throwing darts at a bulletin board," I said. "There are vampires, werewolves, witches, one shape-shifter, a private investigator who can smell the future, and two panthers who seem like they know too much. *Actual* panthers, not CGI."

Nick blinked. "Oh no. Night Nick is about to become obsessed with this."

"Is that your insomniac side?" I guessed.

"More like his evil twin," he said. "Freddie and I have a running joke about how once it gets late enough, Night Nick takes over, and Night Nick is a total bastard to Day Nick. He does things like watch TV for hours, instead of going to bed. Night Nick once watched all three *Lord of the Rings* movies instead of resting up for an official appearance with Gran. Day Nick got his ears boxed for it." He sighed. "At least those are good. Night Nick usually has the worst taste."

This is true. He is the only person I know who has sought out every cut-rate sequel to every dance movie of the past twenty-odd years, and I once caught him voting in the finals of a web series called *So You Wanna Be the Next Real Housewife?* ("It will be a crime if Ashleigh doesn't win this, Bex," he'd told me seriously. "Just look at her lip implants.") I'd almost choked on my breakfast when the *Guardian* recently reported that our go-to TV program is *Morning Worship*.

Nick rewound the bit of *Devour* I'd been watching.

"Amazing," he said. "You'd think the coffin would sink."

"*That*'s the part that's bugging you?"

A knock came at the door. Cilla barged in just as Nick slammed shut the laptop, closely followed by Clive, who tossed him a newspaper. On the front page, in the bottom right corner, a headline read, NICK SAYS NO TO POLO*: "Horses Are Terrifying Beasts."*

"Crikey, who did you plant that one with?" Nick asked.

Clive looked smug. "Penelope Six-Names. I told you she was weak."

"She comes from a long line of fools," Cilla said. "My great-granddad once saved the life of *her* great-granddad after he fell on a pitchfork during a routine game of lawn bowling."

"Oh, 'fell on,' right," Clive said. "Remind me never to play any games with your family."

"How did you pass the security check?" I joked.

"My dad used to be one of Richard's PPOs," Cilla said. "Skills with unconventional weapons were an asset."

"Did you have to say 'terrifying beasts'?" Nick frowned, examining the paper. "I don't have to sound *wimpy* in these things, you know."

"Well, I was feeling colorful," Clive hedged. "And it worked, didn't it? Penelope is busted. Besides, everyone already thinks you're afraid of polo."

"I'm allergic to horses!" Nick yelped. "If this keeps up, I'm going to go on TV and sit on one and then get wheezy and faint and fall off and break my neck and then who will be sorry?"

"Well, I'm glad to see you're not overreacting," Clive said mildly. "Speaking of, I haven't told Gaz about this one yet. I'm not sure how he'll take it."

"Why on earth would Gaz care?" Cilla asked, poking through my mail nosily. "It doesn't involve free beer or potted meat products."

"He's shagging Penelope Six-Names," Clive informed her.

"What?" Cilla was startled. "He never. That useless tart? Since when?"

"The other night at The Bird," Clive replied. "But now he'll have to scrap her, I guess, as she's clearly untrustworthy. Why are you so bothered?"

"*I'm* not bothered in the slightest," Cilla said, nose in the air. "I just had hoped for his sake that he had better taste in girls than he does in shirts. Apparently not."

She turned to me, and I detected a faint blush in her cheeks. "We're going to The Head of the River. Kitchen is open late tonight and I'm dying for fish and chips. Are you in?" she asked.

"That sounds great," I said, but just then I saw Nick's finger twitch. He was jonesing, and besides, I had something that I wanted to ask him. "Um, but I can't. I'm having some trouble with one of the Hans Holbeins, and Nick agreed to help me out."

Cilla let out a braying laugh. "Art, Nick? Can you even draw stick people?"

"It's art *history*," he said. "These people painted my entire bloodline. I'm very useful."

Clive looked disappointed. And, admittedly, rather cute in his England rugby shirt, his glasses slightly crooked, his hair still a Gluggy mess.

"Are you sure?" he asked me. "It's pub trivia night. Hugh von Huber is hosting, which means it'll all be questions about historical Germans who were actually very kind."

"Thanks," I said, getting up to give him a kiss on the cheek. "Another night, I promise. If I screw up the actual university part of Oxford, I'm on the next plane."

"Suit yourselves," Cilla said, closing the door, but not before an appraising look at us.

Nick and I were alone again. There was a moment of silence.

"I don't want you to think—" he began.

"Which story did you plant with me?" I said at the same time.

"See, the thing is," Nick said, fidgeting, "there are always people with big mouths, or bad intentions, or who just can't say no in the face of a fat pile of cash. Father told the press to back off and let me be, but sometimes they try to get crafty with the people on the ground here."

"And you all tell different lies to see which ones end up in the paper," I reasoned. "Like a trap."

"It's harmless," Nick said. "It's not like we're having her executed. Just maybe thrown in the Tower for a week."

"So what lie did you feed me by the bridge the other day?" I crossed my arms, hurt and put off. "Or was the entire conversation a test?"

"I was hardly camped out there waiting for you to come trotting by at dawn," he said, sounding defensive. Then he picked uneasily at my quilt. "When I was a child, you couldn't pick up a paper without reading something salacious about my parents," he said quietly. "A miscarriage my mother had, some terrible fight, a story about her up all night crying because she'd hugged an old childhood friend and everyone decided he was actually my father. True stories that only someone inside our house would know. My mum..." His voice faltered. "I've learnt to be careful. I don't know how else to do it."

I studied him for a second.

"I guess I can see your point," I said. "If every stupid thing I said ran the risk of being in *The New York Times*, I'd have duct-taped my mouth by now and become a recluse."

An expression of sadness crossed his face, and realizing what I'd just said, I wished I could've done exactly that.

"Dammit," I cursed. "I'm sorry, I forgot that your mom doesn't—"

"Never mind," Nick said. "I know you meant well. She's . . . just shy."

I reached over to squeeze his hand, but caught myself and ended up patting his knee like an affectionate old aunt. "I just mean, I don't have a right to be mad. I obviously don't know what I'm talking about."

He met my eyes. "If it helps, it was different with you. Everything I told you that morning was true."

Then he opened my laptop. "And I will buy you *three* plates of fish and chips in exchange for letting me experience this show, and perhaps one of those Twinkies, which look like an equally bad idea," he said, hitting play. "Let's get to work."

# CHAPTER FIVE

Night Nick and Night Bex were equal parts compatible and self-destructive. One *Devour* episode led to another, and one shipment of Twinkies became three (Nick liked to stick his fingers in them and eat them like corn dogs, and also prod me in the face). Lacey sent us her DVDs of old seasons so Nick and I could binge on the whole saga from the beginning while we waited for the newest hours, and she was delighted to have what she viewed as a profound impact on Nick's life.

The more fun I had feeding Nick's obsession, though, the more often Clive found himself displaced from my bed. While I was never in love with Clive—the closest we got to being official was agreeing that, *officially*, there were no strings attached—we definitely were involved. There's no denying it, no revising it, no editing my behavior into something more innocent. Nick's great-grandmother, Marta, the Queen Mum, once asked me if I was nervous about—and I quote—*losing my maidenhead* on our wedding night. I snickered before I could catch myself, and she playfully wiggled the scotch in her hand and said, "Too right. A woman can't bloody well pick her signature drink without sampling the whole bar."

Not looking to fall in love didn't mean I didn't want to sample the cocktails, so to speak, but at Oxford, the bar wasn't as open as I'd have liked. Half the men we met wanted an in with the Crown, were prone to spouting off on the plight of the landed estates, or just wanted to ask endless conspiracy theory questions, like whether the Queen ever rigged the horse races (no) or requested certain *Coronation Street* storylines (she says no, but I don't believe it). Any promising guys without Nick-related agendas lost interest in me once they got wind of who my friends were, and decided I wasn't worth the fuss. It turned out to be less agita just to walk down the hall, and Clive made himself a habit that was hard to break. He was attentive and witty, and with a bit of coaching, his kissing vastly improved (he'd always been skilled at the rest of it). I thought it was sweet that he'd put his hand on the small of my back to steer me through crowds, and that he bought a hypoallergenic pillow in case I wanted to sleep in his room. But it was hard to untangle that warmth and comfort and familiarity—that pure *like*—from the other truth of the circumstance: I enjoyed Clive's company, but I also enjoyed the company Clive kept. Cutting the umbilical cord that yoked me to Lacey for twenty years was so much easier thanks to everyone on my floor *not* named Bea, and over time, their friendship became my cocoon. Especially because the instant the grapevine gleaned that I had gotten tight with Nick, polite nods and interest in the American newcomer gave way to under-the-breath jokes about my nationality, or snickers about the origin of my family's money. Assumptions about my motivations had been made, and I was being assessed and found wanting.

"All hail the Sofa Queen," one guy said at a pub.

"Cheers, BHS!" said another, at breakfast, referencing a British furniture store.

"Are you getting the next round, Bex?" Lady Bollocks said one night in the JCR. "Don't forget, here at Oxford we keep the drinks all the way up at the bar rather than under our bums."

Most of the teasing was casual, except possibly Bea's—although even that I could handle; I wasn't ashamed of my dad actually working for his wealth. But my friends never succumbed to nor stood for those jokes, nor made any of their own, and my gratitude for that loyalty colored and heightened my appreciation of everything. Which therefore kept me from acknowledging the raging case of Clivus interruptus that was developing every time Nick and I settled in for a *Devour* marathon, and I wasn't doing anything to stop it.

What nobody knew, and neither he nor I said aloud, was that my room had become a safe haven for Nick. Although he trusted his friends with his life, he wasn't as liberal with his self, yet something about those uncinematic, quotidian hangouts in my room relaxed his grip on the real Nick. He grew comfortable shuffling in wearing the old Snoopy pajama pants that had been Freddie's Christmas gag gift; bringing in coffee and crosswords when it was too cold to take them outside; tasting and rating the relative wretchedness of the microwaved meals we bought at the market. Certain columnists claim Nick liked me in spite of my being an American, but—not to discount my sweatshirts and ripped jeans, nor the alluring way I stopped bothering to brush my hair when he came by—I think it was *because* of it. Imagine knowing everyone in your life would one day have to stop calling you by your name and honor you as their sovereign. It's impossible for that not to erect walls, even subconsciously. But with me that wasn't an issue, and I enjoyed letting Nick be, for perhaps the first time in his life, unremarkable.

Meanwhile, *Devour*—never exactly a critical favorite—was pulling out all the stops to get ratings in its sixth season, like trapping the shape-shifter in the body of a ninety-three-year-old nun, and delivering a cliffhanger that involved an actual cliff and, unexpectedly, an actual hanger. Night Nick and Night Bex had been fiending, so when a disc arrived in late October with a Post-it in Lacey's perfect script reading simply, *Minotaur alert*, I stuck it under Nick's door and returned to my room to wait him out.

Nick burst in two hours later. "Sorry, I was out with India. We need a bat signal so I can come home as soon as these get here."

He stopped short when he realized I was on the phone.

"Everything's fine, Dad, that's just my horribly impatient hallmate Nick," I said into the receiver.

"He's pretty loud," Dad said.

"He was raised in a barn."

Dad chortled. "I'm going to tell the Queen you said that."

"I'm going to tell Gran you said that," Nick was whispering at the same time.

"Put him on the phone, honey," Dad said. "Prince or no prince, if this Nick fellow is going to run around your dorm room I should at least get the chance to scare him a little."

"Dad, we're just friends. And he probably isn't allowed to talk to you."

"Oh, I most certainly am," Nick said, snatching the receiver from me. "Hello, sir," he said in an absurdly proper-sounding voice. "This is Nicholas Wales speaking."

This is one of my favorite memories. The *put your man-friend on the phone* gambit was the greatest gift my dad gave Nick, because it said from the get-go that he didn't view him any differently than any other guy who hung out in my bedroom.

"What studies, sir?" Nick said into the phone. "Are you quite sure she's doing any?"

I kicked at his leg.

"Oh, indeed, loads of trouble," he said. "I expect she'll get kicked out of the country fairly soon. Sharing humiliating stories might help—you know, really good blackmail material, to keep her on the straight and narrow."

I lunged at the phone but Nick stiff-armed me away from him.

"That is shocking, sir," he said.

"You are dead to me," I called out in the general direction of the phone.

"Oh, that one's even better. That'll do nicely," Nick said. "Thank you, sir. Yes, my royal upbringing should be a wonderful influence. Oh, and if you've got any in Liverpool red, my mate Gaz would love a Coucherator."

"Those things would never fit up these stairs," I hissed loudly.

"Maybe we can fit it in through a window," Nick said. "Right, sir, we'll measure it. Have a wonderful night. Go Cubs."

"Sycophant," I said, reclaiming the phone. "We're already out of the playoffs."

I let my dad know rather colorfully what I thought of that whole scene, and then hung up. Nick was studying me, a mischievous expression on his face.

"You threw your prom date into a rubbish bin?"

"He was being too handsy!" I protested. "He kept trying to hump my leg on the dance floor, and then told me he had a pearl necklace for me in the limo. So I *may* have spiked his punch an obscene amount, and the Dumpster was right outside—"

Nick held up his hand. "Oh, I heard," he said. "Although not the necklace thing; that is disgusting. But there is also the matter of a pet hamster named…let me see if I get this right…Prince Nicky? Whom you tried to flush down the toilet?"

"Lacey named him!" I said. "And he fell in! He was fine! He was aquatic!"

"I ought to call PPO Furrow and have you reevaluated," Nick said.

I held up the latest *Devour* episode. "No sudden moves, *Nicky*. I can end this for you right here, right now."

Nick took his usual spot on the fluffy rug and raised a hand. "Twinkies, please," he said airily. "Be a good subject and pass them along. It's what your father would want."

I threw the pack at his head, which he caught deftly before it smacked him in the nose.

"Treason," he said. "I quite like your dad. I can't wait to meet him."

I grabbed the Cracker Jack and grunted.

When the credits ran—Spencer Silverstone threw supernatural acid at her romantic rival, a mortal named Carrie, and it gave her a mind-controlling scar with a murderous agenda—we plunged back into the end of season two (known to me and Lacey as The Ill-Fated Talking-Candle Experiment), which led to a lively debate about the laws of shape-shifting. Nick finally groaned and rolled over straight into a half-eaten microwave curry from the local supermarket.

"I am numb," he said, picking congealed lumps of chicken off his arm. "Oh God, is it getting light outside?"

He ran to my window. "It has *gotten* light outside," he amended, squinting at my travel clock. "It's seven fifteen, Rebecca Porter."

I yawned forcefully. "Night Bex and Night Nick strike again."

"Rebecca," Nick said in a whisper-bellow. "This is very bad."

"Why?" I peered up at him, crunching my pillow under my cheek.

Nick began pacing, picking things up and then immediately putting them down again.

"Well, for starters, I have spent another full night in your room and Clive is not going to like that," he said.

"Clive underst—"

"And beyond that," Nick said, not hearing me, "I have an event today. Father and I are opening an exhibit of family ancestral writings at the Ashmolean."

I sat up. "That's today?"

"Yes, Rebecca, that is today."

"Why do you keep calling me Rebecca?"

Nick pulled every hair on his head straight into the air. "Because, Rebecca," he said, "I have gone insane. My father is due in three hours. Why did we stay up so late? I am an *idiot*."

He was doomed; I was sure of it. His eyes were bloodshot and his face looked gray. But I decided this was one time honesty was not what Nick needed.

"Everything is going to work out," I said instead. "Here's what you're going to do. You're going to leave my room and you're going to take a cold shower."

"This already sounds like the worst plan."

"It'll wake you up, dumbass."

Nick didn't even flinch at that, which I now know is because Freddie has called him worse at least once a day their entire lives.

"Then," I continued, "chug a pot of coffee and, like, a gallon of water. The caffeine will wake you up and the water will keep you hydrated. And get some greasy food. But *no pastries*, Nick. Pure carbs will make you crash."

"How do you know all this?" Nick asked, rubbing his eyes.

"Nicholas," I said. "You may have named her, but Night Bex has existed since long before I met you. One day, I'll tell you about the time I only slept two hours before my aunt Kitty's wedding, where I had to give an insanely long reading in German, which I don't speak."

"How much more could there be to tell?" he said.

"Focus," I commanded him. "You are not going to blow this. I promise."

Nick grabbed me in a tight hug. Improbably, he smelled delicious, an indescribable scent that I will always only be able to define as *him*. And maybe a bit of tikka masala.

"I'd be lost without you," he said. And as he scampered off to his room, I turned around and passed out on my bed.

Everything about Prince Richard is narrow, from his body to the oval of his head to the line of his longish nose. But his bearing, the way he carries his position with just enough pomposity that you feel it but not enough that you wholly dislike him for it, gives him an aura of being good-looking even though the sum of the parts is fairly plain. I'd long been familiar with his face, because my parents went to London in the eighties and brought back a commemorative Royal Wedding wastebasket that's in their downstairs bathroom ("He's going to be king. He *should* live in the throne room," Dad had said). But seeing someone in magazines—or tossing used Kleenex into him—is different than watching him move and speak in person, especially after the passage of more years than my parents or Richard might care to admit.

That night, Richard and Nick were hosting a grand reopening of Oxford's Ashmolean Museum after a large renovation. The new modern lobby and balconies were packed with donors, rich alleged art lovers, local looky-loos who'd won a ticket lottery, and us, Nick's motley support crew—stuck upstairs against a glass railing that put us nose-to-nethers with a giant naked statue of Apollo from the fifth century BC. This delighted Gaz, who loudly wondered if he could distinguish one huge dick from the other.

"It gives me great pleasure to have my son with me today, in our first joint venture since he gave up polo," Richard was saying into a microphone. His speaking voice is not the rich baritone I always expect; it's higher, thinner, a touch raspy. The Queen Mum once told me she thinks his tantrums as a young boy made it that way forever. I love her.

Nick—just behind his father, who stood at a podium on one of the angular atrium staircase's landings—remained serene and impassive, despite the hot-button polo issue. I'd become fluent enough in Nick's facial expressions to recognize this veneer as Advanced Pleasantness. It meant he was annoyed.

"We're delighted to christen the new Ashmolean with never-before-seen private writings of our Lyons ancestors," Richard continued. "The Princess of Wales wishes she could have been here. She'd have been immensely proud to see Nicholas contributing to Oxford's history and culture. Especially as she once practically had to drag him through the Louvre."

Nick gave a hearty belly laugh, as did the crowd, and Richard preened. I knew he and his staff had swept Nick out of Pembroke for Official Princely Duties at bang on ten o'clock that morning—I woke up at the sound, then passed out again—but he seemed as rested as if he'd gotten ten hours. Lean and handsome in his navy suit, Nick had worked the crowd like a pro, shaking hands, chatting up old ladies, posing for photographs with museum dignitaries, and making merry with his father. It was like he'd been born to do it, and of course that's exactly what he was; *this* Nick was utterly in command, with none of the jagged edges and endearing goofiness that I was used to, and it made him a bit alien to me.

Richard finally yielded him the microphone.

"I'll have you know my mother never dragged me through the Louvre," Nick said, practically twinkling. "Because I wouldn't let her get me past the entryway. She had to sit there and play cards with me while Freddie and the others got a private look at the Mona Lisa." The crowd roared. "It was worth it. I won," he added, cheekily, as Richard reached out to squeeze his son on the shoulder. It was a warm moment in complete opposition to the frosty one in the paper a few weeks back—the news would later call it *an affectionate father-son volley, presenting a united front in the face of rumors of friction*—and the elderly, wealthy benefactors loved it.

For different reasons, so did our friends.

"Better laugh than his father got. Take that, Prince Dick," grumbled Bea from behind me. I turned to look at her, surprised. "May I help you?" she asked haughtily.

"I hope you'll take the time to enjoy the exhibit tonight before it opens tomorrow," Nick was saying. "I know I must, because during term—"

"Blah, blah, blah." Clive whispered into my ear, giving it a nip.

"Shh."

"No one's paying attention to us," Clive said. "They'll never notice if we sneak off and find a dark corner. Everyone's too busy gossiping about him and India."

"Look at her down there," Bea grumbled. "The cat that got the cream. The cat that got several *pints* of cream."

Even from up high, I could see the glowing face of India Bolingbroke, who had not arrived on Nick's arm but whom the rumor mill—so, Clive—insisted had been placed specially in the front row on the ground floor, along with a clutch of Richard-approved luminaries. The appearance caused reporters to use words like *adoring* and *ladylike* and *exceedingly well matched* in the papers the next day. I couldn't imagine she and Nick were actually that tight. Nick had shortened or rescheduled several outings with her in favor of hanging out with me, and I never saw her on our floor at all. I assumed she'd been inside his room, but I couldn't have guessed when, and although I'd seen them holding hands surreptitiously in a dark bar, he'd never so much as given her a peck on the cheek in public. But that night I had witnessed him guiding her gently through the throng, leaning in attentively, drawing her into conversations. If she was besotted, he was at the very least protective.

"Richard loves her," Clive said, in reporter mode, as we watched India applaud exuberantly. "Fancy parents, rich enough not to be grasping, not a whiff of scandal."

"Nor a whiff of personality," Bea said. "I've known Nick since we were tots"—Gaz mouthed along at this behind her back—"and she'll bore him to tears in a week."

But unquestionably, India looked like the sort of person who ought to be dating a prince: model-gorgeous with a megawatt smile, wearing a dress that easily cost two thousand pounds. Given that nearly everything I owned at this time was from Old Navy, I'd greeted Nick's group invitation to the gala with a panicked phone call to Lacey, who pointed out that I had a clothing designer living next door. This turned out to be a mistake: Joss had insisted I wear her favorite new design, a stretchy crushed-velvet-and-leather dress that twisted strangely across my torso, in which I resembled nothing so much as a lampshade at a biker bar. Cilla had taken one look at it and lent me a very large coat.

We drank flute upon flute of free Champagne while Nick made the rounds, introducing India to a series of elaborately bearded lords. She certainly seemed to charm Nick's father. To the outsider and even to many insiders, Richard seems like a relic, a man meant to rule five hundred years ago when a mere flash of his sword could vanquish his enemies and oppress the peasants. But with India that night, Richard laughed and was as solicitous as Nick, which the news claimed was tantamount to him anointing her as his future daughter-in-law.

It was two hours before we got anywhere near them.

"Thank God," Nick said, excusing himself from whomever Richard was speaking to; Richard never abandoned the conversation, yet kept a firm eye on Nick's back. "I have answered the same two questions forty-five times." He eyed my massive coat. "Are you cold?"

"Joss," Cilla said.

"Say no more." He grinned.

"Dick bringing up the polo thing was a bit much, given the papers," murmured Clive.

"But your speech was great," I said. "That Louvre story is super charming."

"And apocryphal," he said. "Father told me we needed Warm Family Stories, and obviously most of mine are fictional."

I started to laugh, until I saw nobody else was, and that he wasn't joking.

"Where's India?" I asked, changing tacks. "I've never officially met her."

Nick pointed across the way. "I left her with a woman who kept asking me how I plan to defend myself in case of kidnapping."

"How attentive of you," said Bea.

"She'll be all right. They're talking about Pilates," Nick said. "It's awkward bringing someone to these things, but Father insisted, and I was too tired to fight it." His gaze flickered toward me.

PPO Furrow stepped in, his signature wrinkle in full effect. "The Prince of Wales prefers you to stay with the VIP guests," he said in a low voice.

Nick closed his eyes for a brief moment and then shifted back into work mode. "Yes, I must get back to my duties," he said. "Thank you all for coming. I really appreciate it."

"What a piece of bloody work Richard is," Cilla said as we peered through the crowd to see him greet Nick with a slap on the back of ostensible gaiety—but with a slightly harder thump than was strictly necessary.

The five of us spent another half hour people-watching. We weren't so much in a crowd as in the middle of an impromptu receiving line—as if the hive mind told everyone to arrange themselves in a way that might hide their essential purpose of waiting for a touch of the royal hand—and as soon as the princes were whisked away, the alleged art aficionados disappeared along with them. They may have said they were there to support the Ashmolean, but they bolted as soon as the bar had closed.

By that point, as occurs in nearly every story from my Oxford year, we had gotten a wee bit drunk—or at least, moderately tipsy, enough so that when I insisted we be cultured and look at the manuscripts, Gaz actually booed. I didn't care. I wanted to linger at the glass cases containing so much sloping, dated cursive on yellowing pages—the intimate and sometimes illuminatingly banal correspondence from back when people cared to do it longhand. Eleanor had very precise penmanship; her father, King Richard IV, was prone to decorating state documents with doodles of the Crown Jewels. But the best were the letters between King Albert and his queen, Georgina Lyons-Bowes, whose untimely death during World War I broke his heart and—my old syphilis joke aside—eventually his mind as well. It was that first torrent of grief that prompted him to adopt Lyons as the dynastic name, and it's endlessly romantic to me that his progeny have reigned under that name now for over a hundred years, all because Albert really, really, *really* loved his wife.

"Oh, Bertie, my pet, do be a love and stay true forever and ever. You *are* a dear," Clive mimicked as I studied one of Georgina's letters.

"Don't be like that," I said, elbowing him. "These are amazing."

"You *look* amazing." Clive's voice reverberated in my ear, as he reached under my coat and ran his fingers over my dress.

"I look like a lunatic."

"A gorgeous lunatic."

"Don't bother me with your hormones. I'm reading," I said playfully.

"These are so bloody formal," Clive complained, leaning over the case, so close to me that I could feel his breath on my cheek. "Look, this one uses the royal we. 'We do love you ever so much.' That's about as romantic as an appendectomy."

"They stood on ceremony back then," I said. "Imagine taking the time every day to write pages and pages to someone about how wonderful they are. Now people just send texts with half the right letters missing."

Clive turned me toward him. "I solemnly swear never to use abbreviations when I text you sweet nothings," he said, "if you will do me the honor of going to get a cocktail with me."

He looked so eager, so sincere. Inexplicably, a memory of India Bolingbroke and Nick together at the party popped into my head. I pulled Clive toward me by the tie and kissed him.

"Let's go. These shoes are killing me," I said. "But just one drink. I was up late."

As usual, one drink became three. But when fatigue set in at around eleven, I extracted myself from The Bird so I could go home and get a little work done before crashing. Clive walked me to a cab, clearly hoping I would tell him to get in after me. I sincerely needed to do some reading, but I was feeling extra warmly toward him—he'd entertained us with the latest rugby news of the brother he called Thick Trevor; rubbed my feet, swollen from being shoved under duress into borrowed stilettos; and told a great story about the time Freddie shot Nick in the butt with a BB gun—so I told him to knock on my door when he got home. With Nick, I had Night Bex, and with Clive it was Beer Bex. Everything seemed grand after a few pints.

When I got back to Pembroke, I found a new DVD of *Devour* from Lacey in my mail slot. This time, the enclosed note read only, *!!!!!!* The very sight of it sent Night Bex into a lusty tizzy. Beer Bex tapped out and she tapped in; I ripped off my heels and tore up the stairs. Nick's door was ever so slightly ajar.

I burst through it waving the DVD in the air. "Ten pounds says the Minotaur tramples one of those judgmental panthers."

"—completely unacceptable. I have made my decision. Respect it!" Richard was bellowing, his face an unsightly shade of purple. Spittle shot like darts onto the floor.

This was the first time I'd ever even seen inside Nick's room. It didn't look bulletproof, but now I know that appearances are deceiving—those old windows were actually full of special glass (and obviously soundproofed, given that I hadn't heard Richard yelling until I'd stumbled inside). In fact, it looked mostly like mine, except Nick's comforter was tartan, and there was a bobblehead of Queen Eleanor on the desk that I later found out was a gift. From her. That was all I could take in, though, because both Nick and Richard whipped around to face me, and I briefly went blind from nerves.

"What are you doing in here?" Richard snapped.

"Father," Nick said in a low voice. "She's a friend."

"My apologies," Richard said, not sounding apologetic at all. "I was having a private conversation with my son and you caught us by surprise. I don't believe we've met."

I immediately felt completely sober. We could eliminate drunk driving altogether if Prince Richard would just be willing to stand outside of pubs at closing time and indiscriminately yell at people.

"I'm Bex, er, Rebecca, Your... sir... Highness," I stammered, resisting an urge to curtsy.

"Ah, yes, the American," Richard said, studying me. "And is disrespect for protocol so ingrained that you're in the habit of barging in on an heir to the throne?"

"I'm so sorry. No disrespect intended," I said, trying to sound very composed. "I was just returning some, er, study aids."

"Father, this is un—"

Richard held up a hand mere inches from Nick's face, without even glancing at his way.

"I'm sure you can return your *study aid* at a more convenient occasion," Richard said to me, his tone dipping several degrees below zero. "Nicholas and I are enjoying some father-son bonding time. I'm sure you understand."

I peeked at Nick's face. He was red-eyed, and not just in a tired way, although he looked that, too. Right there, as in most future interactions with Richard, I decided it was probably wisest to toe the line and escape as quickly as possible.

"Oh, and my dear," Richard added. "I know that nobody will ever hear anything about any trifling family disagreements you may have thought you overheard."

His voice was now bordering on pleasant, but his eyes most definitely were not.

I gulped. "Sure," I said, feeling and sounding incredibly American in that one short word. "See you later, Nick."

That was my first brush with just how barren Nick's family life was. I felt a flash of gratitude for my own parents, who are frustrating sometimes, but who at least don't issue veiled threats to my friends specifically so they will shit themselves with fear, and have never starved Lacey and me of their love or attention. It's not entirely Richard's fault; he didn't become a tyrant in a vacuum. He was raised by a painfully proper mother and her army of uptight nannies, and barely knew his own long-deceased father—and thus was totally unprepared to be one. He was never comfortable with Nick and Freddie until they were walking and talking and could see reason, and when that day came, it was too late.

Holed up in my room, I felt nauseated thinking about leaving Nick alone to wilt under Richard's wrath. I had several elaborate fantasies about storming back in and giving him hell on Nick's behalf, but in the end, I just turned out my lights so I could feign being asleep when Clive's knock came (which it did, inevitably, with a tapping that became slightly insistent before giving way to his footsteps creaking away). I wasn't in the mood; Nick's misery consumed me. I rested only fitfully before finally sneaking into the hallway to go the bathroom—just as Richard was walking out of Nick's quarters. I dipped back and hid behind my door, but couldn't resist watching him through the crack. He shot Nick one last look of fury, which for a split second dissolved into something else—regret?—before he put on his public mask of indifference and slipped away down the stairs.

Day Bex wanted me to give it up and go to sleep, like a rational person, but Night Bex never obeys that boring old shrew. So I grabbed a pen and the *Devour* DVD and crept toward Nick's door, careful to avoid the squeaky parts of the old floor. Underneath the string of exclamation marks on Lacey's note, I scribbled, *Dear Night Nick: Take two and call me in the morning*, then smoothed the Post-it back over the DVD and shoved it all under his door.

The next morning it came back under mine. *Day Nick is dead. Long live Night Nick.*

# CHAPTER SIX

When she was eight, Lady Emma Somers's dog Yoghurt died, and she wept on the shoulder of her best friend Rupert at the backyard funeral while her brother murdered "Amazing Grace" on the bagpipes. Emma told this story herself, back when she was engaged to Richard and the press was keen to learn about the fetching, rosy-cheeked innocent who'd stolen his heart. Shortly after her wedding, Rupert became Emma's trusted bodyguard, and the fall of my year at Oxford the *Sunday Express* ran an exposé in which Rupert Caulfield—promoting an upcoming book—insisted he'd fathered at least one of England's beloved princes. The fallout was swift. The *Mirror* ran a photo of Emma and Rupert on the beach together as children, juxtaposed with a shot of them laughing cozily a year after her wedding. The *Mail* got a recent picture of Rupert driving near Trewsbury House—where the reclusive Princess of Wales was known to hole up—at a time when Richard was in London. Reporters scavenged for anecdotes that either refuted an affair or confirmed it; an anonymous maid claimed Rupert had "lain with" Emma one week after her wedding and twice monthly since, whereas Emma's former butler swore Rupert was just a friend. Reports of DNA tests were combatted by rumors that Rupert and the *butler* were involved. It was, in short, a hot aristocratic mess.

Nick took a brief sabbatical from Oxford, which Clive confirmed was to hunker down at Clarence House and strategize how to handle the crisis. (Freddie coped by bravely visiting Monte Carlo. This is typical Freddie. He throws parties where a simple tantrum would've been sufficient.) I felt terrible for him. Everybody did. Clive made all the academic arrangements Nick needed to stay on track. Joss made him a tie out of motorbike gears, which Nick still doesn't know because it sliced into Gaz's thumb when he tested it out, so she scrapped it. Cilla dusted Nick's room and put flowers in a vase on the desk, then replaced them every time they died before he came home to tend them. And I stockpiled *Devour* episodes for when Nick needed them—and me.

One morning at the beginning of November, when Nick had been absent for a little more than a week, Cilla, Joss, and I studied the latest papers from a bench at the Oxford bus station. Lacey was coming to visit for our birthday, and she was due to arrive from Heathrow any minute.

Joss let out a low whistle. "This says Emma and Rupert were together during that Ashmolean party she skipped," she said.

"Oh, please," Cilla said, grabbing the paper from Joss and examining a shot of Rupert coming out of a Tesco, looking jolly. "As the saying goes, 'Any Yorkshirewoman worth her birthright can smell a lie,' and I can tell you that tosser reeks something awful."

"That is not a saying. *Nobody* says that."

"What is the deal with Emma?" I jumped in.

"Nick never talks about it and we never ask," Cilla said, flipping to the horoscopes. "She backed away from the public eye not too long after Freddie was born and hasn't been to an event in ages. The official line is that she decided she preferred a private life of philanthropy and reflection, or something."

"Bollocks," said Joss.

"Maybe she's agoraphobic," I said. "Like the Japanese crown princess." It was a theory Lacey had advanced on the phone.

"No, I mean, *Bollocks*," Joss said, gesturing toward the entrance.

Sure enough, stomping toward us was Bea, in gorgeous brown leather boots and a wool pencil skirt, her olive peacoat pulled tightly around a thick scarf.

"You lot should be ashamed, reading that trash in public," she said, snatching our papers.

"Oh, blow it out your arse, Bea," Cilla said. "What are you doing here, anyway? Stalking us? Are you going to report back to the Crown that we've been caught *reading*?"

"I'm looking at a horse at a stable near Swindon. My dressage mount is getting altogether too horny to focus." She shook her head. "Don't change the subject."

"Aren't we being respectful to Nick by boning up on what *not* to talk about?" Joss suggested. "See, this one claims that he's going ring shopping for India Bolingbroke, another one says Davinia Cathcart-Hanson wants him back, and then *The Sun* thinks he's gone to Africa to beg Gemma Sands for another shot."

"Bollocks," sniffed Lady Bollocks in a wonderful moment of synergy that almost made me laugh right in her face. "India is so stupid it's a wonder she can still breathe. He'll never marry any of them."

"You sound awfully sure of yourself," Cilla said.

"I know things," Bea said loftily. "Besides, who wants to be tied down in university or right after it? Use your brains, ladies." She poked at the papers. "And be more careful. You know how he feels about gossip." She narrowed her eyes at me specifically. "Not everyone is so American about letting it all hang out all over the place."

And with that, she marched right on past us and boarded a waiting bus.

"Do you think she's really going to Swindon, or she just needed to make an exit?" Joss wondered.

"I think that bus actually goes to Newcastle, so good luck to her either way," Cilla said.

"She does *not* like me," I said.

"Pay her no mind," Cilla said, waving her hand dismissively. "She's twitchy when it comes to him. Her mother is Emma's best friend, so she's seen a lot of his life firsthand."

"It probably doesn't help that you're juggling Nick and Clive," Joss added.

"I'm not juggling anyone," I protested. "Nick and I just hang out sometimes, which I think is specifically because he *knows* I'm not trying to date him. He's like... a brother."

Both girls chortled.

"Anyway, he's with India!" I protested. "Or whoever. One of these girls."

"I think he's mad for Gemma," Joss said, unwrapping her scarf as if the gossip warmed her up. "Apparently, he proposed to her on her family's reservation when he was really young, *and* that's where he spent his gap year."

"See? India, Davinia, Gemma, maybe even Bea for all we know," I counted off the prospects on my gloved hand.

Cilla shot me a knowing look. "I hear you two laughing in your room until the wee hours. You think we don't notice, but we do."

"Nick is taken," I said. "And I don't want to be."

Cilla raised a russet brow. "Don't you?" she said. "You're with Nick most days, and when you do open your bedroom door, Clive is waiting. Sounds taken to me."

"Whatever you do, definitely don't keep seeing Clive." Joss yawned. "He's such a slave to the Palace."

"Says the girl whose father gives Eleanor her mammograms," Cilla said.

"Clive can't be that much of a slave to the Palace if he wants to be a reporter," I said.

Joss shook her head. "The media is an indentured servant. Tank says—"

"Tank is as thick as one," Cilla scoffed.

"And Clive is lovely," I said defensively. "You're friends with him, too, Joss!"

"I'm friends with a lot of people I think are too boring to snog," Joss said.

"I don't think anyone ever really wants to end up with a bloke they call 'lovely,'" Cilla added. "My great-great-aunt married one, and the man made her so potty that eventually she poisoned him, and to get revenge his spirit possessed a garden rabbit that stared at her through the bedroom window for years."

"Why didn't she just poison it, too?" Joss asked.

Cilla looked at her as if she were crazy. "It wasn't the rabbit's fault." She then turned to me. "My point, Rebecca my love, is that it's hard to be free and clear for whatever comes along when you're not making any room for anything to come along."

This profundity was interrupted by the halting growls of a bus carefully turning into the station's tight entrance. Within twenty seconds of the doors opening, Lacey hurtled out of it and threw herself right at me. We shrieked and hugged for five full minutes, as startled-looking passengers waited by the luggage hold for their bags.

"This is amazing!" Lacey crowed. "The scenery is amazing. This bus station is amazing. That chocolate bar I bought at Heathrow was amazing." She looked at Joss, who was wearing crookedly stitched pleather leggings with homemade knee socks over them that read *Welcome to Soxford* in cross-stitch. "Those socks are amazing. England is *fucking* amazing."

"Oh, I like you," Joss said.

"It's so good to have you here," I said, squeezing Lacey again. "Come on, let's get back. I think Gaz is hoping you'll want to party away your jet lag."

"Great! I can't wait to meet Gaz," Lacey said. "And . . . everyone."

"You mean Clive?" Cilla asked innocently, as we began to head to the parking lot. "If you haven't heard, he's lovely."

Lacey turned to me. "So you're officially not into him."

"Told you!" Cilla was triumphant. "She's clearly the smart one."

"Great. I already regret introducing the two of you. Maybe I should send Lacey back," I said, but I didn't let go of my sister the whole walk to the car.

I showed Oxford off as proudly as if I'd discovered it myself, and Lacey was a satisfying audience. She loved the juxtaposition of Oxford's old architecture with its zebra-striped crosswalks and drugstores and Starbucks and McDonald's. She loved the slim alleys that opened into unseen pubs, their patios and flower boxes and famous meat pies kept secret from the streets. She loved the small piece of the Bodleian Library that she could see, and the archaic rule that new students and visiting researchers had to recite a vow of good behavior just to venture into the parts she couldn't. She loved the beef-flavored potato chips, and the shrimp-flavored potato chips, and the chicken-flavored potato chips. She even loved Clive. Our first night unfurled in a pleasant whirl of introductions and jokes and pints. Gaz proposed, Cilla smacked him for being lecherous, and Clive was chivalrous to a fault, even carrying Lacey to my door when she joked she was afraid she'd fall asleep walking up the stairs.

"I can't figure out why you're not in love with him," Lacey said fuzzily.

"Because he's lovely, I guess," I said, mostly to myself.

As usual, Lacey was a rock star. Where I'd originally been the one who piqued everybody's curiosity, I was old news now, and she'd packed her A-game for this trip, dazzling everyone with the infectious fizzy energy she always pulled out whenever she wanted people to fall in love with her. It was a trick I could never help but to admire, like a spectator, and it worked in Oxford the way it had always done. Joss proclaimed her a genius after a lengthy three-hour discussion of fashion. Cilla liked her because they shared a tendency to shoot straight with me (which translated to a lot of ribbing about Clive). And Bea ignored her except to note that she had better taste in shoes than I. It pleased me, how much everyone liked Lacey—I felt like the person who'd brought the most popular dish to the potluck—but there was also the smallest sense that I'd lost something that had been wholly mine.

"You do sort of look alike," Clive mused. "Lacey's teeth are straighter."

"Different noses. Lacey's ends in that little ski-jump bit," Gaz narrated.

"And Bex is more angular. Everywhere," Clive said.

"That can't be good," I said, and it did sort of prickle.

"I wonder if you'd look more the same if you went blond, Bex. Have you ever considered it?" Gaz sounded hopeful.

"Bex is perfect just the way she is," Lacey said loyally. "Besides, both sides of the same coin can't be exactly alike." She winked flirtatiously. "Otherwise no one would flip it."

"I don't know what that means, but I think I want to try it," Gaz said. "Are you sure you have to go home at the end of the week?"

"I probably should stay," she twinkled. "I haven't even met Nick yet!"

Nick's absence was the only failure of her trip, it seemed, and as her departure neared, Lacey fixated on it. And while I understood her disappointment, I caught myself feeling a little defensive of him: Nick was my friend, not an animal at the zoo who was refusing to come out of his cave. It's the first time I ever empathized with Lady Bollocks.

Near the end of Lacey's stay was our birthday, the fifth of November, which coincides with Guy Fawkes Day—so named for the mustachioed ex-soldier who, in the early seventeenth century, got busted guarding explosives that were supposed to blow up Parliament. Much of England observes it with fireworks and bonfires, commemorating the big bang that wasn't. But when Gaz had found out Lacey and I like celebrating our birthday with a costume party, because we're so close to Halloween, he—as Pembroke's social chair—had a brainwave.

"Fawkesoween!" he'd proclaimed. "Two parties for the price of one."

Lacey and I got ready for the party in my room, just like we had our entire lives. (On prom night, she'd spent an hour on my hair, leaving her only five minutes for her own, and voted for me for prom queen; she won unanimously but for that one vote.) Gossiping with her while we primped, and snacked on British cheeses and crackers I'd bought as a surprise, felt like old times. Like home. If I had looked out my window to see our parents' backyard instead of the quad, I would not have blinked.

"Do you think Nick will finally show up?" Lacey asked. "I didn't fly all this way just to walk past his closed bedroom door."

"I have no idea," I said. "No one's heard from him."

"I find it very suspicious that you two are in here all night watching *Devour* and nothing has ever happened," Lacey said. "Are you holding out on me? Or are you not interested? Do I get to be interested?"

"He's got a girlfriend!" I said, though to my own ears I said it a little too fast and a little too protectively. "Actually, she kind of looks like you."

"So does that Ceres chick," Lacey said blithely. "Although I only saw her twice before she dropped out to go work for that party planner. I can't believe she thought Cornell was in Manhattan." She gazed out the window as church bells rang peacefully in the distance. "I sort of sympathize with her, though. It'll suck going back to Ithaca. It's so *alive* here."

"I told you to apply with me."

"I couldn't, you know that. Med school beckons," Lacey said, although she sounded less convinced of that here in my room, staring out at the light dusting of snow that had turned the quad into something from the pages of those old boarding-school stories we read by flashlight. She shook her head quickly, and then came over and threw her arms around me from behind.

"I miss you," she said, her voice tight. "I keep worrying that you're going to forget me now that you have this whole other life."

This was an impossibility; even the suggestion made me sad. As she squeezed me, I had a vivid flashback to our first year at Cornell, at the café in Balch Hall. I'd spied her on my way in and shuffled over to say hi, still sweaty and disheveled from morning practice with the intramural flag football team, only to discover Lacey was being figuratively wined and dined by some power players at a sorority. I wasn't much interested in pledging, myself—which was convenient given that none of them were particularly interested in me, either—but as usual, Lacey went after whatever looked the most prestigious on her resume, and she'd made sure her reputation preceded her.

"This table is full," one of the girls had said, giving me an extremely hairy eyeball. "Consider taking your sweat elsewhere."

I had been prepared to leave quietly, but Lacey grabbed my arm and stood, calmly picking up the rest of her toast. "Maybe you should consider not being such a bitch," she'd said, to their obvious shock. "I'll let you bus my tray. Bex and I have better places to be."

She never did end up joining a sorority. "How could I find any better sisters than the one I already have?" she'd said, with a hug much like the one she was giving me right there in my room at Pembroke.

I rubbed her forearm affectionately. "I could never forget you," I promised. "It's in our genetic contract."

She sniffled. "That better be true."

"It is," I said. "And you're here now, and my friends love you, and there's a party full of guys down there who'd like a crack at the blond twin."

Lacey grinned. "In that case, I'd better do my hair," she said. "No, wait. I need to fix yours first. You're a danger to yourself with a curling iron."

In an hour, Lacey had transformed my head of fine hair into springy, innocent curls, and straightened her own plentiful waves. We were reusing a costume we'd worn last Halloween to great acclaim: I would be an angelic Little White Lie, and she—winking at being the better-behaved twin in real life—would be a Dirty Little Secret. This involved snug-fitting white (for me) and black (for her) V-neck T-shirts—Lacey is all about Just Enough Cleavage, although she has more of it than I do, and so the V on mine fell almost low enough to be indecent—and silver Sharpies tied to our belt loops, so that people could jot down on our bodies their various anonymous fibs and close-held truths. In other words, we would look good, Lacey's main requirement, while everyone else did the real work.

The music was pulsing when we headed into the lovely old Hogwarts-style Dining Hall, with its high ceilings and wood panels and dramatic candelabra. It was well chosen because of the decent-size double staircase leading down from the door, meaning all guests got to Make an Entrance and be ogled from the throng below them. As soon as we hit the top of those stairs, half the room turned, and Lacey broke into a confident smile.

"I have missed *that* since high school," she said.

"Write that on your shirt," I teased her.

"Is *he* here?" she asked as we made our way down the steps and toward the bar, where Gaz had set up several punch bowls full of potent-looking mixed drinks, steaming with dry ice.

"It's dark. I can't tell yet," I said, feeling a twinge at the tenor of her eagerness. "I'll introduce you if he is, I promise."

Gaz had triumphed. All the Fawkes dummies had eerie jack-o'-lantern heads, and were suspended from the wood-beamed ceiling in various grisly positions. The lighting was flickering and spooky, but ripe for romantic shenanigans, and the drinking and dancing were in full swing. Clive met us at the bar in a costume that was split down the middle: half of the pipe, mustache, and hat that make up the classic Sherlock Holmes, and half a set of glasses, a thinner waxed mustache, and slicked-down hair that screamed Watson.

"The Sexy Sherlock I'd envisioned had other plans," he said, gesturing at me, "so I decided to do a Jekyll-and-Hyde thing and go as both of them."

"That must have taken you forever," I said, impressed. "It's really good."

Clive beamed. "If I may," he said, turning to Lacey, "there is a gentleman chemistry major who, when you came in, expressed an interest in seeing if the two of you have any."

He gestured to an extremely good-looking blond who shot Lacey a seraphic smile.

"Damn," she murmured appreciatively. "I haven't scored this fast in a long time."

"Well, you're a busy woman," I said. "But you're on vacation now."

A grin spread across Lacey's face. "*And* it's my birthday," she said.

Just before Clive led her to her prey, he shot me an endearing smile, and I felt a rush of gratitude toward him for caring so much that my sister had a good time. With Nick gone and our TV nights on hold, I'd slipped right back into my old habits with Clive, but I knew it looked like—and, honestly, felt like—I was just killing time until Nick returned. I could hear Cilla's voice in my head from that afternoon, and stubbornly muted her as quickly as I could. Clive was more than lovely. He was smart and cute and available and interested, and maybe I should try to look at him the way I'd noticed him looking at me.

And yet, the first person I scanned for was Nick. Instead, I got India Bolingbroke—dressed, in grand Halloween tradition, as Sexy Person of Vaguely Hawaiian Origin As an Excuse to Wear a Coconut Bra—who was herself surveying the room with a deflated air, apparently she didn't know Nick's whereabouts any better than I did. I saw Joss in one corner dressed as Karl Lagerfeld, sprayed silver hair in a frizzy ponytail. Lady Bollocks, perched on one of the deep windowsills, sported what looked a fortune's worth of Marie Antoinette garb and had brought three boys dressed as peasants, to whom she was feeding cake (which made me wonder if Bea had very well-hidden fun depths). Cilla had done herself up as Ginger Spice, in a Union Jack dress, and she appeared to be berating a large, lumpy burrito with a head. As I inched closer, I recognized Gaz, stuffed into a flesh-colored nylon body stocking. He'd paired it with a long, red wig and the world's most garish pair of massive, hollow plastic breasts. They looked like Jell-O molds with nipples. My gaze, against every ounce of my judgment, drifted between them to the large sparkling heart-shaped bauble resting unluckily there.

"Oh my God," I said, starting to giggle uncontrollably. "You're Kate Winslet. From the scene in *Titanic* where he paints her naked."

"Right you are," he said. "See, Cilla? People get it."

"But it's not accurate," she hissed, pointing to the tufts of black, curly hair glued to Gaz's crotch. "The Heart of the Ocean was not green and she did not have *pubic hair* in that scene."

"Well, we never saw for certain," Gaz offered. "Anyway, it's for modesty. The bloody stocking stretches too thin—I had to put something there or you'd see all my bits."

"I can't believe that your objection to this is on authenticity grounds," I said to Cilla, stealing a sip of her dramatically steaming glass of pitch-black punch.

Cilla uncapped my Sharpie and wrote *Gaz is a genius* on my shirt.

"There. The first enormous lie of the night," she said.

Gaz tacked onto the end of her sentence: *at pretending he is not dynamite in the sack.*

"Much better," he said.

It took me fifteen minutes to find Clive and Lacey, and then another fifteen to get a drink (so I got three, for maximum efficiency). The more the cocktails flowed, the less little and white the lies scribbled on my shirt became—someone wrote *Bea is SO NICE* on my breast—and the sweatier and looser our dancing was: me, Clive, Lacey, Damian the Incredibly Hot Chemistry Student, and whoever else happened to be in our radius, including a guy dressed as Captain Hook whom I'd noticed staring at me with increasingly sexy intensity. I was wrestling with whether to strike up a conversation when the pirate beat me to it, putting his lips right to my ear.

"Yer makeup's runnin' down your face, innit," he yelled.

I ran a finger across my cheek and it came away dark from rivulets of sweaty mascara. I had to laugh. This was exactly what I deserved for breaking a promise about Clive that I'd barely even made to myself.

I waved at Lacey. "Be right back," I shouted, mopping at my face.

But as I headed out to the nearest bathroom, I caught sight of a familiar figure turning tail and sprinting up the main stairs, and like a magnet to metal I shot toward it.

"Hey," I called out, but Nick was already most of the way upstairs. I followed him straight to his own open door, which I caught before he could close it behind himself.

"Welcome back," I said.

He jumped. "I almost didn't recognize you without your ponytail," he said. I could swear his eyes flickered to my cleavage and then immediately away. "What's *that* costume?"

"I'm a Little White Lie," I said, catching my reflection in his mirror and wiping again at my cheeks. "Feel free to add one. I suggest, 'I have every intention of going into this party.' "

"I am going," Nick said, but it was thin.

"Bullshit," I said. "You're hiding."

Nick turned away and stretched, his shirt riding up slightly and revealing an appealing side-ab muscle.

"You've seen the papers. My head's been a bit scrambled," he said. "I thought getting torched with you lot would make me feel right again, but I'm not quite sure I'm ready yet."

I imagined India having a drunken *Where have you been?!?* hissy on the dance floor. I wouldn't want to deal with that in front of two hundred people, either, especially after a half-baked paternity crisis. Nick just looked so downtrodden; I felt suddenly, fiercely protective.

"Come on," I heard myself say. "We're getting you out of here."

"But I just got here," Nick said.

I put my hands on my hips. "Right now, 'here' is alone in your bedroom," I said. "Tell me something. When did you last have any fun?"

"You've been out with me—I'm terribly fun."

"Sure, *you* are fun, but that's not what I asked."

"I do have a good time," Nick insisted. He sat down on the bed and tugged on his hair. "I just sometimes get tired of it being contractually obligated. Being a prince involves a lot of luxuries, but getting to be in a bad mood is not one of them." His face was downcast, but then he shook himself. "Ugh. Poor little royal boy. I'm sorry I even said that. I should be smacked."

I closed his door. "Listen, I don't know if you're aware of this," I said. "But you are allowed to have feelings, even if you did spring from the loins of Norman vanquishers or whatever."

"Can't we just stay in and watch *Devour*?" he said hopefully. "Wasn't that chap with the bad wig going to suck the acid out of Carrie's scar?"

"Nice try," I said. "But you need actual social fun. And you're right that it's not going to happen at this party. Everyone down there's either going to suck up to you or freak out on you."

"Or just stare at me to see if I'm about to crack," Nick said glumly. He looked resigned, then determined. "Right, as you're clearly the delinquent here, where do we go?"

I grinned. "Anywhere. People here might recognize you, but who's going to tell the people milling around out there?" I gestured expansively at the window. "If we can find you a mask, they'll just think you're some deranged guy who's a week late with his costume."

He considered this. "I think we're going to look back at this one day and agree that it was a bad decision."

"Even better," I said. "Let's get out of here."

# CHAPTER SEVEN

Nick still claims I stole the wheelbarrow by announcing, "No fence is bigger than I am," before hurtling over one and then running out two seconds later screaming, "Your chariot, my lord." But I swear that the wheelbarrow found *us*, proffering itself in the middle of a random driveway, practically begging us to let it cradle the Royal Carcass.

"Are we there yet?" Nick asked, lolling his head to the side.

"We have moved about twenty feet since you last asked me that," I said, heaving the wheelbarrow with great effort.

"Your problem," Nick slurred, taking a swig out of his Guinness can, "is that you need to learn the metric system. It will make you whole. Are we there yet?"

His volume was loud, but Nick didn't care. That was at least two parts due to the booze, but I also write it off to something we still affectionately call the Oxford Bubble. Prince Richard had struck a deal with the press to steer clear of Nick while he was at school, in exchange for occasional official sit-downs with him—a level of access previously denied them. Miraculously, the media honored this deal. And somehow both the townspeople and most of our fellow students were protective enough that they kept their mouths shut about Nick's specific comings and goings. Even if they were woken up by the sounds of someone who looked like him being dragged off in a neighbor's wheelbarrow.

It was going to be a long walk with that infernal thing, capping an even longer night. We'd snuck out to the nearest Boots and found, amid the cosmetics and snacks, a junk aisle with Halloween masks on clearance. While Nick hid around the corner—I had lied that I was going to shoplift, just to make him feel rebellious—I picked out a rubbery Darth Vader helmet and a Batman mask that would go all the way down over Nick's shoulders.

"Ultimate Evil, or a hero who never speaks above a whisper?" I asked him.

"Ultimate Evil is obviously you," he said, grabbing the Batman mask, which mashed his nose into a baby snout and made him sound congested. "It smells weird in here."

"Stop stalling."

On the way to Boots, we'd passed a billboard covered in posters advertising various events around town. Nick closed his eyes and I spun him around, and then he ripped a flyer off the wall at random, which is why we ended up at a dive bar named The Hedge Maze, where some regulars were duking it out in a profoundly impassioned and unironic karaoke contest.

I sidled up to the bar and waved at the portly, buzz-cut man pulling pints, whose neck was wider than his head.

"Is there a fee to enter?" I asked.

"Five quid," the guy said, looking skeptically at both of us. "But I don't trust a man if I can't see 'is face. Might 'ave a gun up in there or summat."

"His only weapon is his talent," I said. "He's just got terrible stage fright."

"'e's in a bloody mask," the guy said. "S'not Halloween. What kind o' prat does that?"

"Listen, sir," I said, plonking a ten-pound note on the bar. "My friend Steve here is having a rough year. His, um, brother threw acid on his face and it has scarred him for life."

"Blimey," the man said. "Poor Steve."

I nodded serenely. "The acid burned his throat. They said Steve would never sing again."

"Yes, and he might never," hissed Nick.

"He will," I said. "Steve will sing."

"He *will*," echoed the barkeep. "I'll waive the fee."

"No, Steve would want you to have it," I said. "He stole it from his brother's wallet."

We made our way to a table near the front, Nick pulling nervously at his mask as a balding old man sang "My Way" like he was Frank Sinatra's long-lost brother.

"I was right, this is a bad plan," Nick whispered. "That man is a marvel and I am nothing."

I rolled my eyes, grabbed my Sharpie, and wrote on my own shirt, *I have the voice of an angel.* Then I went up and sang the first song I knew from the list: "Umbrella" by Rihanna. It was a rotten choice. Chances are, if you are not Rihanna, you sound fairly stupid singing that chorus. But going first allowed me to write down *Steve* after my own name, pick his song for him, and buoy—or shame—Nick into stepping up to meet or beat my weak challenge.

"What song am I doing?" he asked.

The opening bars to Wham's "Wake Me Up Before You Go-Go" played. Nick froze. The first lines came and went without him.

"Can't read, eh, Batman?" shouted Faux Sinatra. "Get off!"

"Pay 'im no mind, Steve," shouted the barman. "Let 'er rip."

And rip it he did. Once Nick started, it was hard to get him to stop, as if every suppressed public-partying impulse erupted out of him. I could swear he was working steps from his beloved dance movies into whatever weird prancing he was doing, and the crowd of forty- and fiftysomething cigarette-puffing locals were so enamored of the mystery bat that they cheered his every move. Four pints later, he'd performed a novelty song about fast food, "Bye Bye Bye" by NSYNC complete with the dance, an exaggeratedly wrenching rendition of an Oasis ballad, and a Shania Twain song that was popular when he was at Eton (for which I served as his air guitarist). By the time we rolled out, to wild cheers, Nick was exhilarated.

"That was the worst best thing I have ever done," he announced, tipping over slightly before catching himself. "I am very happy sad that everyone did not see it."

"Congratulations," I said. "You just passed Teenager 101."

"I think I lost eight pounds from sweating," he said. He swiped the Sharpie still hanging from my belt loop and started writing on the back of my shirt. "Where to next?"

"Are you sure you don't want to head back?" I asked. "It's one in the morning."

"Absolutely not!" he said. "Bats are nocturnal, just like Night Nick."

"Well, I did have one other thought," I said, patting my purse.

And so it was that we rambled over to South Park, a fifty-acre expanse east of Oxford's heart. It was big enough for us to hide in plain sight when, after obtaining a cheap cigarette lighter, we lit some Roman candles I'd purloined from Gaz's party stash. And it was when we were fleeing from burning a very slight hole in the park's hallowed ground that Nick realized he was way too drunk to get home under his own power.

"You are really heavy. What did you eat while you were in London?" I asked, huffing heavily as I inched the wheelbarrow down a slender side street.

"My feelings," Nick slurred, his Batman mask now dangling from the tips of his fingers. "And rocks. I love rocks. Rocks rock. Roxford rocks."

"At this rate your eventual biography is going to come with its own drinking game."

"And a long chapter on paternity," he said, bitterness seeping into his voice. "The DNA test came up in my favor, you know. If you could call it that."

I said nothing. What could I say?

"The esteemed Prince of Wales made me and Freddie take one. Thought it might be 'useful information,'" he said. "Never mind what he thought he was going to do if it turned up negative. And the pathetic thing is, I caught myself hoping..." He traced the wheelbarrow bin with his finger, without much accuracy. "Because maybe if I weren't his, it would explain why he never felt... why *we* never felt..."

He shrugged helplessly. I was glad I was behind him, because I know I looked so sorry that it would have made him feel worse. We traveled the rest of the way in silence, and when I carefully parked the wheelbarrow alongside Pembroke's back entrance, the college was as quiet as he was. But before I could head up to give PPO Twiggy the Too Drunk for Stairs code knock, Nick's hand grabbed my wrist.

"Thanks," he slurred. "For not telling anyone what you saw. With Father. They know, but... they don't *know*, you know?"

"It's in the vault," I promised, kneeling next to him. "I saw nothing, I heard nothing."

"No, you did," he said, giving me a beseeching look. "It's important to me that you did."

I reached out and touched his face before I could help it. His head lolled into my palm. It felt so natural that my thumb moved to stroke his cheek.

"Happy birthday, Bex," he murmured.

And then I remembered myself: He wasn't single, I was hooking up with his friend, and I had missed midnight with my sister. Lacey and I had developed a tradition of spending the very last minute of our birthday slamming a bolt of liquor we liked to call the Parting Shot. But tonight I had ditched her. And forgotten I'd ditched her.

Yet still I let myself linger one more second, before withdrawing my hand.

"Let me get Twiggy, okay? You need to get some sleep."

Once Nick was safely in his quarters, I snuck inside my own room and promptly tripped over a body on the floor. It appeared to be Smoking Hot Chemistry Guy, and he was completely naked except for one of Ceres's leftover throw pillows placed discreetly atop his junk.

Lacey stirred and pushed up her sleep mask.

"Bex?" she whispered. "Where did you go?"

"Long story," I said, pulling off my costume and putting on my nightshirt, a jersey Dad wore when he coached my Little League team. "I'm so sorry, Lace. I don't even have a good explanation. It just sort of *happened*."

"You missed the Parting Shot," she said sleepily.

"I know. And I'm so, so sorry. I promise I will make it up to you."

Lacey snuggled deeper under the covers. "I consoled myself by dancing on the bar and then getting very naughty with Damian on your bedroom floor. It really helped."

She tugged her mask back into place. "As long as you don't do it again," she added.

I hated that I'd disappointed her. I'd just gotten so swept up in the heady feeling of delighting Nick when he needed it most that everything else flew out of my mind. I was still electrified by the residual feel of his skin, and as I lay next to my sister, I felt a creeping awareness that maybe, just maybe, I'd wanted to keep Nick to myself a little bit longer.

Lacey's breathing regulated as she slipped back asleep. Crawling back to the foot of my bed, I grabbed my crumpled Little White Lie shirt and used the light from my alarm clock to search it. Nick had doodled in various spots all night, but there was one where I knew he'd written something longer. And right where my shoulder blade would have been, I found his lie.

"You are not my favorite," it read.

And near it, in Clive's handwriting: "I don't want strings."

# CHAPTER EIGHT

Cilla took the T-shirt and spread it out on her lap.

"That's Clive's all right," she said. "And that's Nick's writing for sure."

Lacey practically swooned into her teacup. "Sexual geometry. That's so hot, Bex."

"Only you would call a love triangle 'sexual geometry,'" I said, taking back the shirt and jamming it into my purse. "But it's not a love triangle. That shirt isn't love. It's a craft project."

Cilla slammed down her teacup so hard that it rattled both the saucer and the patrons around us. "Is she this difficult at home?" she asked.

"Mmm," Lacey nodded, scone crumbs tumbling from her lip, which she tried to catch with her napkin.

Cilla had insisted high tea was a must for any visiting relations, but not anyplace she deemed too stuffy. So we'd gone to London to do some sightseeing before Lacey's red-eye back to New York, and capped it at a funky, artsy spot near Liberty called Sketch—a gleefully odd place that fancied itself equal parts a restaurant, a club, and a museum. (To wit: Its bathroom is a unisex, sterile space whose multicolored glass ceiling hovers over a futuristic cluster of toilet eggs—literally, pods with lavatories inside—that are buffed periodically by a woman in a French maid costume.) We sat in a small tearoom done up like a tiki lounge, with dark, tropical wallpaper, and a giant chandelier made of intertwined branches that hung over us like a very glamorous threat.

"You guys can't tell me to believe what Nick drunkenly wrote on a T-shirt," I said, snagging a delicate *croque madame*, wrapped like a gift in tissue paper and yellow ribbon. "It doesn't mean anything. It could just be a compliment. I'm more worried about the Clive one."

Cilla turned to me with a piercing, all-business glare. "Let's look at the facts here, Bex. Number one: Do you actually like Clive?"

"Yes," I said. "He's way better in bed than he is at just kissing."

The mother of two German girls at the next table gave a pointed cough in our direction.

"That's not technically what I asked you, but regardless, what about Ni— *Steve*?" Cilla amended, lowering her voice.

That was more complicated. I couldn't deny that whenever I thought of Nick, or caught his eye across a room, or even just spied him in the quad from my window, my heart practically bruised itself against my ribs. I'd previously written it off as Extreme Friendship, but the events of Fawkesoween had made it hard to keep up that fiction. And then there was the matter of Clive, and India, and the magnitude of the man Nick would be to the rest of the country, versus the boy he'd been in my room and that wheelbarrow. My heart and mind were doing a bang-on impression of one of Nick's cryptic crossword puzzles—so, speaking to me in tongues.

"I can't pretend he's not really hot," I finally said, as Cilla poured me a fresh cup of tea. "But what if he doesn't even remember writing this? I don't think I should bring it up. Do you? It's not worth it. Right?"

Lacey wriggled to the edge of her squashy, low-slung chair and reached for a petite egg salad sandwich wearing a tiny poached quail egg on top.

"I've never seen you be this unsure of yourself," she said. She turned to Cilla. "When we were twelve, Bex decided she liked this smoking hot soccer player in the grade above us, so one day she marched up to him and kissed him, right in front of the Coke machine. And then she just walked away and didn't talk to him again."

I shrugged. "We didn't have any chemistry."

Cilla smirked. "Well, you can't say that about *Steve*," she said.

"*Steve* is the future king," I said, "and he's taken, therefore I can't—"

"Stop assuming you have the whole story. You'll never know it until you talk to him," Cilla said, pointing lightly at me with a knife coated in strawberry jam. "And as my great-aunt Gladys used to say, 'Don't mess about so long that someone else shags your man.' "

"*Steve* is getting plenty shagged, I'm sure," I said, opting for a second scone. "I don't even know if I *want* to shag him."

Cilla rolled her eyes dramatically. "Of course you do," she said. "You can lie about your feelings all you want, but for God's sake, let's not lie about that."

"Good afternoon, ladies."

Nick suddenly appeared, in olive cargo pants and a button-down shirt, swinging a chair over from a nearby table and straddling it to sit down between Lacey and me. She gasped, and our server, Jacques—a French guy who was surprisingly supercilious given that we were at a hipster tea and he had a Mohawk—nearly fell over from shock. He grabbed the sandwich-and-pastry tower off a nearby table just as an elderly woman was reaching for a macaron, and whipped it under Nick's nose.

"As many as you please, Your Royal Highness," he sputtered.

"Thank you very much," Nick said, helping himself to a tiny fruit torte and a lemon bar.

As Jacques frittered off to check the structural integrity of his Mohawk in the mirrored kitchen doors, Nick offered a friendly hand to Lacey. "I'm dreadfully sorry I missed you last night," he said. "I was being a gloomy, selfish git, and your sister had to save me from myself."

Lacey, who had turned bright red when Nick sat down beside her, recovered nicely.

"Great to meet you," she said, shaking his proffered hand. "Not that I've heard anything about you at all. And I for sure don't have any DVDs in my suitcase that would be of interest."

"Pity. I was hoping for some home movies. There's a certain hamster I'd been wanting to see," Nick said, filching a cucumber sandwich from my plate. Cilla's eyes bored into me.

Lacey laughed. "There wasn't much resemblance," she said. "He was on the short side."

"Better hair than you, though," I said.

Nick grinned. "This is the kind of abuse she hands out regularly," he told Lacey. "I'm considering having her deported."

"What are you doing here, Nick?" Cilla asked, trying to sound casual.

Nick glanced at his watch. "Family business, Miss Nosy, and I'm actually running a bit late," he said. "But as for how I knew where to find you, I have sources everywhere."

Lacey's eyes grew huge.

"I'm having you on. It was only Gaz," Nick said. "I ran into him in the hallway when I went by Bex's room to apologize for being so rude yesterday, and to give you something."

Nick fished around in his pockets and pulled out two small enameled pins, each one depicting an American and a British flag on poles that crossed at the bottom. He passed one to a stunned Lacey, and when he dropped mine into my palm, it felt surprisingly weighty in my hand.

"I know Bex misses you," Nick told Lacey. "And it's your birthday, and these made me think of you two. Like a nod to both places you can call home."

Nick addressed the last part more to me. My mouth went dry.

"This is so *sweet*," Lacey said.

"Thank you, Nick," I managed.

"Let's *Devour* later," Nick said to me. "I think the jig is about up for one of those panthers."

The Germans next to us looked up from their guidebooks just in time to hear this and frowned, while Jacques, back with a bonus plate of cookies and two hot pots of tea, looked despondent to see Nick leaving so soon.

"Tremendous food and service," Nick assured him, clapping him on the back. "I'll be sure to tell Her Majesty."

And with that he was gone. The Germans stared at us with naked curiosity, and Jacques bustled around with a much more approving air, even leaving us the extra snacks. Cilla plucked the pin from my hand and studied it; Lacey looked as shell-shocked as if Nick had kissed her.

I met Cilla's eyes. She set the pin in front of me on the table, where it landed with an almost *I told you so* click. I picked it up and spun it between my fingers, feeling my pulse accelerate as the little stars and stripes started to blur with the iconic British crosses.

"Oh, hell," I said. "I think I'm in trouble."

Nick's Little White Lie made it extremely hard to tell any more of my own to myself. I became so much more conscious of his every move, of the times our bodies brushed, of how snug his shirts were on his biceps. I could not stop thinking about how he smelled, how his hands looked, about how the hair on the back of his neck curled when he needed a haircut. In the period after Lacey's visit, I seesawed between wanting to throw myself at him and wanting to escape to the safe, familiar confines of Cornell and my sister, where I always knew where I stood, and where it felt as though nothing I valued could possibly be lost to me.

I began ducking Clive. Lacey was right: I'd never known myself to be so gutless—there are several incidents from my youth in the vein of that barbwire fence—but I'd also never been confronted with a complicated romantic situation, and I didn't trust myself to say the right thing to him. And, as time passed, I was afraid he was going to get mad at me, and that I would deserve it. So, because I was exactly the kind of emotional coward a lot of people are at age twenty, I chickened out and rested on the laurels of our no-strings policy, hoping Clive would see on his own that the wind was blowing him into the Friend Zone.

I'd also curtailed my *Devour*fests with Nick, although in fairness, we'd also run out of episodes. It was a handy excuse to step away while I sorted out my feelings, but I couldn't—and desperately didn't want to—avoid him forever. I took to suggesting safer, more academic outings where there would be crowds of people and no inviting-looking beds, like studying at the library, or group movie outings, or one particularly amusing foray to a local theater revival of *Cats*. We'd bought last-minute tickets in the back row after a long Sunday at the Bodleian, and watched agape as the legendary musical unfolded like a disjointed feline fever dream. Everyone tumbled into the dark night after the show, laughing at the absurdity of it, feeling very young and superior.

"That was the oddest thing I've ever seen," Nick said.

"I can't believe you tripped that actor," Cilla said to Gaz. "He's probably going to sue."

"A man has a right to stretch his legs without worrying some bloody great giant in spandex and cat makeup is going to come running past him," Gaz protested.

Cilla threw her hands wide. "You were at *Cats*! What did you think would happen?"

"I should sue him for terrifying me," Gaz said.

"I wish I could have had a crack at those costumes," Joss ruminated as we began to head back toward the high street. "All those catsuits were so *obvious*."

"THEY ARE PLAYING CATS. IN *CATS*," boomed Cilla. "I am going to need a drink to deal with you lot. Come on, there's a pub 'round the corner."

"I can't. I promised India I'd stop by Christ Church for a nightcap," Nick said apologetically. "And it's already...Crikey, it's almost nine o'clock."

I cursed under my breath. "I'm supposed to be on the phone with Lacey. She'll kill me if I'm any later than I will be already."

Clive made a move toward me, but Joss stuck out a hand and grabbed him.

"Oi, not so fast! You owe me a pint because you never wore that shirt I made you."

"It said *SKIRT* on it!" Clive protested.

"Well, I'm still practicing," Joss said. "It looked like *shirt* if you squinted just right."

She dragged him off, and Cilla corralled Gaz, with a backward wave at me that suggested my situation had been discussed.

Left alone together for the first time since Fawkesoween, Nick and I smiled gamely at each other, pulled our coats tight, and began the walk to Pembroke. Cornmarket Street was lit with the glow of warm lamplight from upstairs windows, the occasional peal of laughter echoing from passing couples huddled together against the chill. A wave of intense happiness washed over me, and I told myself to carry this moment as a talisman of a time in my life when I was both truly content and lucky enough to realize it. In a very short time, Oxford had stamped itself on me, and everything back in the States—for the first time, I didn't use the word *home* in my mind—felt so far away.

"...although in Julian's defense, he didn't know Gran kept Sergeant Marmite's ashes in any of the urns on the floor," Nick was saying.

I jolted. I had been too busy enjoying being with Nick to *listen* to Nick.

"Works every time," he said triumphantly. "I knew you'd vanished on me. Where did you go?"

"I was just thinking how much I love being here," I said.

An unreadable look washed over Nick's face. "Bex," he said.

And then the clouds parted like they'd been slit with a letter opener, pelting us with massive drops of a cold November rain that wasted no time leaking through the soles of my flimsy old sneakers. We broke into a run straight down St. Aldate's toward the intersection that divided Christ Church and Pembroke. India's home and mine.

Water streamed down my face. "This is my first hard-core English rain," I called out to him, my words almost drowned out by the rhythmic pounding of the drops and our feet.

"It reminds me of the first time we met," Nick panted. "You looked so put out from that tiny drizzle, I didn't have the heart to tell you how bad it would get."

"Please," I said, grinning even as the rain got blown up against my teeth. "Winter at Cornell would make your face crack."

We ducked down our cobbled drive and stopped outside the main doors, still giggling and breathless. The porter was long gone, so I had to fumble for my keys; Nick pulled off his coat and held it over us so that the contents of my purse wouldn't get drenched. Not many guys would think of a girl's handbag. If I hadn't already started swooning for him, that would've sealed it.

"You've got some mascara on your cheek," Nick said, his teeth starting to chatter. "Very Fawkesoween of you."

He reached out to wipe it away, which meant half his coat-canopy sagged, so I tilted up my face and scooted closer to stay under it. His expression changed as he moved a wet hair off my cheek. My skin felt warm even with the cold rain hitting one side of it.

"We should get you inside," Nick said, his lips so close to my face that his breath and mine were basically the same puffs.

"India is waiting," I agreed.

"And your phone call."

But we didn't move. A jolt passed between us. I thought of high school English, and that part of the Keats poem "Ode on a Grecian Urn" about how the breath right before you kiss your beloved is the sweetest one of all, because you realize you're about to get exactly what you want.

Then something in my periphery twitched, and I jerked my head sideways. Pembroke's main drive bent around and connected with a slim back street alluringly named Beef Lane, at the corner of which I could swear a camera lens was poking out at us.

"Nick," I said, nodding toward it. "I think we've got company."

Nick whipped his head around and squinted. "Are you fucking serious?" he said.

The heat between us evaporated as his coat fell down to his side, and I felt the frigid raindrops crash anew onto my head. As if he were conjured by magic, PPO Twiggy crept up Beef Lane and shoved the camera lens with his hand, as PPO Stout blocked me from sight and unlocked Pembroke's door in a fraction of the time my freezing, stiff fingers could have done it.

Nick looked shaken and irate, the very image of a guy whose careful bubble had just burst. But he had nothing on the murderous expression on Twiggy, who had a cameraman by the scruff of the neck and was waving Nick over, his face scarlet with rage.

Lady Bollocks appeared in the open doorway, ready to pop open an umbrella. She stopped short at the kerfuffle.

"Now you've bloody done it," she said to Nick, not unkindly.

"Can you get her inside, please, Bea?" Nick pleaded.

"Wait, is that seriously the paparazzi?" I asked.

But he'd already turned to go, Stout by his side. Bea all but lifted me inside the college and closed the door. I skidded on the wet stone entry and had to stabilize myself on her arm.

"Did they see your face?" she demanded. "What have you done?"

I was too breathless to do anything but stare blankly at the closed door. Bea grabbed me and forcibly turned my face to her.

"Were you snogging him?" she snapped, eyes narrow, which was their default state where I was concerned. "I could throttle that boy, carrying on with the Sofa Queen in public. You'd best hope you're not the ruin of him."

And she barged out the door, leaving me hot and bothered in several senses of the word.

The camera crew turned out to be from Prince Charming Productions, owned by Nick's uncle Edwin, who is something of a gadfly and entirely a fool. After quitting the British Royal Navy claiming that he had raging seasickness, and then catting about being of extremely little use for two decades, Edwin was told in no uncertain terms that he had to do *something*. Evidently he chose the movie business, and planned for the first Prince Charming production to be a documentary about growing up royal, including candid footage—so he called it—of Nick being a university student. A documentary he'd told no one about, much less gotten approved.

"It was all a terrible misunderstanding," the round, red face of Edwin had told the BBC. "The camera wasn't even on. We've all had a tea and some biscuits and sorted it out."

The papers had a field day with this, until a pop star on *Celebrity Lawn Darts* came down with necrotizing fasciitis. Never a speck of footage emerged, but Nick vanished to Clarence House yet again, presumably to figure out if further PR spackle was required, and I hadn't seen him since that evening. I could still feel his hands on me, and I wanted to feel them again. It was like reverse electroshock therapy: one jolt and I was out of my mind.

"So, you two were just huddled up in the doorway. How close was he to you, exactly?" Lacey asked for the umpteenth time, on our umpteenth phone call, the week after Edwingate.

"Pretty close," I said. "And he touched my face, and then it was like we froze."

Lacey sighed dreamily. "Oxford is so romantic," she said. "I went out the other night with a guy who spent the entire time talking about Tom Brady, and you're five seconds away from making out with a prince. It's really not fair."

"I wish I knew what to do," I said, getting off of my bed and going over to my window. "The old Bex would just march up and kiss him, but I can't seem to find her right now."

"That's because you actually care what happens for once," Lacey said wisely.

"But what if *he* doesn't care?" I lamented, pressing my forehead against the cool glass of the window.

"I know it's scary," Lacey told me. "But you can't pretend you don't feel anything, Bex, and you'll be miserable if you do."

I hung up the phone and tapped it lightly against my chin, then wrapped myself tighter in my giant woolen cardigan and poured another glass of boxed wine—the official drink of emotionally confused women on a budget. Suddenly, a soft knock came at my door in the cadence Nick usually used. With embarrassing speed, I leapt up and threw open the door, and Clive saw every inch of how far, and fast, my face fell when I realized it was him.

"And there it is," he said, pained.

"What do you... um," I stammered, unable to salvage it.

Silently, Clive pushed inside, at which point I noticed he was clutching his laptop. He opened it, tapped a few keys, and turned it so I could see what was on the screen: a grainy still of Nick huddled up with a woman right outside the Pembroke door. You couldn't see my face, but the intimacy was as screaming as my red scarf.

"I *knew* that camera was on," I said. "Where did you even get this?"

"I have sources," Clive said. "The only people who've seen these are in the very innermost circle."

I stifled the urge to tell him to cram it. Clive did so love being in the know.

"I owe you an apology," I said instead. "I've been a total jerk. I should have talked to you about...well, I should have talked to you. Period."

"No arguments there," Clive said, closing his laptop with a click.

"But I swear this was totally innocent. It was pouring and my hair was stuck—"

"Come on, Bex," Clive interrupted with a reproachful look. "I'm obviously not a *prince*, but I'm not stupid."

I opened my mouth, then closed it. Clive deserved the honesty I had been too scared to give to myself.

"I care about you, for whatever that's worth," I said. "But yeah, there's something there with me and Nick. At least on my side."

Clive sat down on the edge of my bed, deflated. He'd known the score, but it didn't sting any less to hear it.

"Congratulations," he said. "You just added yourself to a long list of girls who've decided Nick is their destiny."

"I know, it's predictable as hell. I hate that," I said, sitting down next to him. "Girl goes to England, girl meets prince..."

"...Girl sleeps with his friend a *lot*..."

"...Girl fucks up royally. Pun intended, I guess," I said with a wry but unhappy smile that Clive did not return. "Look, I don't know if you and I would have worked out even if Nick didn't exist. But he does. And I guess I kept thinking it would be easier if you and I could just...drift apart. How do you break up with someone you're not officially dating?"

"But just fading out, Bex?" Clive asked. "You knew I liked you. You knew it wasn't just sex for me. You had to know."

I closed my eyes. Clive's Little White Lie drifted past them. He had told me. In that way and a thousand others.

"I did know." I felt like a jerk. "And I tried to pretend I didn't, because I was having fun and I wanted it to be simple. And when it wasn't anymore, I chickened out. I'm sorry, Clive. I am the worst. I never meant to hurt you. You really are great."

Clive cleared his throat and blinked hard, then took off his glasses and rubbed his eyes.

"Right. I'm just lovely," he muttered.

In that instant, I realized the first guy I hooked up with in England was, basically, the man version of my beloved Chicago Cubs: never the big winner, no matter how promising it looked. I was hit with a flood of sympathy for him, and anger at myself. Why hadn't I sacked up earlier and been honest?

"I'm not in love with you or anything," he said suddenly.

My lips twitched. "Nor should you be. I snore."

"Yes, it's untenable." He shot me a rueful grin. "Mostly I just thought I'd gotten to a good thing first and might get to see where it went," he said. "And this is where it went."

Clive put on his glasses again. "But you've got bigger problems than me, anyhow," he said. "You're up against at least three other posh, moneyed girls the papers have already latched on to, and *they* know what they're doing."

I didn't expect Clive to hug me and wish me good luck, but the emotionless speed with which he transitioned into business mode startled me even more than his frankness.

"You're also too trusting," he added for good measure. "You got lucky this time, but what if that had been a paparazzi camera?"

"There is nothing going on in that photo," I reiterated.

Clive rolled his eyes. "If you say so. But it doesn't matter, anyway. To an outside eye, it's Nick kissing some random tart in the street."

"Gosh, 'random' seems kind of harsh," I joked.

"And you're completely naïve if you think that footage wouldn't have gotten picked apart," he rattled on. "They're going to eat you alive."

"Okay. I think you are getting way, way ahead of yourself here. I don't even—"

He held up a hand and took a folded square of newspaper out of his shirt pocket. "You should also know that the *Mail* columnist is reporting that Nick got a Lyons ancestral ring for India."

He had come armed and ready. My hands shook slightly as I unfolded the paper to reveal an article headlined GOING FOR (BOLING)BROKE. Nausea hit me as I tossed it onto the bed, next to Clive. I'd gone and uncorked myself and now the jealousy was flowing.

"Hurts, doesn't it?" Clive said, sounding satisfied.

"I'm glad to see you're enjoying this," I said. "I guess I deserve that."

"I'm not," he insisted, softening. "But this is what you're up against."

"It's just a rumor. The *Daily Mail* is full of them."

"India is Richard's pick," Clive reasoned, standing up and stretching. "Someone is working hard to make this happen. And if it's not Nick, it's the family. Which is actually worse for you. You can't compete with that. You're an American and you don't have any kind of background. Will the Queen even agree to meet you? And if not, what then? You mess about for a bit in secret? Regardless, it all ends the same way: He marries someone else."

"I'm not looking to—"

"And neither is he, yet, but he will, and he has to. It's his job," Clive said. "And then you'll be out in the cold."

I must have looked miserable. Clive may have enjoyed that, but to his credit, he reached down and tucked my hair behind my cheek with a sad smile, bringing with it the memory of Nick so recently doing exactly the same thing and inspiring completely opposite feelings.

"You always would have been my first priority," he said.

I felt remorse, but not regret. "You deserve better than what I can offer," I said softly.

Clive nodded, resigned, and turned to leave. "I'm not rooting against you, Bex." He paused, searching for words. "His world is messy. It's not like being with the homecoming king, or... whatever you have in the States."

"I know," I said, touched. "Thank you. And—"

"Right, I know, it's not me, it's you," he said, allowing himself the levity as he walked to the door. "It probably is you. Fortunately, I covered my bases and have plans with another girl in twenty minutes. Good luck."

As the door closed behind him, I flopped onto the bed, my head spinning. Then I grabbed the *Mail* article. It was much easier to scrutinize it now that Clive was gone. There was a photo of Nick and India leaving Clarence House a day or two earlier, his hand on her back, and two different shots of India and Prince Richard in recent months, looking very compatible. I didn't believe for a second she and Nick were getting engaged. Bea was right; it was too soon. And it seemed impossible that the Nick I knew—the one I'd seen almost every day for so long, the one I would have sworn was about to kiss me—was in so deep with a person he barely mentioned to me. Even with the evidence of a united front plastered all over the papers, a voice in the back of my head kept telling me I couldn't have developed my feelings for him in a vacuum. I wasn't a stalker sociopath inventing stories and scenes and memories, seeing things the way I wanted to see them instead of for what they were. Was I?

Then again, India was there, and I was here. Maybe Nick, right now, was assuring her of exactly what I'd been assuring Clive: that nothing had happened, that the grainy still from Edwin's camera was grossly misleading. Maybe, unlike Clive and me, they'd both believed that. And maybe Nick's universe, the whole machine of the monarchy, was bigger than some fleeting foreign friend in his residence hall who liked crappy TV shows and Cracker Jack. Clive was right—it was absurd to imagine me in all of that. India was the crystal decanter of brandy, while I was wine poured from a plastic spout, and Nick and I were doomed before we even started. I curled up with my glass of Shiraz and cried.

In the dramatic film of my story, the camera would have pulled back on me lying there, fetal, weeping all over my quilt, then cut to me bravely soldiering forth until my prince returned and swooned at my sexy dignity. In the rom-com, I'd go get a sassy new haircut and realize Gaz is the love of my life. In reality, the crying and wine slurping lasted about ten minutes before I sat up and glared into the mirror at my red, puffy face.

"Get a grip," I said.

I may not have come to England to fall in love, but it had happened anyway. And I'd never been the sort of girl who willingly took a seat on the bench without fighting for a starting spot; I wasn't going to let England change that about me, too. If Nick didn't want me, that was his call, but I couldn't just sit back and wait to see if it occurred to him to pick me. I wasn't going to play dirty, but I *was* going to play.

# CHAPTER NINE

Nick comes from a long line of people who love a grand romantic gesture—the grandest and arguably most romantic being the statue that the first Queen Victoria commissioned of her cherished husband Prince Albert, sitting golden and humongous across from his eponymous concert hall. King Arthur II delivered his proposal on a white horse—the 1930s version of Lloyd Dobler hoisting the boom box in *Say Anything*—and Queen Victoria II sent her beloved Smudgy a daily carrier pigeon bearing one letter on a scrap of paper, which all would have unscrambled to profess her desire for him to get *on* with it already, but poor Crown Prince "Smudgy" Sigmund of Germany was never one for puzzles and died of a dog bite before he solved it. Still, I now understood where all of these people were coming from: Keeping the secret of my feelings for Nick was torture. I wanted to confess myself and either move on to the euphoria or the Grief Ice Cream phase. But above all, I just wanted to see him.

I was thwarted on all counts. I didn't even know where Nick was, or when he was coming back to Oxford; I was fidgety, and I could barely sleep. My solution was to stay busy. I hung out in the Pembroke JCR a lot more, doing everything from schoolwork to watching part of a three-day test match between the England cricket team and Sri Lanka, which was nearly as incomprehensible to me as Gaz's rhyming slang, as much as he tried to explain both. I went for long runs, and this time, I actually *ran*. In a rare moment after one too many gins, Bea even attempted to teach me chess. Unlike cricket, I had no problem mastering the basic rules, but strategy—seeing three moves ahead in a way that forged my path to victory—was, and is, completely beyond me. Bea got so fed up after ten minutes that she dropped my king in my beer and swept out of there.

The first week passed agonizingly slowly. During the second, I had just started to settle into a rhythm of distracting myself, when Lacey sent me a photo of the annual Thanksgiving Cake that we usually make together—neither of us likes pie, which is thoroughly un-American of us—and it hit me how much I missed my family. While they were snug at home in Iowa gorging on my mother's biscuit stuffing, homemade Chex Mix, and several pounds of turkey, I spent Thanksgiving huddled over a table with my distinguished tutor discussing the noteworthy differences in the iconic portraits of Queen Elizabeth, and gagging on my homesickness: for the Muscatine Turkey Trot, rooting against the Dallas Cowboys with Dad, even my mother's fussy questions about why my jeans are so ratty and whether I might put on a little lipstick. Cilla took pity and corralled me for a late lunch at one of our regular spots, The Grand Café, a thin blue building on the high street that was allegedly the first coffeehouse in England (but noteworthy to *me* for making a decent Bellini). Joss had insisted on meeting us there, for reasons that became clear when she blew in and pressed into my hand something she claimed was a Thanksgiving gift: a white long-sleeved T-shirt with the word *heart* written on the sleeve.

"Get it? Heart on your sleeve?" she prompted. The words were stamped on crookedly. "It's part of my submission to a fashion school in London. If I get in, I can finally blow off this place." She nudged me. "You should wear it when Nick comes back to town."

"No," Cilla said firmly.

"You're right. A drawing of a sleeve on a heart would—"

"*No*," Cilla said, and gestured for another round of drinks.

When we returned to Pembroke, PPO Popeye jumped out from near the mailboxes like he'd been watching for me.

"*Steve* is in Windsor," he said, handing me a packet of what looked like instructions. "He says the castle is closed to the public tomorrow if you want a squizz."

I was so programmed not to expect any movement on the Nick front that I had nothing whatsoever to say in response, and PPO Popeye seemed taken aback by what he perceived as my hesitation. He hadn't presented this excursion as merely an option. He wiggled the folder under my nose and then poked me in the arm with it.

"Um. Of course. Thanks," I said lamely. "Oh, and there's something in your teeth."

"I know," he said, walking away with the awkward gait of a man trying, and failing, to mask his military precision.

Windsor Castle was favored by at least four of the eight Henrys, several Georges, the lone Elizabeth, both Victorias, and Queen Eleanor, and it's also the royal residence that I love best. Unlike Buckingham Palace, which is protected by a large courtyard and a fence and feels rather isolated from the bustle around it, the town of Windsor directly abuts the edge of the castle grounds, like it's merely the fanciest house on the block—which, technically, it is. But the true wonder of Windsor is that it has survived a thousand years and a fire, and is still in active use. In fact, the day I went, the Royal Standard was flying, indicating that Eleanor was staying there—and possibly looking down on me as I ate my fatty, three-quid sausage roll on the walk to the gate. I'd been up so late talking to Lacey that I slept through my alarm and almost missed the train. I'd barely had time to brush my teeth, much less my hair, and I'd thrown on the first shirt I found. I didn't even realize until I took off my cardigan on the warm train that it was Joss's design. She'd gotten what she wanted: I was going to Nick with a heart on my sleeve.

The one in my chest pounded as I loped up the hill. As much as I'd been dying to see Nick, now that it was *happening*, all I could hear in my head was every piece of advice from last night's well-intentioned emergency summit.

"You need a plan, Bex." Lacey's voice crackled through the speakerphone. "You are not suave enough to do this without a plan."

"What if you show up and he acts indifferent?" Cilla said.

"Or you blurt it out, but the magic is gone?" Lacey again.

"Are you going to wear my heart shirt?" Joss asked.

"Are you going to ask about India?" Lacey barreled on, ignoring her.

"Say nothing about your feelings," Cilla said. "Not at first. It's been a while. Just be yourself and let any awkwardness ebb."

"Then jump him," Joss offered.

"No, then watch for a sign that it's time to be honest with him," Lacey said.

"Then jump him." Joss again.

"No, then keep your distance. Say your piece calmly and then look him square in the eye," Cilla said.

"*Then* jump him," Joss said. "Jumping is the whole point."

"But Bex can't be trusted," Lacey said. "She jumped Clive, and look where that got her."

"You guys, I'm *right here*." I said. "Look, I will be careful, I promise. No jumping."

But while being dignified and self-possessed seemed executable at three a.m., now that I was actually at Windsor, I didn't know how to keep the truth from hurtling out of my mouth—or even stop from jumping him. Before I knew it, I was through the entryway and Nick was loping down to greet me, his hands stuffed in the pockets of a blue hoodie that brought out his eyes. My brain clicked on and reminded me to control myself. To wait for the right time. Cordial, civil, normal, poised. These were my watchwords.

"Hey!" I called out, walking toward him.

"Bex! How are you?" he said, leaning toward me.

I didn't trust myself to hug him, so I turned away a bit, forcing Nick to stop short. Strike one for normal.

"This is amazing," I said quickly. "I can't believe you have a home with an actual moat."

"I knew you'd love it," he said. "Lots of history, and today, no tourists. Hope you brought your pencils." He took my arm lightly to point me in the direction we needed to walk. "I thought you might need something to distract from the big family holiday in America."

"That's really nice of you," I said, touched.

His eyes caught my flag pin, affixed to the collar of my coat. I smiled amiably and said nothing else. The platonic, civil, cordial Bex had to be on guard against random acts of feelings. (Although I did quickly ogle him a little. Unlike the castle around us, I was not made of stone.) We walked in silence uphill toward the castle's giant circular turret, pausing only to admire the regrettably nonfunctioning moat that had been landscaped into what would, come spring, be a stunning garden.

"I miss Oxford," Nick said eventually. "I've been gone too much. How is everyone?"

"Cilla and Gaz haven't killed each other yet," I said. "Joss thinks she has a shot at a design school, so she quit going to her tutorials. And Clive, um, started seeing someone."

"Oh?" Nick's voice was even.

"Someone named Cordelia? He said you guys met her your first year?"

"Ah, yes, I know her well," Nick said.

I snickered before I could stop myself.

He grinned. "Not *that* well. Here, let me show you the view."

He led me up to the battlements along the back of the castle, where I found myself staring down an extremely steep hill at an unruly expanse of land.

"William the Conqueror set up a bunch of fortresses within a day's march from each other, and picked this spot because the high hill made it quite protected from one side," he said. "And with the Thames as a transport or supply route, the town grew up around it naturally." He pointed into the distance. "If you squint, you can see Eton."

I peered across the fields and saw the spires of a cathedral in the distance. Eton was the town across the river, home to the fancy boarding school that had housed nineteen eventual prime ministers, ten iconic writers, and Nick and Freddie.

"I loved it there," Nick said. "We used to walk around over the bridge in our dress clothes, and we all looked the same. Nobody bothered about who I was. No one even noticed."

"What were you like then?" I asked.

He leaned against the stone wall. "Much the same, I suppose," he said. "Scrawnier. Quite sporty. Obsessed with the Wall Game."

"You are definitely going to have to explain that one," I said. "It sounds like something you'd play in prison."

Nick laughed. "I oughtn't be surprised news of the Wall Game didn't make it across the pond. It's only ever played at Eton," he said. "See, there's a curved wall running the length of a field that's five meters wide and—"

"Sorry, hang on, I still don't speak metric," I interrupted.

"You nonconformists are so tiresome," he said. "All right, it's as wide across as Cornmarket Street, and about the length of an American football field with all the end bits."

"I spent this whole week learning cricket lingo and the best you can do is *end bits*?"

"Is that what you get up to when I'm away? That's not at all what I imagined," Nick said. "Anyway, the Wall Game is incredibly hard and tactical, and vicious, like rugby. You can't punch people, but if you're quite sneaky, you can sort of press really, really hard on their faces with your fist."

"That is an amazing technicality," I said. "But what's the point? I mean, I get that's fun to push someone's face into a wall, or whatever, but is there a *ball*?"

"Indeed there is," Nick said, warming to his subject in a way that was both boyish and endearing. "Two teams form a scrum against the wall called a bully, and you try to work the ball over to your opponent's end of the field, but you can't use your hands, and only your hands and feet can touch the ground. You can't furk the ball unless you're in the calx, obviously—"

"Well, *yeah*," I said.

"—but when you get into the calx end, you *can* furk it, and you get a shy if you work the ball up on the wall with your foot and someone else touches it, which earns you one point and the right to try a nine-point goal by throwing the ball at the target, which is either a door or a tree depending on which side of the field you're on."

"That is by far the most creatively pointless aggression I have ever heard of," I said. "It's actually almost impressive."

"*The Economist* called it 'the world's dullest game,'" Nick said fondly.

"And as I'm saying this out loud I realize it sounds totally bonkers. I will never make fun of baseball again."

"You'd better not," I said. "In fact, in exchange for all of that, I'm going to make you listen to me explain the infield fly rule."

Nick laughed, and I couldn't help laughing with him, even though most of me just wanted to turn to him and say, *Speaking of the infield fly rule, I love you.*

Then I saw Nick shiver. "It's chilly out here," he said. "Let's start in the chapel."

I exhaled. Cordial, civil, normal, poised. I could wait. I think I needed to wait.

St. George's Chapel is at the bottom of the hill inside the castle walls, and though it is quaint compared to Westminster Abbey, I love it—the spectacular fan vaulting in the ceiling, the surprisingly intimate chapel with its wood-carved stalls, and the graves of at least ten monarchs, including that infamous cad Henry VIII (buried with his third wife, Jane Seymour, his favorite on account of her not living long enough to irritate him). It was stirring and beautiful, and Nick seemed delighted by how much time I wanted to spend lingering over the details.

"Why is he Arthur the First, and not the Second?" I asked of the marble monument to the second Lyons king. "Does Camelot count for nothing?"

"Rebecca, not everything from a Monty Python movie is real," Nick said. "There is no Camelot, nor a Holy Grail. Although the bit with the killer rabbit is true."

"One of Bea's ancestors, I'm guessing," I said.

"I won't tell her you said that," Nick said loftily. "Anyway, *that* Arthur is considered legend, and for dynastic purposes, they don't count anyone from before William the Conqueror, anyway. Too bad for poor Sweyn Forkbeard. Perhaps I'll revive that name with my firstborn."

"So Arthur the First, then," I said. "Died of pneumonia, it says."

"Officially. But Great-Grandmother told me Artie actually drank himself to death because he was in love with his best friend's wife." Nick shook his head. "I can't believe he gets a sculpted marble effigy, and my grandfather, who actually did die of pneumonia, just has a slab with his name on it behind an iron fence." He pointed just ahead to the right, where a large bust sat atop a comparatively plain rectangular stand. "Even my great-granddad got better. He was Richard the Fourth. Took a boat out on holiday and fell off and drowned because he couldn't swim, the idiot. What was he even doing on a boat?"

"We've all got one," I said. "My great-uncle died falling off a barstool. In his own bar."

"My great-great-great-uncle Charles was supposedly obsessed with holistic medicine, so when he got whooping cough he wrapped himself in brandy-soaked bandages as a cure," Nick said. "Naturally, a servant dropped a candle on him and he went up in flames. *Brilliant* bloke, that one."

I laughed. Nick's dead relatives already seemed more entertaining than his living father.

"The Lyons women have been impressively hardy," I said. "You've got a bunch of incautious men, and then two long-ruling queens."

Nick tapped absently on the top of Richard's marble head. "Hardier, or at least cleverer," he said. "I'm probably destined to trip over an ottoman and die two years in. Just as long as whatever gets me is embarrassing. I have to do my part."

We strolled past a short exhibit of watercolors and sketches done by the artsy members of the dynasty (I was surprised to learn Prince Richard was a capable landscape painter) and then into the main castle. Because it's been open to the public for so long, Windsor's halls have the patina of use about them—frayed carpets, creaky floorboards, stray scuffs and scratches—and it is as easy to imagine that a tourist from Scandinavia nicked the floor with an umbrella as it is to picture George IV taking a chunk out of it during a tantrum. Nick peppered the tour with stories that definitely aren't on the official audio guide, like how he and Freddie used to stretch out on the floor by the Grand Staircase, snacking on cheese and onion crisps while trying to count every piece of weaponry that was fanned out on the walls and behind display cases; or the time he caught Agatha's awful husband Julian throwing up in a sixteenth-century enamel box after a long day at Royal Ascot. Before he even got to a reenactment of playing hide-and-seek with Freddie using the old servants' doors and hidden corridors, the castle had started to look like a home to me, too.

Eventually, we came into a very long rectangular room, with knight statuettes in niches on the walls and an elegant wood-beamed, slanted ceiling. Nick fell quiet and seemed to need a minute to absorb the view before explaining that this was the room dedicated to the highly selective and very ancient Order of the Garter, one of the highest honors in England.

"Those belong to everyone who's ever been invested," Nick said, gesturing to the thousand or so colorful shields adorning the ceiling. "The number underneath corresponds to the spot on the wall where the honoree's name is engraved. I used to spend hours in here, trying to pick out the crest I liked best, imagining what mine would be." He grinned. "Freddie preferred mooning the guardsmen through that window. Once he even left a mark behind. Imagine, this room dedicated to chivalry, and my brother's disgusting bum print fogging up the glass."

I snorted, and Nick looked pleased.

"His name will be carved in here, too, someday, like most of the rest of our ancestors, and no one else knows about that but me and the guard, and now you," Nick said.

His gaze flickered to a nearby section of wall, where the names had stopped after the most recent new members were inducted two years ago, including his uncle Edwin (a grudging but obligatory addition on Eleanor's part).

"And that's where yours will go," I inferred.

He reached out and ran his finger across his father's name. "He wants me in now," Nick said. "I think it's disrespectful. I haven't done enough—no military service yet, not nearly enough charity work. But he is so anxious to get good stories into the press."

Nick dropped his hand. "That's why I'm out here, actually," he said. "To talk to Gran about it. I think Freddie and I should have our own team, and get to manage our own affairs. I'm so tired of Father putting out bollocks stories without running them past us. I once woke up and read that I'd agreed to be patron of a charity I'd never even heard of."

He clearly needed to vent.

"There are worse things, I know," Nick continued. "But the press is hard enough on its own, without him stirring the pot. And he should know better because..." Nick's voice seized for a second; he fought to control it. "Well, he should just know better. But instead he plays puppet master, leaking farcical stories like my getting a ring for India. As if I'll see it and decide it's what I want. As if I can't be trusted to find someone suitable on my own. That's the main reason I've always said I won't look for a real relationship until I'm older. Can you imagine being dragged into that?"

I couldn't resist the opening. "Clive implied India was a done deal."

"Clive knows better," Nick said.

"Clive said—"

"Clive," Nick interrupted, sharply, "is perfectly aware that I broke up with India because I found out Father had nudged her toward me for positive press. Everyone loves a royal romance." He rolled his eyes. "I did like her, and it was real for a bit, but never real enough, and I knew it. So now she's stuck looking heartbroken and Father's hoping I'll cave and take her back because I look like a wanker, but I won't." He looked sideways at me. "It reminds me of you in the meadow that day talking about Lacey. I'm done rolling over for Father just because it's easier than fighting him."

I was about to reach for him when he nodded briskly, as if to shake off the blues. "All right, enough of *that*. I've got one more thing to show you."

We doubled back to the Waterloo Chamber, an enormous banquet hall dedicated to the defeat of Napoleon. But unlike the first time we'd tromped though, there was a feast for two set up at one end of the twenty-foot-long dining table. Slowly, I walked toward it, stunned and delighted, because before me—on a dinner service older than Queen Eleanor herself—was roast turkey, mashed potatoes, and my mother's biscuit stuffing and Dad's homemade Chex Mix. It smelled wonderful; it smelled like home. My eyes filled as I whirled back to face Nick.

"Happy Thanksgiving," he said softly.

"I'm so in love with you," I blurted.

Nick's eyes widened, and I clapped a hand over my lips.

"Oh my God," I said. "That wasn't how I wanted to say it. Shit. It's just that this is the nicest thing anyone could have ever done for me and I'm sorry, Nick, but I'm totally crazy about you, and it's so *dumb* to go another minute and not tell you that."

He remained stunned. So I let the words pour out of me until there weren't any left.

"I should have figured it out sooner, I guess, but there was India, and Clive, and he's your friend, and you just said that you don't want to date anyone seriously so this is probably really uncomfortable for you right now, so I'm sorry," I rambled. "But I'm actually *not* sorry, because I can't apologize for falling in love with my best friend. And you *are* my best friend. There is every reason in the world for you to be terrible, Nick, but you're not. You're amazing and thoughtful and funny, and I am in love with you, and yeah, to be honest, I also really want to jump you. But if you don't feel the same way, please just tell me now. I swear someday we can pretend this never happened. I will get over you and we'll both go back to normal."

Nick tipped his head to the left. "And why on earth," he said, "would I want to pretend this never happened?"

He came over, reaching out to wipe away the tear that had snuck over my lashes. His fingers stayed on my cheek, as they had once before, but this time he reached up with his other hand and slowly, softly, ran it down my hair, then traced my jaw, the line of my neck, my arm, the whole time looking at me with a blazing, intimate intensity. As his hand came to rest on my own, he twined his fingers with mine, and my knees wobbled like the heroine out of one of Lacey's bodice rippers, several of which were probably set right here.

"I've wanted to do this ever since you showed up and started talking about syphilis," Nick said, a smile playing around the corners of his mouth. "I told myself I couldn't, because—"

"Nick, if it's too awkward—"

"It doesn't matter. It can't matter," he said. "Because I am completely, utterly, irrevocably in love with you. And if you really feel the same, then please don't ever get over me and go back to normal." His left hand snaked around my waist. "Besides, Bex, you've never been normal."

"Nick." My voice found me, throatier than usual, thanks to my acute awareness of his right hand letting go of mine to glide up my back, under my shirt, against my bare skin. His blue eyes were brighter that I'd ever seen them, searing my face as if committing it to memory.

"If we start this, I don't think I can stop," I managed. "I can't just have a fling with you."

"Good." His breath was hot on my neck as he pulled our bodies together.

"Except for all your excellent reasons for not dating anyone right now."

"Suddenly," he said, his lips landing on the tender spot below my left ear, "none of those seem terribly important."

I felt drunk, off-balance, elated. This couldn't finally be happening, and yet everything from my heart to my hormones swore it was. I dizzily leaned backward so I was perched on the large banquet table.

"You are the best thing that's happened to me this year," Nick said huskily, pulling back to look at me. "And I want nothing more than to let your mother's biscuit stuffing get stone cold, because if I spend another second not kissing you, I am going to go mad."

I let out a shaky breath. "That stuffing tastes great cold."

We both laughed, and in that same second, we were kissing. The moment of anticipation peaked, and passed, and as Keats had predicted, it was poetry. I don't recall when exactly Nick laid me back onto the table, or when my legs wrapped around him. We were totally lost in each other.

"I don't want to be forward," Nick said, breaking away after a gloriously indeterminate period of time. "And I have never longed to defile a table so badly in my life. But there are guest rooms very nearby for state occasions and dear *God*, what *is* that shirt?"

"Joss," I said simply.

"Say no more," he replied. "Except...?"

He searched my face. I pushed him up and got to my feet, then took his hands.

"Yes," I said.

Every week, thousands of tourists tromp down Windsor's exit staircase, past an unremarkable door, never aware they're at the place where Nicholas Wales carried his future fiancée—and then had to put her down, leave her briefly to go fetch the keys because he hadn't realized the door was locked, fumble through a ring of old skeleton keys to see which one worked, swear creatively, try the ones on the second ring, then whoop and pick her up again for a night of little talking and less sleep. The turbulent love and lust we gave in to that day felt like completion, like kismet, like the beginning of a story that was always meant to be written. Nick and I had discovered a gravitational pull of our own, and it changed everything.

# PART TWO

# SUMMER 2009

*"You have no idea how hard it is to live out a great romance."*

—Wallis Simpson

# CHAPTER ONE

My favorite urban legend about Freddie claims he got caught in flagrante delicto with the daughter of a Russian political leader, a week before she was to be married off as part of a covert alliance. But the very best part is that it isn't an urban legend at all. Every word of it is true. Two hours after being threatened with a rapier hanging on a nearby wall, Freddie was doing shots with Petr and Petra while discussing the pros and cons of yachting as a sport.

This is Freddie's superpower. Even when he's infuriating, or obnoxious, or just plain wrong, he is also charming and cheery and naughtily funny, and that side always wins the day. He's twenty months younger than Nick, but bolder and brasher and ballsier, from his sense of humor to his build: Nick is leanly muscular, strong but streamlined, while Freddie's sturdier pecs have their own twelve-month calendar. Where the public is protective of Nick, it lusts for Freddie; it is Nick's communal parent, but Freddie's collective mistress, and I have never met a more gleeful rogue. His deepest commitment is to being a scamp, dropping his pants as often for pranks as he does for sex—the latter being an arena in which Freddie zealously made up for being the kid brother, starting earlier than anyone wants to acknowledge, romancing as many beautiful women as the world could offer. But for all that, he's also got Nick's big heart, even if he's occasionally lacking in his brother's better sense in how to use it—or better sense, period.

I had anxiety dreams about meeting Freddie, which was uncharacteristic. But with their mother all but invisible and Richard so cold and removed, Freddie and Nick had been the one person each couldn't live without—a sibling bond I keenly understood, and so I knew I needed both to mind that, and meld with it. But beyond that, Freddie represented the first of the Lyons dominos to fall, pushing us closer to the day we'd expose our relationship to the family and to the harsh light of day.

In short, a lot was riding on the introduction. I'd rather not have done it in my underwear.

"Hang on. Isn't that Prince Nicky? With those three blondes?"

The bass beat so loudly through Club Theme's speakers that my drink wobbled on the bar. I was deep into my third Raspberry Beret, and simply blinking—much less pretending I didn't already know exactly where Nick was, and who he was with—demanded as much focus as forming a sentence. The London nightclub was run by an old Eton chum of Freddie's called Tony, and, true to its name, it opened only for very specific and thorough gimmick nights, then closed like a West End theater while it mounted the next. This month, Club Theme was devoted to Prince: a playlist of the pop legend's music, an endless loop of his videos projected onto a giant screen lining the dance floor, and specialty cocktails based on his song titles. Cilla, for example, was sipping a Purple Rain while looking very chummy with Tony himself, and the last time I was anywhere near Nick, he'd been doing shots out of an array of test tubes called the Let's Go Crazy. I'd only looked long enough to notice he was wearing my favorite of his shirts—cornflower blue, like his eyes, soft and inviting.

"He's taller than I thought he'd be," the guy mused.

"Right," I said, leaning in and getting a nose full of his aftershave. It smelled like artificial bananas. "But what were you saying before? You *don't* believe in evolution?"

"You don't even notice the wooden leg," he added. "Blimey, the tail he must get."

I couldn't feign interest any longer, so I knocked back my half-empty cocktail before picking up the new one and walking back to the VIP area. In my periphery I noticed Nick glancing in my direction, and resisted the mischievous urge to toast him as I settled into a swanky chrome-and-leather chair (although I might have flipped my hair a little, for his benefit). It had been almost a year and a half since we lit the fuse at Windsor, and although we were still every bit as explosive behind closed doors, pretending we weren't had become my new normal. Outing oneself as a royal girlfriend was a lot more complicated than firing off a social-media alert, and so we'd chosen to stay undercover, including shacking up for the idyllic remainder of my Oxford stay unbeknownst to anyone but his PPOs—who, with the exception of a covert thumbs-up from Popeye, didn't bat an eye—and our closest friends. Although they would have figured it out even if we hadn't told them. I, in fact, *didn't* tell Cilla. She guessed it the second I got home from Windsor, still flushed. But for mind reading, she had nothing on Lacey, who knew just from the way I said hello on the phone.

"You slept with Prince Nicholas Alexander Arthur Edward!" she squealed. "Was it awesome? Please tell me princes do it better."

"Is that really his full name?"

She gasped sarcastically. "Rebecca Porter, do you mean to tell me you had sex with a man whose name you don't even know?"

Lacey wanted to scream the news from the rooftops—"We're going to be royalty! Should we do *Elle*, or hold out for *Vogue*?" she crowed, only half teasing—and I knew it was killing her to keep this secret, but I was barely ready for *my* people to know, much less *People*. But after Nick and I exorcised all that lust at Windsor, we confirmed an infinite reserve of yearning underneath. This was no one-and-done. So when I went home for Christmas that year, I sat down my mother and father and explained to them that I'd stumbled into a relationship with someone whose rather famous grandmother might never allow him to own a Coucherator. Dad was unfazed, saying he was just pleased I'd met a guy who didn't cheer for the Yankees. But Mom was atwitter, immediately reorganizing, cleansing, and replenishing her closet in case she was called upon for a royal audience.

"I should call my friend Mabel's genealogist," she had said. "For all we know, there's a lord or two in our bloodline. I've always felt such a kinship to the mother country, you know? In an ancestral way."

"Your family is from Kentucky!" I protested.

It had been a huge relief to have that short holiday in Iowa, talking where I knew no walls had ears. Lacey and I took turns sleeping in each other's rooms just like when we were kids, whispering and gossiping—me asking about Cornell; her daring me to confess how much Nick already meant to me, and peppering me with unanswerable questions about when I might meet the Queen. Most of all, though, she wanted to know all about Freddie. Dreamy, dashing, ginger-haired Freddie. But I didn't have any firsthand dirt on Freddie. Not yet.

An empty glass jangled under my nose, snapping me out of my reverie.

"Oi, I said, do you want another?" Joss asked, apparently repeating herself. "I can't think where our waitress has got to."

"I'd better not," I said, standing up and teetering in my heels. I was not getting any better in them, no matter how hard I tried, and the Raspberry Berets weren't helping. "I'm chugging mine too fast as it is. I'm going to sneak into Tony's office and use his bathroom."

I spotted Nick looking at me again, and stretched a little so that my shirt rode up for his benefit. He completed his Oxford degree at the end of my time there, but I'd still had a year to go at Cornell, so I'd returned to the States as planned and spent a confined, hormonally challenging semester doubling up on credits in order to earn my diploma early—in aid of hustling back across the pond, finding a job that would keep me there, and resuming having real sex with my boyfriend instead of the phone variety. Our reunion had come right on schedule in January, about a month after I graduated, at the hands of a Hallmark equivalent called Greetings & Salutations that wanted new artists to revamp its line of sympathy cards. I never asked Nick to pull strings to convince someone I was worth the work visa, but I also never asked if he'd done it anyway, and he probably had. We were incapable of making decisions that weren't guided by our libidos, and the months I spent back in the States were torture. So I grabbed the first smudge of a flat I could afford, in a shady end of London's artsy Shepherd's Bush, and just like that we were a *we* again.

Well, in private, anyway. Richard was very peeved when Nick and I got together—I heard his father through the phone loudly calling me "the crass American mess"—so he kept trying to foist the more suitable India Bolingbroke on his son at official functions, especially while I was conveniently stashed away at Cornell. Around Thanksgiving, when we'd survived our first year together (and about five months long-distance) with no sign of stopping, Nick finally refused to attend anything unless Richard backed off—and then a day later, the paparazzi nabbed a shot of India crying her way out of Clarence House. SICK OVER NICK? the *Evening Standard* had wondered. INDIA BOLINGBROKEN: *She Gave Back the Ring!* the *Mirror* screamed. After that, we agreed we shouldn't provoke the press anew, and drag her back into the crossfire, by sharing our relationship with the world. Not yet. But keeping such a huge secret took an army—specifically, our coterie of Oxford friends. Even Clive. He'd bounced back from the breakup by turning himself into our unofficial press strategist, and when he wasn't busy expounding on how the truth about Nick and me would scandalize England's approximately eighty-two million daily newspapers, he reveled in showing off his connections to London's bouncers by brokering our covert entrances and exits from their nightclubs. And inside the clubs, in front of the crowd's curious eyes, Nick and I kept up our pretense, flirting with other people and never touching each other. The charade was sexier than I'd expected, and made it that much hotter when he snuck into my flat at the end of the night.

I found Tony's office door and punched in the code—1999; he was nothing if not committed. Ten minutes later, I heard a light tapping on the bathroom door.

"Just a sec, I'm washing up," I called out.

"I can't wait that long."

Nick squeezed in and slammed the door, a bottle of vodka dangling from his hand. In seconds, his mouth was on mine, the liquor dropped and forgotten as we tore at each other. I bumped against the sink, and he lifted me on top of it.

"I can't believe this old tank top was so effective," I joked when we came up for air.

Nick retrieved the vodka and took a nip. "Anything you wear is effective," he said, tugging my shirt over my head. "When I saw that idiot talking to you, I couldn't..."

His voice got muffled as he went for one of my ears. I laughed and wrapped a leg around his waist, pulling him to me.

"Couldn't what?"

"Aha," he said, his right hand closing around the flag pin he'd given me, which—as part of an ongoing game—I'd hidden right in the center of my bra. "Someplace nice and direct this time. I like it."

I tipped his face up so our eyes met. "Couldn't *what*?" I repeated with a slow smile.

Nick flashed a wicked grin as he unclasped my bra. "I told you. I couldn't wait."

"What if someone catches us?" I asked, even as I reached for his belt. "Won't they notice we're gone?"

"Let them," Nick said. "I haven't seen you all day and I'm going mad."

Thirty-five minutes and one mildly bruised tailbone later, we were sweaty and spent, and the ill-advised vodka made it urgent that I go home. Unfortunately, a large contingent of paparazzi was outside, waiting for a glimpse either of Nick, or a certain redheaded actress from *Neighbours* (who'd most likely called them herself). So Tony threw dark glasses and a purloined hat onto Cilla and had Clive smuggle her out while shouting loudly about recent *Neighbours* plot points, distracting the photogs long enough for me to pour myself into the back of Nick's waiting car and camouflage myself on the floor under a chunky dark blanket—where I promptly conked out, my cheek pressed ingloriously against the mats. I awoke just as Nick was tucking me into the most glorious of beds, explaining with a grin that he'd brought me to Kensington Palace because hauling me up into my flat would've made him and Stout look like they were hiding a dead body. It was my first time bunking in Kensington, thanks to Eleanor's strict policies about unmarried couples sharing royal bedchambers, but I was too groggy to register it; I barely got out a thank-you before I collapsed back into sleep.

The next morning, I awoke facing a robin's-egg blue wall, the weight of a body next to me on the bed.

"I thought your grandmother didn't approve of sleepovers," I said, closing my eyes and rolling over to spoon him.

"Yes, but I was in the mood for a proper pillow fight," came an unfamiliar voice.

My eyes flew open and I screamed, whacking at the man lying next to me with my fists before leaping out of bed.

"Who the hell are *you*?" I spat, before taking in the familiar-looking person lounging on the bed in front of me, all mussed ginger hair and ratty track pants, rubbing his arm where I'd cracked him. I don't know if I've ever seen another human being laugh so hard.

Nick burst in, panicked. "Bex! Are you all right?"

He stopped when he saw his guffawing brother, the infamous Prince Frederick of Wales, rolling on the bed and clutching his chest with mirth.

"I should've known," Nick said, affecting what looked like a full-body eye roll. "What are you even doing here? I thought you were in Somerset."

"I'm on leave for a bit," Freddie said. "As far as you know. I shouldn't discuss classified details with a half-naked civilian standing right there."

If Freddie thought this would make me blush, he miscalculated.

"Don't worry, I'm not interested in your secrets," I told him. "I am interested in punching you again, though, for scaring the hell out of me."

"Go on, a nice young lady like you?" he said, sitting up against the baroque carved headboard with a grin that could charitably be described as shit-eating.

I leaned over the bed and socked him hard in the other arm.

"Easy, Killer!" Freddie yelped. "Where are my PPOs when I need them?"

"Where are *mine*? No one even stuck his head in to make sure there wasn't a murderer in here," Nick said, tossing me some sweatpants from an ornate dresser. "You're lucky she didn't punch you someplace less polite."

"I would have," I told them, "but I think it's treason to break the Crown Jewels."

Freddie shot me an appraising look. "Funny," he said. "And pretty. Natural. Like a toothpaste commercial. I don't know why Father was so sprung on you and old India *Boring*broke, Knickers. Must have been her massive—"

"I'm sorry, Bex," Nick interrupted. "I'd like to tell you that he's not usually this crass."

"It's true," Freddie said cheerfully. "I'm much worse."

I smiled as I tied the drawstring on the sweatpants. I couldn't help it; that's Freddie's charisma at work. Nick sank down next to him on the expansive bed—the future king, dwarfed by his king-size.

"What *are* you doing here?" he asked. "Father'll have your head if you've skived off your job."

"At least I have a job," Freddie taunted Nick. "What've you been up to? Staring blankly at the *Times* cryptics? More juicy trips to the library?"

Nick's face darkened. This was a sore subject. To Nick's endless envy, Freddie had joined the Royal Navy immediately after Eton, and was training to be a helicopter pilot at a Fleet Air Arm base near a town called Yeovil that sounded more like a medicine than a place. But Richard, in a move I suspect was to keep Nick under his thumb, ordered Nick to bypass military service for the moment and instead divide his time between a postgraduate course in global development through Oxford, and reams of outside reading so he could converse fluently with farmers, politicians, dock workers, even bookmakers. Essentially, Richard was guiding Nick toward both an *actual* master's and an unofficial graduate degree in all things Great Britain and Northern Ireland. This was useful, but because it primarily involved staying indoors, it also had the press calling Nick a layabout when, in fact, I'd never seen him work so hard.

Freddie must have regretted his comment, because he abruptly sprang up from the bed and saluted me. There was a hole in the armpit of his T-shirt.

"Madam, I'm Frederick Wales, pilot in training, at your service."

"Bex Porter," I said. "Hired thug."

"Oh yes, Nick's told me all about you," Freddie said, moving to a wingback in the corner of the room and gesturing for me to sit next to Nick. "Although I'm now the second Lyons you've met without wearing any trousers. What's going to happen when you meet our father?"

I glared at Nick as I climbed onto the bed and stretched out my legs. Nick shrugged sheepishly and then crawled over and rested his head on them.

"You cannot blame me for telling my brother about the adorable American running around in a hand towel," he said, blatantly trying to suck up.

"To be fair, that was the second time we met," I corrected.

Freddie nodded. "Of course. The first time you went on about sexually transmitted diseases."

I flicked Nick's earlobe gently. "If you know all that," I said to Freddie, "then surely you heard I already met Prince Richard. Sort of."

Freddie rubbed his hands together. "I can't believe you left out this part, Knickers."

"It wasn't exactly one of our better memories," Nick said.

"No, that'd be Windsor, wouldn't it?" Freddie said with a mischievous gleam.

I fully pinched Nick's ear this time, but I was laughing. "Jealous we beat you to it?" I teased Freddie.

"Who says you did?" Freddie fired back. "Rebecca, I've got secrets that would curl your hair and cripple the monarchy. And you know horny old Henry the Eighth sullied every one of those antiques with his great greasy bum." He smacked his hands on his thighs. "Right, let me guess: Prince Dick was screeching at Nick and you overheard and he got all growly and menacing."

"Got it in one," I said.

The words were barely out of my mouth before Freddie jumped up and walked to the window. Freddie is nearly always moving. He's athletic enough that it doesn't come across as fidgeting—more like he's a very handsome perpetual-motion machine. He pulled apart the thick silk curtains covering the floor-to-ceiling windows, revealing a gray, foggy morning, then fished a thin silver cigarette case out of his track pants pocket and pushed open the top half of one of the windows.

"Freddie, don't smoke in here," Nick said as a cold draft blew into the room.

"Too bloody freezing anyway," Freddie said, slamming the window closed and tossing the engraved case onto the floor. "You win this one, Knickers."

"Please pick that up. When did you start smoking again?" Fatigue and strain crept into Nick's voice, as if a lifetime of being forced to nag his brother was wearing on him all at once.

"It's just every so often."

"It'll kill you, and so will Gran."

"Thanks, but I already have a mum," Freddie snapped.

An unsettling current passed between them. Nick looked away. A flicker of something like guilt crossed Freddie's face, before he turned to me.

"So, you were saying Prince Dick was a complete fuckhead to you," he said.

I laughed, despite wanting to be irritated on Nick's behalf. "I did *not* say that."

"And is old Dickie just thrilled about this romantic development?"

"Is he ever thrilled about anything?" Nick countered. "We don't discuss it."

"Which means his army of spies has skulked around and reported back all manner of sins," Freddie concluded. "Run while you can, Killer, before they tell him you chew with your mouth open and have been seen sniffing around Aunt Agatha's collection of Fabergé eggs."

"I can't run," I said. "I'm really gunning for those eggs."

Freddie nodded approvingly, then checked his watch. "Stay for lunch, won't you? Surely there's something decent knocking about in the kitchen."

*Something decent* proved to be cheese, salad, a standing rib roast, Scotch eggs, and four different kinds of potatoes. It was the first of many such meals where the three of us would take refuge and stuff our faces. We ate this particular one in the second, smaller dining room, which has a view of the public park that used to be the palace's front yard. Compared to some of the other state holdings, Kensington Palace looks the most like a regular old manor: The careworn, faded brick main building houses a museum, and fronts a village of well-concealed, sprawling private apartments for a variety of royal relatives. And given that the green space around it is now royal parkland, gawkers get a whole lot closer than you'd expect. Imagine if you could walk right up to the White House lawn and sunbathe topless while the president looked out of his window. It wouldn't happen, and yet right now there was a girl in Kensington Gardens stretching in the most perfunctory of shorts.

"Your next girlfriend, mate," Nick teased.

"Or an old one," Freddie joked back. Then he squinted through the window. "Actually, she does look familiar."

I had heard about Freddie's addiction to dating gorgeous women—the more the merrier—who were also either odd or ragingly inappropriate enough to keep him entertained for more than a week. The stories he regaled me with over that day's lunch more than confirmed the rumors, including one about his comparatively lengthy three-month dalliance with a Scottish actress named Turret who'd had to be paid off by the Palace to stop her turning the relationship into a one-woman musical. She was now a party planner in Ottawa. Little wonder Nick's own taste in women had been the subject of so much media curiosity.

"So when is the big coming-out?" Freddie asked, passing a Bloody Mary pitcher around and then taking a loud bite out of his celery stalk. "Bex should meet the family."

"Isn't that what we're doing?" Nick replied.

"You know what I mean. I don't count," Freddie said. "I'm barely even frightening."

"*You* know what *I* mean," Nick said. "I'm just not ready to hand this relationship to the wolves yet. Any of them."

The brothers exchanged a silent look, again, that seemed to say a lot in a language that I didn't yet speak. Freddie nodded slowly.

"Quite right, as usual, Knickers," he said. "Your secret is safe with me. This particular secret anyway."

Freddie bounded away and returned with some leather-bound photo albums to show me what he called "all fourteen years of Nick's awkward period." They were notable in that both boys were as appealing then as they are now—it was a teen girl's dream scrapbook—and that there wasn't a photo of Emma anywhere, although to be fair, Richard wasn't present much, either. It was largely nannies; Clive's father, Edgeware; and their uncle Awful Julian, who, despite his reputation as a drunk and a bounder, was clearly adept with the boys. (Freddie once told me that this is because Awful Julian likes them better than his own equally awful son.) We dallied until nine, at which point Freddie suggested we hit up a club he'd been wanting to try in Soho, because he was chasing around a part-time model and party planner called Tuppence.

"And I intend to collect." He winked.

"Appalling," Nick said, but he was smiling.

"I should actually get home," I said. "I'm wiped out, and I need clean clothes."

"It's dark already," Nick said, nudging me affectionately with his knee. "Stay."

"Won't that be scandalous?" I asked. "Two nights in a row?"

"Probably," Nick said. "But Freddie rudely hogged all my time with you today, so I don't want to say good-bye yet."

Freddie hopped up and took my hand. "*Enchanté*," he said, kissing it lightly. "It was a pleasure being abused by your fists. I hope you hit on me again very soon."

Then he turned to Nick and waved a mock-scolding finger. "Now, Nicholas, you simply mustn't sleep in the same bed. Gran will be furious." To me, he added, "Knickers is a stickler for duty, have you noticed? Oh—speaking of..."

He pulled out his wallet and rummaged through it, before pulling out a folded piece of paper and flicking it at Nick. "Finished yesterday's cryptic," he said. "Consider it your new duty to study it and learn."

Nick threw a coaster at Freddie's back as his brother fled the room, and we spent the ensuing hour chatting on the couch, our legs in a cozy tangle, until our yawning could no longer be denied.

"We probably do have to aim for propriety here," Nick said. "Gran is very persnickety about sleeping arrangements. You can stay in mine again, or if the flashbacks to Freddie's appearance this morning are too horrifying, you can take the Howard Bedroom."

He escorted me to a cozy, wood-paneled chamber with deep-set windows overlooking a private courtyard, and an intimate seating area with fresh flowers and magazines scattered artfully on an end table. Against the opposite wall was an imposing four-poster bed, begging me to flop onto it. I am a world-class flopper. I can heave myself onto a couch so hard it's still vibrating five minutes later.

"Despite Freddie's appalling behavior, that went well, right?" Nick asked, collapsing onto a love seat. "You're the only girlfriend of mine who's been able to keep up with him. The one time I invited Ceres for a nightcap, Freddie sent her to a pub down the street. He told her we were out of cups."

Affection washed over me. In all my nerves about meeting Freddie, I never stopped to think that Nick might have been just as worried.

"Freddie's great," I said, sitting down and sticking my feet on the table. My socks didn't match. As usual. "It would've been fun to have a brother like that, although I probably would've wanted to throttle him for a few years because he'd have been letting his pervy friends go through my underwear drawer."

"I often still want to throttle him," Nick said. "Promise me he didn't stress you out about meeting the family. Honestly, I don't have much that's just *mine*. I want to keep you to myself for a bit." He grabbed my foot and started rubbing it. "Mismatched socks and all."

"Mmm. It's a shame I'm going to have to turn you out of my maiden bedroom," I said.

Nick dropped my foot. "Oh, you sweet naïve commoner," he said.

He pulled me up and led me to one of the bookcases flanking the bed, where he tugged on a peeling volume called *Historic Houses of England*. The entire bookcase swung inward.

An actual secret passage.

"The hidden perk of the Howard Bedroom is that it connects to mine, which is where the Duke of York slept back in the day. This is where he housed his..."

"His mistress?" I supplied.

"I didn't realize until the end of that sentence that it was somewhat insulting to you," Nick said. "Let me try again. Ahem. This room is where the Duke of York housed, ah, the guest he might most wish to visit in the middle of the night, for a variety of respectable reasons, one of which is her advanced taste in hosiery."

"Of course," I said. "But that still doesn't solve the problem of your grandmother not wanting us to defile a royal bedchamber."

"I thought of that," Nick said smugly. "Being as this is a guest suite, it isn't a *royal* bedchamber at all. In fact, it's a wickedly *unpopular* bedchamber because it's haunted. We'd be doing it a service."

"Giving it a reason to live," I agreed. "Or giving the ghost a reason to pretend to live."

"Quite selfless, really."

"Sexual philanthropy."

"Fancy term. Now you're just showing off for the ghost," he murmured, lowering his mouth to mine and sliding my sweatpants to the floor. If the ghost was scandalized by what happened next, he certainly never complained.

# CHAPTER TWO

"But *why* haven't you met them?" my mother asked, picking up the white and mint-green teacup and jerking her pinky finger impatiently out to the side, as if scolding herself for it not being innate. "It's suspicious, Rebecca."

It was a reasonable question, and not unexpected: Almost a year had passed since I woke up to find Freddie in my bed instead of Nick, and I still hadn't encountered anyone else in the Lyons family beyond that old, unofficial—and still secret, even to my parents—dustup with Richard. Mom and Dad, in fact, had flown over with the express purpose of meeting the esteemed Prince Nicholas, and yet there were no current plans for me to have a sit-down with the opposite side. Certainly, there were reasons for this; royal life always came with reasons, almost all of them Reasons, some of them even typed up and filed in a manila folder. But as much as I swore I didn't need family dinners at Balmoral to validate my relationship, I couldn't help being stung by the math: A thousand days without a handshake was hard to explain, even to myself, and absolutely not something I wanted to psychoanalyze during a ritzy high tea.

"I can text Nick and tell him you aren't comfortable meeting him without knowing his intentions," I offered, dropping a cube of brown sugar into my exotic blend. "We can really draw a line in the sand, if that's what you want."

Mom patted the neatly curled ends of her silver-streaked bob. "We cannot be so rude," she said imperiously.

"Not when she packed special steam-powered hair curlers," Dad said.

Mom swatted him. "Appearances matter," she said, tugging at her tweedy Chanel suit jacket. "And Nick needs to know we take this seriously. I just don't want him treating Bex like Ms. Right Now if she thinks he's Mr. Right."

"Oh God. Please don't quote some decades-old *Cosmopolitan* that you found at your hairdresser," Lacey said.

"I suppose next you're going to tell me I gave him the milk for free," I said.

"I am an extremely modern woman," Mom said defensively. "I use text messages and the Skype and everything. That doesn't mean I can't be concerned."

"Come on now, Nancy. Nick seems like a good guy," Dad said, patting her arm. "And Bex is no slouch. She has my keen eye for reading people." He winked at me over the tea sandwich dwarfed in his large hands. "I am sure everyone's intentions are good."

Mom blew on her tea, frowning, not having heard a word. "Isn't his *mother* even the slightest bit curious about you?"

Another eminently fair question, and one that I treated as rhetorical, because I had no answer. Nick and I had talked about almost everything else: how he'd lost his virginity (to Gemma Sands, at fifteen, about ten minutes after feeding the giraffes at her father's wildlife preserve), how he got the scar on his chin (Freddie clipped him with a polo mallet), that he had a recurring nightmare about one of his grandmother's porcelain soup tureens. Emma, however, was inhospitable territory. The times she'd come up organically, Nick either changed the subject, or clammed up completely. I wanted to draw him out, to be there for him, but was afraid it would come off like prying. So I let it go.

But I was tired of telling him eccentric bits and bobs about my own family—how Dad helped Lacey build a working model of an intestine for our high school science fair, or the way Mom buys a new summer and winter suit each year for the purposes of being buried in seasonal attire, should the worst happen—that I had to qualify with, *You'll see when you meet them.* To his credit, Nick was delighted when I suggested an introduction, and immediately had his people book Mom and Dad a suite at The Dorchester—one of London's poshest old hotels, and the one the Queen most trusted for discretion. So far, my family had enjoyed a great visit. We traipsed around the Tower of London, hopped the train to Hampton Court, even took a boat ride on the Thames—all the lively touristy stuff that I couldn't do with Nick. Dad made it his mission to eat in as many of the ubiquitous pubs with *Arms* in the title as possible, and sought out an antiques shop on Kensington Church Street that kept all the most fabulous items under the floorboards, hidden from view except to those with a large enough wad of bills. Dad claimed he just wanted to investigate, but left with a walking stick concealing a sword, and an old leather book that was actually a hiding place for a lady's gold-and-ivory-handled pistol. Never mind what he thought he was going to do with any of them. We ribbed him about it the whole week.

Still, the prospect of this day hung over me the entire time. Our tea was a strategic prelude to make sure Mom felt properly civilized, and my dad properly fed and watered. The Dorchester's Champagne high tea is as elegant as its marble-floored lobby dining room, which was infused with the gentle tinkling of utensils on fine china. Down the way a piano player tapped out "I Dreamed a Dream," eyes closed, head bobbing in deepest passion.

"Nothing like a song about a dying hooker to wash down your scones," I said.

"Bex, be regal," Mom said. "For once. *Please.*"

Lacey wiggled into perfect posture. "This is the life," she said. "Sleeping in, wandering through Harrods, gorging on Champers and tea and cakes... I could so get used to this."

Lacey often chose to forget that I didn't live like this all the time. My appalling flat didn't have any water pressure, but it did have mice, and I spent any leftover money on cheap art classes and highballs rather than Harrods and bubbly. I'd never even been inside Harrods until she took me. But Lacey had always been wistful with respect to England. She'd just finished her first year of med school at NYU, but she was never as interested in discussing that as she was in planning her next trip to London. She'd arrive here with a fresh head of highlights and a meticulously curated suitcase, primed to dazzle every guy in her path, reeling in admirers the way she used to friends at summer camp—but unlike when we were kids, she used the phone numbers she brought home. I wanted her to love London, but this felt more like trying to conquer it.

The piano player switched into the theme song from *Phantom of the Opera*, banging it out so violently I was sure his hands would bleed out all over his instrument.

"This guy's repertoire isn't very uplifting," Dad noted.

I checked my watch. "Fortunately that's our cue. Finish your scones. Nick will be upstairs any minute."

In addition to getting my parents a lush suite for their stay, Nick had reserved one specifically for our meeting that boasted both private access for him—for maximum discretion—and breathtaking views of Hyde Park, for maximum brownie points.

"Hideous," my dad said, stepping out onto the terrace.

"The worst," I said, threading my arm through his.

"Intolerable. How does anyone live like this?"

"With ten thousand pounds a night, according to the website," Lacey said, coming up next to us. "Can you imagine being able to snap your fingers and get this whenever you want? Your life is insane, Bex."

"This isn't my life," I said, feeling like I was repeating myself. "This is one day in my life. The rest of the time, I have ants and no central air."

"Ah, but the ants provide such a tremendous distraction from the spiders," came a voice.

Nick walked out into the most insanely cinematic beam of light. It honestly did look as if the Heavens were kissing him—exactly, I suspect, the way my mother (and *The Bexicon*'s Aurelia Maupassant) had imagined it would be, minus Handel's Hallelujah chorus. His sandy hair gleamed slightly red in the sun, his jeans were perfect yet perfectly broken in, his Pumas worn but not dirty, his rugby shirt the exact level of sporty my parents always expected from a boyfriend of mine. The only hint of his status was the gold vintage Rolex that had been a gift from his great-grandmother Marta on his eighteenth birthday.

Mom immediately dipped into a curtsy. Lacey buried her face in her hands.

"Nancy's been practicing for weeks," Dad said, clapping Nick on the shoulder while shaking his hand. "If she needs bionic knees after this, I'm sending you the bill."

Nick laughed. "Mrs. Porter, it's a pleasure," he said, bowing deeply and kissing her hand. "Your form is miles better than Mum's, but if you breathe a word of that to anyone I'll deny it."

"Well!" My mother blushed, speechless. He was good.

"Hey, Nick," Lacey said, giving him a quick hug. "Good to see you."

"And on such a miserable day," Nick joked, gesturing at the clear blue skies. "Father once booked this suite for some of our European relatives, and it bucketed down rain the entire time. Couldn't see a thing. They swore never to come back." He winced. "That may have been a blessing. One of them kept telling us we were all supposed to be German by now."

My father let out a booming belly laugh, and I could tell Nick was tickled by Dad's warm reaction. "Dreadfully sorry about the Cubs, though, Mr. Porter," he added. "I heard the Padres swept them."

"Call me Earl. You should shoot over for a game!"

"Yes, Bex swears Cracker Jack is much better when it's fresh," Nick said.

"It's better in the *stands*," I corrected him. "It's never really fresh. That's part of its charm."

Nick grinned at me before gesturing for my mother to head back into the hotel room, where what looked like yet another tea service—and two cold lagers in pint glasses—had been set out on the glossy coffee table. We'd all turn *into* scones before long.

"So, Nick, I could use your advice on a small weapons issue I might've gotten myself into," Dad said. "There's this antiques shop, see…"

Their voices trailed off and the door clicked shut. Lacey and I stayed on the balcony, enjoying the sun.

"So what now?" Lacey asked.

"I figured we'd hang for a bit, then send Mom and Dad to the theater."

"I mean with Nick."

"We're going to usurp the throne, and invade Switzerland just to be cute," I said.

"Be serious, Bex."

"Okay," I said. "*Seriously*, why does anything have to happen now? We're young. We're happy. Why does everyone want to rush this?"

Lacey threw out an aggrieved hand. "If that's how you want to play it," she said. "As long as you're not going all Bex about it and avoiding reality. Isn't that how you ended up stringing Clive along?"

"That's a low blow."

"Well, it's tough love time," Lacey said. "And those two are basically falling in love with him right now, too, so get ready. The longer you go without meeting his family, the more questions they're going to ask."

I knew she was right. Nick swore he loved me, and he emphatically acted like it—including his willingness to hang out with my dad and discuss, by the sound of it, the nuances of televised darts. But I was beginning to feel unsettled. Like Nick had a hidden reason, or Reason, for keeping me on the down-low.

"I'm good. It's handled," I lied. "And speaking of Nick's family, I have a surprise for you. He'll be here in about three hours."

Lacey's face lit up. "Freddie," she breathed, throwing her arms around me in glee.

"Freddie." I grinned, squeezing her back.

*The Bexicon* glosses over Lacey and Freddie. In fact, it whitewashes almost all the supporting players, as if Nick and I got where we did in some kind of vacuum, untouched by anyone except the fairies of true love who'd drawn us together. That unforgivable turn of phrase is a direct quote—pure Aurelia Maupassant. As is this:

> It is natural to imagine an attraction between England's premier charming rogue and Lacey, a dynamic golden-haired sprite. But such rumours are utterly fantastical and spurious. As Rebecca and Nicholas yachted the oft-tempestuous seas of romance, Lacey and Freddie came together only as their siblings' invaluable confidantes. Nothing more.

Glorious bullshit.

Nick left the massive Dorchester penthouse with plans to return, Freddie in tow, after their slate of meetings at Clarence House. With Mom and Dad off seeing something deliriously British on the West End, Lacey and I had plenty of time to primp for a night out with the princes. Meaning, I watched the worst TV I could find while Lacey took a bubble bath, and then she shoved a dress and a pair of heels into my hand and told me if I so much as tried to put on flats, wedges, or jeans, she'd throw them off the balcony.

"I mean, those aren't even skinnies," she said. "They're *straight leg*."

The dress was undeniably flattering: sleeveless and short with a lightly flared skirt, the plunging V-neck counterbalancing the relatively innocent silhouette, especially after Lacey accessorized it with a delicate lavaliere that rested right between my breasts. She tucked in my bra strap, then stood back to admire her work, rolling her eyes when I futilely tugged the fabric over whatever cleavage I had.

"For someone who has streaked as many places as you have," she said, undoing what I'd just done, "you are so uptight."

"I have to be careful," I said. "It would be just my luck if Nick and I got caught on a night when my boob was hanging out. It's Murphy's Law."

"Well, Murphy is a killjoy," she grumbled, smoothing her stunning, snug leather mini.

The guys were twenty minutes late. Lacey spent that time wiping off her lipstick and trying different shades, then chucking her entire outfit and going through four other options. She was mid-change when I heard the suite door open and the sound of two male voices.

"Stall!" she whispered.

Freddie let out a low whistle when I walked into the living room.

"Nice legs, Killer!" he said, taking my hand and ogling me exaggeratedly. "I never figured you for a miniskirt kind of girl."

I blushed. "Lacey is a bad influence."

"I certainly hope so," Freddie said.

"You look amazing," Nick said, then pulled me in to whisper, "I'm dying to know where the pin is. Maybe we should stay in so I can conduct a thorough search."

Nick made it difficult for me to behave sometimes.

"Where are we going, anyway?" I asked, tearing myself away.

"To Shoreditch, if you lovers can stop manhandling each other," Freddie said. "This bird I'm sort of seeing wants to have a look at Tony's new club."

"Ask her name." Nick nudged me.

"I don't know what you find so amusing, Knickers," Freddie said airily. "Fallopia is a beautiful name."

I nearly choked. "Fallopia? Where did you meet *her*?"

Freddie's lip twitched. "The Tube, of course."

I burst into laughter. Freddie looked delighted. Even Nick giggled.

"What's so funny?" Lacey asked, sauntering out from the bedroom doors.

I'd recognized her whole wardrobe-indecision gambit from high school—last one out of the bedroom makes the grandest entrance—and it worked just as she'd clearly imagined. She'd decided on a sleek black halter dress, which managed to seem classy while simultaneously leaving very little to the imagination; if Freddie had been a cartoon, his eyes would have dropped out of his skull and rolled along the floor until they landed at Lacey's feet, looking up her skirt.

"Nothing is funny," Freddie said, offering Lacey his arm. "There is absolutely nothing funny about the fact that Bex has selfishly kept a blond goddess to herself all this time."

"Well, now we've fixed *that*," Lacey said, never once betraying that she was flirting with a guy whose picture used to be tacked up on her wall, "let's not waste any more time."

Nick and I traded amused glances as Freddie escorted her to the elevator.

"I don't like Fallopia's chances too much, do you?" I said.

"Hurricane Freddie," was all he said.

Plush, a pop-up offshoot of the original Club Theme, was not Tony's best effort. Its fur-covered tables and chairs, damp from perspiration and sticky from spilled drinks, couldn't be cleaned and were unpleasant to sit on, which may be why so many people opted to dance in the cages suspended from the ceiling. Clive and a very drunk Gaz immediately goaded me and Lacey into the two above the VIP section while they catcalled appreciatively—and, in Gaz's case, clambered up to join us.

"This is brilliant!" Gaz shouted, jerking into a triumphant pose that had the cage swinging perilously (and Tony flinching).

"Yes, our Garamond is a font of bad ideas," Cilla cracked from the floor beneath us, loudly enough for Gaz to hear and salute her comically.

"What's the matter, Clivey, can't lift yourself in there?" shouted Martin Fitzwilliam, whom Clive referred to as his stupidest brother. "Worried you'll pull a *journalism* muscle?"

I saw Clive shake his head. Then he drained his drink and climbed in with me.

"If I can't beat them, I'll join you," he quipped. "And if there's one thing they've proven over the years, it's that I can't beat them. I broke a finger once punching Thick Trevor in the chest."

"I thought Martin was the stupid one," I said.

"He is," Clive said. "And Trevor is thick. You'll understand the difference if you see them together."

I grinned. "All I know is, Martin *must* be stupid, or else he'd be the one up in a cage with a girl."

Lacey always says club dancing looks like a seizure—as with Halloween, she'd rather look cute if she plans to be the center of attention—so she and Gaz started some deliberately exaggerated dirty dancing that eventually morphed into a facetious dance-off against me and Clive. He made a good partner in our pseudo-lambada—even his stupid brother Martin ended up cheering for us—although I did feel a twinge seeing Nick out of the corner of my eye and knowing he and I could never do this, even in jest. Freddie, however, seemed to be considering it. He hadn't taken his eyes off Lacey's cage.

"Isn't *she* a dynamo," Bea said to me during a break in our revelry. "What's next for you two? A trapeze?"

I smiled sweetly. "Can't," I said. "I believe it's currently jammed up your ass."

"While I fetch it," Bea said through a matching smile, "you might enjoy the view of Nick with his old flame. Don't they look cozy?"

I peered around her at Nick, talking to a lithe, fair-skinned blonde who was positively overloaded with jewelry.

"He was devastated when Ceres cheated on him," Bea continued.

At that moment Nick laughed loudly and put an arm around Ceres's shoulder. A jealous pit blossomed in my stomach, but I ignored it. Insecurity had never been my style.

"I'm sure he's just thrilled to hear about the cutting-edge world of party planning," I said.

"Yes, well, it's not so avant-garde as greeting-card design, but what is?" smirked Bea, drifting back to them.

"What was that all about?" Lacey asked, coming up behind me. "Do you need me to crack some skulls?"

"You sound like me," I said, hugging her around the waist.

"I'll take that as a compliment," she said. "Now, forget Lady Bellatrix Hyphenate Whatever, and let's give the Wales brothers a night they'll never forget."

We did our best, and I'll wager Freddie returned the favor: I caught him the next morning tiptoeing out of Lacey's bedroom. She immediately extended her trip—blowing off the beginning of her med-school semester in a giddy lather—and he rebooked the penthouse, and the two of them embarked on a full-fledged fling. Lacey particularly enjoyed the covert shenanigans of sneaking in and out of bars to avoid the paparazzi, although once she mistimed her exit and got caught in a shot with Freddie. Fortunately, he was blocking most of her body and all of her face, except for her ear, and a couple of curls. She bought four copies of the story, even though it included shots of him with two other girls under the headline FRISKY FREDDIE BLAZES THROUGH BLONDES.

"Isn't it funny?" she'd said brightly. "It's the perfect souvenir for when I'm back at school dissecting kidneys, or whatever, and I want to remember what it was like to be in Prince Frederick's little black book."

"That little black book is more like an encyclopedia at this point," I said.

She grinned. "At least I'll go down in history."

Nick wasn't as amused.

"You don't think you're being bit careless?" he asked Freddie one night shortly after Lacey returned to the States. The brothers were teaching me cribbage at Kensington. "You've spent the last fortnight leading around half of London, including my girlfriend's sister."

"Beats hiding girls under a blanket in the car," Freddie said. "How long can you keep pretending you and Bex aren't actually together? I'm even bringing Fallopia to Klosters and we barely know each other."

"Then why bring her?" I asked.

"Her name is Fallopia. Father will hate her," Freddie said patiently, as if this were too stupid to be discussed.

"It's none of my concern if you burn hot and fast with these people we'll probably never see again," Nick said. "But Lacey is someone we care about. I've no interest in denying you the great love of your life, but if she's *not*, then—"

"It was two glorious weeks, and everyone went home with a smile," Freddie said.

"Then what about the next time she visits? And the one after that?" Nick asked. "What happens if Bex and I get found out? Leading Lacey on is one thing, but *carrying* on with her would make both Bex *and* Lacey look bad. The last thing we need is that stodgy old *Mail* columnist squawking that they have a royals fetish."

"I know you're the heir and I'm the spare, Knickers, but that doesn't mean you're also meant to be my nanny," Freddie said. "Let me have my fun."

"Not everyone would call baiting the press *fun*," Nick said curtly.

"Screw Prince Dick."

"I don't mean him."

"Why are you always bringing her up?" Freddie asked hotly.

"Why are *you* always forgetting?" Nick slapped his cards down on the floor.

Freddie slammed down his cards, stood, and angrily swiped his coat from the back of a flowered armchair. He disappeared out the door of the apartment with a bang.

Nick rubbed his eyes. I crawled over and hugged one of his knees to my chest.

"Lacey knows it was casual," I promised. "And nobody recognizes her, and nobody even knows about us. They won't put two and two together that she was out with Freddie. "

"It's just..." He let out a frustrated breath. "We have to talk about something, and this isn't the way I'd wanted to do it."

My mind flashed to his arm around Ceres at Plush. My stomach sank. I really hate *We have to talk*. It never goes anywhere good, and for me, it brings back memories of the day Mom sat me and Lacey down on the couch and said *We have to talk* because Dad had a heart attack. I will never forget the sensation that if I opened my mouth, my own heart would come up out of it and land on the coffee table.

I steeled myself. "Talk about what?"

Nick tucked a stray strand of my hair behind my ear and tugged on it gently. "Well, you may not want to after that display, but I rather thought I'd like to bring you on the family Klosters trip at New Year's."

The longer I sat there in shocked silence, the more Nick's amusement turned to nerves.

"Obviously, you don't have to," he said, fidgeting. "I just enjoyed your parents, and—"

"Yes, of course, yes. I want to," I said happily. "You just caught me off guard."

His face was a picture of relief. "I wanted it to be a surprise," he said, folding me into his arms as we leaned back against the faded green love seat. "I did *not* want it to seem like Freddie goaded me into it, because he didn't."

"I believe you," I said. "I'm just...I'm totally excited, but I also want to throw up a little. Is that lame?"

"I'd be worried if you weren't slightly jittery," Nick said. "It's not like Father recently hit his head and woke up all cuddly."

I snorted.

"Definitely do as much of that as possible," he teased.

I elbowed him, he tickled me, and we spent a few minutes poking at each other and laughing until he finally caught both my wrists and gave me a long kiss.

"London stresses me out," he said when we broke apart. "It's full of people who want something from me, or expect something." He smiled. "But Klosters is like Oxford. Ten minutes with the cameras and everyone leaves us alone."

"Is there ever a time when you're *not* looking for everyone to leave you alone?"

Nick rolled onto his back, carrying me with him until I was straddling his chest. "Right now?" he said, and tugged at my jeans with a wicked gleam.

I grinned and uncurled myself. "Race you to the Howard Bedroom. Last one there gets the lumpy side."

"Oh no, that's not on," he said, leaping to his feet. "I know another secret passage you've not seen," he shouted, tearing off in the other direction.

And indeed, I slept on the lumpy side. It was worth it.

That December, a huge snowstorm they were calling the Arctic Sinkhole socked in the entire Midwest. I turned down kind invitations to spend the holiday with Cilla's and Gaz's respective families because I kept hoping for a last-minute break in the weather, but it became clear that even if I somehow got to Iowa for Christmas, I was fifty-fifty at best to return in time for Klosters. Nick called from the annual Lyons gathering up at Sandringham to tell me everyone would understand, but Lacey and Mom were adamant that I shouldn't risk it, Mom even threatening to disown me if I tried. So I spent the holiday alone in my flat with a radiator that worked only half the time but clanged monotonously all of the time, and a toilet that wouldn't stop flushing unless I hit the tank with the broad side of a dictionary.

But I embraced the unplanned quietude, which I had jokingly

christened my Solitary Refinement. I bought a pint-size fake tree and decorated it with tinsel and ornaments from a local drugstore. I hung the holiday cards I'd gotten above my imitation fireplace, and I stocked up on port wine and fancier beer. And every day I spruced up my blue Oxford sweatshirt with Nick's present to me. Eleanor decreed long ago that the Royal Family must give only gag gifts at Christmas—which makes perfect sense; Sephora gift cards don't quite cut it for a woman who has her own Gutenberg Bible—but I think Nick missed the satisfaction of giving actual *thoughtful* presents to his loved ones, because he blew past our amiably low price cap and bought me a delicate diamond solitaire pendant on a long gold chain (so I could wear it under my clothes, next to my heart, without anyone being the wiser). I gave him a sweater and a cheat guide for cryptic crosswords. In my defense, he is almost as hard to shop for as his grandmother, and he needed both.

On Christmas Day, I luxuriated in changing out of my sleeping pajamas and into a new flannel set specifically for loafing around, and spent the day watching movies. Just as I got antsy for human contact—right at the part of *The Sound of Music* when the Von Trapp kids are parading around Salzburg dressed in nothing but some old drapes—I heard a sloppy knock at my door.

"Who is it?" I shouted. My peephole was permanently fogged.

"Gaz. I bring delicacies."

I fumbled at the chain and tugged open the door. Gaz charged through, a burst of frosty air around him as he made a beeline for my compact kitchen, carrying several grocery bags from Harrods. He dumped his quarry on whatever counter space he could find and surveyed my place.

"Cilla said your flat was small, but I didn't realize she meant you could see into the lav from the kitchen," he said. "I could probably *use* it from here."

"Go ahead, you just metaphorically peed all over the place anyway," I said. "What are you doing here? I mean, I'm glad to see you, but I'm not exactly company-ready."

"My family is all done in by about two o'clock. Big fat Christmas dinner and then straight into a food coma." He patted his stomach.

"But I'm a growing boy and I need my third meal, see, and Cilla said you wouldn't go with her to Yorkshire to have her eighteen nieces and nephews blow their noses all over you, so voila, your savior is here."

Gaz started pulling things willy-nilly from the bags. "I brought all kinds of goodies. Come have a butcher's. We've got cheese and onion pasties, a pork pie; have you ever had one? Bloody brilliant. Oh, and a spot of cheese and caviar, and some chocolates."

It was the sweetest gesture, and one he'd clearly planned well in advance. I gave him a sniffly, tight hug.

"Now, now," he said, reddening, but clearly delighted. "I know I'm a sexy beast, but I can't have my mate's girl throwing herself at me."

We carried the food into my living room and spent a lively night yelling at the remainder of *The Sound of Music*, cheering so vibrantly at the nun with the carburetor that my downstairs neighbor banged on the ceiling to shut us up.

"God, what a film," Gaz said when it ended, folding his hands onto his stomach. "That naughty baroness was the first woman I ever saw who drew on eyebrows. I didn't know if I was afraid of her or in love with her." He screwed up his face. "Probably both. Might explain a few things."

"Yes, when *are* you going to declare yourself to Cilla?" I asked casually.

Gaz looked startled. "Is it that obvious?"

"Maybe not to most people," I said. "But the way you two thrive on goading each other always seemed suspicious to me."

"You're bonkers," Gaz sighed. "She thinks I'm a stuffed git."

"Cilla doesn't suffer fools. She wouldn't spend so much time needling you if she thought you were one."

Gaz brightened, then his face fell again. "She's seeing that Tony bloke, though," he said. "Never mind whatever shady business he's probably up to with that nightclub of his. All that white powder in the loos doesn't get there on its own."

"You're almost a solicitor. Or a barrister. Whichever it is," I asked. "Can't you sue the pants off him for something?"

"That's tempting," Gaz said. "I'll be a solicitor in about a year, and then I can get into business. Maybe that'll impress her." He frowned and rubbed his nose. "Maybe if I weren't such a fat oaf," he said harshly. "Maybe if I lost a bit of weight and stopped drinking. But I can't help it. That's who I am. My feelings have loads of flavors."

I laughed, but not unsympathetically. "Lose it for yourself, if you want to, but not for anyone else," I said. "Cilla will see through Tony eventually, and she clearly knows you were the only person for the job of cheering me up tonight. She'll come around. Maybe even while we're all in Klosters and Tony is stuck here."

Gaz shot me a grateful smile. "You're a real mate, Bex," he said. "Let me at least return the favor. What do you want to know about this whole Klosters bit? Or have Nick and Clive already briefed you?"

"Hardly. When Nick and I talked about it, I got so fixated on the etiquette part that I didn't even ask him about the other people coming," I said. "And I haven't seen Clive for ages."

"Yes, too busy doing world-beating reporting like COUNCIL APPROVES PLAN FOR NEW LIFT AT HOLBORN STATION," Gaz joked.

"Poor Clive. I admire how hard he's trying," I said. "But I do need it explained why the Palace isn't more worried about him coming to Klosters. He's essentially the media now."

"*Top News* hardly counts as media. It's barely a step up from words printed on bog paper. People only even see it because it's forced on them when they're getting off the Tube," Gaz said. "But we also sign our lives away, as I'm sure Nick told you. And the Fitzwilliams are thick as thieves with Richard. If Clive ever violates that, Thick Trevor will twist him up so that his nose unloads into his bowels." He grinned. "This trip is quite good people-watching, actually. I can't wait for you to experience Pudge."

I coughed around a piece of pork pie. "What is a 'Pudge'?"

"It's a *who*. Bea's sister Paddington," Gaz said. "She was an eleven-pound baby, and the nickname stuck. She's... how to put this delicately... a total drooling gobshite."

"That's the delicate option?" I laughed.

"Just you wait." He rubbed his hands together.

Gaz made it all sound so entertaining, but I was increasingly nervous. Intellectually, I knew I wasn't being introduced to the extended family as anything more than Nick's friend, and that Cilla and even Bea being there would bolster that cover. But I wasn't the kind of moneyed or titled aristocrat with a plummy accent and a Bentley that Nick's relations were used to; I was a first-time skier whose father made comfortable appliances for beer lovers. I didn't know how any of that would go over with them, no matter what they thought he and I were to each other—and on that score, Richard was still in severe, sometimes apoplectic denial.

Gaz studied me, then raised his glass. "No need to panic," he said. "We'll keep you out of the blast radius."

As we clinked wine glasses, mine cracked and squirted thick red port all over my couch.

"Don't tell Cilla about that," Gaz warned. "She'll say it's an omen."

"I don't believe in omens," I said.

# CHAPTER THREE

Freddie calls Klosters "ten degrees below narcolepsy" because of its lack of nightlife, but I have always found the sleepy mountain village enchanting: clusters of pitched-roof cabins flanked by towering pines, their branches heavy with snow—like Whoville without the Grinch, unless you counted Richard. But for jaw-dropping grandeur, the Swiss Alps might meet their match in the two chalets Richard always rents, for something like forty thousand dollars each. Each spread has four floors, a staff of maids and cooks on loan from Balmoral, a guesthouse for the PPOs, a seventy-two-inch flat-screen, heated bathroom floors, and Champagne on tap. Literally. Champagne actually comes out of a faucet. Once the Coucherator debuted in the SkyMall catalog it had changed my family's life, but every Fourth of July we still holed up in the cabin in Michigan my mom and Aunt Kitty inherited, with its one bedroom and broken futon. So luxury purely for the sake of luxury was new to me, and as I unpacked in the fourth-floor master that I was sharing with Nick, Lacey's words echoed in my head: *Your life is insane, Bex*. It hadn't felt true then. It did now.

"May I come in?"

When I looked up to see Clive standing in the doorway, it struck me that all the gradual tweaks he'd made since Oxford added up to a comprehensive, carefully planned upgrade: He was now more muscular, his hair was artfully spiked rather than slicked, and his recent LASIK offered a better view of the indigo of his eyes. He looked great, even though I missed the brainy cuteness of his specs.

Clive stuffed his hands in his back pockets. "I just wanted to get any initial strangeness out of the way. We haven't done a lot of sober socializing recently."

"Good thinking," I said. "A lot has changed."

"And in a way nothing has," he said. "Gaz and Cilla still haven't had sex or stabbed one another, you and Nick are still a secret..."

"Is that what you came in here to talk about?" I asked, bristling, his words taking me right back to that night in Pembroke.

"No, no," he said. "I just wanted to make sure everything is good." He touched me on the arm, never breaking eye contact. It brought back more pleasant memories. "It's important to me that you're happy."

"I care about you, too. Sorry to be so defensive," I said, sinking onto the bed. "It's just...well, you know. My situation is complicated. How is life at *Top News*?"

"Dreadfully dull. They made me do a story on holiday shopping," he said, sitting next to me. "I had to hang about outside stores, flagging down anyone with a decent amount of bags, asking how the economy is affecting their spending." He grimaced. "The ones that don't run away immediately will talk for ten minutes and then say, 'Oh, but you're not using any of that are you?' and *then* run away. It's maddening. I'm so tired of working for a crap free paper doing the stories nobody else wants. I've paid my dues, but they keep saying, *one more month*."

"You'll get out of there soon enough," I assured him.

"How's the art?"

"I'm currently very occupied drawing comforting landscapes for the bereaved."

He put an arm around me and squeezed. "We'll *both* get there," he said. "I'm sure it's also quite time-consuming being the secret girlfriend of Prince Nicholas."

"It's hard not being able to grab a sandwich together on my lunch hour, like normal people. Especially with him being so busy," I said. "And, I mean, look at this disgusting slum he's foisting on me."

Clive laughed.

"Cheers, Clive," Nick said, walking in from the balcony, a pair of binoculars hanging from his neck.

Clive slowly lifted his arm from around my shoulder, standing up to give Nick a handshake.

"Just catching up with Bex," Clive said. "We haven't had a proper talk in ages. But I wanted to chat to you, too. I'm seeing somebody and I wanted to be the person who told you about it." He took a breath. "Gemma Sands."

Nick cocked his head. "My Gemma?"

I didn't miss that. Neither did Clive.

"*My* Gemma," he corrected.

"She never mentioned to me that she was seeing anyone," Nick said.

This sounded a trifle like jealousy, and my mind screamed, *How often are you talking to her?*

"She may come by, actually," Clive added. "She's trying to find a flight so we can ring in our first New Year together."

"Well, I can't wait to meet her," I offered.

I was, in fact, very curious about the mysterious virginity-grabbing Gemma Sands, whose very name had the glamorous, smooth finish of an expensive glass of wine, and whose family conservancy in Namibia Nick visited at least once a year. The last time, they'd washed elephants together and helped deliver a baby zebra. A wobbly part of me decided it was in my best interest for her to be romantically occupied.

"You really think Gem is coming?" Nick asked skeptically.

"Hope so, hope so," Clive said, rubbing his hands together. "We're both so busy, with my work at the paper and hers in Africa. It'd be nice to steal a moment together." He smiled widely. "Now come downstairs, you two. Cilla and Gaz are fighting over whether one of her ancestors died while inventing the T-bar lift, and Freddie's Icelandic party planner has lips that seem to vibrate. You *must* see it."

Once Clive was gone, Nick turned to me and rolled his eyes. "He and Gemma are about as meant to be as Penelope Six-Names and my grandfather."

"Your grandfather is dead."

Nick was in the middle of taking off his sweater to put on another.

"Exactly," he said, through a layer of wool. His head popped out through the top of the crewneck, his hair standing on end like a child's, and I felt a rush of love for him. "*Exactly,*" he repeated.

I did not have a lot of love for his tone.

"A toast. To the woman who is responsible for us all, who is the mother of our beloved kingdom. God save the Queen."

Richard raised his glass to the sky in solemnity, and everyone else followed.

Agatha shot me a reproachful look from down the rectangular table. "She's not *your* Queen."

"No, but..." I faltered. It had felt weird to glom on to that salute, but it seemed like it would be even weirder if I had ignored it and implied I didn't think God should help Eleanor out at all.

"Oh, just let 'er drink," Awful Julian slurred. His foot found mine under the table. I shifted without changing my facial expression.

"What if she doesn't even believe in God? They have all kinds of atheists in America," said Lady Bollocks, in a way that suggested she was enjoying adding fuel to this fire.

"They've got atheists here, too," boomed Clive's brother Martin. "I'm in the running for captain of the national rugby side!"

"Better hope they don't give IQ tests," Clive said under his breath.

"Perhaps the girl can say, 'May a higher power of some sort preserve the Queen of this realm,'" offered Agatha, still fretting.

"For my money, both God and Gran would want us to let it go and tuck into dinner," Freddie said. "Bex lives in England. She pays VAT. She can jolly well rent the Queen for a while."

"Enough!" Richard boomed. "Eat."

Our first evening had been relatively tame. It had begun with subtly studying the cheerfully oblivious Fallopia—her lips did vibrate and even seemed to emit a mild hum, as if her last injection had gone bad—and then took a turn for the militant when our chalet was invaded by Clarence House's best generals. Marjorie Hicks had worked for either Eleanor or

Richard for Nick's entire life, and Nick and Freddie had selected her personally when Eleanor granted their wish for their own dedicated staff. Marj tended toward woolen cardigans with floral buttons, and wore her iron-gray hair in a close-cropped coif that was too long to be a pixie, but too pixie to be a bob; the boys both greeted her with great and genuine affection—as if she, too, were their grandmother, an Eleanor proxy who could do all the constant hugging and reprimanding the Queen's schedule didn't allow. Marj's equivalent on Richard's staff was a heavy-lidded fiftysomething man called Barnes, who had a coiffure so elaborate it made Donald Trump look like he suffered from alopecia. Barnes had handed Fallopia and me, as the newcomers, a lengthy nondisclosure agreement and cowed us into signing it in about seventeen different places. Then he and Marj had distributed a personalized schedule outlining which social events we were expected to attend at either Richard's chalet or those of his titled friends, the dress code for each, and when we'd have free time. Nick's packet ran at least ten pages. Mine was two.

And yet somehow Nick and I still managed to be late for Richard's dinner party. We'd had a long day on the mountain, where his attempts to teach me to disembark from the believably deadly T-bar ski lifts were hampered by the fact that we couldn't stop laughing, and I'd healed my bruises in the hot tub and then passed out on the bed. We didn't wake up until five minutes before dinner, which is why I'd arrived at Richard's chalet out of breath, with my hair shoved up into a bun because it was only *nearly* dry and thoroughly frizzy.

"The schedule said your cocktail finest," Barnes growled, unimpressed by the black long-sleeved dress Lacey had helped me buy. "And you are three minutes late."

I wilted a little under his stare. I hate being late. But I've also never mastered the art of estimating how long it takes me to get anywhere or do anything. Now all my official schedules are done in BST—Bex Standard Time—which is elaborately coded and changes every day in case I accidentally crack it. If only we'd thought to invent it sooner.

"My fault," Nick covered smoothly. "I could only find one sock."

"I hope Frederick's excuse is as compelling," Marj said tartly. "His Royal Highness is also tardy."

Nick squinted at the floor-to-ceiling glass window, into the pitch-black night.

"Is that him out in the snow, Marj?" he asked. "He's not wearing a jacket."

Marj tsked and bustled to the window. "That boy. He'll catch his death. It's below zero."

She knocked on the glass and began to call out Freddie's name, when a thunderous thwack sounded, followed a split second later by Marj's scream, and gales of laughter. A giant snowball, easily half ice, had hit the window right where her face had been.

"NICHOLAS!" she thundered. He was doubled over, gasping with mirth. "I NEVER."

"Wasn't me... don't know what you mean..."

"You were in it as much as your no-good brother and you know it," Marj panted, fanning herself. "That rapscallion, I ought to—"

"Ought to what, Marjie?" Freddie asked innocently, walking in and whistling under his breath. "Gosh, have you had a fright?"

"You're as good a liar as you are a person," Marj scoffed at him. "Conspiring to give heart failure to an innocent old woman. I ought to staple you to the table."

"That's my Marj," Freddie said, looping an arm around her neck. "It's just not the holidays until I'm victimized by her bloodlust."

Freddie was my salvation that night. With Nick on the other side of the elaborately carved dining room, Freddie kept me talking, deftly drowned out his seventeen-year-old cousin Nigel's announcement that I held my utensils in the wrong hands, and now had stuck up for me during the inane argument about how, or whether, I should pledge my allegiance to the monarch of the country that was allowing me to live and work in it.

Gaz had been right about the people-watching, at least. Clive's divorced father was arguing boisterously with Agatha about Western-style riding, and Clive's brothers' limitations had indeed proved distinguishable: Martin was boomingly stupid, confident he was always right even though he never was, while Thick Trevor came off like his brain was working very hard yet going nowhere (it made me sad the one called

Dim Tim hadn't come, just for the comparison). Bea's parents were her clones, patrician and perfect with chins like upside-down Gothic arches. Conversely, her sister Pudge was the apple that fell so far from the tree that it rolled into a ditch and landed in a pile of snortable substances. Alarmingly gaunt, with a haircut she might have given herself with safety scissors, she'd disappeared to the bathroom six times already that night, and seemed to view everything with a deep, miserable hatred. Even from three seats down I'd caught her blitz of f-bombs about the food, the company, even the butter dish, though everyone pretended not to hear.

And after three long hours of this dysfunctional family dinner writ large, the menfolk—Richard's exact word—excused themselves for brandy and cigars (and presumably talk of topics too weighty for our tiny ladybrains). On my way out the front door, I found Bea trying to lug a clearly queasy and spaghetti-legged Pudge out of the bathroom, a spot of vomit on her shirt and an indiscreet smattering of powder under her left nostril.

"Come on, Pads," she was saying, as gentle as I'd ever heard her. "Let's get you home."

"Can I help?"

She looked up at me, startled, and then a flash of embarrassment flickered across her face. It wasn't an emotion I generally associated with Lady Bollocks. But she was in a pickle, and she knew it, so she nodded and let me drape Pudge's arm around my shoulder.

"Easy, Paddington, we'll get you," I said, trying to use her full name out of politeness, although frankly I'm not sure it was much better.

Pudge's head lolled on her shoulders until she jerked it in my direction. "Your hair smells like violets."

"Thank you."

"Violets fucking stink," Pudge snapped.

We trudged outside, saying nothing but stopping three times to let Pudge decorate a variety of bushes with the contents of her stomach. Bea's resentment about depending on me for help fairly radiated off her. Once we got inside our chalet, Bea and I hustled Pudge to the room they were sharing, I brought her water and a puke receptacle, and we spent a wordless period putting them alternately to her lips until she passed out on her bed.

"Thank you," Bea said grudgingly.

"Sure," I said. "This can't be easy, and—"

"I don't actually want to discuss it. I am simply being polite," Bea said sharply.

Then her phone beeped, and she pulled it out to check a text message. "Ceres," she said. "She's on her way over."

I said nothing.

"Yes, Nick's ex is in town." Lady Bollocks's radar for other people's insecurities is as precisely groomed as she is. "And his other ex could be dropping in at any minute. Are you jealous?"

"No," I said, mostly honestly, although I was starting to feel intimidated. And outnumbered.

"I doubt they want the job," she said. "Or else they'd already have it."

"Nick isn't a job."

"You'll soon see," Bea said, tapping the air with a stiff, well-manicured pointer. "Those hungry mobs at Oxford were just sycophants and desperate, disgraced blue bloods. The real catches don't want any part of this."

"So you're saying I'm here by default."

"Those are your words, not mine," Bea said.

"Well, I don't believe them."

"Suit yourself," Bea said. "But someone should inform you that being Nick's partner isn't actually a partnership at all. It's accepting a position. You're on display, and on trial."

"Why are you telling me this?" I asked. "To help, or to *pretend* to help until I run away screaming on my own? Because we all know you don't want me and Nick to end up together."

"That's neither here nor there," she said. "You're who we're stuck with at the moment, and Nick is my friend, and I don't want him going any further with someone naïve or unsuitable, or weak. He doesn't need it, and honestly, if you are the spineless sort, neither do you. So if you do not think you can handle it, step aside before it ends badly for both of you."

No one has ever accused Lady Beatrix Larchmont-Kent-Smythe of mincing her words.

"You know, for someone who says she's Nick's friend, you are really bad at being friendly, Bea."

"Someday you might disagree," Bea said. "Cheerio, Rebecca. Enjoy your prince."

And with that, she sailed out of the room, leaving me unsettled as Pudge snored softly.

"How's the snow looking, sir?"

The BBC News photographer got off the first question over the rustling and clacking of the rest of the press corps. Richard and his staff at Clarence House arranged this photo op for the royals in attendance every year, in the exact same spot—atop one of the gentler slopes, the Alps cresting behind them—in exchange for total privacy the rest of the week. It was a deal not unlike the one that had kept Nick protected at Oxford, and which everyone observed, again, because both sides essentially needed each other more than anyone cared to admit.

"The snow is as perfect as my lovely wife," Richard said, his attempt at a romantic tone contrasting with his villainous black ski suit and polarized wraparound shades. "She wishes she could have been here, but she is no longer so partial to sport."

He laughed lightly, at odds with the actual sentiment he'd expressed. It made me think of the most famous of the Klosters photos over the years: Svelte in a red ski suit even though she'd had Freddie only six months earlier, Emma had two-year-old chubby, cheeky Nick standing on his stubby skis between her own, giggling as she kissed him. Even Richard had been smiling. It was one of the last family photos on record.

"Freddie! There have been reports that you've brought former glamour model Fallopia Jones as your personal guest," a reporter shouted. "Can you confirm?"

"I believe she has been sighted on the slopes," Freddie replied with a cheeky grin.

"What a coincidence," Richard said, jaw clenched.

"Perhaps, but we are extremely good friends. *Allegedly.*" Freddie winked broadly, which got a laugh.

I glanced at Fallopia, obliviously drawing faces on the fogged-up glass of the medical cabin where we'd been stashed to watch and wait for the press conference to end. She had probably, whether she knew it or not, just served her last purpose. Freddie's frowned-upon girlfriends arrived on a schedule as regular as the crosstown bus and were just as interchangeable, and Fallopia had just left the station.

"Nick!" called the royals reporter from the *Daily Express*. "We're also hearing rumors that *you've* got a new girlfriend. Care to comment?"

"Uh-oh," Cilla muttered, next to me.

"Come on, Annalisa. You know I've no comment on my personal life," Nick said, his expression hardening subtly from Perfectly Pleasant into Aggressively Pleasant.

Freddie must have noticed this, too, because then he chimed in: "One minute it's girlfriends, the next you'll be wanting our inseams, eh?" he chirped. "Although personally, I'm always delighted when you lot do us the favor of believing that my brother has any game at all. I mean, *look at him*. You'd have to be—"

"And that will do it," Barnes interjected. "Thank you, everyone. Enjoy the slopes."

Nick, Freddie, and Richard shooshed swiftly away, giving off the convincing air of resuming a jovial family adventure, even though Nick had actually spent the morning popping Nurofen between sips of the darkest coffee he could make. (Our chalet—still minus Gemma, who never left Africa, to Clive's dismay—had only even woken up forty-five minutes ago after a long night of compensating for the lack of nightclubs by inventing drinking games, like the instant classic, Take Three Sips If Anyone Does Anything. That any of us has a working liver left is a miracle of body chemistry.) But as Gaz, Cilla, Clive, and I huddled around our ski maps to figure out where to meet later—and in my case, what runs I could take without breaking my face—my mind wandered to what mood Nick would be in when he reappeared. Because the *Daily Express* was onto something, somehow. I knew our sneaking around was on borrowed time, but I hated that it might've run out when I was stuck in an enclosed space with his less-than-welcoming relatives.

"He's with *which* one?" I heard Agatha hiss as she and Awful Julian tumbled inside after kicking off their skis.

"The one in that terrible sweater," Nigel rang out.

I suddenly felt several eyes in the cabin turn to me.

"The *American*?" Agatha breathed, in the same tone of voice as you'd expect from someone saying, *The Satanist*? "I thought she was just some fancy of Clive's, or I wouldn't have been so kind to her at dinner."

I nearly spat out my coffee. Agatha seemed to approach the world as if people she didn't care to acknowledge therefore automatically did not have the privilege of hearing her.

"Her sweater looks like vomit, Mummy," Nigel prodded. "It hurts my eyes."

"He's a wonderful argument for birth control," Gaz muttered.

I looked down at my sweater. "Is it seriously that bad?" I asked. It was a thank-you gift from Joss for being her fit model for her latest fashion school project, and I was trying to be supportive.

"It is a bit...scribbly," Cilla allowed, gesturing to the neon scrawls knitted into it.

"Nicky! Nicky! You're not really seeing the American in the terrible sweater?" Agatha wailed.

I looked up to see Nick, Freddie, and Richard shaking snow off their boots inside the cabin. Nick and I made eye contact, but for once, his face was inscrutable to me. I plastered an expression on my face that I hoped looked confident rather than arrogant or smug. Jumping into this wouldn't help anything, but I also wasn't going to let them shame me into staring at the floorboards so they could add poor posture to my list of obvious faults.

"I can assure you my son is not seeing anyone seriously," Richard said, with a pointed look at Nick. "And certainly not the American in the terrible sweater."

"Told you it was horrible," Nigel singsonged.

"Bit saucy, American girls, eh?" Awful Julian said, wiggling his eyebrows at Nick.

"Nick can see anyone he wants to," Freddie insisted. "It's not like Bex is going to topple the dynasty."

"You will not engage me on this here," Richard said.

"Just leave it, Freddie," Nick hissed.

"Why should I let him be such a prick about it?" Freddie asked. "Why do you always—"

"*Just leave it,*" Nick said frostily.

I remember once waiting for the Tube and thinking, as its oncoming headlights gleamed brighter in the tunnel, *I could just jump*. Not because I wanted to die, but because sometimes your mind dangles the worst-case behavior in front of you specifically so that you can be aware that you're choosing to resist it. They call them intrusive impulses, and mine stacked up high: throw my arms around a clearly reeling Nick; scream at Nick that Freddie was right; smack Richard upside the head and ask him why he was such a raging douchelord; take Agatha and Nigel and crack their skulls together like the Neanderthal they apparently thought I was. Instead, I casually studied my ski map as if none of this was unfolding in front of me. I just wish Clive had told me sooner that I'd been fake-reading it upside-down.

Suddenly, Gaz patted his stomach. "I'm famished," he said loudly. "Anyone care to dive into some fondue? My treat."

"Not likely. You'd faster see a yeti than Gaz with cash," Cilla said.

As they bickered, Clive gently turned us all toward the door as if it were the most natural time in the world to take our leave. As the three of them swept me out of there, I heard Agatha's voice.

"Oh, Nicky, just don't go off and get engaged until I've at least introduced you to Ursula Northrop-Cumber's daughter Ruth," she pleaded. "She's *so* aristocratic. She speaks four languages!"

"I'm *not* getting engaged, Agatha," Nick said firmly, and that was the last thing I heard before the door slammed behind us.

There was something undeniably awkward about hearing him say that so staunchly, particularly after Bea's lecture the previous night. Cilla seemed to feel like she had to distract me from it, dispatching Gaz and Clive in the direction of the ski lift and regaling me over lunch with the latest details of her on-off relationship with Tony. He had not been invited to Klosters, most likely to prevent headlines like PRINCES HIT POWDER WITH SOHO COKE HO.

"He swears it's his business partner who's doing it," Cilla said, poking at her bratwurst. "I know you think it's mental of me to still be with him. He's just a sight better than any of the blokes 'round my sister's village. And nannying her children takes it out of me. All I want is a bit of fun when I'm in London."

"But there might be plenty of fun guys who don't also potentially sell drugs," I said.

"Is my bar that low?" she groaned. "Am I turning into Joss?"

"Just as long as you don't start giving me sweaters," I told her, a rueful glance down at my own. It was not the last time that my wardrobe would publicly be found wanting.

Nick caught up with Cilla and me as we were strapping on our skis for another run. He had changed into an orange ski suit with green piping, and with that and a knit cap and goggles, he looked totally anonymous.

"Irish colors?" I asked. "Interesting pick."

"They'll never expect it," Nick said.

The three of us carried our skis to the enclosed gondola and rode it all the way up to the top, passing quaint mountainside cafes and looking down at skiers of every ability carving through the fluffy powder, and occasionally wiping out. In fact, we were about to disembark when a round-looking figure careened down one of the steeper runs, totally out of control, screaming as he went past.

"There goes Gaz," Cilla observed calmly.

He rolled like a ball and then skidded to a stop, spread-eagle, in the snow.

"He can barely ski at all," Cilla added. "He just doesn't like Clive to feel superior." She sighed. "I'd best go make sure he hasn't broken his leg again."

"I'll take you down the hill, Bex," Nick said as she skied away. "It'll be nice to slow down and actually see the views."

"Speak for yourself," I said. "I will be watching my feet."

We pushed over to a patch of snow-covered trees and plopped down in the powder to get our gear in place. Nick sat with his back to most of the other skiers and pulled up the hood on his parka while rubbing sunscreen onto his face.

"My family has been in rare form," he said. "I'm sorry about that whole scene down there today. That reporter's question had me in such a mood, I didn't even defend you properly until you were already gone."

"Don't sweat it. I understand."

"I just can't believe we've got a leak," he said. "I promised I'd keep you out of the papers."

"It's not your fault," I insisted. "You can't control the entire world."

He blew out his lips. "Clearly, I can't even control my own corner of it." He stared out at the mountain. "I just wanted it to be on our terms, always. What's the bloody point of being who I am if I can't even make it safe for you to be with me?"

"Nick. A question from a reporter is not going to scare me off," I said.

He gave me a grateful smile, then fell silent, fiddling with the straps on his poles.

"Gaz seems happy in his legal training. Clive's a reporter, just like he always wanted. Joss is busy making clothes. Even Cilla seems to enjoy taking care of her sister's children," he finally said. "I'm going to sound ungrateful, but I'm so jealous that they get to *pick*. They can be *anything*. Even Freddie gets some choice, but I have none. I'm stuck hanging about looking cheerful until everyone around me dies and I'm given a job I am required by genetics to do."

His voice cracked. I'd never heard him sound so dark about his life.

"I am a placeholder," he said. "And I am a chess piece. And obviously, this comes with a lot of advantages. I know I am extraordinarily lucky. But do you know what it's like to never, ever be asked what you want to be when you grow up? Or being told not to bother about it because it doesn't matter?"

"No," I said softly, wanting to hug him and hating that I couldn't.

"I do sometimes look forward to military service," he admitted. "But is that because it's the best of the options I have, or because I actually want to do it? It's so bloody hard to tell. I might never know."

A certain sense of déjà vu crawled over me. "You mean, is it good on its own, or is it just good by default," I translated.

I saw how stuck he felt, and it tore at me. This was also the most monumental confidence he'd ever shared, and I wanted to choose my next words carefully.

"I think," I said slowly, "that you can't change what you were born into, or what your life has been up to now, but you *can* control what it's like going forward. Listen, you are who you are. Richard is your father, and one day, you are going to inherit the throne. That's just the reality. But you are not a job, Nick. You're not a title. You're *you*. And there has to be a way for you to make this into a life you want to live. You're still in charge of yourself. That has to be the key, don't you think? That's the touchstone."

He poked me in the leg with his pole. "You're the only touchstone I need," he said, his voice blazing with feeling.

Looking back at this conversation, I want to hug both of us. We really did think we could handle anything as long as we had each other.

"You know that if I weren't... the person I am... it would be totally different, right?" he whispered, urgently. "I would be going up to strangers in the street and telling them about you. The last thing I want to do is pretend we're just friends."

"I know," I said, and I blew him the tiniest, most imperceptible peck, then looped my ski poles over my wrists, planted them in the snow, and heaved myself to my feet gracelessly.

"And now you've seen our seedy underbelly," Nick said. "The press, the leaks, the squabbling, Julian drunk before noon. And Nigel. I wouldn't blame you if you walked away."

"You'll have to do a lot worse than Nigel to spook me," I told him. "Now, quit stalling. Unless you're afraid to race me. Ready?"

He rose and studied me intently.

"I'm ready," he said, leaning over and kissing me, briefly, tenderly, perfectly, not for more than five seconds.

We never even saw the flash.

# CHAPTER FOUR

## 'POSH AND BEX?'

### Nicky Goes Snoggers in Klosters, says XANDRA DEANE

The Prince has a pauper: Single since breaking the heart of his most recent socialite, Prince Nicholas was caught on vacation kissing an Oxford classmate.

And she's an American.

Nicholas, 24, was giving lip service to the plain brunette during the annual Royal Family trip to Klosters, the Swiss resort favoured by the Lyons clan for its privacy. Sources identify her as Rebecca "Bex" Porter, 23, an exchange student who met Nicholas at Oxford three years ago, and seduced him before the Prince broke it off with cuckolded party planner India Bolingbroke.

"She's quite persistent," one former classmate says of Porter. "Not bad looking. Bit heavy on the eyebrows, maybe. But she set her cap for him early on, and she got him."

The Palace hasn't issued a comment, but sources claim the Princess of Wales is particularly distraught...

"Well," Bea said, drumming her fingers on a folded copy of the *Daily Mail* that sat on my dining table. "The good news is, they think you're unemployed."

"If that's good news, then I'm in trouble," I said, accepting a mug of cocoa from Cilla.

"Don't drink that. It's going to ruin your skin." Bea snatched it and handed it to a brooding Pudge, whose face presumably was sacrificial. "And it *is* good news, because at least nobody is making fun of your ridiculous job yet, although it's only a matter of time."

The paparazzi snaps had hit the Internet the night they were taken. Nick was so upset that he put us on a charter straight back to England—where it turned out photographers were already lying in wait at Kensington. So he had PPO Furrow take us to my flat instead, refusing to spend New Year's Eve apart; by the time we woke up the next morning, though, the press had found and surrounded my hovel in Shepherd's Bush, forcing us to hole up there for several more days. It was us against the world, except for the occasional moments where Nick's mood would char and I'd lose him to the wilds of whatever was whipping through his brain.

Once Nick had safely escaped, Cilla called an emergency summit at my flat with Joss and Bea (with a typically bleak Pudge in tow; so far she'd kept her New Year's resolution of sobriety, but there was no cold turkey plan for rage). Lady Bollocks may not have been my biggest fan, but she is never intimidated by a crisis and she loves telling people what to do.

"Right. You'll need basic dresses, nothing too short, and no blouses you can't wear with a bra," Bea said, starting to check off her list items on her finger.

"Oh, I've got some frocks," Joss piped up. "Made a few at school the other day that got the attention of an investor, actually."

"Don't be batty. She can't go all experimental and psychotic now," Bea said, then turned back to me. "Get some skinny jeans, not those wretched things you had on the other day. I don't know where you even got those. Cilla, write this down."

I expected a protest, but Cilla was already looking for a pen.

"Map out three alternate routes to work and vary them every day,"

Bea continued. "Also find a shortcut branching off from each one, as an escape valve, if you need it. Carry the number of a car service. Don't let Nick pay for it. Link it to your credit card."

"He won't like that," I said.

"I don't care," Bea said.

"He can't be seen paying your way," Cilla said, scribbling furiously on a notepad.

"They'll start going through your rubbish, Bex, so take it out in the wee hours and change up the bins you use," Bea went on. "And for God's sake, shred anything interesting and divide the pieces into separate bags: credit card bills, prescriptions, receipts. If Nick is in the habit of writing you love letters, burn them. Or bury them, I suppose."

"Fucking *eat* them," Pudge said.

"Am I not allowed to *keep* them?" I wondered, archly.

"Certainly, if you want a ticking time bomb," Bea retorted. "Have you ever read a tabloid? They'll use anything they can get their hands on, however they can get their hands on it. Do not get comfortable with any reporters and do not wave at the paparazzi, even if they seem sympathetic. If you engage, they draw you in, and then suddenly you're on the front page looking like you want to whack one of them with your umbrella."

"Like Britney Spears," I said.

"No," Cilla said. "Like Bea."

"Fuck it," Pudge said, sitting up from her slouch on my sofa. "Fuck it all. They want your soul. Don't let them take it. They'll eat you alive."

She then slumped back, as if someone had hit the "off" switch. Bea rubbed her temples and stared out the window. Outside, the clouds had whipped themselves into fat, dark puffs, promising something cold and wet that might at least give the paparazzi pause about continuing to camp out on my doorstep.

"Pudge's second trip to rehab was right after my eighteenth birthday party," Bea finally said. "She rode a horse into the living room. Paparazzi were on our family for days because Prince Richard had been at the party, and..." She looked again at her sister. "Well, don't talk back. We've all done it and we've all regretted it."

I'd seen paparazzi coverage of other celebrity couples; I wasn't naïve about the news cycle. But when the lenses turn on *you*, at first it's hard to reconcile the thoroughly regular person you are with the person everyone else suddenly finds extraordinary. I was still a half beat behind, so while Bea's advice was intense, I was also grateful for such a proactive to-do list. My mother, on the other hand, had been so excited by the photo's appearance in *People* (under the headline A STAR-SPANGLED PRINCESS?) that she'd turned a recent dinner party into an English tea, to the great surprise of the guests who'd come over expecting a barbeque.

"Don't come home for a while," Dad teased on the phone. "She's got it bad. If you turned up now, she'd make you walk around with a book on your head."

Mom's voice came down the line: "Bex, that's a good point, actually," she said. "You've got to stand up straight if you're going to—"

"Lay off, Mom," Lacey hissed, and I could picture her wresting the phone from both of them. I felt a rush of affection until she added, "Let her deal with her eyebrows first. They do need a little work, Bex. You're going to be a public figure now." I heard a puff of contentment come down the line. "It's all moving forward. *Finally.*"

But if Lacey could have seen Nick's face every time he looked at the paper, she wouldn't have been celebrating, and ultimately, neither was I. We'd lost control, and we were now reacting instead of acting. In retrospect, the Palace should've been the one giving me the practical and psychological tools to deal with the aftermath of being discovered. Instead, there was a lot of criticism, but not a whole lot of help. Richard, in fact, gave us the silent treatment for two full weeks. When we were eventually summoned to his private meeting room at Clarence House, the mighty Prince of Wales spent ten minutes glowering before slamming the article on the table and spitting that he wasn't sure if he was madder at the photographer or at Nick.

"I can't believe that's even a question," Nick had said. He looked exhausted. His insomnia was at full strength; he probably got three hours of sleep a night.

"You were stupid," Richard accused. "You got careless."

"It's Klosters; it's supposed to be safe!" Nick said. "And it's not like I was having an orgy. I was kissing my girlfriend."

"We've all wanted to kiss our girlfriends," Richard snapped. "You're the only idiot who got himself photographed."

Nick flinched at *our girlfriends*, and I bumped on it, too, but I kept myself from acknowledging it. It was seriously not the right time.

"So now what happens?" I ventured.

Richard's eyes bored into me. "We can't lie," he said. "But we don't have to tell the truth, either. A *no comment* will do."

"We cannot go public until your relationship is stable," Barnes informed us.

"I didn't realize it was unstable," I said before I caught myself. Under the table, Nick took my hand.

"There can be no ups and downs," Richard hissed. "Once you are out, you are happy. Period."

It sounded like a threat. And two hours later, Marj added an ultimatum to the pile.

"Her Majesty would prefer if you and Nicholas refrained from any more overnights in royal residences, even in separate bedrooms," she relayed to me by phone, in the imperious tone she uses when she's working from Eleanor's script. "Premarital coitus cannot be tacitly sanctioned by the Crown."

"I...right," I said, unable to deny that one even for sport. "So... does that mean Nick is allowed to sleep here now? Or...are you asking us to...?"

"We're not *that* old, Rebecca," Marj said in her regular voice. "No one wants to stop you from having a shag altogether." She cleared her throat. "But, er, Her Majesty wishes to convey that if His Royal Highness insists on spending the night, your current situation is undesirable."

I felt backed into a corner. The Palace could not be perceived as setting up Nick's good-time girl in a fancy flat, and nor did I want that to happen, but as a lowly greeting-card artist I couldn't afford to satisfy the decree on my own. However, this gave my dad the leverage he'd been waiting for, because he'd been itching to move me somewhere nicer for ages, and I'd refused to accept his financial help. So on what remained of Lacey's winter break, he sent her over with a budget and a mandate, and together we found a gorgeous place in Chelsea: the top floor of a smart redbrick building in a mews just off Old Church Street, with a cloistered back entrance and a petite front garden that set it slightly back from the road. We signed the lease and I spent the year taking gentle teasing from my father that he was spending my entire dowry but was relieved he didn't have to give up any livestock. Lacey was so taken with my reality inching closer to her England fantasy that she insisted I needed her, and by April, she'd convinced my parents and, somehow, NYU, that she should take a short leave of absence because my unusual circumstance required her moral and emotional support. It would be our first time living together since before I went to Oxford, and I was happy about it, even if it was only for an extended summer. Everything was changing so quickly; maybe having Lacey back in my life would help things feel the same.

It was an impossible wish. That one unguarded second in Klosters marked a sea change in Nick. He stopped drinking or dancing, and started getting frustrated if he felt any of us was imbibing too much, reveling too loudly, lowering our guards. When Lacey returned for the summer and rekindled her dalliance with Freddie, Nick fretted about how careless they might be, what media stoning Lacey or I would receive—or, almost worse, what admonishments would come from Eleanor or Richard. The clouds over his head rivaled anything the British climate could conjure.

"Pipe down and untwist, Knickers," Freddie would say, handing him a drink that would go untouched. "You're not the king *yet*."

"But this is how it starts," Nick insisted. "You think no one is watching, so you stop being vigilant. And then they pounce."

It bothered me that Nick was so daunted. Before, it had been easy to live like we'd begun everything together, like nothing of consequence happened to either of us before that rainy day at Pembroke. But Nick's almost pathological fear of the headlines, larger than the headlines themselves, reminded me that there had been twenty or so mile markers before me, and I knew surprisingly little about the journey between them.

The paparazzi wasted no time finding my new flat, and furthermore became my regular greeting and salutation anytime I entered or exited Greetings & Salutations. The pictures landed on blogs and message boards that dissected my nose (natural?), my boobs (too small?), my taste (emphatically too boring), and even though Lacey meticulously helped track what I'd worn each week so that I didn't look like I was living in my own laundry pile, the occasional comment would pop up from within G&S walls with precise details about how often I repeated my shirts. By June, the colleagues who were once disinterested in anything but their own professional frustrations started guiltily closing papers whenever I passed, and I couldn't grab a Diet Coke from the fridge without hearing whispers about my clothes, or which columnist had spied Ceres at Nick's favorite club, India at Clarence House, or Gemma Sands at Heathrow. Even the woman who read *The Economist* every day had swapped it for *Hello!*

One especially sweltering summer afternoon, the heat outside causing the industrial carpet in our office to reek even more strongly of chemicals, I was plugging away on a new line of sympathy cards with the meaningless directive "The Modern Condolence." Two of my coworkers loudly discussed how my gray suede kicks had sold out online since being featured in *heat*, and even the usual din from Piccadilly Circus—a constant soundtrack of roaring buses and honking horns—wasn't drowning them out. I couldn't focus. I had ten cards to illustrate and no inkling whatsoever about which blossoms conveyed a hipper sense of sadness than usual. Frustrated, I pushed my chair backward to stretch my legs, and crashed into something human.

"Dangerous as ever, Killer," a familiar voice said.

"Freddie!"

I leapt up and hugged him, as everyone within gaping or gasping distance did one or both of those things. Freddie seemed unperturbed by their curiosity, perching rakishly on my desk, a fluorescent light flickering its way to death just over his lavishly cute head. Two extremely unlikely worlds were colliding. The office grapevine would never recover.

"What are you doing here?" I asked.

"Just passing through," he said blithely. "Piccadilly Circus is wonderful for quiet reflection." He caught the eye of Pandora Millstone, the old battle-ax who sat in the cube next to mine and wore an endless rotation of olive cardigans. "How are you supposed to have juicy, private conversations if everyone is out in the open, listening to each other?"

Pandora dropped the highlighter she was holding.

"Just teasing," he said, winking at her. "I am here to discuss, er, a commission. A card for, ah, my father's beloved manservant Barnes. He's such a . . . special creature."

"Let's go in the conference room."

"Right! Cheerio," Freddie said to the people in our vicinity. "You look lovely in that cardie . . . Pandora," he said, reading her nameplate. "Makes me crave a martini."

I grabbed a notepad and all but shoved him into the conference room. It had windows, but at least we could speak privately.

"Nick is going to kill you," I said closing the door with a firm click. "People will totally gossip about this."

"You'd be surprised. A spot of charm goes a long way," Freddie said smugly.

"Humble as always," I said. "What's up? Don't tell me you just dropped by to give Pandora a thrill."

"It's a fringe benefit. I rather enjoy flummoxing people," he said. "Mostly I just wanted to say hi. I had bits to do at Clarence House that were hopelessly dull, so I thought, why not pop by for some greeting-card intrigue?"

"I didn't realize Frederick Wales could just 'pop by' anywhere," I said.

Freddie shrugged as he took a seat at the head of the table, spinning in the chair like a child. "Don't tell, but this area is so full of tourists that I often wander around by myself and nobody notices," he said. "They never think to look. It's quite relaxing."

"I know." I sat opposite him. "That week before the press found my office was fantastic."

"I'm surprised they even bothered looking," he said. "It's much better for them to report that you're a lazy money-grubbing shrew."

I ripped a page off my notebook, crumpled it up, and threw it at him.

"You always make me miss my PPOs, Killer," he said, swatting it deftly. Then he cocked his head. "How are you handling all of this?"

"I'm getting by," I said. "The paparazzi itself isn't even that bad, honestly. It's how much Nick hates it that makes it tough."

Freddie drummed his fingers on the table. "That's another reason I stopped by. I wanted to chat about him when I knew he wouldn't be around."

"I knew it."

"Knickers is wound tighter than I've ever seen him," Freddie said, leaning forward earnestly. "He's got veins in his face that don't exist in most humans, and they're all bulging out at once. He's got to get out of his own head. And he won't listen to me about it at all."

"He doesn't listen to me much, either," I said. "He's not dismissive, but there are subjects where he doesn't let me in, and I haven't pushed."

"Perhaps you should," Freddie said. "He internalizes things more than anyone I know. I tease him about being so serious and duty-bound, but sometimes I worry that he forgets even poncey future kings are allowed to have feelings."

"I said the same thing, once," I said. Then I smiled affectionately at him as he rubbed his hair, so like his brother. "I've never seen you worried like this."

"Don't look at me all misty," he said. "This isn't entirely selfless. I'm also bored of him staying in all the time, so I want you to fix him, and then we can all go to Hell."

I laughed. Hell was Tony's latest enterprise, full of drinks laced with spicy peppers, music that only had the words *hot*, *warm*, or *burn* in the titles, open-flame light sources that I knew did not have the proper permits, and no air-conditioning. It was quite literally London's hottest club.

"I can try to talk to him, but if I have to be patient then you probably do, too," I told Freddie.

"It's just that we were having such a good time," Freddie said, leaning back and resting his feet on the table. "Knickers and I have always been close, but we never actually hung out together the way we have since you came along. It was nice. Like being real best mates." He swallowed. "I miss my best mate."

I reached over and squeezed his forearm. "For you, Your Highness, I'll push him as hard as I can."

Freddie gave me such a stunning smile that even my heterosexual male boss, whose turn it was in the rotation of people pretending they needed to walk by the room, gave an audible gasp as he passed. My phone rattled in my pocket, saving me from giving away that I'd heard him.

I pulled it out. "Lacey's here," I said, quickly texting her to find me in the meeting room. Everyone at G&S was knocking off soon so that maintenance could pretend to fix the climate control; Lacey and I had plans to get manicures (her idea). "Are you guys on this week, or off?"

Freddie pulled a face. "We're mostly just friends, Bex."

I cocked a skeptical brow.

"Not everything is about getting my kit off," he insisted. "Only about sixty percent. Perhaps seventy."

I chucked another paper ball at him.

"Fine. She's been a very *nice* friend and I'm glad she's back," he said, swatting away my missile. "I like Lacey. I also like Tara and Naomi and Farthing—"

"I thought Farthing moved to Ireland."

"That was Tuppence. Farthing is someone different entirely," he said impatiently. "Do try and keep up."

"Usain Bolt couldn't keep up."

"We're consenting adults," he said. "You can't dangle that twin of yours in front of me and not expect me to jump."

The conference room door burst open and Lacey sailed inside.

"Twice as many paparazzi today," she said by way of greeting. "And three of them totally whistled at my *oh my God*, Bex. I hate that shirt. Is it *polyester*?"

"My loving sister, ladies and gentlemen," I said.

"No gentlemen in here," Freddie said, getting up to give Lacey a peck on the cheek.

"What are you doing here?" she asked delightedly, putting a hand on his arm and then rubbing it slightly. In her defense, once you touch Freddie's bicep, it's hard not to linger. "Are we still on for tonight?"

"Of course," Freddie said. "I never offer a lady something I don't deliver."

Lacey giggled, then came over to me and stared very intently at a spot on my neck.

"It *does* look like a hickey," she announced. "About an hour ago someone tweeted that they saw you in the elevator with one."

"I had wondered," Freddie said. "Doesn't seem like Knickers' style, though. I've always been afraid he was one of those rose-petals-on-the-bed sort of blokes."

I clapped a hand over it. "It's a curling iron burn!" I protested.

"I believe you. I know what you're like with that thing," Lacey said. "But no one else will think you were actually using a curling iron when they get a look at your hair today."

"Ugh. They're going to want a picture of my neck," I said. "Any chance you can distract them, Fred?"

He shook his head, guiltily. "I might have blown off Prince Dick and pretended it was for a Navy thing, so...?"

I let out a sigh. "I'll take the bullet," I said, pulling my hair out of my ponytail to cover my burn.

"No. It's all stringy. Put it back up," Lacey ordered me. "We can stop in the bathroom and use real concealer on the fake hickey." She sighed. "Too bad we can't conceal your shirt. I thought I told you to run all new purchases past me."

Freddie clapped his hands together. "Right, you two do your thing, and let's see who gets to the flat faster," he said. "Remember, when all else fails, just chuck it and run."

He saluted and was off, exiting the conference room with a very loud, "The Crown thanks you for your service, Miss Porter. Barnes will be giddy with girlish glee."

Lacey shook her head. "What a goofball," she said affectionately.

"A goofball and a man-whore," I said. "Which I say with love. For both of you."

Lacey looped her arm around my shoulder. "Don't worry, I know what he's like," she said.

This made me feel better, until she followed it with, "I'm playing it cool, and it's working. If you haven't noticed, I'm the girl he keeps wanting to spend time with." She sighed happily. "I have this weird feeling we're *both* going to get our Prince Charmings."

Lacey had been right: As soon as we exited the building, a sprawling group of at least twelve photographers, rather than my usual six, sprang to life with a new nosy aggression.

"Where's the love bite, Bexy? We know you've got one!"

"Come on, girls, over 'ere, look 'ere."

"Got a hickey from Nicky, eh?"

"Give us a smile—yes, Lacey, that's right, I saw that, you love it."

I nudged Lacey. "Head down," I hissed.

"That's not my best angle," was her reply.

The photographers gave chase in an agitated cluster. Lacey and I picked up the pace to try to get away, but half the pack broke off and darted ahead to get in front of us, their frenetic flashes bursting in our faces. With every step, they encircled us tighter and tighter, like hands crumpling a piece of paper. They bumped and buffeted us, swiping at our bags, almost plowed us into traffic, and at least twice I felt hands roughly grab *me*. Even Lacey—who'd never felt like she was born for the spotlight so much as spotlights were born for her—looked unnerved.

And that's what lit my fuse. I stopped short, which caused pandemonium among our stalkers. I turned sharply, and when the ensuing shuffle of bodies created a hole on the opposite side, I darted through it, yanking Lacey along for the ride.

"Until next time, boys," she shouted at the confused pack.

But rather than concede the point, the pack started running after us full bore. We picked up the pace, sprinting around the corner and up Regent Street, dodging in and out of the paths of oncoming pedestrians. I could hear the paparazzi panting behind us, and the click of their cameras, but the further ahead of them we got, the less I cared. It felt so good to act on the sum of all my impulses to run, just *run*, to do the Bexiest goddamn thing I could imagine, that I actually heard myself let out a delighted cackle. I didn't want to be careful. I just wanted to be me.

We wove through side streets to throw them off the scent, burst through various clothing stores that Lacey knew like the back of her hand, and even dodged into Hamleys, the massive seven-floor toy store. We giggled manically, hiding behind pyramids of stuffed toys, as the paparazzi flew past. But when we triumphantly burst onto Regent Street again, we saw they'd tricked us: four of them lay in wait, on all sides, and there was nowhere left to run.

"Bus, Bex!" Lacey breathed as a double-decker lumbered toward where we stood.

Without even thinking about it, I dove at the opening in the back and grabbed the chrome pole for stability, the momentum swinging me into the bus and temporarily off my feet. Lacey followed suit, and we saw the photographers, red-faced and frustrated, hunching over, panting, with their hands on their knees. Lacey waved cheekily, and then—after a lecture from the incredibly disgruntled driver, who didn't care for shenanigans—we paid the fare and hunched down in our seats, feeling like we'd won. It was only once we changed buses toward home that I began to smooth myself out again, and realized that something felt off. Paper, once crumpled, never does go back to being whole again.

When we finally made it through my front door, any remaining exhilaration wore off when we were greeted by a frowning Nick and an incredibly sheepish Freddie.

"And how was your day, Bex?" Nick said, a note of challenge in his voice. "Anything exciting to share?"

Nick had never spoken to me before with anything approaching condescension, and here he was talking to me like I was a child and he was tapping my knee to see if my kick reflex worked. And it did.

"By your tone, I'm guessing you already know how it went, *Richard*."

Both men sucked in a breath. Freddie let his out first.

"I told Knickers this was my fault," he said, handing me his smartphone. "I'm the one who said to chuck it and run."

His phone was cued up to a *Daily Mail* story about me and Lacey leading the paparazzi on a chase through London, painting us as two brats endangering tourists on our selfish lark—as if the whole thing were just a Benny Hill sketch. They even had a photo submitted by a bystander, in which we're hanging onto the bus poles and giggling, a sweat stain thoughtfully starting to form under my left pit. The article wondered if I had hyperactive glands.

"Freddie, none of this is your fault," I said, looking up. "I knew you were joking. I wouldn't have run if I hadn't wanted to."

"My legs look fantastic," Lacey murmured as she peered over my shoulder. "I should run in heels more often."

"She's kidding, Nick," I said, at the sight of what that did to his mood. "I'm sorry. Things got intense and I had to get us out of there."

"Please don't be angry at her," Freddie said earnestly.

"I'm not. I'm angry at you," Nick said, turning on him. "You were there, for some reason. You should've called for PPO help, or gotten her a car, or something, *anything*, other than just being Freddie. I don't know why neither of you called *me*."

Freddie and I looked at each other. *This* was why.

"I did this to myself, Nick," I said. "Freddie wanted to figure out how to make things better for you, and I'm the one who made it worse. Running was entirely my decision."

"And was it your decision that had Freddie and Lacey getting caught doing...whatever the hell that is...at Soho House the other night?" Nick asked. "Scroll down."

Lacey obeyed and let out a whistle. "THE OTHER PRINCE AND THE OTHER PORTER," she read aloud. "It's a picture of him whispering in my ear."

Freddie threw his hands out in exasperation. "How the bloody hell else are you supposed to hear anyone in a loud bar?"

"I had a lot of guys whispering at me that night," Lacey added, trying to be helpful.

"You know this has to stop," Nick said, barely listening. "This whole Princes and Porters bit is only making the media hungrier, and Father thinks it makes us look sleazy."

"Bollocks to Prince Dick," Freddie said rudely. "Bollocks to all of them."

"You know I don't have that luxury," Nick said, ice cold. "And now it looks like my alleged girlfriend is running around London angling for attention. I've been saying all summer not to give the press anything to feed on, and you have no excuse, Freddie. You of all people."

Freddie stood up from his perch on the arm of my sofa.

"You're *so* right, Your Highness," he said. "I'm just sorry we can't all live up to your lofty standards of having an *alleged* girlfriend who doesn't know the half of it."

He retrieved his phone from Lacey's palm and dropped it into his pocket, then brandished his engraved cigarette case. "Text me later if you come to the club," he told her. "We can blink in code at each other from across the room."

To Nick, he added, "Hope I see you in Hell," before jamming a defiant cigarette between his lips and slamming the door, leaving the three of us in suffocating tension.

"Um, I should probably, uh, there's a..." Lacey began. "You know what, forget it, I'm just going to take a shower so you two can fight in peace."

She scurried off and closed her door as quietly as if a sleeping baby were inside. Nick was practically breathless with frustration. Gingerly, I walked over and put my hand on his.

"Hi," I said.

He looked at the floor. "Hi."

"Can we talk about this?"

He finally turned to me. His face was angry and upset and something else, something indefinable. I stood on my tiptoes and kissed him, slowly, softly, letting it last.

"Let's start there," I said. "I love you."

"I love you, too."

"I did a dumb thing," I acknowledged.

"For an understandable reason," he conceded.

"They were squeezing up around us and I couldn't breathe, Nick. And one of them grabbed me, and I just sort of..."

"...snapped," Nick finished for me, emptily. "You snapped."

"Exactly," I said. "That's exactly it. And it looks stupid now, but soon enough someone on *Strictly Come Dancing* will have her septum collapse and everyone will forget that I jumped onto a bus in front of Hamleys."

He turned to me. "*This* is why I never meant to get serious until I was older. Exactly this. It's too early in our lives to have this much pressure about what we're doing, or not doing, or whether we look sufficiently happy. The press is always waiting to pounce on any fuckup. They will be vultures about it, and they will destroy you."

Somewhere in that speech, he had stopped talking entirely about me. I reached out and grabbed him by the arms, stopping his pacing.

"What else is going on here?" I asked. "I know you hate the press. Trust me, I know. But I can't just never go out and hope that fixes everything. I can't give them that power. I won't."

"It doesn't matter. They'll take it anyway," he said, his voice breaking. "And no matter how many times I tell you that, you don't seem to want to listen."

"I'm listening now," I said.

I had seen Nick happy, sad, lustful, loving, bored, irritated. I'd seen him with the flu, running on no sleep at all, enraged with his father, engrossed in a movie. But I'd never seen him look at me the way he did here—as if he was making a judgment—and then as soon as I'd registered it, the whole thing melted at the edges and fell away, and I just saw a little kid, scared.

"You snapped," he echoed, sinking into the couch and putting his forehead in his palms.

"Yes."

"*She* snapped."

"Who?"

"My mum, Bex," Nick said. "I'm talking about Mum. She's...she's mad."

"At me? If I could just *talk* to her—"

"You can't talk to her. No one can," he said, his voice so painfully flat and expressionless. "She's not *angry*, Bex. She's insane."

# CHAPTER FIVE

The truth about his mother poured out of Nick in a rushed tangle of words and tears, like he was a soda bottle shaken for a quarter century and suddenly uncapped. Until that night, the biggest secret anyone had ever told me was sophomore year at Cornell, when Lacey confessed she had a crush on her physics professor—and that one, she'd recanted a day later after she saw him with food in his beard. I was out of my depth here. So I just lay beside Nick, our fingers twined, and imagined with heartache the scenes he described playing out on the stark white ceiling of my bedroom.

Lady Emma Somers grew up in a stately home in Wiltshire and spent summers on the Isle of Wight, right near Osborne House, the Royal Family's retreat at the time. Emma was fascinated by Osborne—the rooms decorated during the imperial rule of India, the crazy trailer-like contraption on the beach that Queen Victoria I had used for private naked swims in the sea—and Richard had been fascinated with her. He was a shy kid, emotional, extremely self-conscious; his father's death meant Eleanor expected him to act like the man of the house even though he was still a boy, and he did not flourish under those circumstances. Edwin and Agatha were allowed to attend to grubby, childish pursuits, but the heir had to have his hair just so at all times, his socks pulled up high, his clothes immaculate, even during their summer breaks. He never had fun; he simply wasn't allowed. But rosy-cheeked, blond, blue-eyed Emma *embodied* fun. She handled the stiff, lonely Richard with the same care and spirit that she used to rescue birds with broken wings and tame local feral cats and even once shoo a fox away from an actual henhouse. And when Richard returned to Osborne the summer of his twenty-seventh birthday, as England's most eligible yet desperately unattached bachelor, it was the beautiful nineteen-year-old Emma who found him thrown off his horse, Emma who got help, Emma who was permitted to keep him company while he recuperated from a broken leg, and Emma who, two months later, was given an immaculate emerald and the promise of becoming queen.

And so Emma married her broken bird, and then became one. She went from being a civilian to being under a constant microscope: Her clothes were found wanting, her hairstyle too modern, her smile too big or not bright enough. Her confidence dwindled to nil, she became resentful and barbed, and Richard—distant by nature, unused to anyone talking back to him, and never skilled at affection of any stripe—was brusque and judgmental in return. The softness and vulnerability of his convalescence evaporated when his need was no longer so naked, and their union became the very definition of *marry in haste and repent at leisure*. It seems unfathomable that Nick was conceived at all, other than out of the strictest sense of duty. Freddie came mostly because Emma viewed Nick as her best friend, and she wanted to build a team. But if she hoped delivering the expected heir and spare would also decrease the scrutiny, she learned quickly that it actually made her a bigger target. Demand for photos in the pre-Internet age was so astonishing that a photographer snuck into the hospital on the day of Freddie's birth, and a nurse cracked him over the head with a bedpan. Emma grew so paranoid that she came across as shifty, and the mounting strangeness of her every public appearance with Richard, as if they were uncomfortable touching or perhaps never truly *had*, ignited a buzz that never stopped. She clammed up, and then shut down, sunny one moment and a total eclipse the next; provoked shouting matches, jealousies, and accusations, and then welt and wilted under them. She stopped going outside, closing all the windows and curtains in their Kensington Palace apartment and refusing to let in the daylight. By the time Nick turned five, she was lost to them, and then buried under a carefully scripted fiction that the Palace thought was less troublesome than the facts.

"Basically, she doesn't live in any sort of reality anymore," Nick explained. "Occasionally she'll speak, but it's always about things that only live in her head. Most of the time it's like she just unplugged. She doesn't recognize any of us. She doesn't even seem to know herself anymore."

"She snapped," I echoed him.

"The doctors had a lot of theories," Nick said. "Anxiety. Some form of rapid-onset dementia. An adjustment disorder. Her brother overdosed when she was eighteen, and her parents died within months of each other when I was two or three, so she may also have slipped into a severe depression. I'm sure she felt terribly alone."

I carefully wiped his tear before it dribbled into his ear.

"It's all guesswork, though, at this point," he added. "Nothing anyone's ever tried has helped, and she certainly can't tell us herself." He let out a mirthless laugh. "One day it'll probably be called Emma Somers Syndrome."

"What does Richard think it was?" I asked. "Does he talk about it?"

Nick frowned at the ceiling. "He's not forthcoming, which I'm sure is no surprise," he said. "I've heard more about her as a *person* from her friends, her butler, even Great-Grandmother, after a bourbon or six."

He clasped and unclasped his watch absently. "My own memories of the end are mostly snapshots. I remember a lot of screaming. Her smashing the telephone into a mirror. I remember being scared, and trying to keep Freddie busy so he didn't hear or see anything, although I suspect I was too young to do a very good job at it." Another tear snaked down his face. "Finally, one day, Nanny took me and Freddie to Buckingham Palace to get us out of there. We ended up staying for...weeks, I think."

I snuggled up to him and kissed his shoulder. "I'm so, so sorry," I said, feeling the inadequacy of the words.

"Me too," he said. "I try so hard to be there for her. That's what I was doing half the time I left Oxford. Visiting, moving her from place to place. Father acts like it's a waste, but she's in there somewhere, even if she's buried deep. She needs to see life around her if she's ever going to..."

He put his hands over his face, letting out a quiet sob. I rolled away and let him have it to himself. I didn't want to ebb a flow of tears that was clearly a long time in coming.

"I do remember bits from when she was herself," Nick eventually said. "There was nobody like her. She could laugh so easily, and she had this way of talking to you, *right* to you, that made you feel like the most important person in the world."

"I'm sure that's exactly what you were to her," I said. "And still are. That never goes away, not deep down."

Nick shrugged. "I don't know about that. I do wish we didn't have to hide it. But Father and Gran made that decision a long time ago. God forbid there be human imperfection in the blessed Royal Family," he said bitterly. "But every time there's a story about her, it's so obviously made up. It's a transgression of the worst sort and they don't even know it, and I can't tell them. Like that thing about her taking up with her bodyguard. We couldn't very well come out and say it's impossible because she's out of her mind and we've been lying about it for years."

His tone grew frustrated. "And even worse, I catch myself wishing they were all true," he said brokenly. "Because if she was saying those things, if she did have an affair, it would mean she was capable of it. And that she wasn't lost to us."

"This was all such a weight to put on you," I said softly. "Have you ever asked them to come clean?"

"No, Bex. I can't."

"Why not? Wouldn't it be easier on everyone, not having to explain away her absence?"

"People would see the liars, not the lie," he said. "Besides, I don't want *them* to have the satisfaction."

"The press," I translated.

"They hounded her," he said. "My mother was the biggest celebrity in the world. The *Guardian* did a special edition about her wedding that still holds the record for the most papers ever purchased in the UK. Two girls in Devon *died* waiting overnight in winter just to meet her. The press hid in the bushes, tapped the phones. They paid off bodyguards and cooks and one of our nannies. The press was the trigger for all of this, for everything that went wrong for her, and my mother would not want them to know they won."

I curled into him, my head on his chest, the way we lay together almost every night. He clasped me tightly.

"That isn't going to happen to me, Nick," I said firmly. "Or to you."

"I'm sure my mother would have said the same thing."

The hopelessness on his face unsettled me. I had only seen Nick like this from the outside. The place he was showing me now, the one he disappeared to when Emma came up, was so much sadder than I had imagined.

"So," Nick said. "Now you know my big family secret." He paused. "In fact, it is *the* big family secret. Please don't tell Lacey, or your parents, or anyone. No one outside the family knows. Well, Bea does, but only because our mums were best friends."

"I'm honored that you shared it with me," I said. "I think you needed to tell someone."

"I needed to tell *you*," Nick emphasized. "Things are already out of control with the media, and the more you and Lacey feed the beast, the hungrier it gets. We sell papers. The more they sell, the more money they make, the more they come at us. The more they own us."

"Only if we let them," I said gently.

"I'm sure Mum would've said that, too," he said, picking at a loose button.

"Would she?" I asked. "I don't mean to be disrespectful. It's just that we're all savvier about how these things work now. And she didn't have you. Not the way I do."

"All she had was Prince Dick," he said. The distaste in his voice was obvious even without the nickname.

I hugged him tighter.

"She wasn't perfect, and I know that, but I miss her like you wouldn't believe," he continued, his voice breaking again. "It's almost worse to miss someone when they're standing right in front of you." He shot me a sideways look. "I used to feel that way about you, sometimes. When we were at Oxford and I wanted so badly to reach out and touch you, and I couldn't because you were with Clive and I was with India. It was like I missed you even though I'd never had you."

I kissed his hand, then pressed it to my cheek. Nick looked at me pleadingly.

"Now you see why it's so important for you and Lacey to be careful," he said. "If anything ever..."

He covered his face, unable to finish. I loved that he worried about me; I believed he was underestimating me. I wished, desperately, that I had known sooner so I could've been more careful, and considerably less blithe. I wished the Palace had more faith in the public's capacity to bear the truth. And, frankly, I wished I could punch Richard for not protecting his sons from carrying this burden alone and in silence. But I said none of that. Instead, I kissed Nick with every feeling I had in me, and when we had sex, it was a sacrament, Nick's hands reverent on my body, sealing a bond forged through his confession and his tears. But as the heady afterglow of our catharsis ebbed, I felt haunted by something. As if somewhere in our turning point we'd forgotten to make sure we were still going in the same direction.

In the ensuing weeks, my fears were confirmed: While I'd hoped the truth about Emma would unite Nick and me with a newfound bravery and team spirit, it mostly just united him to his pajama bottoms. Fortunately, Richard was finally satisfied that Nick had absorbed enough about British exports and the migration habits of the red-breasted goose, and had approved his entering the Britannia Royal Naval College in Dartmouth. I prayed that once Nick had a real, tangible duty he would feel better equipped to make his way in this world, and less like the world was lying in wait for him. Then surely he'd realize that what happened to his mother wouldn't happen to me, and everything would go back to normal. I wanted to be supportive. I *was* supportive. I was a good listener, a loving confidant. I tried.

But we had started arguing. All of our friends were going out to parties, to clubs, to art openings and movies and football matches and music festivals; while Nick never forbade me to go out, it was impossible to ignore that *he* never did, and I felt guilty ditching him to party with his brother and our friends. Worse, Lacey was clutching ever tighter to Freddie's arm. Her leave of absence would end when summer did, and with real life looming large once more, she was doubling down on the pleasures only he—and London—could offer. Nick was cross with them both for continuing to bait the press with all their cozy cuddling, and I was loath to get involved, which made him cross with me. We were both touchy and terse, and low on patience.

The honeymoon was over.

One Sunday morning over toaster waffles, Nick and I were reading the headlines on our iPads. He always went for hard news first, in case Richard quizzed him on foreign affairs, so I had decided it was my valuable role in this partnership to scan for gossip. The *Mail* didn't have much that morning—one of the girls on *EastEnders* had worn a shirt made of cling film—but when I clicked on the *Mirror*'s website, a slideshow came up with the headline LACEY THE LYONS TAMER. As far as I'd known, Lacey was in New York, sorting out housing for her return to med school (NYU's patience, and that of our parents, could logically and logistically only extend so far). She must have come back and gotten a hotel room somewhere. I couldn't think why, except that it started with an *F* and ended with an *E* and was spelled *Freddie*.

"Shit," I murmured.

"Did you say something?" Nick asked, looking up.

"Oh. Um." I had spoken by accident, but I also couldn't avoid this. "Just, you know, some creepy new restaurant threw this crazy opening party."

"The one that went into that old crypt?" Nick asked around a piece of waffle.

"Yeah. I guess it uses coffins as tables," I said. "There's a really funny picture of Lady Cressida Morningstar wearing a giant velvet scrunchie, trying to climb inside one of them with her boyfriend..."

"That prat looks just like her prizewinning pug," Nick said.

"...and Gemma Sands talking to Bea..."

"Weird. Bea usually avoids Gemma," Nick said.

"...and Lacey with your uncle Edwin and Freddie, and then some pictures of the owner's prosthetic hand. I guess he lost the real one in a paddleboarding accident..."

"What?"

"It's silver-plated, really ornate," I said, hoping I had distracted him sufficiently.

Nick tilted his head in classic *give me a break* body language. Then he leaned over and studied the entire piece.

"'...the real star was Lacey Porter, the sun-kissed twin of the serious brunette who betting shops believe will be Prince Nicholas's first fiancée,'" Nick read aloud.

"*First* fiancée," I repeated. "So, like, the test model. Thanks, guys."

"All this bloody wedding speculation makes my head hurt," Nick said. Then he continued reading. "'Porter was spied with at least three of London's dishiest bachelors, but she got the most attention on the arm of our famed Ginger Gigolo. Freddie frequently cold-shouldered his date, model-turned-party-planner Arabesque DuBois, to whisper what looked like very sweet nothings in Porter's ear.'"

And amid pictures of her beaming at Prince Edwin and listening rapturously to Cressida Morningstar's pug boyfriend, there was a raft of photos of Lacey with Freddie—at one point caught laughing so hard that her head apparently had no choice but to loll on his shoulder. It gave off an indisputably intimate vibe.

Nick tossed my iPad aside. "Wonderful. Bloody great."

"Come on, it's not like they had sex on the bar."

"How many times do we have to talk to them about being indiscreet?" he said, exasperated. "Gran and Father are going to think we haven't even tried."

"Well..." I hedged.

Nick's eyes widened. "You didn't talk to her about it?"

Busted.

"She's going back to med school!" I defended myself. "She can't go out with Freddie if she's all the way across the Atlantic."

"You shouldn't have avoided this," Nick snapped. "It's important to me."

"And Lacey is important to *me*," I argued. "There was no point in getting heavy-handed with her if the whole thing was about to become moot anyway."

Nick rubbed his eyes. "I'm so tired of all this. The same conversation, the same fight. I don't want to have it today, Bex. I can't."

He grabbed the last of his waffle and got up and walked toward the bedroom.

"Hey," I called out to him. "I'm on it, Nick. It'll be the last time."

He looked sheepish, then doubled back to give me a syrupy kiss before heading to the shower. I, however, was becoming increasingly cranky, as if he'd passed his irritation to me by mouth. While I hadn't had the larger discussion with Lacey about all this, she was standing right there the day Nick lectured Freddie about it, and simply hadn't listened. Where had she stayed? When had she come back? And why was I finding out about it from a newspaper, and not my own sister?

Lacey was waiting by the Basil Street entrance of Harrods, looking crisp in a day dress and heels. I had texted her to join me there for a prescribed shopping outing, because I'd known she would accept, and now she'd beaten me there—along with six or seven paparazzi, who would doubtless multiply. Two Porters were better than one.

"Bex! Over here!" one of them called, and the cameras turned away from Lacey and the store's iconic terracotta façade when they spied me spilling out of my cab. Most of these guys were my regulars, who'd shown up every day since we'd fled Greetings & Salutations, hoping I'd crack again and give them something similarly juicy. My boss was losing his patience, although that might've been because the press made *greeting-card artist* sound so foolish and inconsequential, or worse, made-up.

"Shopping for Nicky's birthday?" That one, I'd dubbed Voldemort.

"Not getting him a Coucherator, then?" asked Too-Snug Safari Vest.

"Is he ever going to marry you?" Mustache boomed.

I turned a deaf ear and pressed toward Lacey, the cameras tracking my every step.

"Let's get inside," I said through my smiling, clenched teeth.

"Just give them what they want, Bex," she murmured.

"Just give us what we want!" Mustache parroted as the men advanced on us, the flashes from their cameras bright and disorienting. My breath quickened. That day we ran up Regent Street, I'd at least known *somewhere* around us lay air and space. But at Harrods, I didn't have anywhere to go other than through a plate glass window. I couldn't control Lacey, but I was not about to stick around and get shoved through it by twelve hundred pounds of loudmouthed testosterone, and bleed out on a display of beaded evening bags.

"Have a nice day, gentlemen," I said tightly, pushing inside to the complicated air of men's promotional fragrances.

Harrods takes up an entire city block and sells everything from handbags to riding equipment to foie gras, to elephants like the one Queen Eleanor bought Nick for his ninth birthday—although in fairness, they had needed to special-order that. (Now it lives at the London Zoo. His name is Patrick. Nick likes to visit him.) It was hardly a soothing place for me to regain my bearings—I once had to ask directions five times just to find the restrooms—but I'd been forced there for a very specific reason: I, my friends, and my immediate family had all gotten the same gold-edged, cream invitation with elegant script requesting the honor of our presence at a birthday celebration in late August for His Royal Highness Prince Nicholas of Wales, black tie required. Eleanor had stuffed the invite list with important diplomats, politicians, and foreign relatives, making it more of a coming-out party than anything else—and in a much smaller sense, it felt like mine as well, given that the handful of approved reporters in attendance would all know who I was, or what they suspected I might be. Which left me with one very large problem, and apparently I wasn't the only one who knew it.

"You're going to bungle this, aren't you?"

I had flinched and held the phone away from my ear. "Hi, Bea. I take it you got the invitation today, too."

"Has he gotten you a stylist? No, of course not. He cannot be seen paying to tart you up, especially when you don't officially exist," Bea mused, as if she'd called just to monologue at me. "And yet if you insist on banging about with him, it's in everyone's best interest that you do this correctly. I *suppose* I can help. Meet me at Harrods on Sunday, and for God's sake, bring the right underpinnings."

And then she'd hung up on me.

I spied Lady Bollocks waiting at the foot of the ornate Egyptian escalator, which probably seemed like the height of opulence when it was built but now feels like something on loan from a Vegas casino. Bea looked wan underneath her typically cross expression. I'd heard from Clive that Pudge had fallen off the wagon, and also off *a* wagon, at Glastonbury.

"Where is Lacey? I haven't got all day," she snapped in her usual tone.

"Out making friends with the paparazzi," I said.

"Naturally," she said, her lips tightening with disapproval. "You have got to put a stop to this. She's getting more and more indiscreet. You should've seen her and Freddie at that party, breathing all over each other. It was almost worse than snogging."

I groaned. "She is addicted to Freddie. He shouldn't be legal."

"He is irresistible," Bea affirmed. "Everyone's slept with him."

"Have *you*?" I asked.

"Of course," Bea said.

"Sorry!" Lacey bounced over, tucking her phone in her purse. "One of the photographers wanted to know where I got my shoes." She grinned. "They've given me a nickname. Racy Lacey. I think it's cute!"

"You would," Bea said, giving me an arch look. "It's not a compliment. It means they think you're unsavory."

"Nah, it's just their way of saying I'm fun," Lacey said. "I like it."

"*It's not a compliment*," Bea squeaked, almost losing her composure in what would have been a historic first.

Bea had arranged for a private fitting area, a beautiful sanctuary of a room where racks of pre-pulled gowns waited for us, along with petit fours, chilled glasses, and an ice bucket holding an open bottle of white wine. There was a bell to ring if we needed any assistance, but otherwise, we had complete and utter solitude.

"Discretion," said Bea, "is nine-tenths of success." She glared at Lacey again for good measure.

"I may never be able to shop another way ever again." Lacey sighed, ignoring Bea in favor of sampling the sweets.

The three of us spent the next hour zipping and unzipping some of the most perfect dresses I'd ever touched, and I relaxed and let out the breath that I'd gotten accustomed to holding every time I felt a stranger staring at the side of my head. Lacey and Bea put aside their squabble and seemed to have fun—or as close as Bea ever got—bandying about opinions on what I should choose. In the end, Lacey knew best; her first pick for me was a magnificent forest green strapless gown with gossamer gold thread woven into the bodice, then shooting through the skirt like a sunburst, and it won easily.

"It's even a British designer. They'll love that," she said, as she fastened the hook-and-eye closure at the back.

"Quite. You may not be *totally* useless," Bea said to Lacey, which for her was rapturous praise. The dress cost three times my rent, but if Lady Bollocks approved, there could be no other choice. Sabotage was not Bea's game: I might be a foolish American, but as long as I was with Nick, I was *her* foolish American.

"Right, now that I've done my patriotic duty, I've some choice words for Giles in the saddlery and he's not going to like them," Bea said. She eyed Lacey sipping her drink. "Do try not to pocket the Waterford."

I almost wanted Bea to stay, so that I could delay this inevitable Freddie conversation a bit longer, but when the door clicked shut behind her I knew there could be no more stalling. Lacey and I were heading into uncharted twin territory: I'd always been content to take a backseat when she needed to shine, and she'd never had to step back and return the favor. But Nick had begged Freddie to tone it down and it hadn't made a difference, so Lacey would have to step up.

I weighed carefully what to say. Maybe I could just be casual. Maybe she'd bring Freddie up organically, apologetically, and I wouldn't have to put my foot down at all.

"So Lace," I said, deliberately taking a long time to zip my boots over my jeans. "How was New York? I didn't know you were back."

"I like giving you and Nick space when I can," she said. "Freddie had a room at The Dorch that he wasn't using."

"Uh-huh."

"I slept alone, Bex."

"Uh-huh."

"What's got you in such a mood?" she asked, sitting down on a tufted ottoman.

"This paparazzi stuff is really bumming me out," I said.

"Well, it shouldn't," Lacey said, draining her glass. "You're world news, after all. And speaking of news, I have some that ought to cheer you up. I'm staying."

I blinked. "You're *what*?"

"Isn't it awesome?" she asked. "I just started thinking about it, really seriously, and I realized that I'm not enjoying med school. The thought of going back and spending the next however many years locked in a lab..." She shuddered.

"But you've been talking about med school since we were fifteen," I said incredulously. "It was awesome of you to put it on hold to help me, but it seems crazy to give up completely."

It was, in fact, totally unlike my sister to do that. Lacey simply never quit something before she mastered it.

"It's not giving up. It just didn't feel right anymore," she insisted. "Look, if you must know, my grades haven't been so great. It's hard to concentrate because I miss you so much, and I'm not happy there the way I am over here. So I told NYU that I'm done."

"But what—"

She held up a hand. "I'm way ahead of you. I had an interview with Whistles the other day to be one of its new buyers. That would be a lot more fun than studying the inner workings of the colon anyway, and it means no more transatlantic flights and months apart. We can get the band back together, once Nick gets out of his mood. You and me and Freddie and Nick..."

I leaned forward to rest my elbows on my thighs. At the sight of my face, Lacey stopped talking.

"I thought you'd be more excited," she said, genuine hurt in her voice. "Do you not want me here?"

"No! It's not that, it would *never* be that," I insisted.

And it wasn't that; not really. But I could no longer pretend the problems that came with Lacey would dissolve once she went back to her real life—and it gutted me that she might've done this hasty one-eighty on her future in service of something I now had to ask her to walk away from entirely.

My hands shook. Asking her to pick me over Freddie was effectively telling her that she played second fiddle to Nick. And yet I couldn't see any other way. I needed them both.

"You can't keep seeing him," I blurted.

She held my gaze. She knew the score. "It wasn't a date. We were just talking at a party," she said evenly.

"More like Racy Lacey snuggling up with Freddie in public again," I said, sitting back up. "And then you add us running through London, and you taking an extra ten minutes to pose in front of Harrods on the pretense of a photographer complimenting your shoes."

Lacey opened her mouth immediately and then closed it. "Yeah, I was enjoying that," she grudgingly admitted. "People want to talk to me, Bex. It's flattering! I don't know why everyone's so uptight about it, or about Freddie, for that matter. He's not the one who's going to inherit the throne someday. Let him enjoy his life."

"No one has ever accused Freddie of not enjoying his life," I said, my lips twitching. "It's coming from the top, though, Lace. It's not coming from me."

"Isn't it?"

I froze on that. Because she knew me better than anyone else, and she had me.

"Maybe it is coming from me, too," I said. "Because everything that keeps *you* in the papers keeps *me* in the papers, and you know that whenever I'm in the papers, it's a problem. Everything you and Freddie do ties back to me and Nick, then to Richard, then Eleanor. It goes up the chain, and then comes back down on me again twice as hard."

"You're exaggerating," Lacey said.

"I'm not. The last time you and Freddie went out together, Marj lost her mind," I said. "I believe her exact words were, 'All this cavorting with American twins looks like a bloody beer commercial.' "

Lacey rolled her eyes. "That old crank. She doesn't get it. We're *twins*. We're connected."

"But we're not a package deal, Lacey," I said.

Her shoulders sagged. Her whole *being* sagged. I think even her hair uncurled a little bit.

"We used to be," she said.

I flashed on one of those Best Friends charms, the kind that splits in half so you can each wear a piece. I gave Lacey one when we turned ten, and we still keep them in our wallets. But the thing about them is, even when you hold them back up to each other, they never look whole again. Once broken, there's always a crack.

"I hate this," I whispered.

"I know," Lacey said, and I could see she meant it.

"You know I wouldn't ask if—"

"I know," she repeated.

"But you're right that I can't do this without you. And I don't want to," I said. "Can you do that, though? Can you be here, but stop with Freddie, and the press, and just... be my sister?"

Lacey glanced over at the dress she would be wearing to Nick's party, hanging in a bag, ready to be sent back to our place. It was sexy as hell and it fit her like it was born on her body.

"Well, I can't promise he'll be able to control himself when he sees me in that," she said, aiming for lightness. "But he'll have to learn."

She scooted next to me and drew me into a hug. "I'm sorry if we made it harder for you, or for Nick," she said. "Of course I'll be there for you."

"Thank you," I whispered into her hair.

"I am going to miss him," Lacey confessed, pulling back. She let out a short laugh. "Other than the fact that he's hotter than the sun, I think it was just fun to imagine the Porter twins having this whole crazy adventure together, you know?"

"Lace, we'll always be a team," I said.

"I hope you're right," she said. "And besides, I'm going to be living here now. I *should* pledge my allegiance to the future queen."

I let out the loudest snort of my life. "I am so not going to be the queen."

Lacey gave me a strange look. "Of course you are," she said quietly. "Otherwise, where is this going? What is all this for?"

I thought about what Lacey had said all the way home from Harrods. Obviously I was keenly aware of Nick's station in life, but somehow I hadn't properly considered the notion that following my relationship through to a happy conclusion meant me becoming... if not a queen, then certainly the wife of a king. And, as I looked back on all those years of secrecy that had no end in sight, doubt crept in about how much that simple fact might be coloring our current status—which suddenly felt more like a stalemate. By the time I got home, my head and my heart and my feet were throbbing, and I just wanted to lose myself in some deliriously lousy TV.

Three hours later, after a *Celebrity Big Brother* marathon crowned with a riveting confessional in which a contestant fell asleep for five uncut minutes—*Big Brother* is considerably less produced in the UK than it is in the United States—I channel surfed until I heard a familiar name on the nightly news.

"Prince Nicholas is at the National Portrait Gallery tonight," an entertainment reporter gushed as Nick's picture came up, "and you won't believe what he said about his future!"

It was the Queen Mum's birthday, and Nick was at the gallery to unveil a painting of her in her youth, crisp as usual in one of his navy suits. This channel's cameraperson was in the phalanx of media stuffed behind a metal barricade; Nick had obviously agreed to answer a preapproved question or two, but as he'd finished, someone went rogue. The news subtitled it even though I heard it plain as day.

"Oi, Nick! When's the wedding? None of us are getting any younger!"

I knew the voice. It was Mustache. I sucked in a breath, but on the TV, Nick played it off with a comedic head shake.

Until.

"I don't know why you lot are in such a hurry to chain me down," he said. "Getting married is the last thing on my mind. Talk to me again in a decade."

The station cut back to the studio, where the newscaster was chuckling.

"Someone better tell Rebecca Porter," she said. "Although maybe Prince Nicholas just *did*. Up next, part three in our report on the common household pets most likely to kill you."

I told myself it was nothing. I told myself Nick loved me, and that everything else was just smoke and mirrors. I told myself we'd laugh about it when he came over later, the way he always did. But his glib reaction was all I saw, on a loop, every time I closed my eyes and tried to sleep. Because I ended up being wrong about one very important thing: Nick never did come home to me that night.

But he was waiting on my bed the next morning when I got out of the shower, annoyingly huggable in gray heathered cashmere (he'd had breakfast with Marta, who'd wanted to celebrate turning ninety-nine with a full English fry-up that would make her arteries "really work for it"). By this point, I was in a state: poorly rested, emotionally wounded, fresh from my twentieth dramatic imagining of how this conversation would go, and ready to take off his head with whatever blunt instrument I could find. Including my tongue.

Nick reached for the pile of newspapers next to him and wordlessly tossed me *The Sun*. Near the photographs of Lacey from Harrods were shots of her with some guys I vaguely recognized from the society pages. The only solace I could take was that she wasn't with Freddie—Lacey had, at least, followed the letter of that law—but the headline read POSH AND BEX AND THE PARTY GIRL, and that was bad enough. But it was also clearly a sidebar to something larger. I unfolded the paper, and found a photo of Nick in front of the gallery, under the words MATRIMON-OH-NO!

"Good morning to you, too, Nick," I said, brandishing it and then throwing the paper back at his head.

"Sorry. Good morning," he said guiltily.

"Too late. I'm mad," I said, dropping my towel and giving my wet hair a vicious rub. "You spend all that time lecturing me and Lacey, but now it's okay for *you* to feed the beast?"

"If we're going to fight about this, would you mind putting on some clothes?" Nick said. "You're very distracting right now, and I want to be at my best."

"Stop trying to flirt your way out of this," I said, stiffly tugging on my bathrobe.

His face fell. "I didn't actually mean it."

"Which part?"

"Any of it," he insisted.

"If I had done anything like that, Barnes would deep-fry my head for lunch," I said.

"How do you know he didn't deep-fry *mine*?"

"Because I'm sure he's extremely relieved to have it confirmed that I'm just keeping your bed warm," I said, choking up. Nick looked as surprised as if I'd just handed him my acceptance letter to Hogwarts. "Did you even think about how this would make me look? Like some tragic American girl you're just toying with, until someone better comes along."

*Or in case no one better does*, I didn't say.

"I promise, that bloody photographer just caught me off guard," he said. "This marriage nonsense and their obsession with our relationship drives me up a tree, and it slipped out. I should have ignored him. I don't know why I didn't. I suppose I'm not immune, either."

"You snapped," I said meaningfully.

"I'm so, so sorry, Bex," he said. "Hurting you was the last thing I wanted to do. If we were two normal people..."

"But we're not," I said. "We're one normal person, and then you."

Nick attempted a wan smile. "How many times do I have to tell you, Bex? You've never been normal."

This reference to Windsor made something inside me unfold. I crossed the room and kissed him.

"You know I don't care about getting married, but I do think I care about the hiding," I said, sitting next to him. "It's been almost four years. *Four*, Nick. I don't know how much longer it's fair for us to live in a cave."

"Well, this cave has satellite TV and a very enticing bed," he said, nudging me.

"Be serious." I smacked his leg.

"Sorry. The bathrobe is too flimsy to keep me focused," he said, picking up the satiny tie and rubbing it between his fingers. He sighed. "It's not like I've ever done this before. Not really. And it's not like I can ask my parents for advice. They were miserable even when Mum was well."

"So neither of us knows what we're doing," I said.

Nick looked at me and although his lips smiled, his eyes didn't. "Haven't a clue," he said.

I took his hand, almost as if to bridge the silence that fell between us. My eyes landed on my flag pin, our private little talisman, sitting on the dresser staring back at me, daring me to put it on and feel the same as I ever had.

"Maybe you're right," Nick said suddenly. "Maybe that's the answer. Maybe we just stop running."

"You mean, go public?" I asked, my jaw swinging open wider than was strictly ladylike. "Are you ready for that?"

"I guess this is as ready as I'll ever be," was his reply.

Not the answer I'd hoped for, but it was all he said.

# CHAPTER SIX

Very few people in this world look, in person, exactly as you imagine them. I, for example, am told I look taller and not nearly as American, whatever that means. David Beckham, conversely, is more compact than expected, but also sexier, which evens it out. The first time I stood in a room with Queen Eleanor, I expected a similar revelation—albeit not about her level of sex appeal—but the surprise was that there was no surprise. She is one of the rare public figures who looks the same in the papers, on TV, and in your mind, as she does in the flesh: supreme, authoritative, every inch the icon that she is on the postage and the pound.

Then again, maybe it's unsurprising that I reacted that way, given that my first encounter with Eleanor was on her turf—Buckingham Palace being the ultimate home-field advantage. Before Nick's party I hadn't done anything more than whiz past Buck House in a cab, because I felt weird taking the pricey tour when I was suspected of dating someone whose birth had been announced on a placard in the courtyard. *Suspected*, but still not confirmed: Word from The Firm was that no personal gossip could take precedence over the dawn of the Navy career that represented the next phase of Nick's fastidiously plotted life. I hadn't honestly expected them to give us the green light the first time Nick asked, but that didn't make it any easier to know that on a night when I'd loved to have celebrated *with* him, I'd have to settle for *near* at best.

At least I'd have my parents, who'd jumped at the chance to fly over for the party. My mother would have brought lemon bars to a ritual human sacrifice if the Queen had invited her, but this gala legitimately tickled her fancy bone. Proving that Lacey takes after her, Mom promptly invested in a library of etiquette books, studying them and the potential guest list to the exclusion of everything except her trips to the Men's Wearhouse Big and Tall section, to make absolutely sure Dad—who laughed at the price of the Burberry tux she'd been eyeing—had the right clothes.

"Are you nervous? I'm nervous," she tittered as our Mercedes sedan inched forward.

"Don't be nervous. You look beautiful, Mom," I said.

"Queen Nancy of Muscatina," Dad joked. "Most fun shopping spree I've ever been dragged on."

"Oh, pish," Mom said, but she was beaming.

I had no doubt that a hefty percentage of people expected the King and Queen of Coucherator, Inc., to be tacky, vulgar Americans, but Mom looked sleek and elegant in her midnight blue gown with beaded bolero. Dad's tux fit to suave perfection. And Lacey had outdone herself: Her red sweetheart-neckline gown, matching lip, and delicate finger waves gave her an Old Hollywood glamour-girl look, flashier than I'd expected but still somehow pitch-perfect. When our car finally turned into Buckingham Palace's giant iron gates and crept toward the porte cochere, I felt an intense wave of affection and appreciation for what they were doing—putting themselves on display, up for judgment. All because of who Nick was to me.

"Before we get out, I just... I don't really know *how* to, properly, but I want to thank you guys," I said, beating back tears. "For being here. For the flat. For these clothes. It's beyond generous. I mean, when will we ever need these gowns again?"

"Well, when will Dad ever need those dueling pistols?" Lacey cracked.

"You never know. Let's see how tonight goes," Dad said.

"You know what I mean!" I said. "We should've borrowed stuff somehow."

"Oh, sweetie," Mom said, patting my knee. "What's the point of inventing what Hammacher Schlemmer called 'The World's Foremost Seating-and-Cooling System' if you can't spoil yourselves with... well, the spoils?" She gave me a loving, and more serious, smile. "Besides, you needed the best tonight."

Impulsively, I grabbed her hand. "I love you," I said. "I don't know how to repay you."

"You can stop biting your nails," was her reply, though she squeezed me back.

Our car ground to a halt, the door swinging open as if by magic, and I caught myself hanging back as if I were about to trespass. Buckingham Palace is so symbolic that you almost forget it's a real place with plumbing and heating, linen closets and washing machines, and the occasional creaky floorboard. It felt like a transgression somehow to step inside and solve some of its mysteries. The magnitude of my luck hit me then—followed by my sister's hand, nudging me forward. I felt eyes on us as we climbed out, and mentally blessed Lacey's hairdresser for my romantic, low, loose bun, and the Harrods tailors for making sure my dress wouldn't need a public hoiking. My gut roiled, but my exterior, at least, looked the part I needed to play.

We were ushered directly into the Grand Entrance, a sunken rectangular room that appeared to be constructed entirely of cream marble, columns, and gold trim. Some of the statues that usually live there had been replaced for the bash with festive topiaries, including a giant one of an archer drawing his bow.

"That's in honor of Saint Nicholas," Clive said as he materialized next to me, dashing in his tux, and an endearing nick near his ear from his efforts at a close shave. I hugged him, relieved to see a friendly face that might depressurize this occasion.

"Where's your other half?" I asked, craning my neck. Clive's dalliance with Gemma Sands had, as Nick had predicted, proven so short-lived that I never met her, and he'd rebounded with another glossy girl from an upmarket family. Philippa Huntington-Jones made up for her lack of personality with a vintage Aston Martin that she let him drive around London. The two of them looked like a Cartier ad in it.

"Philippa is coming with her parents." He cringed slightly. "I'm trying to wriggle out of that one, to tell you the truth. The other day she asked about our family land holdings."

"Speaking of family," I said, "have you met my parents?"

"Delighted," Clive said, shaking Dad's hand and then kissing my mother's. "You are as stunning as your daughters."

"Hey, thanks," Dad said. "I try my best."

"I was just going to tell Bex that Nicholas is the patron saint of archers, hence the massive shrubbery up there." Clive grinned. "He's also the patron saint of repentant thieves, but that's harder to capture in horticultural form."

"*Our* Nicholas is more of a patron saint of our couch these days," Lacey said.

Clive let out a surprised laugh. "Careful," he warned. "You don't know who's listening." Then he bit his lip. "Blast, Philippa's spotted me. I'd best go put in my time so I can have a bit of fun the rest of the night."

He set off across the room, squeezing against the tide of guests that the palace's red-coated, white-gloved footmen were ushering gently up the famous double staircase. The dark wood banister was cool and substantial under my shaking hand as we curved up and around to the second floor, through a series of beguiling reception rooms, every couch supported by a carved lion armrest and every throw pillow punched into a perfect hourglass. Still, there are tiny things that make buffed and burnished Buckingham less intimidating—the odd candle askew in its holder, the light odor of menthol, cords still dangling inelegantly from the marble lamps to the wall. It's almost comforting. Some logistics, even royalty can't circumvent.

We were eventually deposited in the Picture Gallery, a dusty-rose rectangle of a room with an arched ceiling whose skylights, by day, toplight the original works by the Old Masters that hang side by side with portraits of royal ancestors.

"Bex, the *fire extinguishers* are *gold*," my mother breathed.

The room swam with VIPs: foreign royalty in ornate baubles that distinguished themselves from the mere dignitaries, who in turn wore whatever medals and sashes they could to outdo us commoners. The motherly hand Mom laid on my arm on the Grand Staircase had gripped me tighter as we'd been led deeper and deeper into the palace, and I had five fat red finger marks on my bicep. I think she just had to squeeze me or squeal, and squealing was too unbecoming.

"You could live here one day, Rebecca," Mom said, subtly leaning over to fuss with my pendant. "Can you imagine?"

"Please don't," I whispered to the statement as much as the fussing.

She just shot me a knowing look and reached out with a curious finger to touch the diamond in my lavaliere.

"That's from Nick," Lacey told her.

Mom arched a brow excitedly. "I wondered," she said. "Oh, Bex, when was this?"

"Ages ago," I said. "It doesn't mean anything."

It actually did, to me at least. As a surprise for Nick, I'd had the diamond put on a shorter fine-filigree chain so that I could wear it out in the open, for the first time, the way we'd wanted to be but couldn't—like a show of solidarity, a sign that even apart we were still together. But I couldn't think of a less ideal place to say that out loud.

Gaz to the rescue.

"Not too shabby, eh?" he said, coming up and clapping a hand on Dad's shoulder—which required him to reach up higher than was strictly dignified. "Quite tolerable, in fact."

"It's no Chicago Yacht Club, but it'll do," Dad said, shaking Gaz's hand. "Ever been to Chicago before?"

"I've never even been *here* before, much less to America," Gaz said.

"You should see this place when it's set up for a garden party," Clive said, squeezing in between me and Lacey, and bringing with him that familiar air of enjoying his one-upmanship. "Stunning. There's a giant vase out there that Napoleon commissioned to celebrate his assured victory at Waterloo."

"What a stupid short git," Gaz said. "And I say that as someone who has a soft spot for stupid short gits."

"I like you," Dad said to him. "You seem someone who'd know where they keep the beer at this thing."

Gaz brightened. "A gentleman after my own heart," he said. "The bar is over where Nick's face is melting." He nodded toward the ice sculptures that flanked either side of a bar set against the silk-covered east wall. "I would be delighted to take you there."

"I'd better go, too," Mom said. "I don't know if I trust your father on his own here. He's done none of the reading I assigned."

Gaz escorted them away with gallantry. Clive swiftly scooped three flutes of Champagne off a passing server's tray, and he and Lacey and I made our way as gracefully as we could over to where Cilla and Joss had carved out a spot near a particularly famous Rembrandt.

"Joss, that's... what an *interesting* dress," Lacey said, eyeballing the word *dress* scrawled up the skirt of Joss's white gown.

"Isn't it?" Joss said. "I've got this really posh investor on the hook if I can do a whole line of them. Says he likes my whimsy. I'm thinking of calling it Soj, because it's like Joss backwards, kind of, or maybe The Queen's Bits, to stick it to my dad for—"

"Soj," we all said immediately, as Lacey choked on a slurp of Champagne.

"A clear winner," Clive added quickly, thumping Lacey on the back. "Though they're both... so special."

"What's the matter with Gaz?" Cilla asked, pointing across the room. Gaz was listening intently to my father, who was wearing what I recognized as his Pitch Face.

"Nothing that isn't already filed under 'Being Gaz,'" Clive said.

"He's plainly wasting away," Cilla said. "That girl has been starving him."

Gaz had lost about thirty pounds under the influence of his girlfriend, Penelope Six-Names—who'd redeemed her Oxford faux pas one night by helping Freddie avoid a fight between his latest fling and a weeping ex called Mauritius he'd hooked up with in Aruba (or was it a girl named Aruba he'd slept with in Mauritius? Freddie should come with CliffsNotes).

"I think he looks really dapper," Joss offered. "Very trim."

"He looked perfectly good just as he was before," Cilla said irritably. "He's a solicitor. He needs brain food, not some fitness model who feeds him leaves and berries."

I raised an eyebrow. "And where is Tony?" I asked.

Cilla's confidence slid. "He decided not to come."

"He wasn't invited, you mean," Joss said.

"He may have failed the security check," Cilla admitted, not fully looking at any of us.

"Cilla," I groaned. "You have got to break up with him."

"But he's dead sexy," she protested.

"So is Gaz," I said boldly, nudging her.

"And dead *skilled*," Cilla added pointedly.

"So is Gaz," Clive teased, taking a swig of his martini.

"Tony is so shady, Cil," I said. "You know this. Where is it even going, anyway?"

"From the pot to the kettle," Joss said blithely.

Lacey set her jaw. "That's below the belt tonight."

"Oh, come on, we've all said Nick should man up and go public," Joss said.

"We have?" I asked. "When were *we* talking about it?"

Joss rolled her eyes. "All the time," she said.

"Leave it out, Joss," Cilla said.

"If Cilla is willing to be seen in public with Tricky Tony, then what's Nick's problem?"

"*Not here*, Joss," Clive said.

I felt myself turning red. It made sense that they had discussed it—hell, I would have, if one of my best friends had been treading water in her relationship for this long. As much as I appreciated their collective allegiance, though, it hit me that there was more to it than pure protectiveness: They *pitied* me.

"Where *is* Nick, anyway?" Lacey asked, rising up on her toes and scanning the room. "I don't see Freddie, either."

Suddenly, I felt a hand on my arm. We looked around to see the Queen's footmen silently, discreetly, arranging the guests in long, parallel receiving lines of sorts that created two aisles in the Picture Gallery.

"Asked and answered," Clive murmured. "Here they come."

At her coronation, the leading columnist of the day wrote that Eleanor was so beautiful she'd have ended up Queen even if she'd been born a peasant. At seventy-seven, the florid march of love and death had conspired to fold that beauty into something less refined, like taking a gentle eraser to a pencil sketch. But she was still striking, with unmarred bone structure and the same cornflower-blue eyes that she'd passed down to Nick. That day, they glowed as she entered the Picture Gallery in a glorious royal-purple frock, emerald drops in her ears and a glittering tiara perched on her flawless pewter bob. Age had stooped her slightly, but she still walked with the elegance of a younger ruler and the confidence of a woman accustomed to being obeyed.

Richard, Freddie, and Eleanor's mother Marta entered next, the men in full military dress—Prince Dick, coldly chiseled, and Freddie eliciting an inadvertent intake of breath from Lacey. The guest of honor emerged last. The sight of Nick in his tux melted me, and I was proud of how composed he was even though I knew it killed him that his father and brother had military regalia to wear and he didn't. Across the way, I caught Lady Bollocks staring at me, her black gown's bodice as architectural as her features. She gave me a half nod that was as approving as I was ever likely to get, and so brief that she could plausibly deny having done it.

Richard and Freddie strolled up our aisle, Marta on Freddie's arm, with Eleanor and Nick taking the other. I faced them with my back to the wall, and pretended not to watch as they acknowledged people in the crowd, Nick's face brightening at the sight of a redheaded girl I recognized with a sinking heart as Gemma Sands—currently on the cover of *Tatler* in a glowing profile featuring her both as London's most eligible bachelorette, and in the majestic environs of her father's wildlife preserve while wearing a fluffy feathered couture. She'd looked fantastic. She did again, in tonight's sleek blue gown, which irritatingly matched Nick's eyes.

I tore away my gaze when I sensed Richard approaching. As his eyes swept down our line, he looked for a moment like he was going to speak to me, so I opened my mouth.

He passed right on by.

In the void where his body had been, I saw Eleanor across the room flicking her gaze toward me. I was gripped again with one of those intrusive impulses: to stick out my tongue, or scream, or announce *I left a pair of underwear at Windsor Castle—did anyone find them?*

Instead, I smiled. She ignored me, too. Bea, in the distance, raised a brow at me as if to say, *What did you expect?*

Marta and Freddie passed by in a cloud of cigarette smoke (she smokes two packs a day).

"Nice dress, Killer," he murmured.

At least I had one ally.

We ate in the Ballroom—paradoxically, the formal dancing later would happen in the Throne Room—which is like stepping inside a very fancy music box, right down to the gargantuan early-nineteenth-century pipe organ across the back wall of the room. The chandeliers had been dimmed to give way to the candles on each of the thirty or so round tables, scattered below the long, raised rectangular one where Nick and his family and some carefully selected seatmates were placed. With one noteworthy absence: This time, the official story was that Emma had bronchitis. Prince Dick's seatmate for the evening was instead Princess Christiane of Greece, a fleshy and foxy middle-aged woman Richard had (per Nick) come very close to marrying thirty years ago. Freddie, wisely forbidden to select his own date, was placed next to the British prime minister's daughter, to her obvious delight. Lacey did not even look at him when we entered the Ballroom. So far they had done their level bests to steer clear of each other—but Lacey was already on her fourth refill of bubbly, so it was anybody's guess whether either of their level bests would hold.

Lady Bollocks was stuck at a table nearby with her parents and a variety of poncey-looking middle-aged folks who were carrying on in stage whispers about the relative gaucheness of the fish knives that had been included in the place settings (only among Britain's upper crust would there be a cutlery scandal). Bea was feigning interest in a hilariously dismissive way, until something at the head table caught her eye. I followed her gaze. The clusters of cream roses in our centerpiece partially obscured Eleanor and Freddie from me, but I had a clear view of

Nick, who'd just entered with his dining companion for the evening: one Gemma Sands.

"*That's* interesting," Clive said, reading my mind.

Prince Nicholas in his spit-shined capacity was distant enough from my slovenly, Twinkie-inhaling boyfriend that I could, at first, consider Gemma's placement with anthropological curiosity. And then the meal began, and I had to sit through six courses of the two of them putting hands on each other's arms, telling rip-roaring jokes to other members of the table, and being solicitous of each other to the extreme—and I had to do it in a room full of people who read the papers, and thus recognized me and saw that I was plonked in the worst seat in the house. But it was during the salmon course that I felt the Queen's particular gimlet eye on me once more, and was suddenly quite sure that she was gauging my reaction to her seating chart. In the face of our denied request to become official, giving the nod to Gemma Sands in front of everyone Eleanor cared to impress felt like a chess move. And everyone knows the Queen is the most powerful piece on the board.

*Screw that,* I thought.

So I straightened my back and resolved to have an epically delightful time. I threw myself into every conversation, smiling, laughing at Cilla's story about how one painting in the Portrait Gallery had belonged to her great-great-great-aunt until the Prince of Wales won it in a high-stakes game of whist. I sipped daintily at the tremendous wine from the palace cellar of more than twenty-five thousand bottles, dredged up some stories from the greeting-card trenches that were passably entertaining, and overall ensured I visibly held my own as a lively—but not overtly loud nor showy—dining companion. If anyone in the House of Lyons wanted to beat my spirit into submission, he or she would have to strike harder.

Which eventually, Nick himself did. The evening closed with a giant cake, lit with sparklers, and a round of "Happy Birthday," which Gemma punctuated with a highly affectionate kiss on Nick's cheek—a moment I instantly knew would be the lynchpin for all the gossipy reports in the papers. Lacey reached under the table and took my hand, Cilla and Gaz swapped a look, and my parents, bless them, betrayed not even a flicker of surprise nor irritation. Then Nick took his seat and leaned over Gemma to speak to the prime minister, and I looked at Lacey, who had just dropped her butter knife onto the floor and was trying to fish it out from under the table with her toe. I felt extraordinarily out of my depth.

"You're spending this entire party just watching Nick," Lady Bollocks accused me.

We had moved into the throne room for digestifs and traditional ballroom dancing (designed to appeal to the Olds, as Freddie called them, until they retired and a DJ took over). My parents were taking a surprisingly graceful turn around the dance floor, and I felt a surge of pride at how fleet of foot Dad looked, and how beautifully that simple act thumbed its nose at anyone who'd painted him as a beer-swilling baseball hooligan. But, although I'm loath to admit it even now, I was paying more attention to how many people Nick greeted and spoke to before he made it to me (currently, he was stuck with a posse of Danish relatives who were hugging him copiously). I knew I was being watched, so I couldn't even spy as flagrantly as I wanted to, and if Bea had noticed, then possibly so had other people. So I turned my back on him and pasted on the most contented smile I could muster. Nobody bought it.

"Has he even spoken to you yet?" Cilla asked.

"Does this morning count?" I said.

"This is a lot to deal with, Bex," Lacey ventured sympathetically.

"Stop encouraging her tiresome moping. It's not as if he can stroll up and ask her to dance," Bea said. "The reporters here would be all over *that* bit of foreplay."

Cilla looked at the whirling couples wistfully. "Pity. The dancing looks quite lovely."

Gaz drew himself tall and held out a hand to Cilla. "And *you* look stunning, and Tony is a deep-fried wanker for missing the chance to twirl you around this room," he said, as gallantly as anything involving the word *wanker* can be said.

Cilla blushed. "Go on, you," she said, but she was beaming, and took his hand, and Gaz whisked her away like a man who'd been practicing for weeks.

"He's been practicing for weeks," Clive said.

"You read my mind," I said.

Clive offered me his hand. "I hope I'm reading it again."

I involuntarily glanced again at Nick, and saw him give Gemma a quick hug in passing.

"You are," I said, accepting.

And so Clive and I performed a passable waltz, giggling as we tried not to step all over each other. Freddie and Bea even joined us, the latter holding her dangerously pointed chin high in the air as Freddie tried whatever goofy move he could to upset her iron posture. When the music ended, I noticed Eleanor's eyes pausing again on me.

"Stop checking the approval meter," Bea hissed.

Gaz bowed low to Cilla. "Can I interest the lady in a drink?"

"Bloody hell, yes," Cilla said, her cheeks sweetly red.

"Me too," Clive said somewhat obliviously. "And I saw Joss's father going blue in the face yelling at Tom Huntington-Jones about something, so I'd best buck up and go fish for the scoop from Philippa. Coming, Bex?"

I scanned the room again. I couldn't see Nick, but I did see my parents at the edge of the dance floor, entangled in a conversation with Nick's agitated-looking Aunt Agatha.

"You go ahead. Let me check on my parents first."

". . . show jumping in Great Britain simply hasn't been the same since he threw his hat in with the Dutch," Agatha was saying when I reached them. She sounded accusatory.

"I am sure you're right," my mother said, in a tone I recognized as the one she used when she wanted to be conciliatory and also had no idea what the other person was talking about.

Agatha seemed pleased by this response, before turning to me with a stare that was evaluative at best. "Can I help you, Rebecca?" she asked after a beat.

I gestured at Mom and Dad. "These are my parents, Your Highness," I explained.

Agatha looked at them, then back at me again, an expression of consternation on her face. "Really?" she said.

"I'm afraid it's true," Dad told her.

"I was quite sure you were related to Maxima," Agatha said, in a tone that implied that she was still fairly certain that she was correct. She turned to me, grudgingly. "Rebecca, how are you enjoying the palace?" No one has ever sounded more pained by a pleasantry.

"It's stunning," I said. "One of my favorite Vermeers is hanging in the Portrait Gallery."

"Oh yes," Agatha said. "*The Milkmaid.*"

It was a test. I was about to pass.

"No, ma'am, I believe that one is in the Rijksmuseum," I said. "I'm talking about *The Music Lesson*. Up close you can really see the way Vermeer injected himself into the work by adding that reflection of his easel. It's breathtaking in person."

"Of course," Agatha said, looking almost disappointed that I'd been right.

*In your face*, was my elegant thought.

Then Agatha's face fell even further. "Excuse me. Julian is . . . well, excuse me," she said, hustling toward the bar, where I saw Awful Julian dumping two shots of whiskey into his soda.

"Do I even want to know what that was about?" Mom asked.

"I think Princess Agatha was making sure that I'm not both a greeting-card artist *and* a bullshit artist," I said.

"I can only assume you showed her up magnificently," Nick said, suddenly at my side. "I apologize if she was rude."

My mother burst into girlish laughter. The two old women next to us glanced over and, in sync, raised penciled-in brows.

"Not at *all*," Mom chortled. "I found her quite fascinating, actually."

"Happy birthday!" My father shook Nick's hand. "Quite a place you've got here."

"Thank you both very much for coming," Nick said warmly. "It means a lot to me to have you here, and I know Bex has been missing you very much."

"Well, obviously, we're *delighted* to be here," my mother said, launching into what sounded like a TripAdvisor review. "It's *tremendous*, and the level of *service*! I can't even begin to imagine the planning."

"Luckily, all I had to do is show up," Nick said, smiling. "I don't want you to think your daughter would have anything to do with the sort of person who would approve an ice sculpture of himself riding a polo pony."

"He barely even rides," I said. "Because of the wooden leg."

"Bex!" Mom gasped.

"Don't tell," Nick said conspiratorially. "I'm so sorry I can't stay and chat longer, but Gran will have my head if I don't circulate." He caught my eye, and did a quick double take. "Nice necklace," he added.

"Happy birthday," I said, holding his gaze, unwilling to melt. "My best to Gemma."

Before he could react, he was whisked away. It was the last I talked to him that night.

After another hour, the footmen began notifying the older guests that their cars were lining up outside. I desperately wanted my parents to stay, but Mom and Dad had an early flight back to the United States, where my father had a long-standing meeting with the SkyMall board to discuss the Coucherator 2.0, which came with the option for a full sleeper sofa.

"This was marvelous, Bex," my mother gushed quietly, as we were saying our good-byes. She gently touched my chin. "And you were dignified and composed and wonderful. A credit to any family, even a royal one. Maybe especially."

"Stop it, Mom," I said. "You're going to make me cry."

Mom kissed my cheeks—both of them, European-style—and moved over to say good-bye to Lacey. I went to hug Dad, and he squeezed my shoulders very paternally.

"This is a strange kind of life," he said, looking me square in the eye. "There's always going to be a part of it that looks different from the outside than inside. And that you can't share. With anyone."

Nothing escaped my father. "I know, Dad," I said.

"And you really have to love a person to put up with that," he continued. "Love the *person*, not just the trappings. Because the rest of this..."

"Is fabulous," Mom supplied, bouncing over as Lacey drifted back toward the party.

"Is a lot to hitch your wagon to," Dad said. "Especially for someone like you, Bex."

"What does that mean?" Mom twittered. "She'd be grand at it."

I think this was a beginning of her quasi-English accent.

"It means this is the antithesis of someone as free-spirited as Bex is," Dad said to her. "Or used to be, anyway. And I worry about that."

There was a moment of silence among the three of us. My mother looked thoughtful.

"I really do love him, Dad," I finally said.

But as I watched my parents disappear down the Grand Staircase, I chewed on what Dad had said. I'd had to swallow an awful lot of irregularities to be with Nick, many of them hurtful, and all of them starting to chip away at my core.

While we'd dined and danced, the Picture Gallery had been transformed into a tiki theme, with potted palm trees lining the walls and a thatched roof over the bar, which was dishing out cocktails in coconuts. Someone had even wrangled an enormous tank, full of colorful tropical fish, against the far wall. That someone had to be Tony, whom I spied standing in the corner, talking animatedly to Cilla. Near the door, Gaz slumped against a totem pole.

"Freddie got Tony a gig designing this," Gaz said, gesturing around the room. "He only pretended to fail security. Top secret. So impressive." He sighed. "I feel a right pillock."

"Pillock." I tossed the word around in my mouth. "What is *that* rhyming slang for?"

"Not a bloody thing," Gaz said morosely.

Nick was dancing loosely with a cluster that included India Bolingbroke and Gemma Sands. His bow tie swung open and carefree, his eyes not searching for mine the way they would have a year ago, and I knew there would be no covert rendezvous later. I leaned against the pole with Gaz, my partner in feeling inconsequential and insufficient. The room was buzzing with energy and people and revelry, and even as I looped my arm around my friend, I had never felt so alone.

# CHAPTER SEVEN

Nick and I broke up ten weeks later.

As I'd feared, Gemma's impetuous kiss had made the papers, and the tabloids immediately blared that she was in and I was out. Clarence House didn't want to make a statement either way—"We can't discuss *them* if we never discussed *you.* Consistency," had been Marj's unsatisfying explanation—and Ladbrokes christened Gemma the odds-on favorite for a potential royal bride. I'd been kicked down to twenty-to-one, just inside "Someone He's Related To" and "A Man." Nick and I had barely discussed this, beyond *Don't worry* and *Gem's just a friend*, because he was off at the Britannia Royal Naval College before joining the officers' ranks. The little he did come home, we had sex in what felt less like insatiable need for each other, and more like an insatiable need to do something other than squabble. And despite what Nick had promised, still there was no movement toward going public. The excuses that piled up were everything short of astrology, reasons and Reasons eventually blurring into nonsense. The longer we weren't official, the more I officially felt like his dirty little secret.

Things came to a head during the run-up to Prince Edwin's wedding to a young dance teacher from Sussex, Lady Elizabeth Bewley. Per the official story, Edwin met Elizabeth at a dinner party and, besotted, carefully wooed her out of the public eye. Per reality, no one had a clue how they'd met, and the Palace was caught totally by surprise.

"I think he got tired of Gran nagging him, so he bought himself a quickie bride who'd irk her and get him a lot of press," Freddie said one night over pints in his chambers at Kensington.

"Sounds familiar," Nick said dryly, raising an eyebrow at Freddie.

"What if they don't like each other?" I asked.

"He's fifty-two years old," Nick had said. "Gran doesn't care if he *likes* who he marries, so long as he does it."

"That seems so archaic," I mused. "What if Edwin is gay?"

"You can't expect royal obligations to take pesky little things like sexual orientation into account," Freddie said.

Edwin randomly announced the engagement himself on the morning chat show *Sunrise*, just because it is Elizabeth's favorite (she likes that the weather graphics wear human accessories, like sunglasses and scarves). His press secretary publicly quit in a huff, and Eleanor was in a tizzy—so much so that she actually suggested that Nick bring me to the wedding.

"Wait. You mean...like a date? A public date?" I'd asked when he told me. We were in my living room, him doing a crossword before his phone rang; me pretending to try one, but actually idly sketching various imaginary cartoon ladies (who all ended up looking rather like Gemma with devil horns).

"Yes," Nick said. "It's all been thrown together so fast that Gran is worried it's a bit of a shotgun wedding, and she's keen for a distraction."

"So I'm just part of a gambit," I said, letting out with a sad puff the excited breath I'd held.

"We don't have to go, if you'd rather not." He tugged at his hair, not meeting my eyes. "I agree it's not ideal."

I couldn't tell what he wanted me to say. But I knew that for me, Job One was getting out of this discomfiting personal purgatory.

"No, we should do it," I said. "It'll be nice. Right?"

"Right," he said. Then he did look at me, and warmth crept into his face. "Right," he repeated, more confidently, and we exchanged smiles that were—if tentative—at least sincere.

The one definite upside to this wedding: Figuring out who exactly Lady Elizabeth Bewley even *was* briefly proved more enticing to the public than Nick, or Freddie, or Gemma, or I, and the press dug into her life hungrily. Elizabeth was sweet. Elizabeth taught children how to do pliés and stand in fifth position. Elizabeth had been very popular, but not very academically gifted. Elizabeth raised chickens at her family's summer home and named them all after great romantic heroes of books she probably hadn't read. Elizabeth's blond hair was trimmed every six weeks, and she took a gap year in Chile but then never went to university, so it was hard to say what the gap was technically bridging. But I loved her, even though I hadn't met her, because all the photographers in front of my house and Greetings & Salutations temporarily decamped to her place.

I used the break in media attention to sneak my way into a new, hopefully more compelling job working in marketing for Sir John Soane's Museum, a terrifically bizarre place jam-packed with art and antiquities. I no longer got goose bumps in my own apartment, knowing the windows were being watched, and could actually go outside without the company of a pushy, camera-laden mob. Finally, I felt free again, enough so that I felt comfortable voicing my relief to Joss and Cilla over lunch one day.

"I know it seems weird to feel safer when a street is empty," I told them. "But it had gotten crazy. Nick has trained assassins looking after him. I'm on my own."

And of course, the next day a story ran under the headline LET'S TALK ABOUT BEX, BABY: *Nick's Nosh Begs for Bodyguard*, swearing I'd demanded security from the Palace at great taxpayer expense. (A blazingly mean sidebar titled ME ME ME implied I felt overshadowed by Elizabeth, and was furious that I hadn't gotten a ring when this English rose had snagged one in thirty seconds flat, even though her prince was kind of a frog.) Barnes telephoned specifically to share how unimpressed Clarence House was—"Last I checked, Miss Porter, you are not a member of the Royal Family"—and I'd cursed myself for talking about it at all, much less in public.

Two weeks before the blessed event, I was hat shopping after work with Bea and Joss at a private room in Stephen Jones Millinery in Covent Garden. Joss was pitching me on a hat she'd made herself in which the various flowers on the brim actually spelled out *hat,* which appealed to my limited budget because it would be free. I refused to ask my parents for any more money.

"Come on, Bex," Joss pleaded. "It could be a big deal for me."

"I do actually like this hat," I said, studying Joss's drawing. "Is that weird?"

"Yes," Bea said, ripping it out of my hand. "We are not at home to DIY projects. Not for this."

Joss looked so crushed that I said, "I'll find another occasion, Joss, I promise."

"We'll see," muttered Bea, plopping a spiked fascinator on my head. I looked like a cactus.

Joss brightened, despite Bea's side eye. "Hunt would be ever so chuffed."

"Please tell me you are not referring to Tom Huntington-Jones," Bea said.

"That's what he tells me to call him," Joss said. "Philippa's dad," she explained to me. "My investor. He says I'm an exciting emerging talent."

"That's great, Joss," I said warmly.

"I assume 'investing in emerging talent' is not a euphemism," Bea said, crossing her arms over her silk-clad chest.

"Ew," Joss said. "I mean, I think he fancies me, but he's not my type."

This was a compliment, to Hunt. Joss's last boyfriend had been a guy who wore a large stud in his left ear with a chain attached to it that turned out to be the leash for a hefty white rat called Bob, which prowled around his shoulder and neck. Eventually, Joss dumped him for refusing to take off Bob while they had sex, and we'd been glad to see the back of him before any of us caught rat-bite fever.

My phone rang. "It's probably Gaz," I said, digging in my purse. "Penelope Six-Names wants to take him to her tarot reader. I think he's over it."

I wish it had been Gaz.

"Bex," Nick said. "Have you bought a hat yet?"

"No," I said. "What do you think, tasteful beige, or a potted plant?"

"Um," he said.

My face fell so fast that I'm pretty sure it made a sound. Quickly, I got up and walked over to the window; a banal-looking grill across the street was packed with theatergoers overpaying for a meal before curtain at the *Starlight Express* revival running around the corner.

"What's up?" I asked, trying to sound unconcerned.

"It's off," Nick said bluntly. "With your public opinion ratings so low after the PPO thing—"

"I have public opinion ratings now?"

"It's not—"

"And you *care* about them?" I hadn't wanted to fight, not with Nick all the way at the southwestern tip of England and out of my physical reach. And yet. "What other data should I know about? Did Marj decide she prefers the odds on 'Nick Gets a Fellow Officer Pregnant'?"

"I'm sorry," Nick said impatiently, but not without sincerity. "It's been decreed. It isn't a good time."

"It never is," I said. "And I'm starting to think it never will be."

And I hung up, barely getting the words out before a sob escaped my throat.

Nick and I didn't correspond the next two weeks, beyond quick apologies. It was the longest we'd gone without speaking. I was full of contradictory upset: I didn't want to talk to him, because I didn't want another argument, yet I hated that *he* hadn't tried to talk to *me*. Lacey did everything she could to jolly me out of it—American snacks, Socialite Darts (in which we threw things at the faces of our enemies, tacked onto a corkboard behind my bedroom door), and in a moment of desperation, a DVD of Great Moments in Chicago Cubs History that ended up only enhancing my depression due to how short it was.

The day of the wedding also happened to be my birthday. Tony had invited us to the soft launch of a Club Theme pop-up that was so new he hadn't even released the name, just the address; Nick was supposed to meet us there after the reception, and I was on edge about seeing him. My wonderful friends rallied to my side, planning a casual dinner for me and Lacey before our night out, so that if I was wobbling, I could find strength in numbers. Gaz volunteered to do the food.

"I plan to dazzle Cilla with my secret weapons," he confided, wiggling his hands. "These can do magical things to a chicken."

"That's a very alluring selling point," I said, giving him a side squeeze.

Gaz hosted us in his ancient flat in a mews near the Victoria and Albert Museum. His place looked like a turn-of-the-century time capsule of masculinity: Everything was tartan or leather, there was a deer's head mounted on a wood-paneled wall over the fireplace, and an actual divot in the chair rail in the dining room that Gaz swore was thanks to an errant piece of shrapnel during the Blitz.

"What is he making in there?" Lacey asked, sniffing the air from her perch on his plaid couch. "It smells like... burnt shoes."

"That'll be the Chex Mix, or whatever that stuff is that you love so much, Bex," Cilla grunted. "He's been practicing all week and he still forgets to check it."

"I'll go help," I said.

"No, let me," Cilla said, getting up. "I am excellent when Gaz is in crisis."

"So there is one piece of good news. I've finally left *Top News*," Clive said. He was almost vibrating with excitement. "I'm now at the *Recorder*. It's not very established yet, but at least it's a paper that people pay actual money to get."

"Shut up, that's awesome!" I said, hoping my sincere happiness showed through my bad mood. "I knew things would work out for you."

"Yes, well, technically the job is as a nighttime copy editor, but when I'm not editing, I can volunteer for writing assignments," he said. "It'll be society stuff, mostly, but when you think about it, gossip is the part of the paper that people really read. Perhaps there is no better way to communicate."

"*Seriously?*" Bea asked, dripping with derision as she poured herself a martini.

"The society pages are high-profile," Clive argued, defensively. "This is a great stepping-stone for my career. A bloke can't go straight from *Top News* to the *Daily Mail*."

Bea nearly coughed up her olive. "If you think Nick is going to associate with someone working for the *Daily Mail*..."

"Not this again," Clive groaned.

"Nick knows Clive is a reporter," I said. "It's not new. He would deal with it."

"Yes, because dealing with things is his strong suit," Lacey said protectively.

I snorted. Clive chuckled. Even Joss smiled, although she looked exhausted; she'd been fighting a lot with her father, who'd wanted her to work in reception at his gynecological practice instead of, as he'd phrased it, letting some leering toff bankroll her fancies. (Apparently I wasn't the only one in need of distraction that night.) Bea started to speak, but was interrupted by the buzzing of her phone. She did a double take at it, then frowned at me.

"It would seem," Bea said, "that you are not going to have a very happy birthday."

She handed me the phone. Among the news photos trickling in from Prince Edwin's wedding was a beautifully cinematic shot of Nick and Gemma Sands arriving at the church together through the mist, his elbow proffered, her hand curled around its crook. He was looking back at her, beaming, and she glowed up at him.

"No. *No.*" I tried calm breathing. I tried fast breathing. I tried a combination of the two. Nothing worked. As if on strings, I shot to my feet, my arm in the air. "MOTHERFU—"

"My phone," Bea yelped, lunging at me just as Clive grabbed my wrist before I could hurl the phone at the wall.

"Calm down," he said, rescuing the device. "Calm down," he repeated softly.

"Is everything all right?" Cilla said breathlessly, coming out of the kitchen holding a carving knife that had a piece of chicken impaled on the end. Gaz followed her with a bowl of Chex Mix that smelled shockingly correct.

"Bex almost destroyed my mobile, which I haven't had a chance to back up in weeks," said good old Lady Bollocks, irritably.

"And, not to bury the lede or anything, but Nick went to the wedding with Gemma," Clive reported. "I'm sorry, Bex. I can't believe my sources didn't tell me first."

"Oh, get off it, Clive," Cilla said, handing the knife to Gaz and helping Lacey pull me over to the couch.

"It might not mean anything," Lacey began.

"It *looks* bad," Bea said.

"It could be accidental," Gaz offered, cradling the Chex Mix like a baby.

"It's a slap in the face," Cilla barked.

I internalized all this, mutely, furiously, and then I started giggling. The giggles turned into a laugh when I saw how alarmed my friends were at my reaction. The laugh turned into a guffaw interrupted only when the tears ran into my mouth.

"Oh, come on, guys, it's funny," I said, wiping my eyes, sounding hysterical even to my own ears. "Today of all days. It was supposed to be me. And instead he's with *her*. Happy birthday to me!"

Gaz shook his head. "She's barmy. She needs a drink."

"You are right on one count," I said. "I do need a drink. It's my goddamn birthday and I am going to go out and have the best time anyone has ever had."

Joss brightened. "I have a shirt you could borrow," she said. "It's mostly black lace but there are two patches over the boobs. For modesty."

"*No*," said Cilla, Bea, and Lacey in unison.

"*Yes*," I said. "Nick would hate it. So yes. Give me that shirt."

"... Thanks? Whatever, I'll take it," Joss said.

"Eat first, at least, Bex," Lacey said, throwing Cilla a concerned expression. "If you're going out with a vengeance, at least get your base going."

"That's the only thing I learnt at Oxford," Gaz said melodramatically.

I wiped my eyes and smiled, and felt the emotions I usually funneled into Nick break free and flow at all of them.

"Group hug," I said, signaling for them to come to me. Maybe I *was* barmy.

"Absolutely not," Bea said as everyone else reached around me.

"I love you guys. Thank you so much for being here with me even if... well, whatever happens with Nick."

"We love you, too," Cilla said. "Bea, get your bony arse over here and engage."

"This is not one of Pudge's interventions," Bea sniffed, but she walked over and gave me a crisp pat on the shoulder just the same.

Tony's latest project turned out to be called Misery, an aptness that seemed less funny once we got there and saw it was in an abandoned, recently condemned building on the South Bank that looked like the kind of place you'd visit if you were angling to catch hepatitis. There was yellow caution tape stretched across the front, broken glass from the ruined windows, and floors intentionally (or still?) littered with trash and assorted debris. The drinks were deliberately bad, and the music was the worst nightclub mix you could imagine, from morose Tracy Chapman to endless Gregorian chants. All the artsy, desperate hipsters lined up around the block were proclaiming it Tony's most ingeniously subversive effort yet.

Two good things came out of that night. One was that Cilla dumped Tony for being a pretentious ass who'd tricked me and Lacey into spending our birthday at a potential hotbed for suicide. ("The rudest comedown from Gaz's lovely dinner," she'd rebuked him, and she'd been right in every way.) The other was that even in my emotionally reckless state, I couldn't choke down more than a quarter of one poorly made bottom-shelf cocktail. So there was no false liquid courage when Nick showed up—I was stone-cold sober—and no drunken regrets when the end finally came.

I had actually texted Nick and told him not to bother, and that we'd speak in a day or so. He'd obviously picked up on my vibe, or been self-aware enough to know that this would be coming, because he ignored me and showed up anyway. The second I saw him, I wanted to pretend everything was fine, because... well, he was *fine*: His muscles were more sculpted after his military drilling, and because he'd borrowed Twiggy's motorbike—as he always did whenever he wanted to travel quickly and anonymously—he'd also purloined his PPO's snug, weathered leather jacket. The whole effect was very *Top Gun*. Nick seemed relieved when he saw that I was alive and whole in this den of scuzz, but as he walked toward me, my resolve steeled.

"Proceed with caution," Lacey said quietly, laying a hand on my arm.

"What *is* this place?" Nick asked when he reached us, his motorcycle helmet tucked under his arm. "Are we sure Tony isn't going to murder us all? What is that *shirt*?"

At my expression, he kissed me very chastely on the cheek, which made me go stiff. "Happy birthday . . . ?" he said loudly, the words for the bystanders' benefit and the question mark for mine.

"I told you not to worry about coming," I said.

"But it's your birthday," he said reasonably.

"It is," I said softly. "And it hasn't been the best one."

He sagged a little. "Bex, let's go talk about this someplace else," he said.

"No. Not tonight. I think you should just go."

"Bex," he said, trying to look pleasant for the sake of appearances.

"*Nick*," I said, wiggling the vile potion in a cheap glass tumbler that was in my hand. "Don't harsh my buzz. I'm trying to celebrate."

*"Rebecca."*

I didn't care for his tone—whether he liked it or not, Nick had inherited a sliver of Richard's flinty impatience, though he almost never deployed it—but I'd also known perfectly well my texts would freak him out, and I'd done nothing to correct that. I've never been patient; I wasn't waiting for this fight any longer.

Cilla stepped toward me. "Tony has a trailer parked out back that he's been using as a makeshift office," she whispered. "Go. I'll send Nick in a minute."

The trailer was an Airstream that had clearly recently been a food truck, still tricked out with a restaurant-quality griddle and hot plates, and smelling faintly of old bacon grease. A crusty plastic squeeze bottle of ketchup lay unloved on the counter.

Nick walked in ten minutes later. In that time, my hackles had gone down somewhat, leaving in their place that cold, goosebumpy feeling you get when the sun goes behind a cloud.

"I didn't want to do this tonight," I blurted out at him. "Not here."

Nick set his helmet on the counter. "I am amazed anyone wants to do *anything* here."

He looked like he was wrestling with coming over to me, but I held up my hand.

"No," I said. "Please don't. If you come over here, we'll just end up having sex on the griddle or something and that won't help."

"It might," he said, but he stayed where he was.

My mind raced for what to say first, but as usual, my mouth had its own ideas.

"So, was Clive right?"

"I doubt it."

"Don't be cute," I said impatiently. "Clive told me I was destined to be discarded once you found someone more suitable."

"Clive had an ulterior motive."

"Doesn't mean he was wrong," I said. "Look at the facts, Nick. We've been together four years, and you *still* won't be seen with me in public. I had Bea telling me I'm your safety play. I had Clive telling me I was a fool for doing this in the first place. The press is telling me I've been thrown over for your ex, you're telling the press you'd rather die than be tied down—"

"Please, don't remind me," Nick groaned.

"—and all *you* are ever telling me is, 'It's not a good time,' over and over, before going out and snuggling up with Gemma goddamn Sands. I had to sit there on your birthday and watch her kiss you, and act like it didn't hurt, in front of a room full of people who knew enough to look over at me when it happened," I said, heating up. "Watching you from afar I could take, but watching you do *that*, in front of my *parents*, in front of your family . . . But, you know what? I got through it. I passed that test. And then I got bumped for her *again*. Like I'm some mutt you picked up because it looked cute in the pet store but now you can't make it presentable."

"Is that what you think?" he asked, incredulous.

"What else can I think?" I asked. "I know that being who you are sucks for you sometimes, Nick. But I am who I am, and that cannot be someone who waits by the phone for her boyfriend to call and say she can come outside now. Especially because I'm starting to think that call won't ever come."

He smacked his hand against the counter. "That is not fair," he said. "You know I was nervous about being with anyone so seriously this soon. You *know* how much that scared me."

"And you know perfectly well that *you* said that didn't matter anymore," I spat. "I was there, Nick. You didn't fuck me into amnesia that night at Windsor. You *decided*. We both decided. Let's at least own that."

I hadn't meant to go nuclear, but I was tired of being polite, and we were both past restraint.

"Okay," Nick said. "Then let's also own you making the paparazzi chase you through London. Let's own me telling you about my mother, the reason for everything I'm afraid of, and then *nothing* changing with Lacey for weeks after that. Let's own you dancing with Clive at my birthday party and acting like it was the best time you'd ever had."

"I haven't been perfect. I know that. But I have been lonely," I said. "You left, Nick. Every day, little by little, since Klosters. The second our secret started to slip out, you started backing up. Straight into her."

"There is nothing going on with Gemma!" Nick said, exasperated. "God! I'm so tired of explaining myself."

"But that's just it, Nick," I said, beginning to shout. "You're *not* explaining yourself. Not to the people who pick up the papers and see her walking into a wedding on your arm. You're not explaining anything to the people who used to chase me around London, who are now writing that I'm being deported and that you and Gemma have a secret love nest in Surrey."

"We've been over this, Bex!" Nick said, throwing up his hands. "Talking to them only makes it worse. I will not give them any more ammunition."

"Your silence is the only ammunition they need anymore! How do you not see that?" I exploded. "I endured those people lying in wait for me, and said *nothing* about anything to them, because I love you enough to defer to your request. I told my sister to lay off your brother. I sucked it up while they picked me apart, and I've kept it together while they've laughed at me. I tried to fix what I messed up. I tried so hard to be perfect, to do exactly what you wanted me to do. And apparently I'm still not good enough."

"That has *never* been it."

"You made me look pathetic, Nick. And the worst part is, I let you. I can't believe I put so much of myself into another person that all this petty shit tears me down, but it *does*, Nick, it rips away a piece of me every single time."

"It was never on purpose. Gem was just *there*—"

"Then why does it keep happening?" I asked. "Explain it now. Explain it to me. *Please*, Nick."

"I—maybe *that's* why," he said, running a hand through his hair and staring at the floor. "There's no explaining with Gemma. There's nothing at stake. We're friends, it's easy. And you and I lately . . ." He sighed. "Everything has been a battle. All push and pull. Will we, won't we, what's Lacey doing, where is Freddie. It got so exhausting, and when the wedding got closer I just didn't want—"

He stopped himself, realizing what he'd said in the exact instant that I did.

"The disinvitation didn't come from on high, did it," I said, stating the fact for both of us. "It came from you. *You* didn't want me there."

In that moment the gulf between us widened without either of us moving. I sank against some decrepit old cabinetry and banged my palms onto my forehead.

"Talk about choices," I choked. "That is one hell of a choice. You can't take that one back. You just proved my point. Oh God."

I wrapped my arms around my stomach and rocked forward, as if to hold myself together. There was a real possibility that I was going to throw up.

"I was arguing with Barnes, and I had barely seen you, and suddenly I just got this vision of us going public and everything falling apart," he tried to explain, looking and sounding ashamed. "And I couldn't go through with it."

I fought hysteria with everything I had. "In baseball they call that a balk."

"It wasn't because I don't love you," he said desperately. "I do. I just got tired of *thinking* about everything so much, Bex. I just..."

"Don't say you snapped," I said. "Just *don't*."

"Mum's shadow is over everything I do," he whispered. "I can't shake it. I don't know how not to be paranoid, for me *or* for you."

My heart—my stomach, my head, everything—hurt for him. For both of us. Nick was adrift in something, and I couldn't be his moor anymore. Which meant I was adrift, too.

Nick was sucking on his lower lip hard now, rubbing the floor of the trailer with his shoe, trying to look at me but unable to do it.

"This is it, isn't it," he said. "Is this *really* it?"

"I don't know," I said. "But it feels like it."

Something dawned on his face. "Our pin," he said. "You're not wearing it, are you?"

I think he already knew the answer, but I shook my head anyway. I'd left it on my dresser. I hadn't worn it in two weeks, and I'd known, on some level, that tonight wouldn't end in a game of him finding it.

"Did we ever really have a shot?" I asked almost wistfully. "Did you truly think this would work, or were you just hoping?"

He thought about this. "Both," he said. "I knew—I *know*—how I felt about you. But once the press got wind, I kept thinking that maybe if we stayed where we were, and kept everyone at bay, I could just..."

"Delay the inevitable," I said hollowly.

He shook his head helplessly. "I *always* wanted you," he said. "But I also just wanted things to be simple for a minute." I could hear the emotion in his voice. "And they haven't been with us. They probably never will be, for me, and it kills me, and it ruins things. I hate that we can't just live the way we did in Oxford, forever."

"We were hiding there, too, Nick," I said sadly. "Just because people weren't chasing us doesn't mean your demons weren't."

He met my eyes. They were red-rimmed and wet with tears. "I don't regret it," he said brokenly. "I regret that we're standing here, right now, doing this, in the stupidest location in the world."

That got a laugh out of me, halting though it was.

"But I don't regret trying," he said. "I just wish we'd tried harder."

"Not harder," I said. "Just better. We tried hard enough."

On the last word, I lost it. I heard him crying, too, so I turned away to give us each a moment and blotted my tears with my wrist. "There isn't even enough cloth on this stupid shirt to use it as a Kleenex."

It was his turn to laugh. He pushed off the wall and picked up the helmet, then juggled it between his hands before putting it down again.

"I don't want to go," he said. "Because if I walk out of here, I don't know when I'll get to touch you ever again, or even talk to you the same way, and I..." He swallowed a lump in his throat. "I don't know what that life looks like," he said, his voice tinny and strained.

I nodded, over and over, for lack of knowing what else to say.

"I love you," he said, picking up the helmet again and walking to the door.

"I love you, too," I said as he walked through it.

But it hadn't been enough.

# PART THREE

# WINTER 2011

*"Your image fills my whole soul.... How that moment shines for me still when I was close to you, with your hand in mine."*

—Prince Albert
in a letter to Queen Victoria, 1839

# CHAPTER ONE

The night we split was the last I saw of Nick for months—at least, in the flesh—and the pain from the hole he left consumed me. Our fight had been inevitable, and I'd gone cruising for it. I knew that. But I hadn't thought ahead to *after* I picked it, when, like a scab, it would fall away and expose whatever hid beneath. I hadn't even stopped to wonder what that would be. I certainly hadn't imagined a mutual surrender. Maybe I should have gone after him when he walked out of that trailer, but there was nothing more to say—we'd carved each other up enough as it was—and so in his wake I found myself glued to that cold metal floor, knowing my next step would be the first in a string of them that would take us further and further away from each other. We'd had our last lazy Sunday morning. We'd had our last laugh. We'd had our last kiss—a hurried peck on the corner of my mouth on his way out the door. If only I'd known, I'd have appreciated the casual intimacy. Or turned my face an inch to the right.

The trailer door banged open as Lacey and Cilla barged in, armed with water bottles and Kleenex.

"Blistering hell," Cilla said as soon as she saw my sodden face. Lacey said nothing; she simply snapped to my side and wrapped me in her arms.

"Someone has to check on Nick." I hiccupped. "He's upset, he's on that motorcycle—"

"Bea and Clive went after him," Cilla said, smoothing my hair. "He'll be all right."

I gulped the water, then slowly found my feet and glanced through the chipped window. Misery was so packed that the crowd had overflowed outside. People sat slumped on the stoops of the crumbling converted tenement, or leaned against the carbon-crusted burnt-out walls, all nodding in deep existential appreciation of "Cat's in the Cradle."

"Well, shit," I said. "Now our great memories of this place are ruined."

They just looked at me, sad and sympathetic and worried.

"I can't believe it's over," I said, my voice cracking on the last word. "I don't know what to do. This whole country feels like Nick to me."

Lacey stood decisively. "Then maybe it's time to go home," she said.

I'd expected to touch down in the States and feel healed—by the familiar territory, the beautiful sunsets, the cozy embrace of our two-story converted farmhouse. Mom and Dad sold their starter home once the Coucherator took off, swapping it for a larger, rural spread with a basement for his tinkering and enough bathrooms that Lacey could play with makeup for hours without me banging on the door. In typical Lacey fashion, she'd taken one look at the biggest of our two bedrooms, clasped her hands and spun around in it, and then spent the rest of our tour helpfully exclaiming over how the smaller one simply radiated me. And in typical me fashion, I didn't care enough to stoke the squabble, so I'd expressed an agreeable passion for the garret-like room with the sloped ceiling and the bay window. I painted the walls a funky gunmetal color, positioned my bed so that the angled wall hovered over me when I slept, and hung posters on it of Cubs greats like Ryne Sandberg, Greg Maddux, and Mark Grace (and a small picture of Derek Jeter; it appalled my father to have a Yankee on my wall, but some forces of nature are too powerful to be denied). Art supplies littered the floor as I sat in the window and drew, tapping my foot to music, relishing my refuge—in a way, Lacey had been right—even as Lacey habitually insisted I crash for the night in hers. But now, the old watercolors and pencil sketches were stacked neatly atop a high shelf in my closet, next to a box of trophies and faded team photos. My old quilt with the softballs all over it had been boxed up when I left and replaced with an itchy, girly Laura Ashley floral that gave me metaphysical hay fever, and Mark Grace and Ryne Sandberg and Greg Maddux were, as in life, warped and curling at the edges. (Derek Jeter, also as in life, still looked perfect.) I'd wanted to return to Muscatine to feel like myself again, but instead I felt like a tourist.

My first full day home, news broke that Nick had jetted off for a hunting weekend with Gemma, and it became obvious that I had underestimated the international appeal of my perceived role in this intrigue. The *Mirror* reported I'd flown home in a jealous tizzy; *The Sun* believed Nick and Gemma had been having an affair for years but were afraid to tell me because I am so unpredictably violent. And they all—in a move I knew had to have Nick spitting nails—quoted an anonymous source saying Emma had expressed her distaste for the bawdy American with unrefined hair. Lacey and I used to wonder how it felt for celebrities who couldn't dash out for toilet paper and ice cream without being surrounded by magazine stories about their fictional Baby Joy or their ex frisking someone new. That was now my life, and it was worse than I'd imagined. Two high-school-age girls at the local market started whispering and pointing as they pored through an *Enquirer* story titled JILTED BEX: "I'M KEEPING THE BABY," to the point where I excused myself from the checkout line to grab the largest box of tampons I could find. A girl from Lacey's cheerleading squad pretended not to see me at a gas station, then took a photo of my L.L.Bean duck boots that showed up later in a *Glamour* slideshow about shlubby breakup fashion. The anonymity I'd hoped to find in Muscatine proved as elusive as a warm hug from Barnes.

And Gemma's face haunted me. Of course *she* was the first place he ran. I knew tabloid appearances could be deceiving, but not all of them, not always, and those pictures with Gemma made me feel like the four years Nick spent with me might as well have been forty-five minutes. I wrote him a hundred frustrated emails I never sent. I couldn't eat. I barely slept. I did nothing but go on long predawn runs and then sack out in front of the television, pretending I wasn't Googling Nick and then secretly bingeing on whatever rumors I could find about him and the irresistible, illustrious, insidious Gemma Sands. By the time Lacey came home for Thanksgiving and marched into my room holding an open laptop, I was a stringy-haired wreck.

"Crikey, you look awful, Killer."

Freddie's voice and image burst out of her computer. It was jarring that he should be so much the same when nothing else was.

"For your information, I've been sick," I lied.

"If it helps, Knickers was in a complete glump before he went back down to the base," Freddie said. "I couldn't jolly him out of it. He didn't tease me about my new girlfriend Persimmon. I faxed a photocopy of my bum to Marj, and put her on speaker when she called to scream at me about pornography, and then I prank-called Barnes, pretending to be the Royal College of Taxidermy inquiring about his new hairpiece. Nothing."

That got a laugh out of me, at least. "Aren't you supposed to be on Team Nick?"

"He knows I am," Freddie said. "But he's also not in London, so get your arse back home and let me help with the healing process. I am unofficially a PhD in Medicinal Misbehavior."

In fact, other than one Beatrix Larchmont-Kent-Smythe—whose investment in me did not seem to extend past her sense of aristocratic duty—my English friends all tried to jolt my flatlining spirits. Cilla and Gaz gave raucous, amusingly divergent accounts of his attempts to give her cooking lessons; Joss shared that Tom Huntington-Jones wanted to bankroll an entire Soj store after the paps identified me wearing one of her shirts (I'd forgotten to button my peacoat when I ran out for cheese puffs). Clive gossiped that Prince Edwin ran over an endangered gopher on a golf outing, and Penelope Six-Names now hosted a children's TV show called *Morning Zoo* that involved her dressing up as animals and visiting them in their habitats to promote better interspecies relations. Apparently, a certain group of hens hadn't liked the cut of her jib *at all.* It was heartening to be included even though I'd decamped to American soil, but all I wanted was to laugh at those dishy stories with Nick. After all, he had been my best friend out of all of them.

Three days before Christmas, with no end to my sloth in sight, my parents decided it was their turn to intervene. I was digging around in the Coucherator for a Diet Coke when the two of them descended, Dad parking on the coffee table, and Mom to my right.

"Bex," Mom began. "Honey, this has gotten—"

"You are a disaster, Bex," Dad interrupted, patting my knee.

"Earl!" Mom hissed. "We rehearsed this."

"Well, rehearsal was sort of boring," Dad admitted. "Let's just give it to her straight."

"Give what to me?" I asked.

"It's in the script," Mom said huffily. "You'd know by now if he'd just stuck to it."

"There is a script?" I was confused. "Wait. Is this an intervention?"

"No," Mom said.

"Yes," Dad said.

"Don't take offense, but it's not a very good one," I said, folding my legs up under me.

"You're loafing, Bex," Dad said, smacking his lap. "All day, all night, you loaf. You loaf so much you've *become* a loaf. I could slice you up and use you for sandwiches."

"What your father is trying to say is that we're worried," Mom translated, shooting him a dirty look.

"What I'm really trying to say is that you need to go back to England," he said.

"I wouldn't go that far," Mom said. "That boy ran roughshod all over her feelings, Earl."

I put up my hand and wiggled it around. "Do I get a vote?"

"Yes," Mom said.

"No," Dad said. "You get to listen. Look, hon, I'm very sorry your relationship ended. But I don't care if he was the Prince of England or the Prince of Persian Rugs down on the interstate. You can't hide out here forever."

I pulled a face. "That carpet guy is sort of cute, and in the commercials he does those one-armed push-ups. Maybe I should introduce myself."

"He uses a body double. Costs them a fortune," Dad said.

"What?" Mom and I were both unnaturally shocked.

Dad shrugged. "We all use the same camera-people. The things I know about Hardware Pete from Pete's Hardware would make your toes curl." He shook his head. "Don't change the subject, Rebecca. You don't get to become a mole-person. Pull yourself together and go back to London with your head held high."

"I can't," I argued, faint with rising panic. "Everyone will be watching me, waiting to see if I'll crack. I'm not making that up, Dad. The headline on *In Touch* this week was WILL SHE CRACK?"

"Honey, you said yourself that half the problem was Nick being afraid of the press," Mom said gently, placing her hand over mine. "Don't you make that same mistake."

"Just go *be*, Bex," Dad said. "And, go be Bex. Go find your life again. It's not here anymore, and you know it."

"But what if it's not there, either?" I could barely do more than whisper. "Imagine what it's like, living in the country he's going to rule one day. He's everywhere, Dad. And I don't know if I'm strong enough." A tear slid down my cheek. "It's one thing to crack over here, but if I do it over there, everyone sees. *He* sees."

Dad slid off the table and knelt down in front of me, putting his hands on my face. "The Bex who dumped her prom date into the garbage is strong enough," he said. "The Bex who climbed over a barbwire fence is strong enough."

"That report is still unconfirmed," I muttered.

He kissed my forehead. "Sweetie, it all makes you who you are, which is someone real special, and also maybe a little crazy," he said.

"But—"

My mother stopped me. "I have never worried about you," she said. "Not really. We used to joke you could stand in the middle of a tornado and find a way to enjoy the breeze."

I cracked a tiny smile.

"That's a good thing, Bex," she said. "But it doesn't give you license to sit here and wait for life to find you. It just means you can survive whatever is out there."

This is one of my favorite memories of my parents, because in their faces I saw the most naked love and concern and support—and faith. They believed that I was brave. They believed I was tough. They believed in me, period. The original Bex Brigade.

"You win," I said. "I'll go back."

Dad stood with a groan. "Thank goodness. My knees couldn't take much more."

I scooted over so he could sit on my other side. "I just hope I don't do anything stupid while I'm trying to reconnect with my inner awesomeness."

"You won't," Mom said.

"You will," Dad said.

"Earl, *really*." That one was me.

"What? Everyone does stupid stuff," Dad said. "The Cubs have a rich history of it. But they never stop playing, and I love them anyway."

We heard a throat clearing. "I have an idea, if I may," Lacey said from the stairwell. A thumping noise accompanied her hopping down the last few steps.

"Clive's got a new girlfriend," she began, coming around in front of us. "Her dad owns half the world, basically, and she's throwing a New Year's Eve party on their private island. Staying at their house is free, and he owns Luxe Airlines, so we can get there for like twenty bucks or something insane," she said, at our mother's expression. She bounced on the balls of her feet. "What do you say? Nick won't be there. You can see everyone in a super-fun atmosphere and then we'll all head back to England together."

"Hell, *I'd* go, if I didn't think you'd rather die than party with your old man," Dad said.

I threw my arm around his neck and kissed his cheek. "You'd be great company, but I should probably brave this one on my own."

Lacey's eyes sparkled. "So you're in?"

"I'm in."

And that's how the debauchery started.

# CHAPTER TWO

The room reeked of booze and smoke and stale sweat. My mouth felt like I'd eaten a stick of paste, and tasted about as compelling. My head throbbed. My stomach churned. I was clammy and cold, which I quickly realized was because I was naked other than a sheet covering my ankles.

And some guy's leg was thrown over mine.

His breathing was slow, heavy, rhythmic; whoever he was, he was asleep. I pried open my eyes and saw a very posh hotel room that a cyclone of hedonism had torn to bits. The carcasses of the minibar blanketed the floor alongside heavy glass ashtrays full of cigarette stubs and ashes. Clothes dangled from anything they could; a deck of cards lay scattered as if someone had hurled it up into the air. A trail of powder led to the suite's second room, where I could see a slumbering couple I didn't recognize. Carefully, so as not to stir him, I lifted my head and looked my mystery companion in the face.

It was Clive.

New Year's Eve on Wayne Hanson's island reawakened a sleeping beast in me that would have given my selective biographer Aurelia Maupassant a stroke. I flirted with inappropriate guys. I gave out absurd fake names like Picasso Von Trapp and lied elaborately about my job—neurosurgeon, buttock-implant technician, party planner—while wearing tight shirts and tighter skirts provided by Joss, who seemed to like me a whole lot more now that I was feeling, as Bea might've said, more experimental and psychotic. Clive's new girlfriend, an old ex of Nick's called Davinia Cathcart-Hanson, was generous with the perks of her father's conglomerate and routinely booked us cheap airfare and gratis suites anywhere that had a warm beach, strong drinks, and a throng of people who either didn't know who I was or didn't care. And I went, again and again, to escape the memories that were boxed up in my Chelsea love nest along with a great deal of Nick's stuff. Which apparently he didn't want. He'd simply dropped away without so much as a note to tell me I should toss the chartreuse tie he left behind, which was a gift from the Queen, and which he hated. Of course, I hadn't texted him either to return his cashmere sweater that I was still sleeping in, even though it didn't even smell like him anymore.

Instead, we engaged in a screamingly immature game of cat and mouse. Photos of Nick and Gemma had given way to a mix of reports that he was exceedingly popular at the Royal Naval College, and grainy stills of him inside nightclubs, or leaving them, with a series of pretty women. I insisted I didn't care, that it was all gossip for sport—and yet, when the paparazzi caught me bodysurfing in Portugal, the surf ripping off my ill-advised string bikini top, I didn't hate the gloriously carefree shot of me that made the paper. Nor did I mind when the photographers found me in an even more tenuous Joss-designed bikini in Cinque Terre, the week after the press had hotly dissected snaps of Nick at an Eton friend's wedding reception, his arm wrapped around a gorgeous brunette so that his hand appeared to rest on her breast. And when Nick's ship docked in Majorca (the last phase of his Naval training) and the *Daily Mail*'s Xandra Deane reported he'd done body shots off a bevy of exotic beauties while shouting, "It's good to be free," I was particularly okay with the paparazzi catching me in Cannes perched on the lap of a hot young beefcake promoting his action flick *Venom Has a New Face*. None of it was choreographed—I hadn't alerted the paps, and Marj would never sign off on Nick publicly licking tequila from a stranger's clavicle—but it was definitely satisfying.

But once the pictures of me with the actor hit the Internet, the press decided I was a calculating fame addict, trading a future actual king for a future king of Hollywood (or any other title-adjacent guy who dared to be seen near me). In the following months, the paparazzi's formerly genial tone became toxic: I can still describe with laser accuracy the carpet in Heathrow's terminals, because of how often I hung my head and plowed over it while they took my picture and hissed things like, "Oi, nasty tart, look up," and, "Where's *this* weekend's shag, you dirty bird?" There was even a new nickname: the Ivy League, a pun on Lacey's and my Cornell educations and the fact that the press believed we were, in Xandra Deane's words, "attractive, creeping, climbing, and pernicious," like the vine itself. Lacey thought this was catchy, but I could hear Lady Bollocks's voice in my head: *It's not a compliment.*

"Honey, don't you think you should slow down?" Mom asked about six months into my bender, putting me on speakerphone. "All those trips. That actor. You're looking peaky."

"Never believe what you see in the papers, Mom."

"I believe what I *hear*, which is that you're exhausted and defensive," Dad opined. "You're never home. You're always with strangers. What the heck are you doing over there?"

"Exactly what you told me to do," I said. "Finding myself."

"No," he said. "All you found was another way to escape."

The sadness in his voice filled up my chest and exploded in a way that did not look especially good on me.

"You wanted me to come back and stick it to them," I said. "You told me to act like I don't care. Mission accomplished."

"You should still act like you care about *yourself*," Mom said.

"Oh, please," I snapped. "I'm just having fun. So is Lacey. Somehow I suspect you're not calling to tell *her* she's acting like a skank."

"Young lady, I don't care how screwed up you are right now, you will not speak to your mother that way," Dad said. "We are worried, and we want better for you, and that is that."

And he'd hung up; in a fit of pique, so had I.

Of all people, it was Freddie who came the closest to getting through to me. Lacey and I often ran into him at various clubs of Tony's, where it was too loud to discuss anything but our drink orders, and I knew the two of them had stayed in more constant contact. But I was still surprised when, one Monday in August about two hours after I'd called in sick with another abysmal hangover, he showed up at my flat with a restorative bag of Cornish pasties.

"This is obviously a total nonsense suggestion," he'd said, handing me a warm puff-pastry pocket. "But what if you tried *not* getting pissed off your tree all the time?"

I flopped back onto my sofa and took a bite. "This country's best quality is its belief in butter," I said, pastry debris shooting into the air like greasy snowflakes.

"And its worst quality is that its third in line to the throne will not be diverted from the topic at hand," he said, pulling a newspaper from his bag and unfurling it with a flourish. The front page read IVY LEAGUE VALEDICTORIAN?, with five images—styled to look like they'd been torn from an album—of me dashing in or out of clubs, shaky and smeared.

"Hang on," I said, sitting up and grabbing it from him. "Some of those are from the same night, and one is like two years old. They're making it sound like I did all of this last *week*."

"Clever, I know," Freddie said, nonchalantly propping his feet up on my coffee table. "But you are going rather hard."

"This from a guy who goes rather hard with a new girl every week, just to piss off his father," I said. "At least I'm not dragging anyone else into this."

"Touché," Freddie said. "But all my relationships are mutually beneficial. Trust me, I haven't broken a single heart in England."

"If you say so. But you've never had yours broken, either, so you don't get to tell me how to deal with it," I said, heating up. "You and Nick have whatever fun you want. You don't judge your own girlfriends for it. So you damn well don't get to judge me."

Freddie let that settle for a second. "I didn't say I've never had my heart broken," he said calmly. "And I didn't tell you not to have fun. You've always been fun. Just not reckless."

We chewed quietly until I couldn't stand it anymore. "How is he?"

"Rather well," Freddie said. "He's started training as a warfare officer down near Portsmouth. It's all weapons and navigation and whatnot. He's chuffed."

I'd seen pictures of the parade when Nick finally finished at the Naval College and became an officer. He'd been so hot in his gold-and-red-trimmed black uniform and white hat that I'd fallen into a box of wine and watched *Bridget Jones's Diary* three times in a row.

"He'd want to know you're getting on all right," Freddie added gingerly.

I bristled. "If you're just here to absolve his conscience or something—"

"Don't be so testy, Killer," he said, holding up a hand. "I'm here on my own behalf."

"Good. Because I would love to tell you that I'm doing great," I said. "I would love to tell you that I'm seeing someone awesome, and we're allowed to touch in public, and I've never been happier. But it would be lies, and the only thing that helps is getting far away from Nick and pretending I'm Leona Da Vinci, who wears huge hats and doesn't have any problems. And I'm going to keep doing it until *I* don't have any problems."

Freddie looked at me intently. Then he smiled. "I was Jock Weapon once at a hotel."

"In more ways than one, I bet."

He chuckled. "Well, Killer, this was a terrible talk," he said, clapping his hands together and then standing up. "Just promise you won't go completely 'round the bend. No face tattoos, no running off with a pool boy to Belize."

"I'll try, but Leona Da Vinci wants what she wants."

He chewed on his lip, then added, "Maybe you and Knickers should just have tea and get it over with. Wouldn't it be worse if you just bumped into him?"

"Probably," I said. "But I'm not ready to see him, Freddie. Not yet."

Turns out we were both right: It was way worse, and I wasn't ready.

That particular drizzly, doomed Friday in mid-October was the red carpet opening of Joss's new store on Kensington High Street. I'd worn a series of outrageous Soj bikinis in Cannes that had stirred up even more interest in her as a designer, so she and her walking midlife crisis of a business partner decided they should strike while the proverbial iron was still... if not hot, then at least plugged in, and so they rushed the shop and her clothing line to market. She'd invited socialites, pop stars, party reporters, and any of Tom Huntington-Jones's crew who were still speaking to him—which, for the moment anyway, included his daughter Philippa, who'd recently begun seeing Gaz.

"This is nuts. Cilla is single. I would've thought you'd pounce," I had said.

"Naw, after that smarmy tosser Tony, *any* old git looks good. I don't want to be Cilla's any-old-git," Gaz said firmly. "She needs to realize I'm her destiny."

"Or, you need to man up and show her," I said. "She basically once told me to stop wasting time and lock down Nick before somebody else did. She was right. You should try it."

I'd been anxious about the first real prospect of seeing Nick since the breakup, but Joss texted to say Nick had RSVP'd no. And so, emboldened, I dutifully opened the box containing the other source of my dread: the complimentary clothes Joss wanted her higher-profile guests to wear on the red carpet. Mine were a silky top that read *blouse* around the neck in silver-sequined letters, and white skinny jeans with a foot airbrushed on the ass like graffiti.

"It's symbolic," Joss had explained. "You've been kicked around, but you're still standing."

"It's heinous," Lacey had yelped when I walked out of my bedroom modeling the ensemble. "I assumed you were joking about wearing that. You just can't. You cannot."

"Joss is counting on me," I said. "Think of it this way. She gets my loyalty, and you get to look a hundred times better than I do. I'm helping *two* people."

Lacey downgraded her yelp to a whimper and fiddled with the sequins on my top, as if hoping to make them look less like letters. I did envy her chevron minidress, which she claimed was a sample she'd gotten from work, but which looked more like it came from Harvey Nichols. I suspected a lecture from Dad was coming about abusing her so-called emergency Amex.

"These past few months have been entertaining, and all, but real talk: At some point you need to dress like a rational adult who wants to attract a rational boyfriend," Lacey finally said.

"But I *don't* want that," I said stubbornly. "I just had a boyfriend. Now I want to have irrational fun."

"Okay, but if Nick starts dating someone first, you'll wish you'd tried harder to replace him with someone real," she said.

"Nick's dating life isn't my concern."

Lacey actually laughed in my face, although not unkindly. "Every ex-girlfriend says that, and no ex-girlfriend ever means it."

"You don't care about Freddie and Petunia," I pointed out.

"Persimmon," Lacey corrected me. "And that's different. I've technically never been his girlfriend." She smiled. "The clock's about run out on her, though, and the guy I'm seeing is dullsville, so the timing finally might be right pretty soon."

She stopped. "Oh, shit. I hope you know I'm not—"

"I know," I said. And I did. It was awkward that my brutal breakup was a romantic opportunity for my twin, but she'd stepped back when I'd asked, and now it was my turn.

Lacey hugged me. "Let's just try and enjoy having the Ivy League back on the prowl. You and me again. The package deal."

Soj turned out to be a retro-punky black-and-neon space that felt like Betsey Johnson crossed with old-school Madonna in a way that confirmed Joss once again had absorbed whatever her boyfriend was into—in this case, Tom Huntington-Jones's lost youth. I sensed the Ivy League headlines writing themselves as Lacey and I posed for pictures outside Soj, which I wished were not obligatory, because Lacey had been right about my pants. I should never have worn them, because no one else in the press line bothered: not the soap stars, the socialites, nor Special Sauce, the girl group whose hit "Dip It" was blaring both inside and outside the store. Not even Penelope Six-Names, a woman who'd willingly dressed as a llama last week on national television.

Inside, we rescued Cilla from a conversation with Six-Names and her new boyfriend, and made our way to Clive and Gaz, near a display of bikinis with the Universal No symbol stamped someplace scandalous. Gaz had his arm around a petite, bobbed brunette in a prim shirtdress.

"You all remember Philippa," Gaz said.

"Brilliant. It's the Ivy League," Philippa said, but she was glaring at me. "Daddy said your beach holidays singlehandedly made this happen." This sounded like an accusation.

"Oh, I'd say *his* hands had a lot to do with it, too," Lacey said sweetly, tucking her arm protectively through mine. We all glanced over to where Tom was peacocking with Joss. They were in matching snug leather trousers and identical platinum bouffants, like they were members of a Duran Duran tribute band rather than business partners. Philippa let out a guttural yawp; a tattoo artist set up between the jumpsuits and the tube tops was sketching the word *guns* on her father's right bicep, as he and Joss nuzzled.

"I am going to stab that bitch," Philippa said, stomping across the room.

"Bit crackers, that one," Gaz said. "Always on at me about my family landholdings."

"I did warn you," Clive said.

"There's no future in it, anyway," Gaz said. "She said curry makes her teeth hurt."

"Blasphemy," Cilla said heartily. "You are a magician with curry."

Gaz looked delighted, unlike Joss, who was currently getting the business end of Philippa's rage.

"Poor Joss," I said.

"Poor nothing," Clive said. "She got Sexy Bexy in her clothes again. Mission accomplished."

I groaned. "But I regret these jeans."

"You need a drink," Lacey advised, scanning the room for the bar and then charging off in that direction.

"This party has a very unusual guest list," Clive said, raising an eyebrow at two girls with half-shaved heads loitering near the handbags, whom I suspected were former fashion school classmates of Joss.

"Yes, that's right, only poncey society to-dos for you now," Gaz said. "No one with fewer than three surnames allowed."

"Can't complain. It's been ripping for my career," Clive said, drawing himself to his full height. "I've managed to use my connections without severing any of them. I'm hoping the *Recorder* won't be able to resist giving me a Man About Town column, if the *Mail* doesn't jump on me first."

"I bet they will," I said. "I told you things would turn around for you."

"I really should do an anonymous one with all the dirt I wish I could print, if it wouldn't get me ostracized," he said. "For example, from the rumors I've heard, there's a certain pug—"

Clive was interrupted by a flurry of flashbulbs outside the store, and then my shell-shocked sister pawing through the crowd.

"He's here," she hissed. "Hide your pants."

The whole room slowed down the instant I saw Nick. He was exactly as I remembered—kind face, piercing blue eyes, hair slightly tousled. As if he'd just rolled out of my bed.

"Oh, aces," Joss said, coming up behind us. "I suppose he did actually say *maybe*, but that usually means no."

Lacey and Cilla appeared to be wrestling with which of them would sock Joss first. I opened my mouth to say it was fine—it had to be, I had no choice—but then a blonde walked in beside Nick and took his hand. Ceres Whitehall de Villency looked like a gleaming golden angel in a leather pencil skirt and a sexy white top. I looked like a hobo, and I felt like a fool.

"I can't," I heard myself whisper.

Clive heard, too, and roared with laughter as if I'd just said something amazing. "Come with me," he leaned down to whisper. "We can be on a flight to Paris in thirty minutes."

"Yes," I whispered back. "Take me."

Bad choice of words.

My head pounded so hard that my vision blurred. I crawled out from under Clive and into the bathroom, all indigo and white tile and gold-trimmed fixings (it was, at least, the prettiest place in which I had ever felt like refried death). My makeup had relocated to all the wrong spots on my face, my breath smelled like my downward spiral, and my hair stood up as if I'd been dragged through a hedge. I heard footsteps and lurched to lock the door, then curled up on the cool floor to try to pull myself together. I recalled a bottle of bubbly on Davinia's father's jet, and some limoncello, among other liquid sins, at a nightclub in Montmartre—which unearthed a memory of meeting that random couple, whom Clive then invited for a nightcap at the Hotel Unpronounceable Frenchy Thing. I saw hazy images of strip blackjack, and being goaded into betting a kiss when I lost my last euros, and the other two whooping as Clive collected on that bet. That's where the reel in my head snapped and stopped. But what more did I need to see? I had been telling myself so vehemently that pretending to enjoy the wild life would somehow magically turn me back into the Old Bex, who only ever had vigorously noncommittal fun and never gave anyone her heart to break. But sprawled there naked on the floor with a mottled memory of the night before, I had to accept that this was the opposite of fun. It was dangerous, and it was exhausting.

So I threw up. Four times. I hurled with the might of someone hoping to purge *everything*, not just her stomach, and then did a swish of the complimentary mouthwash and put on the hotel robe. With a shaky hand and a deep breath—but not too deep; even my lungs were pissed at me—I steeled myself and opened the door. Clive had put on his boxers and was lying on the bed, clutching the last intact thing from the minibar to his forehead: an aluminum can of lemonade that had to be, at best, lukewarm. Our guests were nowhere to be seen.

"Why did we drink so much?" he whispered.

"Did we have sex last night?"

Clive lifted up the can, a picture of surprise. "You don't remember?" He plonked the can back into his forehead. "Well. That is not flattering."

"I know we kissed." I closed my eyes. I had a flash of myself removing his pants, of us lying on the bed, of me laughing wildly. "Oh, man. Maybe I do remember."

"It was not," Clive said with a wince, "our finest hour."

I kicked debris off the other double bed and crawled between its cool sheets, where I should have been all along.

"What is wrong with us? You have a girlfriend! And I have..." My voice trailed off. "Issues," I finished. "I got spooked and totally lost control. I'm so sorry."

Clive slowly righted himself. "We both did it, not just you," he said. "Two old friends got too drunk, emotions ran high, we blew off some steam. It doesn't mean anything."

He paused to pick a long brown strand of hair off his chest. "So, no need to tell Davinia. And without doubt I won't tell Nick," he added.

"He has Ceres. He wouldn't care." I sighed at my bruised tone. "It turns out I'm not dealing with this very well."

"Bex," Clive said patiently, "*no one* thought you were dealing with this very well."

I put my hands over my face. "I need to go home."

"It's five thirty in the morning," Clive said.

"Then I need to call Lacey."

"And I need grease," Clive said. "Let's order breakfast. What do you want?"

"Nothing," I said. "Pancakes. Eggs. Sausages. Everything."

I angled myself sideways and scrabbled at the mess on the floor. I found my underwear, a hair band, ten pounds, a torn condom wrapper that was a huge relief, and my passport, and then finally my cell jammed into the rear pocket of my foot pants. Lacey's phone barely rang.

"Why are you calling at this hour?" Freddie's voice asked.

"Why are you answering my sister's cell?"

Across the room, Clive looked up from the room service menu.

"It's not what you think," Freddie said. "Actually it's—what? No, Lacey, I'm not going to lie. We're all safe, Bex, but we're awake, because... well, there's been an incident with Nick."

# CHAPTER THREE

Given the choice, I would've liked my first post-breakup conversation with Nick to have included really good hair—a little *Shakespeare in Love*, a little Gisele—and a preternatural amount of self-possession. Instead, I'd scraped my unwashed locks into a bun, scrubbed off as much makeup as the hotel washcloth would take, and picked up discount mascara and lip gloss at the Chunnel terminal. It wasn't a bad patch job, but I was still green around the edges, on the whole more Zombie Apocalypse Survivor than the beguiling heroine of my own movie.

Freddie had shared only the barest details: Nick had almost decked a paparazzo outside a club, Gaz stepped in front of his fist, and then he popped Nick in the face in return.

"What the hell is the matter with them?" I had squawked.

"Well, we only talked for a second, but... *stop it*, Lacey, she's going to find out eventually," Freddie said irritably. "Er, so it sounds like the photographer said something rather offensive about you."

I clapped a hand over my mouth. "Nick, you idiot," I whispered. "Where is he, Fred?"

"This might not be the best time," he warned.

I rubbed my temples. "Yeah, I'm done hearing that phrase from your family," I said. "I'll find him, but it'd be a lot faster if you just told me."

In the end, it was also faster to take the Eurostar than wait for a Luxe Airlines flight. Clive had been a prince himself, of a sort, dashing down to the hotel gift shop and getting me a cotton shift that might have been intended as a nightgown, but which passed faintly for a casual dress. (Nothing would scream *walk of shame* to Nick louder than the same pair of foot pants I'd been wearing when I ran away from him.) It wasn't until our taxi dropped me at the Gare du Nord that I even looked Clive in the eye again. My hangover was hitting me in waves, as was a deep embarrassment.

"Clive," I said softly.

"Don't mention it," he said.

"I'm serious, I never meant—"

Clive held up a hand. "*I'm* serious. Don't mention it."

The two-hour Chunnel trip sped by as I scrolled through the reports already flooding the Internet, like ROYAL RUMBLE; NICK TUMBLES, and GINGER 'DAVID' FELLS PRINCE GOLIATH, accompanied by photo after photo of Nick falling, then landing hard as his PPOs swarmed him and Gaz. My brain ricocheted between raking myself over the coals for backsliding into bed with Clive, and trying to figure out why I thought I should see Nick in my current state given that I had indirectly caused *his* current state. I'd reached no helpful conclusions by the time my cab pulled up to Joss's place in an unremarkable part of Fulham. Every slender maisonette in the row had a different hint-of-color paint job that failed to hide the crookedness of the windowsills and mouldings. And when I pressed the bell, it sounded like a duck stuck in an air vent. No one would look for Nick here.

The curtains twitched, then Joss ushered me inside, her hair matted on the left as if she'd been woken from a deep, motionless slumber. We shambled into her microscopic white-and-yellow kitchen, where we came upon a very pale Cilla in a snug red tank dress, her heels in a heap near the sink as she blotted Gaz's split lip with a wet cloth.

"God, Gaz. Look at you. What *happened*?" I said.

"You should see the other bloke," Gaz quipped through one side of his mouth.

"I don't know how you caught that punch," Cilla said. "I barely knew myself what was happening until it was over."

"Piece o' doddle. Catlike reflexes, and all," Gaz said, but fatigue and worry blocked his grin from reaching his eyes. "That photographer bastard leant right in at us and said... *the thing*, and I somehow just knew Nick was going to have a go at him. So I sort of swung 'round at the right moment, and bam, Bob's your uncle."

"Didn't even fall down," Cilla said. "He was bloody brilliant."

"Or a bloody idiot, because then I shouted that Nick was a horse-fearing geezer and socked him back," Gaz said. "I just felt like it had to look *real*, like we'd been quarreling rather than anything to do with that mustachioed slug."

"Bowled Nick clean over," Joss said, leaning against the doorjamb. "It was almost hot."

"It was *extremely* hot," Cilla corrected.

Gaz looked proud, but just for a second. "I assumed I'd miss," he admitted.

I snorted and then covered my mouth and nose with both hands. "Shit, sorry. It's not funny," I said. "I just can't believe you were faster than Stout *and* Popeye. You are seriously impressive, Gaz."

"I'm a disaster," he said morosely. "I'm finally a sensational hunk of manhood, and it's going to get me chucked in the Tower."

"No," I said firmly. "It's going to get you a medal. You know as well as anyone how hard that guy would've sued the Royal Family. You totally stepped up."

"Too right," Cilla agreed.

Gaz flushed to the tips of his hair. "Cor," he said. "I just did what any mate would do."

Cilla threw the rag aside and took his face in her hands. "Garamond Bates, you did what only an *exceptional* mate would do," she said. And then she pulled him toward her, practically by the ears, and kissed him so hard he'd have seen stars if he weren't already. Gaz's obvious astonishment eventually faded as he wrapped his arms around Cilla and responded in kind.

Joss and I hadn't been sure our conversation was finished, but after a full minute passed in a fumbling blur of plummy auburn locks and vibrant carrot-colored ones, we backed away into her dining room.

"I had fifty quid on this happening right after we graduated," Joss said. "Could've used the cash back then. Christ, they're loud."

"I should go talk to Nick," I said. "I assume he's upstairs?"

"Is that *moaning*? Can I come with you?"

I just looked at her.

"Oh, all right." Joss grunted. "I suppose the good news is that now Cilla won't need to crash here when she's in the city. I should sublet and move in with Hunty. Maybe I'll go tell him the news."

"Good plan," I said, scooting to the stairs as Cilla roughly backed Gaz against the wall oven and Joss slipped out the front door, a protective hand over her eyes. I stared with trepidation up the steps, then started to climb toward what I'd been dreading.

Joss's flat was decorated in the style of someone with a pathological addiction to flea markets: odd geometric tables, fringed lampshades, colored glass jugs, and one entire shelf of brass candlesticks. Despite my nerves, I still almost snickered at the sight of Nicholas Wales lying on her green and pink-flowered bedspread, holding a bag of frozen corn over his face while a three-foot statue of David made out of chicken wire stood watch. I hadn't thought to ask if Nick knew I was coming, but when his eye opened and he saw me, he answered the unspoken question by sitting up so fast that the vegetable bag dropped onto his thigh. A vibrant bruise bloomed over his right cheekbone and up around to his temple, a butterfly bandage held together a cut over one eye, and his left hand was red and swollen and cut.

"What are you doing here?" he stammered.

I perched on the edge of the bed. It felt too intimate, but there was nowhere else to sit in Joss's room. "I heard the fastest fists in Britain were on the premises and I had to see for myself."

He glanced at his hand. "Pretty gruesome."

"I was talking about Gaz."

Nick's laugh quickly morphed into a sigh. "How's he faring?"

"I suspect he has never been better," I said, "considering he and Cilla are finally going at it downstairs. Apparently getting clocked in the jaw is an aphrodisiac."

Nick looked surprised, then very pleased, then agonized. "Be that as it may, I strongly recommend against getting into a fistfight," he said. "Everything hurts. Even my feet are screaming at me."

"So are Barnes, and Marj, I'll bet," I said.

"I made Freddie talk to them for me."

"You didn't have to do it," I said softly.

"Of course I did." He swung his legs around to sit next to me. "Freddie never does anything responsible. It was glorious making him handle those calls."

"What did he say?" I asked. "And don't give me any glib crap about Freddie. I'm talking about Mustache."

"I'd rather not repeat it."

"What do you think I'm going to do about it, Nick? Punch him?" I gave him a reproachful look. "Who'd be *that* stupid?"

"No one," Nick agreed. "That would be epically stupid."

"Even stupider than drinking Pimm's from a hose," I said.

"Even stupider than *Cats*."

"Even stupider than *Devour*."

"See, now you've gone too far," Nick said. "Don't make me defend your honor and *Devour*'s in the same night."

"Just tell me."

Nick looked queasy. "He said, 'So are you done slumming it with that Sofa Queen slag? Are we shot of that low-class bitch at last?'"

I let that wash over me; surprisingly, sadly, I found I'd heard its equal enough that I was now immune. Nick got up, creakily, and tugged at his hair, as if weighing what and how much more to say.

"He's been needling me for a while. I'd been out with Ceres a bit"—at this, he paused, but I managed to remain impassive—"and he'd started tossing out stuff here and there about your bikinis, or who you'd been with. You know how he is. Loves to get a rise. But he must've really wanted me to crack, because suddenly it got worse. Really misogynistic. I shouldn't have repeated it."

I shrugged. "He's said it to me, too. Nothing as American as *bitch*, but you English have a vibrant array of words for what he thinks I am. *Slapper*, that's a good one."

"None of them gives a toss about Freddie sleeping with half of London, but you chat up a movie star and it's open season," Nick said. "It's vile."

I closed my eyes briefly, and when I opened them again, he was looking at me protectively. But there was also a new emotional distance between us. I had been afraid I would come here and break down and dive at him, but instead maybe the tide was ebbing. I waited to have a feeling—of sadness, or remorse, of lust, of anything—but it was like I'd vomited them out hours ago and a country away, and so it was time, in classic Bex fashion, to just open my mouth and see what else came out of it.

"Thank you. I mean it," I said. "I'm touched that you stuck up for me. But you can't fight my battles anymore, Nick. It'll just make things worse for you."

"I am not going to let people talk about you like that," Nick said fiercely.

"And I lo—" I caught myself. "I *appreciate* you for feeling that way," I amended. "Mustache is a chauvinistic oaf, but let him be my problem. You have enough to worry about on your own."

Nick went quiet for a second. "What happened to you at Joss's party?" he asked.

I hadn't remembered to come up with a suave excuse for that one.

"Are you dating Ceres?" I asked instead.

"It's casual," he said. "Are you dating anyone?"

I thought of Clive. "Not even casually," I said, perhaps too emphatically, but Nick didn't seem to notice. "Did you really yell something in Majorca about being free at last?"

"I think I was referring to being off the ship, but I was rat-arsed at the time, so who knows," he said. "And you didn't answer my question about Joss's party."

"Okay, fine. I ran away," I confessed.

"From me?"

"Did you *see* my pants?"

"Only very briefly. You were moving quite fast," he said.

"Yeah. Well. This whole thing hasn't been easy for me," I told him.

"That makes two of us." He flexed his bruised hand. "You know, in that second before I swung, it felt really good to just do what I actually wanted to do, damn the consequences."

That he'd realized this, months beyond the point where it could have saved us, was something I'd rather not have known.

"Just don't get hurt punching people for me anymore," I said. "I can throw my own."

Nick looked at me for a long time. "I'll make you a deal," he said. "I will try not to assault people in your name if you stop running off anytime we bump into each other."

"I don't know if I can, Nick," I said. "I really *am* okay, or at least I will be. But I'm not ready to pal around London with you like we never happened."

He looked sad. "But this was a good step, right? Seeing each other, I mean. Not the Mustache part."

"It was a very good step. Let's take another one sometime."

We lapsed into silence, companionable, but still more remote than I could fathom feeling around someone I'd loved so much. Back in that stale Paris hotel room, I'd known I had to make some changes, but Nick's black eye drove home that I wasn't the only person who would benefit from me putting down the bottle and picking myself up instead.

"Is it always going to be like this, do you think?" I wondered.

"Like what?"

"Well, it's funny," I said. "When we were together, whatever I did blew back on you. Once we broke up, I assumed that would stop, but it hasn't. People will always connect the dots, and wonder if I'm pining for you, or if we're secretly hooking up, or if we hate each other. It never ends."

"You make it sound so appealing to have been with me," he said wryly.

"It was. I don't regret it for a second," I told him. "But it's just... a strange feeling. To be so tied to you in public now, when we never got to be tied to each other in public *then*. I guess being your girlfriend was temporary, but being your ex is for life." I shook my head. "I don't know. Maybe I'm just annoyed I couldn't go on as many dumb benders as it took to get over you without people judging me for it. And now it's made trouble for both of us."

"Bex, the only trouble you've ever been for me is the fun kind," he said gently.

And as our eyes met, the tide came in again. I had the turbulent thought that I could take his head in my hands and then just take *him*, like Cilla had with Gaz, and that he wanted me to and would let me. There was a softness in his bruised face, a hint of a question in his eyes. But if Nick and I were going to happen again, it couldn't be three hours after Clive's naked body inspired me to ralph in a hotel bathroom. I refused to be reckless with him. So I screwed up my nerve and turned away, and the charge fizzled as quickly as it had sparked.

Nick's phone buzzed. I stood to leave, but he held up a finger before answering.

"Cer, can you hang on a tick? Thanks. I'll just be a sec." He pushed mute. "I'm glad we talked," he said to me.

"I am, too." I meant it.

"Do we hug good-bye?"

"Better not," I said.

"Right," he said, rubbing his phone with his thumb.

As I rounded the corner and crept down the stairs, I heard him take Ceres off hold.

"Thanks, I just needed to fix my ice pack," he fibbed, his voice fainter as I got farther away. "Oh, just a bit puffy. I'm told it will be character-building..."

Joss's now-empty flat was dark and stuffy and, but for Cilla's bra swinging from a drawer pull in the kitchen, devoid of life. The clock said it was just gone eleven thirty a.m. but it felt like eleven at night. I wanted to talk to Lacey. I wanted to apologize to Dad. I wanted to take a shower. But most of all, I wanted to celebrate. I had seen Nick without bursting into tears, or flames, and as Joss's front door clicked shut behind me, I knew, at last, that when I slept I would wake up to some kind of fresh start.

# CHAPTER FOUR

"Four losses in a row, Bex. Twelve total and April isn't even near over." Dad's large, stubbly face filled the screen as he took off his battered ball cap and ran a hand through his salt-and-pepper hair. "The Cubs are going to be the death of me."

"Chin up, Dad," I said, yawning. "Literally. I can only see half your face."

It was a new baseball season, and Dad and I were picking one Cubs game each week and video chatting right after, when, as he put it, the agony or ecstasy was still fresh. I had woken up before dawn for today's rant, and although we were both bleary and bummed, I wouldn't have missed it. I'd spent too long being defensive and evasive with my parents because I was secretly upset with myself. It's the cruelest coincidence that the meeting with Nick that I'd so dreaded turned out to be the exact thing I needed to pull myself together, and I still catch myself wondering what might have happened if I'd reached out to Nick sooner, or at least said hello. But I always come back to the fact that running away was a necessary act of cowardice, begetting a necessary act of stupidity. I needed to hit rock bottom; I needed bleary regret.

Half of Mom suddenly ducked into the video frame. "Good night, Rebecca," she shouted, as if she had to carry her voice across the ocean.

"It's only good night for *you*," I said. "I still have to go to work."

She clucked. "The things you do for that team."

"It's the truest love there is," Dad intoned. "Well, except for one."

"Thank you, Earl," she said, right as Dad and I said in unison, "Cracker Jack."

"Oh, well, that's lovely. See if I make you my famous beef Wellington again," she huffed, as Dad pulled her onto his lap. "It was highly lauded by Hardware Pete and his wife. We had them over for dinner yesterday, Bex. *Much* nicer than Auto Sal from Sal's Auto."

She lovingly touched her screen, where I think my cheek must have been. "You do look so much better, sweetie. Happier. Or at least more solid."

"Thanks," I said. "I mean it. I know I was tough to take for a while there."

"You want tough, try Mrs. Auto Sal's brisket," Mom said.

I smiled as she prattled on about the offending meat. I did feel more solid. The first step in my recovery, not unlike what we used to do before going out and getting blitzed, had been establishing a solid base. I skulked into the Soane museum, apologized for my spotty attendance, and promised my boss, Maud, that I'd fired Jack Daniel's as my therapist. Maud is an extremely nice fortyish woman who is also a bit of a blank canvas—her hair is neither blond nor brown, yet also both; her features and wardrobe are plain, her thick hose as neutral as possible, and she and her mid-height, mid-weight boyfriend seem to eat only at mid-priced chains—and I think she was tickled that I confided in her, confidentiality agreements notwithstanding. I paid back her milky tea and sympathy by throwing myself into my job, the most successful product of which was convincing the Soane to turn an unused basement space into an art studio for at-risk children. We named it Paint Britain, and watching the kids revel in it inspired me to go back to my own art classes. And it was there that I met the first guy of about eight that I would date in the ensuing months—proper guys, employed, called when they said they would, stood when I got up from the table, remembered every detail a well-bred boyfriend ought. The one hitch was that I couldn't make out with any of them without feeling like my heart was stuck in my windpipe. Another stage of my *Irresponsible Ladies' Home Journal* Guide to Healing was supposed to be recalibrating via harmless romps—or, per the old adage, getting over someone by getting under someone else—but after my two-day tryst with the actor in Cannes, I'd lain awake worried that Nick had spoiled me on casual sex, because I couldn't stop making comparisons to him. And yet I wasn't ready for anything deeper; I had to hope someday I would be.

I focused in on my parents again as my mother was launching into an explanation of the origins of beef Wellington, and something caught my eye.

"Mom, what are you wearing?"

"Oh, this?" Mom fluffed the collar of her robe. "I'd gotten accustomed to the ones at The Dorch, so I bought one and personalized it, and now I have a piece of London here at home."

"Does it say *Lady Porter*?"

"Damn right," Dad said, nuzzling Mom's arm. "I *am* an Earl, after all."

"You two crazy kids," I said. "I have to go. I haven't had enough caffeine yet to watch my parents get all gross with each other."

"When will we see you again?" Dad asked.

"Next week, right? The Pirates are going to murder us tonight, and then the Reds . . . ugh."

"No, I mean, in person," he said. "Come for a game!"

Iowa still bore the taint of my post-breakup trip, so I'd avoided it, including convincing my parents to spend last Christmas in England (I know they saw through me, but luckily, they were totally on board). I did pine for that crack-of-dawn pilgrimage to Wrigley Field, though, wandering around Chicago in a daze to kill time before the game, then guzzling stadium food and sodas to fuel the five-hour ride home—as if our electric indignance about their performance, win or lose, wasn't enough. I missed that ritual.

"It's a date," I said. "Now go to sleep."

"Will you be watching Nicholas tonight?" Mom asked.

"Honey, maybe she doesn't want to talk about icholas-Nay," Dad said, nudging her.

"I do speak pig Latin, Dad," I said. "And it's fine. I promise. Lacey and I are going to watch it together."

"He's a very nice young man," Dad said. "I'm sure he'll do great."

"Earl!" Mom rapped his hat brim.

"What? He can be nice and still undeserving of our beloved first-born," he said.

"Good night, guys. I love you," I said, laughing as I closed my laptop.

Nick hadn't taken much of a beating, pun intended, for his fisticuffs with Gaz. Their cover had either worked, or Mustache's colleagues played along with the party line to avoid a blacklisting, and the public forgot about the set-to as soon as something more interesting happened—like Prince Edwin's wife Elizabeth delivering a "premature" baby boy seven-ish months after the wedding, whose weight miraculously reached nine pounds by the time he equally miraculously went home three days later. So on the occasion of Freddie's twenty-fifth birthday, instead of a party the likes of which had been thrown for Nick—if this bothered Freddie, he never said—the boys had agreed to a rare joint appearance on the BBC. Beyond the surface PR objective of showing them grown-up and diligently serving Britain, this interview had a slew of ulterior motives: to remind the public it was rather fond of Nick even if his decision-making was not unimpeachable, and to distract everyone from analyzing Elizabeth's pregnancy timeline.

Lacey had moved to her own place in South Kensington—she claimed having a roommate cramped her personal life—and because I passed out at geriatric hours these days, I only ever saw her on weekends, if she wasn't out with Freddie or a shiny new guy. But we'd both agreed that this weeknight special with the Brothers Wales deserved its own private viewing party, bolstered with port wine and a ripe Stilton. While we waited for it to start, she dove into my pile of newspapers.

"Not *one* report from that film festival in Brixton last night," she complained.

"Since when are you a fan of... what was it? 'Gritty Hungarian noir cinema'?" I asked.

"Obviously I don't care about that," she said. "But Philip emceed it, and he brought me, and I wore the best green dress. I even gave Clive a heads-up, but nothing."

Interest in the Ivy League had waned once I stopped making a spectacle of myself, and it hadn't escaped me that Lacey's subsequent social choices had the warmth of the spotlight in common. She'd dallied with a lawyer named Maxwell, son of Baron Something-Something; an up-and-coming celebrity chef named Dev; and a footballer who'd immediately fallen off his game, and thus broke up with her before his debut with the Dutch national team. She was now seeing both Penelope Six-Names's cohost, Philip Frogge-Whitworth (it was a hyphenpalooza on *Morning Zoo*) and some DJ I could never remember. I didn't know how she had the energy.

Before I came up with anything ego-soothing to say, a graphic on the TV screen coalesced into the words *On Heir with Katie Kenneth*. Lacey plonked a massive slice of cheese onto a cracker.

"Do you think they'll be in suits, or their uniforms?"

"Suits," I said. "The uniforms are too obvious."

"I bet you a cocktail it's uniforms," she said. "For the full impact."

We were both right: The hour-long special opened with Freddie and Nick on the job—Lacey sighed audibly when Freddie landed a rescue copter with extreme panache, although I privately thought shooting finger guns at the camera was a bit much—before transitioning into a sit-down interview in which they wore elegant but not ostentatious jackets and ties. Nick was in high spirits (when asked why he hadn't pursued being a pilot, he cracked, "I can't fly with a peg leg") and Freddie was, well, Freddie.

"Think of me as the court jester," he'd said with a twinkle, when asked about his bad-boy image. "Nick and my father have a heavy responsibility in their futures, and they handle it with care. My job is to get into enough trouble for both of them, to balance the ledger."

"He makes out like he's such a gigolo," Lacey said, crunching through another cracker.

"That's because he *is*," I said.

"Sure, but he'll come around," she said. "I think he wants more than just some flavor of the month. Their phones stop ringing eventually. Mine hasn't."

I turned to look at her, but she studiously did not meet my gaze.

On TV, the fiftysomething Katie Kenneth asked Nick about Emma—he'd lied, with that long-practiced façade of calm, that she was helping them choose charities for their patronage—before segueing into a line of questioning that I was surprised had been approved.

"You've been linked with Gemma Sands, Ceres Whitehall de Villency, and even American Rebecca Porter," Katie said, frowning as if this were as vital as a conversation about genocide. "We're all hungering for a royal wedding. Are you game?"

"Ugh," I said to the TV.

But Nick simply laughed charmingly. "Are you proposing to me, Katie?"

"Please. Everyone knows I'm the real catch," Freddie said.

"You know I don't usually comment on this," Nick said pleasantly. "But I will say that I can't simply decide I want a wedding and plug in the first bride that appears. I take my military duties seriously. I take my royal duties seriously. And I take commitment to another person seriously, as she'd be my partner for life and beside me at the helm of the country someday. I want to make the right choice, and that cannot be rushed."

"That was well done," Lacey said.

"Beats 'ask me in a decade.'" I couldn't pretend that didn't still sting.

"And I know it's tempting to speculate, and to track and trace the movements of the women who are important to me," Nick continued. "But I would like to ask the public and the press to show them some mercy. I accept what comes with my birthright for myself, but I don't have to accept it for them. I cannot brook with a person being made to feel unsafe simply for having cared about me."

As he looked full into the camera at the end, I swear I felt his eyes on me, and in a flash, mine were wet.

"He's a class act, that one," Lacey said, then heaved a comical sigh. "I wish he would have given them the all-clear to hound *me*, though. I have much cuter clothes than I used to, and, like, hi, give some love to a girl who puts on heels to go to Tesco."

She stood and brushed cracker crumbs onto my carpet. "Come on, we officially owe each other a drink."

I shook my head. "I have an early staff meeting tomorrow. And I still don't think I'm fully detoxed from the first year of being single."

Lacey eyed me suspiciously. "You never did tell me what made you decide to dry out."

Our psychic twin abilities had dissipated a bit lately, but she still knew I was withholding something, and she didn't like it. But Paris was too dangerously juicy. Clive and I had only even discussed it to reassert that we would never discuss it. I certainly didn't want to relive it, and he needed to keep Davinia loyal, given that her entire life was one long roster of connections he still hoped to leverage for his own column at the *Recorder* (although so far he'd produced only biased profiles, buried in the middle of the paper, of her father's rich friends and their self-indulgent charity efforts, like a benefit for something called the British Association for the Proliferation of Philanthropic Events—M. C. Escher fecklessly reinterpreted). No, the truth of Paris was nonnegotiable, even with Lacey. Maybe especially with her. Because I couldn't swear she wouldn't whisper it to Freddie, and that was like telling the town crier.

"My liver begged for mercy," I said instead. It was close enough.

"Very funny," Lacey said. "You're going to waste your prime years if you don't get back on the party horse at least a little. Come on. For me? For the Ivy League?"

"Lace, he just asked the press to lay off," I said. "I will look like a total jackass if I run right out and tempt them into a chase."

Lacey fell back against the couch cushions and crossed her arms over her chest. "I miss my partner in crime," she said petulantly. "We don't live together and now we don't have much of a *life* together, either."

I reached out and poked her with my big toe.

"Get that thing off me," she said. So I poked again. "Ew, I'm serious, Bex, you know I hate feet."

But she was laughing, and so was I.

"We can go out next weekend, I promise," I said, wiggling a cheese-topped cracker in her face, another button I knew I could push.

"Okay," she said, but I could tell she was still smarting. "You win. But only for tonight."

To look at the area around Lincoln's Inn Fields, the largest public square in London, you'd think you'd stumbled upon a residential neighborhood—which, in fact, it used to be. The three- and four-story brick or stone buildings once housed a variety of highborn folk who must have had a real thrill in 1683 when a would-be assassin of King Charles II was beheaded there. Maybe watching a public murder during afternoon tea is why they all moved west and gave up their real estate to the business world. Queen Eleanor's lawyers have an office there, as does the Royal College of Surgeons, and at numbers twelve, thirteen, and fourteen, there's Sir John Soane's Museum, my professional home and my refuge.

Sir John was an architect, and an inveterate hoarder, and the space is crammed to the gills with his eclectic souvenirs: almost eight thousand books, sixty or so Greek and Roman vases, three hundred and twenty-three gemstones, a pair of leg irons, and a mummified cat. The byzantine, tight space means the museum only admits eighty people at a time, and it scrupulously bans cell phones, so it could never become dangerously jammed with amateur paparazzi once people figured out I was on staff. This meant I could fill in for a docent without causing much of a stir, and I was grateful not to be treated like a plague (if my notoriety was good for business, the Soane never once exploited that). And in late May, I hit the jackpot. The Soane was so pleased that Paint Britain was a hit—bigger museums were sniffing around about partnerships—that my boss Maud rewarded me with the Picture Room when the regular docent caught a mysterious rash. The Picture Room is a compact space where Soane ingeniously turned the walls into doors as a way of multiplying the amount of art he could display. Every twenty minutes, whoever is assigned to that room opens them to display a layer, sometimes two, of hidden paintings and architectural renderings hiding behind them. All told, there are about a hundred, usually commanding the most experienced historians.

And the space is snug. So after I gave my second pack of gawkers a moment to appreciate the initial view, I hustled all twelve of them back out and pulled open the south planes to reveal William Hogarth's *A Rake's Progress*. The eight paintings depict a debauched evening of gambling, drinking, and whoring in an infamous London tavern before the titular rake is imprisoned and then sent to Bedlam, and in Soane's day it was considered scandalous. As I explained this, an eleven-year-old boy near the front made bored clicking noises.

"If it's so scandalous," he scoffed, "then where are the sexy bits?"

"An excellent question," said a guy in the back in a dark ball cap, a leather jacket, and aviators, whom I hadn't noticed earlier. "Where *are* all the sexy bits?"

And then Freddie took off his sunglasses, grinning, and stuffed them into his pocket.

"Holy shitballs," an American girl hissed.

"Shh, don't make a stir, or we'll lose the intimacy of this moment," Freddie told her. "I love *A Rake's Progress*. Also the working title of my autobiography."

Everyone tittered, except the cranky octogenarian who'd asked me if this was the Tate.

"You heard the young man," Freddie prodded me. "I believe he wanted sexy bits."

I glanced at the boy's mother, but she seemed as interested in where this might lead as the rest of the room, so I pointed to the orgy in the third painting. The kid peered closer.

"I've seen worse on TV," he said.

"I'll be the judge of that," Freddie said, edging to the front. "You're right. Hugely disappointing. What I've been longing to see, though, are some saucy drawings of *buildings*." He rubbed his hands together. "Are there any of *those* sexy bits around, please, madam?"

"But of course," I said, stifling a laugh as I closed up *A Rake's Progress* and opened the opposite planes. I sped through the rest of the spiel, so as not to give Freddie much time to make a spectacle of himself; he did his best PPO Furrow imitation and clapped loudly when I finished.

"Brilliant," he said. "Ladies and gentlemen, please head down to whatever terrifying hellhole that rickety staircase takes you to."

"That's the Monk's Parlour," I explained. "For the imaginary monk."

They stared at me blankly, then clattered down into the basement.

"This Soane chap really was a nutter, eh?" Freddie said, the floorboards creaking under his feet as he took in the sheer quantity of stuff—no, Stuff—all around us. "I only own one piece of art. It's a photo of me scoring a goal past Father at a polo match, and it's priceless."

"I hate to break it to you, but I'm pretty sure you own a lot more art than that," I said. "How did you get in without anyone freaking out?"

"A lady named Maud let me in the back," he said. "She's a firecracker, that one. Told me she's knitting trivets as a wild change of pace from scarves. If you're keeping score, that means changing from a rectangle all the way to a square."

"That's our Maud," I said affectionately.

"I hope to be a steadying influence on her, in time," Freddie said. "But first, come have a long lunch and a pint."

"I can't blow off work anymore, Freddie."

"Aha, but I told Maud I was on a fact-finding mission about fundraising."

"Is that true?"

"Perhaps," he said. "And if Maud thinks you chucked a potential patron, she'll never speak to you again about how the bridge tips from the Sunday *Times* are working."

We dined at one of the ancient gentlemen's clubs to which the monarchy belongs—or, perhaps, which belong to the monarchy. It was a dimly lit cavern full of burnished oak and leather and antique globes no one ever spun, and was staffed solely by cantankerous old men, one of whom seated us with a whiff of mistrust and stepped on my foot as he went.

"Don't mind him," Freddie said. "He's been making that face ever since Gran forced them to let in women."

He ordered a shepherd's pie and I got a big plate of crispy battered cod and chips; we made small talk until the food arrived, at which point Freddie picked up the table's bottle of malt vinegar and deluged my fries before taking a few.

"You're welcome," I said dryly.

"I know," he said smugly, poking one of the chips into the mashed-potato top of his pie. A belch of steam came out. "I miss giving you a hard time, Killer. Why don't you ever come out with Lacey and me anymore?"

"Wait, so first I was partying too hard, and now I'm not partying enough?"

"A mild over-correction," he said. "Easily repaired."

I took an extra-large bite of fish, to our waiter's consternation. "I don't understand why you're not nearly as paranoid as Nick is about the media," I said. "We both know why he's so sensitive, but why aren't you?"

Freddie tapped his knife against his plate thoughtfully. "I think I was too young. Nick actually has memories of Mum." He all but mouthed the word. "I envy him those, sometimes. But then I think maybe his normal memories, of *before*, make the bad ones that much worse. Maybe having nothing at all is better." He stared into the distance. "It's a bit like when you hear about a plane crash, and it's awful, but it also doesn't haunt your life. Nick was on the plane when it went down, and I just read about it in the papers. Does that make sense?"

"Perfect sense." I let it settle for a second. "It's hard to explain to Lacey sometimes, though. Not that I mind keeping your confidence, but I feel bad that she'll never understand the whole story. She's actually *miffed* Nick tried to call off the paparazzi. Like she's being denied her rightful place in the papers."

"I doubt it's that simple," Freddie said.

"Says the expert on my twin."

"In some areas, I probably am," he said, and I snorted. "Not *those* areas," he chided. "I mean, yes, those too, but what I mean is, Lacey is the only other person I know who understands being the spare." He swigged his scotch. "It is a peculiar person to be."

It was disarmingly, alarmingly, honest, and it hit me so hard that I actually leaned back in my chair with a thump.

"Freddie," I said. "Nobody thinks of either of you that way. 'The heir and the spare' is just a jokey expression."

"Perhaps to you," Freddie said. "Truthfully, I think Knickers would rather be that than the heir sometimes. I'm sure he thinks it looks easier, and in some ways it is, but..." He shrugged. "Everyone had expectations of Nick, or for Nick. Nobody ever had any of me. And after a while they didn't have much interest in me, either."

I bit my thumbnail, unsure of what to say.

"But Nick might have it worse," he continued. "My biggest problem is feeling pointless, and his biggest problem is that he basically *is* the point, and that consumes his whole life. So if I can muck about with outrageous people and give Dick something else to fume about, I'll do it."

"Only you could get away with turning serial dating into a selfless act," I teased. "But I hate that you feel so superfluous. Does Lacey honestly feel that way, too? Do I treat her like that?"

"No," Freddie said firmly. "Sometimes it's hard not to feel like *the other one*, that's all. But I probably shouldn't be speaking for her. Just give her time to find her own footing."

"Well, since we *are* speaking for her," I said, gesturing at him with my fork, "she'd kill me for saying this, but I think she feels a connection that may not be there for you, and if it's not, I'm scared she's going to get really hurt."

"I know. I don't want that," he said sheepishly. "I've been selfish about it, because she's hard to give up. She's clever, and she's fun. Even if her sister is a bit of an ogress." He drummed his fingers. "Perhaps in another life, she'd be it for me, but in this one it's not very realistic."

"It could be," I said. "Your roadblock is gone, remember."

"Aha, but I think we both know that even if you're not quite *in* Nick's life, you're never actually gone from it, either," Freddie said.

We lapsed into our thoughts, filling the air with the clattering of our silverware. I felt guilty for talking about Lacey with him, but I couldn't keep turning a blind eye to how much she hoped for more and how little Freddie thought he could give it.

"This lunch took a somber turn," he said. "I thought we were going to trade juicy personal gossip."

"That would have been a lot more interesting for you six months ago."

"Still, let's give it a whack," he said. "I'll go first. Nigel got chucked out of St. Andrews. He had cocaine in his room."

"Damn. Awful Julian must be so proud," I said. "My turn. Gaz and Cilla hooked up the night he punched Nick."

"Finally!" Freddie crowed. "Nick didn't bloody tell me, the bastard. I wonder if I won the pool. Right, let's see. Barnes had a girlfriend for about twenty minutes and it made him into an entirely different and wonderful person."

"I can't imagine a pleasant Barnes," I said.

"He sang a lot of show tunes," Freddie said. "He's quite a good Sally Bowles, it turns out. You're up. With one about *you* this time, please."

"Yours weren't about you, either!"

Freddie frowned. "If I must. Persimmon slept with Tony after I wouldn't let her plan a birthday party for me," he said.

"My last boyfriend had a third nipple."

"My new girlfriend's name is Santa."

I cackled so loudly that our ancient waiter had to sit down and collect himself at a nearby table—which already had three diners at it.

"You made that up!" I accused him.

"It's deadly true." He grinned smugly. "She has a large bag of toys."

"Well, Third Nip and I broke up because he found it erotic to suck on—"

"No! My virgin ears!" Freddie laughed, grabbing them.

"—my *chin*," I finished. "It's rough out there, Freddie. This is why I'm all nights in and quiet country house parties now. It's all I can take."

Freddie polished off his pie. "Shows how much you know. I've gotten into more trouble at country house parties than anywhere else," he said. "I take it you're going to Cilla's do?"

Cilla's sister owned a home in the countryside of Berkshire, which differed from her home in the countryside of Yorkshire by about two thousand square feet and a swimming pool. Apparently she'd refused to leave the family birthplace, so her rich husband bought them a mansion they could remodel, in the hopes of making her fall in love with it and want to live there permanently. Cilla had permission to throw a weekender there before they knocked it to rubble.

"I was thinking about it," I said. "It sounds relaxing."

"It won't be," he said. "But I think you can handle it. You don't need another calm weekend reading some big fat book."

"How about a civilized game of croquet?"

Freddie grinned. "Not unless you think strip croquet is civilized."

"Depends on who's stripping."

He tipped his scotch to me. "There's the Bex I remember."

# CHAPTER FIVE

T*he time Nicholas and Rebecca spent apart was exquisite agony*, Aurelia Maupassant proclaimed, before spending two and a half *Bexicon* pages glossing over my bikini period, Nick's apparent dustup with Gaz, and a variety of other juicy transgressions she could've unearthed if she had wanted to confront reality. Instead, she claimed we were saintly hermits:

> They devoted their time to self-enrichment, firming up the deep strength of character with which they will lead this great nation into the future. While Nicholas bravely fought for our shores, Rebecca immersed herself in professional pursuits and charitable endeavours, and, as the consummate sportswoman, to perfecting her tennis game.

"That ball was out, Bex. DRINK," Gaz bellowed.

"Too close to call," Lacey said from a deck chair that was doubling as an umpire's seat. "That means you both drink."

"What's the score?" I asked.

Lacey blinked. "Whoops. Six? Is that a thing in tennis?"

Gaz invented Drunk Doubles years ago, because he said he wasn't comfortable letting someone club a yellow missile at him unless he was off his head. The rules change a lot because no one ever quite remembers them, but it starts with guzzling something potent if you lose a point or a set, if you ace a serve, at deuce, and at match point. The longer it goes, the harder it gets to *see* the ball, much less hit it, so it devolves into ineptitude and arguments and offers of replacement dares. I had already played an entire game wearing Gaz's trousers, my partner Joss served backward, and for the last two points, Cilla had worn socks on her hands. Freddie had been right; the weekend was not, perhaps, a bucolic PBS-style affair.

We'd drawn up to the three-story ivy-covered manse late Friday night and woken in the morning to an actual rooster crowing and Bloody Marys on the peaceful terrace. Freddie's warnings had seemed misplaced, until lunchtime came, and with it, a steady stream of thirsty guests. By the time we'd reached this late-afternoon stalemate at Drunk Doubles, there was an equally boozy game of lawn bowling down by the vegetable garden, suspicious smoke wafting from the tree house, and some convoluted gin-soaked swim relay. The estate teemed with the kind of young, preppy aristocrats who regularly retired to the country to escape the rigors of day jobs they bemoaned yet could never explain in specific terms. I vaguely knew a handful of them from Clive's glossy party reports, but I wasn't sure how they connected to Cilla, and she was too busy snogging Gaz on the court to ask.

"I think we win by default," Joss declared.

"Hang on, you can't punish a man for being in love," Gaz shouted.

"Love means nothing in tennis," I said. "Literally, in fact."

As I reclaimed my pint from a peeling wooden bench, I spied Clive sitting by the pool, tapping away on his laptop and chatting to the dreaded Gemma Sands and Lady Bollocks—the former of whom I'd still never met and didn't care to, and the latter of whom I was equally pleased to avoid. There were several single guys milling around whom Cilla had invited as a favor to those of us who were likewise uncoupled; one of them, appealingly, resembled Brad Pitt in his prime. He was playing a game of (non-strip) croquet with Freddie, and he was bracingly hot.

"Now *that* is a view," Lacey said, slinging an arm around my neck. "You want dibs?"

"They're all yours," I said.

"Well, yeah, I know you don't want Freddie," she said. "But that other guy might do nicely." She grinned naughtily. "For either of us, if Freddie doesn't get his act together."

"May the best Porter win," I said with a smile.

She pulled my ponytail. "Done. But we have to clean up first. You look like you were just electrocuted."

Cocktail hour coincided with one of England's more cinematic summer twilights, scented by a blooming, exuberant garden growing up around the old stone terrace where we congregated. Movers were coming to the house in three days to clear out the antiques worth keeping—Cilla's brother-in-law bought it furnished—and the rest of the gabled building and its picturesque patio would be demolished and built into something bigger and more modern and probably uglier. I wondered if Cilla's sister had even seen it; to me, its cracks and chips gave this old place character.

I didn't get to luxuriate in any of it, though, because Lady Bollocks marched right up to me as soon as I walked through the terrace doors. I'd hoped to summon enough sorcery to escape her entirely, but the sight of her so inflamed—angular brows, squinting eyes, sequined minidress shooshing as she stomped toward me—against such an august backdrop was so amusing that my nerves abandoned me.

"That isn't awful," she greeted me, flicking a finger at my slim-fitting patterned dress. "Which can only mean you didn't pick it out yourself."

"Oh, buzz off, Bea," I said. "If that's all you have to say, then go back to ignoring me."

Bea took a sharp bite out of her martini olive. "Someone had to pick Nick in the divorce."

"Most people had the strength of character to choose both," sassed Lacey from her perch on the low stone wall of the terrace, where she was nursing a bottle of something orange-flavored called Hooch.

"Frankly, I'm beginning to see why Nick should have picked *you*, having been forced to endure all the other nitwits coming after him lately," Bea said.

"I'm sorry my breakup has been so difficult for you," I said. "How's your sister?"

"Fucking great," said a raven-haired girl who uncoiled herself from a chair near Lacey.

I peered closer at her. "*Pudge?*"

"I go by Larchmont Kent now," she said. She was groomed to within an inch of her life, with luxurious long hair, and wore a slouchy white romper that was insanely ugly in that annoying way where it also looked fabulous. She appeared to be sans underwear.

"She's modeling," Bea said, prickly pride masking a bit of concern. "Discovered by a scout who was in rehab with her at the Priory last time. She just did Japanese *Vogue*."

"Fashion is redemption," Ex-Pudge said dreamily. "No judgment. Just an embrace."

Bea squinted at her. "Are you high *now*?"

"If you mean high on serenity, then yes," she said patiently. "I was meditating. I may need to find the koi pond."

"There's a koi pond?" I asked Bea, looking at her sister's retreating figure.

"Focus." Bea snapped her fingers in front of my face. "I will only say this once, so listen well. You are far less irritating than Nick's other options, so I need you to get back together."

"Oh! Well, if *that's* what you want," I said.

"It is," Bea said, missing my sarcasm. "You were good for him. He was so much lighter with you. If only you'd met last year, it would have been considerably easier for everyone."

"Yeah, Bex really blew it for you," Lacey said.

"Your face need not be part of this, so feel free to shut it," Bea said haughtily.

"Bea, I appreciate what you're trying to do," I said, trying to mean it. "But Nick and I have moved on."

Bea arched her crazy-arched brow, which I hadn't imagined was possible. "Are you quite sure?" she said.

I would have thrown up my hands with frustration, except I didn't want to spill my Pimm's Cup. "I sent him back a box of his sweaters. It's over."

"Oh, please, that's absurd. He probably never even got them." She poked me in the sternum. "I saw you dribbling over the eye candy this afternoon, and my advice is that you do not touch. Nick will be ready soon enough."

"What? Like a pan of brownies?" Lacey asked. "It's not 1925. She's not going to twiddle her thumbs and wait patiently while Nick is off playing solider and sleeping around."

"I'm not suggesting she take up needlepoint," Bea countered. "I'm merely saying that timing is everything."

"And our timing was terrible," I pointed out.

"Once," Bea said airily. "Maybe not forever."

"Stop fucking with my head, Bea."

"I am *fixing* your head," she said. "And before you decide to listen to your sister on this topic, may I remind you which of us has known Nick since—hang on, is that Duddy Fitzherbert? He cheated me out of the most beautiful filly at Tattersalls. I have *words* for him."

She swept off.

"She apparently has words for everyone today," I said to Lacey. "I wonder if she showed up with a list."

"Do not let her get to you," Lacey told me. "Nick hasn't given you any indication that he is coming back."

"I know," I said.

"And you will regret wasting time on a faint hope."

"I *know*."

"You're not getting any younger."

"Now who's acting like it's 1925?" I retorted.

"I just don't want you to get sucked into Bea's magical thinking," Lacey said.

"I doubt Bea's engaged in magical anything in her entire life," I said. "And I don't want to spend the rest of mine talking about how I almost ended up with Nick. Can we move on?"

"Sure," Lacey said, gesturing with her bottle of Hooch. "Freddie's over there with Penelope Six-Names. What's that about? He can't be into her."

"Here's a challenge," I said. "Let's see if we can avoid talking about Wales boys altogether."

Lacey glared at me. "I'm not sure if you're less fun with Nick, or without him," she said, and walked away, leaving me with plenty of people staring but nobody who wanted to talk.

In that moment I decided I might hate country house parties.

Suddenly, a gong rang out; I turned to see Gaz standing near the French doors, beating a giant golden disc hanging from a wooden frame with a carved Chinese dragon across the top.

"Dinner is served," he announced.

"You'll make a great butler someday," I teased. He responded by bopping me on the arm with the velvet-covered mallet.

The dining room had a mahogany sideboard that functioned as a hot-food buffet, and a massive table in the middle of the room covered with cold dishes. I grabbed a plate and fell in line behind Clive, who was juggling his with a white wine spritzer. There are a lot of reasons Clive never turned my crank enough to be the love of my life, and one of them is that he likes white wine spritzers.

"That looked like a fun scene outside," he said.

I stabbed some roast beef like it had insulted me. "The next person who says N... um, *Steve's* name gets a fork through the neck."

"Watch out, Clive. She's always been a danger to others," Freddie said, cutting in behind me. "Who are half of these people, anyway?"

"How it is possible *you* don't know?" Clive asked as we carried our plates to the bottom of the house's sweeping, chipped wood staircase and sat down to eat. "I'd have assumed you'd slept with at least that many."

"A gentleman never kisses and tells," Freddie said. "Certainly not to a reporter."

Clive waved his glass. "This entire party is off the record."

"Nothing is ever really off the record," Freddie said. "I'm actually surprised you're free today, Clive, what with so many important galas to cover, like Lord Whatsit's Charity Pet Statue Auction."

"Reporters need to keep their feet on the ground," Clive said, missing the insult. "I am massaging my sources. Speaking of..."

He nodded at a fetching brunette giving him the eye from across the foyer. Clive and Davinia were still together, as far as I knew, but she was in London, and clearly no handsome, ambitious party reporter—or at least not this handsome, ambitious party reporter—worked a room with total chastity.

"That's Hilly Heath-Hedwig's niece," he told us. "She'll have loads to say about *that* divorce."

As he left, Freddie made a gagging face. "I prefer his brothers," he confided. "They might be clods, but they're also very straightforward."

"Clive is *lovely*," I said, before I caught myself.

"Point proven."

"Why are you here on your own?" I asked. "Santa too busy in her workshop?"

"Making toys for other boys," he said. "If you must know, I'm currently single."

"Are you ill?" I gasped, feeling his forehead.

"Cute," he smirked, swatting me away. "No, I've just been thinking about something you said a while back. It *is* rather juvenile, selecting my girlfriends specifically to annoy Father. So I'm taking a break." He nudged my empty plate. "Which we are supposed to do, too, from each other. At dinner parties it's customary to change conversation partners between courses."

"Please, let's not," I said, pointing to the couple behind us on the landing, who were alternately fighting and feeding each other cornichons. "I can't jump into that."

Through the wide archway into the family room, I spied Lacey leaning against a mantel, twirling her hair and chatting up none other than British Brad Pitt.

"I might have wanted to jump into *that*, but it looks like I'm too late," I added.

Freddie looked guilty. "I believe I led that lamb to the slaughter."

I smacked him in the arm. "Are you saying you pimped out my sister?"

"I merely hinted—in the form of an explicit statement—that he'd do well to talk to Lacey because she's very nice and very available."

"So am I!" I protested.

"Yes, but *you're* not on my scent," he said. "As part of this new leaf

I've turned over, I also considered that since it's inevitable that we'll get drunk and stupid, I should make sure Lacey is otherwise occupied."

My phone buzzed in my purse, which was a surprise. Almost everyone I knew was at this party. But the ID indicated an unknown caller.

"Miss Porter, this is Barnes," the voice on the other end said, sounding a lot more relaxed than the Barnes I knew. "I have the Prince of Wales on the line for you."

I rolled my eyes. "Very funny, Gaz, but Barnes sounds more like he's been impaled on a spike."

At that very moment, I saw Gaz scurry across the hallway, demonstrably not on the phone. Freddie's eyes bugged out and my stomach sank.

"When you're through being hoisted on that petard, Miss Porter, kindly loan it to me so I may resume a more familiar demeanor," Barnes said. "Please hold for the Prince of Wales."

*Richard*, I mouthed at Freddie. He looked utterly nonplussed, and I'm sure so did I.

"Miss Porter, I trust you're well this evening." Richard's voice was as chilly as ever.

"*Fuck* you and your Volvo, Damian. Go park it up your girlfriend's massive backside!" shrieked the girl behind us on the landing, storming upstairs in a tornado of tears.

"Yes, Your Highness, having a nice quiet night," I said, biting my lip and shaking my head. Next to me, Freddie mimed hanging himself.

"I wanted to speak to you about Paint Britain," he said. "It's been mentioned to me that several London museums are helping to grow the program, and as an artist myself, I should like to offer my patronage. Congratulations."

I almost pitched forward off the stairs. Freddie steadied me with his hand. "Sir, that's *amazing*, everyone will be so fuc—er, fantastically thrilled," I said, tripping over my tongue and its more purple tendencies. "Thank you, Your Highness, your generosity and—"

"Let's not prolong this any longer than necessary," Prince Dick said, and rang off.

I stared at the phone in my hand, then up at Freddie, dazed. "I thought you were joking the other day about discussing philanthropic ventures."

"I was," Freddie said, surprised.

"Then tell me how Paint Britain just got itself a patronage from your father." I couldn't even blink. "Did Nick, or . . . are you sure you . . ."

"It wasn't me," he said. "And Knickers is out to sea. Father must've just thought it was a cracking idea. It's a bloody miracle."

Joy shot through me. In that moment, I decided I might love country house parties.

Freddie gave me a *wait right there* gesture and ran off, then returned holding a bottle of Veuve Clicquot. "Do not go into the kitchen. Gaz is weeping over a fallen soufflé and the noises he's making will curdle your soul," he said. "Come with me. We're celebrating. Did I see a tree house?"

We swigged from the bottle and toasted our way outside. Inky night had dropped like a cloak, but still the tree house loomed large, wrapped fully around the massive oak like something right out of *Swiss Family Robinson*. Through the dark, I spied the outline of a homemade bridge high up in the foliage, accessible by ladder, stretched between the fort's roof and another tree. I made a beeline for it.

"I doubt it ever even crossed Prince Dick's mind to get his bothersome sons a tree fort," Freddie said, following me as I scrambled up the ladder. "My future sprog shall definitely have one. Lucky old Galahad, Murgatroyd, and Bob."

I reached the top and found myself on a wooden platform at the mouth of the bridge, which was made largely of rope, old planks, netting, and probably a dash of chewing gum and hope.

"Are you sure this isn't going to kill us?" Freddie asked warily.

I tested the bridge with my foot; it swayed a bit, but seemed sturdy. I darted halfway across and gave Freddie the thumbs-up.

"Man up and get your ass out here, Captain Wales," I said.

"I'm holding precious cargo!" he protested, waving the Veuve bottle. But he took a step and then, feeling more secure, jumped up and down a bit. The bridge creaked cooperatively but did not give.

"Pretty cool," Freddie said. "Galahad will love this. He's going to be an architect, see. Murgatroyd is more into science, and Bob will be a third-rate stage actor."

"Poor Bob."

He shrugged. "Bob's also going to be a bit of a shithead."

I laughed, then raced the last few feet, which made the bridge quiver extra tenuously for Freddie's final crossing; he looked relieved when he stepped onto the tree house roof. We weren't quite high enough up to see over the lush hedges that flanked the property, but from this deep in the garden, the drunken cacophony of the party sounded more like a symphony, and the sky was starting to twinkle. As I retrieved the Veuve from Freddie, he looked at what we'd just traversed.

"Stout should never have let me do that," Freddie said. "Wherever he is."

Suddenly, a low moaning noise escaped from the fort underneath us. I put my finger to my lips and crept around until I spotted an open trapdoor in the roof, then lay down on my stomach and peeked through it. The moonlight bounced off a sequined dress lying in a heap on the floor, and a trail of clothes led partway behind the thick tree trunk. I shimmied further and ducked my head through the opening, and there was none other than Beatrix Larchmont-Kent-Smythe, clad only in underwear, her mouth working its passionate way down a pale leg.

A very pale, very shapely, very female leg.

I had scooted in a touch too far, and started to slip. I gasped, involuntarily, and just as I felt Freddie reach out to save me, Bea whipped around her head.

"This tree house is occupied."

"Oh, it's *you,*" Bea snapped.

"Who is it, pet?" whispered the hidden woman, who must have sat up abruptly, because her long, wavy red tresses swung into view.

Gemma Sands. Whose compelling heterosexuality I had feared was tempting Nick into all manner of disloyalties while we were dating; whose bed I'd assumed Nick took to after we ended. The notion of her and Bea as a couple didn't hit me nearly so hard as the astonishment at how far off my paranoia had been... and the regret over whether I'd made a huge, huge mistake.

"Well, *this* is juicy," Freddie said, sticking his head through the trapdoor.

Bea pursed her lips. "Yes, well, now you know," she said. "I'm a highly erotic creature and I'm seeing a woman. Can we all close our mouths now?"

She crossed her arms over her naked chest with an impressive amount of dignity.

Gemma peeked around the tree. "Er, hello, Freddie. And you must be Bex."

"In the flesh," I said, still stunned. "And I'll be honest, part of me kind of wishes we'd met this way two or three years ago."

"No, this is much better." Freddie wiggled his brows suggestively. "In fact, I might need a closer look. What if it's their first time? They might need an advisor—"

"Pass," Gemma said tartly. "Now, I haven't seen this one in two very long weeks, so would you mind leaving us to it?"

"No, of course! I mean, yes. Good-bye," I stammered, and pulled Freddie out of the trapdoor by the back of his collar.

"You're no fun," he said, pouting, as we scurried back to ground level. "But may I just say, well *played*, Bea!"

We cracked up, although in my own laugh I could hear a manic fringe. Bea had known Gemma wasn't a threat. What if she'd told me? What if, what if, what if.

I grabbed the Champagne and drank deeply all the way back to the house. Our delight—Freddie's genuine, mine distracted—morphed into a tipsy mischief, and we decided it was our mission to ferret out as many other illicit lovebirds as we could find. We poked through everything from paisley-walled guest rooms to an impressive cathedral-ceilinged library, and managed to bust three more pairs—one of them being Clive and his brunette—before Freddie noticed a subtle knob in the large wooden wall under the staircase.

"Oh, *hello*," he said, giving it a tweak. It obliged by leaping open, the way everything does when Freddie tweaks it, revealing a dimly lit box of a room that appeared to be upholstered in red velvet—the walls, the stubby bench, even the telephone table. We barreled inside, and then

Freddie stopped short, and I careened smack into him. Apparently the red velvet room was big enough for exactly one occupant.

"I once slept with Bea," he said, as the door clicked shut and left us in squished darkness. "What if I was the *last* man to sleep with Bea? What if I turned her off men forever?"

I burst into a rude guffaw. "You? The Commonwealth's most notorious Lothario?"

"I can see the *Mail* now: FRED DEAD IN BED."

"SEX IS CRAP WITH GINGER SNAP."

We cracked up harder. "It doesn't work like that, Freddie," I managed to eke out, "so I think your reputation will survive."

"Where *are* we? We need a light," he said, still wheezy with mirth.

His hand searched futilely in the pitch black for a wall switch, and accidentally brushed my waist. We were giggling, in that heady way where the real laughter has subsided into a silly afterglow, and as we awkwardly squeezed around each other, our bodies smashed and collided. I felt a charge shoot through me and tipped up my head.

"Whoops, I didn't—"

"Sorry, is that your—"

The rest was lost, because then we were kissing.

# CHAPTER SIX

That night taught me why exactly Freddie is, fundamentally, so hard to quit. Kissing him was pure, ravenous heat, a thousand gigawatts blowing my every fuse. It swallowed my consciousness, my judgment, even my senses. I couldn't smell or taste or touch or *contemplate* anything that wasn't him.

Until I instinctively wove my fingers into his hair, and thought to myself how much coarser and unrulier it was than Nick's—

*Nick.*

Freddie and I sprang apart, gasping. I heard him stagger backward until he fell onto the bench, sitting with an inglorious plop as I felt wildly along the wall for a switch, finally finding one right about where we'd first fallen into each other. The dying bulb flickered on, casting a strange, jaundiced glow.

"What the hell just happened?" I panted, sliding to the floor. The room was so small that I was now basically next to his shins.

"Bex. I don't know what I was thinking. I *wasn't* thinking," he said, clearly longing to pace but having no room in which to do it. "One minute I was looking for the light and then..."

"We just kind of..." I brought my hands together.

"Like a magnet," he finished. "That sounds rubbish, but I can't explain it. I never, ever meant for that to happen."

"You're like a brother to me—"

"I know. I know! I'd never—"

"And Lacey—"

"And Nick, I mean...God, this room." Freddie flapped his hand in front of his face. "Is there no actual air in here?"

We stared at each other.

"My coping skills are for shit," I said. "I've been off-kilter all night, and apparently I react to that by kissing the least appropriate person within range."

"Bingo," he said with a joyless laugh. "And we are never speaking of this again." He tugged at his hair in exactly the worst moment for me to notice a Nick-like tic. "As soon as we open this door and go back to the party, it'll be like it never happened."

"Deal." I clambered to my feet. "Give me a decent head start, though."

"Wait." Freddie tilted his head to the side. "Are *we* good?" he asked.

He was so handsome, even with his shirt wrinkled and slightly dirty from our tree house escapade, and looked so earnest and sad and guilty. That kiss was blazing, but it had also been missing something—a sense of completion, of bone-deep need, and above all, the quintessential Nickness that would be absent from every boy I kissed until I found one who made me forget that I wanted it. I was hit with a bodily wallop of yearning for Nick more potent than I'd felt in a year, and a strange sense of calm settled over me. I felt a lot of things for Freddie right then, but neither lust nor anger was among them.

"We're good," I said. "We're the dumbest people alive, but we're good."

I swung the door open and left him there. And nearly crashed into Clive, who looked curiously behind me.

I pushed the door shut. "Just snooping," I said, trying to steer him away without raising his hackles. "That's some weird panic room. How's your brunette?"

"Quite fun, and also, full of tidbits," he said. "The Heath-Hedwig divorce is in a ghastly state over custody of their peafowl, and she said the most awkward thing about Rich—" He stopped as we reached the terrace, a strange look on his face. "Is that Lacey?"

"What's wrong?" Freddie asked, appearing at my shoulder.

"Where did you come from?" Clive asked. "Weren't you outside?"

But I ignored them. Everything had become fuzzy except the sight of my twin bolting frantically up the lawn. I could hear her calling my name, but it sounded distant, as if I were underwater. Her makeup was ruined. She was hyperventilating. A cold psychic misery gripped me; she didn't have to say the words. As I felt a piece of me crack and fall away, I just knew.

The weeks following my father's death were a devastating blur that, paradoxically, I can recall in the sharpest relief.

I remember clinging to Lacey as Freddie and Clive hustled us to privacy. Hearing Gaz cry with us. Cilla getting us on a flight. Lady Bollocks waving us off down the long gravel drive, kinder than I had ever seen her. I remember my mother's face, too, stoic and empty, more wrenching than if she had greeted us in tears. I remember how brave she was, moving her trembling finger down the phone list, repeating to friends what none of us could believe. I remember understanding what a brutal thing it is to be the bearer of truly bad news—to break off a piece of that misery and hand it to other people, one by one, and then have to comfort them; to put their grief on your shoulders on top of all your own; to be the calm one in the face of their shock and tears. And then learning that relative weight of grief is immaterial. Being smothered a little is no different than being smothered a lot. Either way, you can't breathe.

I remember saying good-bye. Caressing his cheek. Seeing his lively, joyous face reduced to a remote serenity, his mouth curled into a final half smile that was only an eighth of how big it had seemed when he turned that smile on you. I remember the sense that it wasn't him. Not anymore. And I remember feeling gutted, hollow, as if someone had scraped out my insides. Busywork was all that sublimated the pain: planning, organizing, shepherding, greeting, hugging, hosting, organizing the casseroles—an endless parade of aluminum-wrapped apologies from friends who wished they could bring Dad back instead. I'd flip the switch and plow through the list with robotic efficiency, then flip it back and lie awake, destroyed, disbelieving, devastated.

It was such a stupid damn thing, too. He'd missed going to games, so he drove to Cincinnati to see if he could break the Cubs' five-game losing streak. He never made it. The doctors said it was fast, that he may not have known it was the end, likely never felt his heart quit on him, much less the median. And the Cubs still had the indecency to lose. There was cold, dark comedy in realizing he was right; the Cubs *were* the death of him.

The church was packed. Dad would have been so embarrassed and so pleased. I kept making fruitless mental notes to tell him about all the people who'd come, from grade school friends whose soccer teams he coached, to employees at Coucherator, Inc., tearstained and swollen. There were the regulars and bartenders from his local, The Shortstop; classmates of ours who'd deemed him the parent they'd most like to acquire in a trade; and teachers from as many as two decades ago, armed with stories about what a great guy he was. Hardware Pete, Auto Sal, and Electric Bruce of Bruce's Electric sat shoulder to shoulder in the same pew, with the barber who cut his hair. I don't remember giving a eulogy, although I know I sat up all night trying to write it, my Hot Cubs of Yore looking at me with silent, yellowing support. I'd been compelled to chip Derek Jeter off the wall and hide him in a drawer, because my father thought the Yankees were Hell's foot soldiers, and it seemed disloyal to let one stay.

My friends called, kind and helpless: "Bex, I'm so sorry," "Bex, if there's anything I can do," and from Gaz, whose mother died when he was fifteen, "Bex, this is the worst thing that's ever happened. I love you all." Bea sent a beautiful wreath, Cilla sent a ham. An enormous bouquet that required three men to carry it was simply signed *Steve and family*.

For the better part of three weeks, we Porter women wandered around like zombies, every room full of Dad's echo, as if he had just stepped away and would be back any minute. We avoided his spot on the couch like it was sacred, yet Lacey and I surreptitiously repositioned whatever might remind Mom too much of him. We emptied the Coucherator, we threw out the Funyuns, and I smuggled all the Cracker Jack up to my room, then binged on it while crying over the box of baseball souvenirs, still tucked under my bed—every gaudy plastic ring I'd ever found in the box of sticky sweet popcorn, every ticket stub, shirts I'd outgrown, and old cards and pencil nubs from when Dad and I would score the games together. I read about a change in the pitching rotation and thought, "Earl Porter will have *feelings* about this," before realizing that he wouldn't, that he'd never even know, and it seemed pointless suddenly that they bothered playing at all. And every night Lacey and I crawled into Mom's king-size bed, the three of us a human chain, as if hanging on tight would prevent the universe from ripping off another link.

"I'm sorry we fought," Lacey had whispered one night.

"Me too. Never again."

"Never again," she repeated.

It hurts to think about how much we meant it, lying there, crying into each other's hair. We used to joke that we needed a safe word whenever we wanted to complain about subjects we'd already covered ad nauseam, so that we could save time by just saying *Altoids*, or whatever. I wish we'd made up one that could take us back and remind us how essential we are to each other, more priceless than any of Eleanor's antiques.

And yet, the whole time, I also yearned for Nick, the only man in the world I'd loved as fiercely as I loved my father. The criminal loss of one dredged up the egregious loss of the other, and I started to develop a very real antipathy for my hometown. My two most recent stays had coincided with two suffocating hazes of grief, and Muscatine had become synonymous with a dull, comatose emptiness. The people who would one day so glibly coin the name Fancy Nancy didn't understand that England was an escape, that the ghosts in Iowa would sometimes become as unbearable to Mom as they already were to me. And as our third week without Dad drew to a close, my mother poured me and Lacey coffee at the breakfast table and, in the Lady Porter robe that had become her uniform, ordered us go back to London and to our lives.

"Earl would not have wanted you to mope around with me," she said. "Your aunt Kitty isn't that far away in Michigan, if I need her, but I have to learn how to be on my own."

"But I don't want you to be," I said stubbornly.

"Neither do I," she said with a sad smile. "But we can't always get what we want. And I think it *is* what I need."

The three of us hugged tightly at the airport, extracting promises to visit frequently, to call often, to be honest about our good days and bad. I cried through security in Des Moines, through the movie on the plane, through the sweltering customs line in London and the cab ride to Lacey's flat, in Lacey's arms when we dropped her off, and up the path and into my home. I was drained and devastated when I walked through that front door, and the last thing I expected to find inside was a miracle. But there he was. Nick. Waiting for me.

# CHAPTER SEVEN

For a long moment, we just stood there, Nick on the verge of motion, me swaying, still holding my luggage, wondering if the grief was making me hallucinate the one person in the world who could help me feel whole again. He wore a Cubs cap Dad sent for Christmas one year, and his cornflower-blue eyes were red-rimmed and wet.

"I still had my keys," he finally said awkwardly. "I pulled some strings to get off the ship. I just... had to be here."

My knees buckled. I let out a low sob and dropped my bags, and in a flash Nick crossed the room and scooped me into his arms. I felt his own tears on my hair, his body shaking as he wept with me, to the point where I don't even know what we were crying for anymore: for Dad, for us, for the way my face still fit into that spot of his neck where it had always belonged. All the feelings I'd tried to ignore for the past two years came pouring into the empty spaces Dad had left, as if by magic an essential something was being restored to me, even though hours earlier I could've sworn my life would never have any magic in it ever again.

I lifted my head and searched Nick's face. He searched back, brimming with exquisite care and worry, and something deeper—something I hadn't seen in such a long, awful time.

So I kissed him. Our arms slid around each other in desperate sync, pressing us closer, tighter, dizzier.

He broke away. "Are you sure?" he whispered.

I silently pulled my sweater over my head, and then my tank top, and took his face in my hands. "I don't want to be sad anymore, Nick. Please, help me not be sad. Just for a little while."

"My love," he murmured, kissing me again, his hands warm on my body.

Afterward we lay in my bed, my head pillowed on his chest.

"I'm so sorry," he said, stroking my hair.

"Surely not for *that*," I told him.

"Definitely not for that." I could hear his smile. "But it's wretched about your dad. I liked him so much. He treated me just like any other guy you might have been dating."

"Dad had a good eye for people." My voice cracked.

"I keep thinking about when I phoned to get the Thanksgiving recipes," Nick said, running a hand down my arm and lacing our fingers. "He shouted, 'Nancy, he's in love with her, you owe me a steak.'"

"You never told me that!"

"If memory serves, we were otherwise occupied that night," he said. "Anyway, he rang off by telling me I should only use the Chex Mix if I really, really meant it. I swore I didn't have any impure intentions, and he made the most amazing noise. He knew before *we* even said it."

"And you used the Chex Mix."

"Well," he said, "I really, really meant it."

We were still holding hands. He squeezed mine. "Every day, I wake up and tell myself that today is the day I'll feel normal again," he said. "And it never happens."

"I've tried not missing you. I've tried so hard," I said, rolling onto my back. "But if it works, it never lasts." I shook my head. "Sometimes I just wanted to talk to my friend Nick about my ex-boyfriend Nick."

"And I wanted to tell Friend Bex that Ex-Bex can wear trousers with a foot printed on the bum and still look devastating," he said. "Friend Bex probably would've told me to stay away tonight in case I upset you more, but I couldn't let you leave your mum in Iowa without me here when you walked in that door. And if that was inconsiderate, or arrogant, or presumptuous..."

"It wasn't any of those things," I said. "It was perfect. You were perfect."

I sat up and wrapped the eiderdown around me, suddenly feeling extremely exposed even though he'd seen it all and then some.

"That being said," I started, "I don't have any delusions. My dad died, and we're both messed up about it, and I'm crazy vulnerable, and you're probably taking extreme advantage of a bereaved lady because you're a dangerous sex addict."

"That would be the headline in the *Daily Mail*, yes," Nick said.

"You're off the hook, is what I'm saying," I continued. "I loved this. I needed this. But I will not be *needy* about this. I'm not the kind of person who assumes that sex is a cure-all and that suddenly all our old problems are gone. Or even that this has to mean anything."

Nick heaved himself upward and sat against the headboard.

"That's marvelous," he said, "except that I've no interest in being off the hook. I came here thinking I could just hug you and give you this possibly terrible lasagna I tried to make, but when I touched you, it was like I'd finally woken up after sleepwalking for two years."

I can't truly have stopped breathing while he talked, but broken ceiling fans push air with more purpose than my lungs did.

"I tried dating other people, and it felt so insincere, like I didn't really mean it. And I didn't. Because I am, as ever, completely, utterly, irrevocably in love with you," Nick said, and as he quoted himself from Windsor, the tips of his ears began to vibrate, that old embarrassed tic I hadn't seen since Oxford. "I don't even know if you want to hear all this, and I'm certain this is the worst possible time for me to be telling you. But I learnt from you that sometimes just blurting things out leads to the best outcome."

He closed his eyes. "And there's one more thing I need to confess," he said. "Which is that I believe I've burnt the lasagna."

It was then that I noticed the acrid smell of charred tomato sauce floating through the flat.

"My father is dead, and you torched my dinner so that we could have sex," I said, after he'd turned off the oven and crawled back into bed. "If you're not being sincere, things may take an ugly turn. You know how I am when I get low blood sugar."

Nick pressed his hands against his eyes and laughed. "Always so glib."

"Okay, how's this for sincere," I said. "I am, as ever, completely, utterly, irrevocably in love with you, too."

He sat up and pushed a stray strand of my hair behind my ear, such a familiar, comforting gesture, one he'd done a thousand times before and I never thought he'd do again. "Please don't feel you have to say it back," he said. "I just couldn't *not* tell you any longer."

"I have never wanted to say anything more," I said, and it wasn't until he tenderly wiped them that I realized my cheeks were wet again. It is amazing how many tears the human body can produce once it gets going. "I love you. And I am so, so sad. Those two things can be equally true. I learned that the night we broke up."

"I went about us all wrong, Bex," he said ruefully. "I took the wrong lesson away from Mum. The press might've been the trigger, but she was a loaded gun." His eyes were bright with feeling. "Every day, I've thought that if I could do it over, I wouldn't be so scared. I would tell Barnes and Marj and my father to get stuffed, and I wouldn't keep you a secret from anyone. God, that last time I kissed you, I didn't even do it properly."

"Well," I said, choking up again, "it turns out it *wasn't* the last time. We got another chance."

"We got another chance," he affirmed. "And I want you to know I don't intend to waste it. But most of all, there is something else I want, and it doesn't involve any more talking."

My feelings whipsawed between sadness and euphoria during those few days Nick and I had together before the Navy reclaimed him, but he didn't seem to mind. He took care of me. He let me cry. He kept me fed, and hydrated, and brought me frozen spoons for my puffy eyes; mostly, we spent more than half our time in bed and the rest of it doing only the essentials so that we could get *back* into bed—as if we owed it to ourselves to recoup every single lost touch.

"I am the world's biggest idiot," Nick said, kissing my back the second morning. "We could have been doing this all along. I made a bloody mess of things."

"Give me a little credit. I worked hard to help screw things up," I said. "Like wasting all that energy on Gemma, for one thing. I'm guessing you didn't know she's a lesbian, either?"

Nick's eyes widened.

"I caught her with Bea," I told him.

"*Bea?*"

"In a tree house," I added.

"Cripes, I don't know which part of this story is more interesting," Nick said, bemused. "I had no clue. I've known them both my whole life. Gem was my first." He looked thoughtful. "You know, I honestly never considered trying to have it off with her until after you and I broke up. And even that was partly because you were out wearing those cruel bikinis. But she wasn't interested. I assumed I'd just been *that* crap when I was fifteen. Perhaps I was. Perhaps I revolted her."

"Why do guys always assume women being lesbians is about them?" I asked. "It's not like quitting pasta because of one bad burned lasagna."

"Touché," he said, grinning. "I think a bloke just hopes that if he's someone's last, he provided a lovely send-off."

We laughed, but remembering Freddie's similar reaction gave me a guilty pang. I had zero remorse about ignoring the Clive incident, but Freddie was Nick's brother, his best friend, his teammate in that chilly hierarchy of a family.

"Speaking of Gemma," I began. "We can't ignore the past two years. Things happened. With other people. I need to tell you—"

He held up a hand. "Freddie told me about Three Testicles Guy. That's all I can take."

"It was three nipples," I said, "and I should have known Freddie wasn't to be trusted."

Nick wiggled to a sit. "Seriously, I will be happy to discuss the particulars of our time apart." He paused. "Well. Not *happy*. I'll do it, if that's what you want, but I can't think what good will come of it. I didn't take a vow of chastity when we split up, and I certainly didn't expect you to, either."

"We can't pretend it doesn't matter, though."

"Did you kill someone?" Nick asked.

"No."

"Have a love child?"

"Not that I know of," I said.

"Good. We could've made that work, but Barnes would've needed a raise," he said. "Eat any babies?"

"Not for ages."

"Root for the Yankees?"

"Now you're just being disgusting," I said.

He smiled. "Then I sincerely don't care. Nothing counts except what we do now."

I looked at Nick and knew he meant it. And if I said that one particular petty sin out loud, it might spin us back into the dark place we'd just left, so instead I kissed him and buried it deep.

Next to him, on the bedside table, my phone rang. Nick picked it up impulsively.

"Hi, Lacey," he said, then chuckled. "I don't know why I answered this. Sorry."

"Nicely done," Lacey said when I came on the phone. "I just read an article in *Cosmo* about the importance of the Grief Bang. It's when you deal with bereavement via a sexual affirmation that you yourself are alive. Nick is an extremely classy Grief Bang."

"Well, it's not *exactly* a Grief Bang," I said, looking over at him. He had pulled out a folded cryptic crossword from his wallet. "I think we're back together."

"And no more bossing you and Freddie around," Nick said loudly, for Lacey's benefit. "Ring him whenever you like. Part of the New World Order."

"Did you get that?" I asked.

"Hard to miss it," she said, a little flatly. "Tell him not to write checks the Crown can't cash."

"Nah, you heard the man. Live and let live," I said. "Grief bang and let grief bang."

"If you say so," she said. "Well, I just called to see how you're doing. Obviously, you're in good hands. Maybe I will call Freddie." There was a pause. "I'm glad something good came out of all the sadness. Just promise me there'll still be room for all of us."

"I promise."

"I really am happy for you, Bex." Her tone was light again.

"I know. I love you, Lace."

When we hung up, I turned and looked at Nick. "So this is really happening."

"As long as you're in," Nick said, putting down the crossword and reaching across the bed to take my hand.

"I'm in," I said.

"Then there is one thing I'd like to do straightaway, before we go any further. Before I have to go back to my ship." He swallowed hard. "I want you to meet my mum."

Since her disease eclipsed her mind, Emma, Princess of Wales, divided her time at Richard's behest between verdant Trewsbury House in Gloucestershire and a cottage in Cornwall overlooking the water. Emma had loved the sea, but Osborne House—where they'd met and fallen in love, of a sort—was too impractical for Nick and Freddie to visit. Cornwall, on the other hand, is the duchy of every sitting Prince of Wales, so no one blinked when Richard bought himself a bolt-hole there. Nick enjoyed the four-hour trek, which he routinely made in rented cars to avoid press scrutiny, and so we set off the next day in a boring, borrowed white sedan, expertly tailed by PPO Popeye. It was the first time I'd sat next to Nick in a car instead of under a blanket in the back.

"I don't know quite how to prepare you for this," Nick said as he shifted gears. "She's always different. Sometimes she doesn't seem to know I'm there. Sometimes she'll talk, although it won't make sense. Sometimes she'll get angry, and sometimes there will be times where she seems like herself..." He cleared his throat. "But they're illusions, really. Like a stopped clock being right twice a day. Whatever's happening in her mind accidentally lines up with the real world for a split second and I can see what...things might have been like."

I rubbed his shoulder. He smiled before turning back to watch the road.

"It's nice being based near her," he said. "I see her loads. I don't think Freddie's been lately, though, and Father never bothers at all." His tone was cross.

"Freddie told me it's hard without any real memories of her to speak of," I said, hoping this wasn't violating a confidence.

"I know. I'm not actually angry at him," Nick admitted. "It just always gets ugly whenever anyone discusses Mum. Freddie has never cared one way or the other if it's a secret. I've always felt like we owe it to her not to let the press know it beat her. But I also think it's wrong to trot her name out falsely, and that's where Father disagrees. He puts her name in family statements as if she's actively involved, and it doubly hacks me off because he can use it like an alibi. If there is a perception of a functioning Princess of Wales, it gives him some benefit of the doubt if he's seen in town with other people."

"That seems incautious," I said. "At best."

"Too right," Nick agreed, glancing in the rearview mirror. "He almost got caught with India Bolingbroke."

"I'm sorry, *what*?"

Nick groaned. "That's right, you probably haven't talked to Clive," he said. "I guess he was chatting up India's friend Helena Heath-Hedwig at that party, and she let slip something about India being at Clarence House lately. Which is odd because her only reason for being there before was supposedly me, right? So Clive went nosing around, and I gather he saw her leaving rather late one night. It looked suspicious."

I gasped. "I can't believe he went snooping around."

"Don't worry, he came straight to me," Nick said. "Jolly good of him, too, because that scoop probably would have made his career. He's a mate, through and through. I told him I'd try to give him something he can print, as a thank-you. It's the least I can do."

Then it hit me. "Wait, if she was... does that mean India and Richard have been—"

"It looks that way," Nick said.

"Since when?" I winced. "Do you think it was while *you* and India—"

"Please do not go any further down that path," Nick said, shuddering. Then he brought the car to a halt, and punched a code into his mobile. Between two walls of mossy rocks, a well-camouflaged gate squeaked open.

"We're here," he said.

This was only technically a cottage. Yes, there was a thickly thatched roof, but it crowned a house two stories tall, with a perfect view of the Cornish sea, riotous flower beds, and an immaculate, sloping green lawn.

Nick frowned at the large black sedan in the driveway.

"I've never seen that before," he said, setting his jaw.

I leapt out of the car before he could open my door for me, so we reached the cottage's stoop in unison. Just as Nick reached for the doorknob, it turned.

And Richard walked out.

Nick stood up so straight, so fast, that it knocked him backward. Richard was dressed down to the point of being incognito—khakis, a polo shirt, no hair gel. He looked... like a dad. Which may have been part of what stunned Nick so much, given that he'd never *been* much of one. Richard did not seem surprised to see us, but he definitely acted uncomfortable; I got the sense he'd known we were coming and hoped to be gone before we arrived. He was holding a briefcase, and his hand tensed around the handle.

"Miss Porter," he said.

"Your Highness," I replied, bobbing into a slight curtsy. Years ago, I had resisted the urge. Today, I was different. Everything was.

"What are you doing here?" Nick asked.

"That is no one's concern but mine." Richard's tone was defensive, but it ebbed. "She is quiet. Sometimes that's good. It means she'll know you're here. I... Well. Good day."

And with that, Richard climbed into the backseat of what was presumably his own rental, and PPO Rambo appeared from out of nowhere (the shrubberies?) to chauffeur him away. Nick gaped after him in confusion.

"Don't let it throw you off," I urged him. "Enjoy our time with your mom. We'll figure him out later."

Nick still looked dazed, but he nodded and then ushered me inside the quiet house. The warm décor—comfy furniture, sunny walls, bright knickknacks and paintings—was lovely but ordinary, with none of the opulent panache of the other royal residences.

"I was twelve when Father bought her this place," Nick said. "He asked us what color to paint our rooms, and we ended up bossing him around about the whole thing. It's the only time he's ever really listened. We told him we wanted it to feel comforting, like a normal person's house. The kind she might've had..." He gulped. "In another life."

"Oh! You're here, Your Highness."

The words appeared to burst out of an enormous arrangement of roses bustling into the foyer, which revealed themselves to be attached to a petite, plump woman in her mid-fifties. She tried to curtsy, but threatened to tip over onto the floor.

"Don't you dare bow to me, Lesley," Nick said, gallantly taking the arrangement from her with a peck on the check.

"Aren't they stunning?" she said, smoothing her starched white apron. "Every few weeks he brings the most cracking bouquets."

"Every few weeks?" Nick parroted hoarsely. He glanced over at me, and then appeared to right himself. "I'm terribly sorry. Where are my manners? Lesley, this is Rebecca, whom I've told you about. She's here to meet Mum."

"A delight to meet you, my dear," Lesley said warmly. "Ring if you need anything."

I followed Nick to a rectangular living room done up in nautical tones, which looked as if Richard had simply opened a home-furnishings catalog, pointed to a page, and handed it to Barnes. The southern wall of windows faced the sea, and a staircase led down to a garden with a gated pool, which Nick told me was closed off so she couldn't wander in unsupervised. The entire house, in fact, was Emma-proofed so that she couldn't slip out and get any further lost than she already was. This was a lovely cell inside a lovely, but unmistakable, prison.

And there, in the left corner, in a chestnut rocking chair, sat Emma. Nick gently set the roses on the coffee table as the most profound sorrow crossed his face. I saw a childlike yearning to have his mother back juxtaposed with the achingly adult knowledge that this wish would never come true. Then that melted away, leaving behind pure love.

"Mum," he said, walking over and kissing her on the cheek. "There's someone I'd like you to meet."

Emma's eyes flicked up to Nick, expressionless, and then over to me.

"Nice day for a ride, Agatha," she said, then turned back to the waves lashing the rocks.

The last time I'd laid eyes on Emma had been in a photo of her at about twenty-five. Her sandy hair had been short and feathered, a style that was on the way out but which had no easy exit door; she wore it now in a pixie overdue for a trim. She was a year away from fifty, but the look in her eyes belonged to someone much older—and yet her skin seemed ageless, as if the houses that confined her had also preserved her. I've always known Nick resembles his mother, but it wasn't until I saw them in the same room that I realized how strong an echo he is. Every time Richard looked at his son over the years, he surely saw Emma looking back at him.

I followed Nick's example and simply chatted with Emma, or really *around* her. We talked about everything from my sister and mother, to Freddie, to whether Nigel was salvageable as a human being and how lucky Edwin and Elizabeth were to get away with their outrageous preemie lie. Occasionally, Emma would flit about the room, moving a book, playing a note or two on the piano, or jotting down something at the rolltop escritoire. When that happened, Nick would wait patiently, never demanding any more than she could give, and she'd inevitably drift back to him. And that's where she spent most of the hours we were there: sitting, possibly listening, Nick making sure to squeeze her hand or rub it with his thumbs every five minutes or so. She never said anything else to me; she only absently asked if Nick remembered to feed the cat they didn't own, and, in a mercurial moment, barked whether "that bitch Pansy Smythe" had been on the phone with the *Evening Standard.* It was the whole smorgasbord Nick had described.

I did want them to have some private time, so when Nick took her for a walk by the sea, I ducked into the adjacent sunroom to wait. Three walls were windows, and the fourth was covered with framed family snapshots, as if surrounding Emma with where she came from might bring her back to who she was. There was chubby toddler Nick, holding baby Freddie; a fading Polaroid of teenage Richard and Agatha at what looked like Ascot; Nick and Freddie with Richard on Freddie's first day at Eton; and a photo that I knew was from Nick's twentieth birthday trip to Mustique, because I spied a bandaged Gaz lurking in the background (he'd legendarily been bitten by a turtle that he described as "a dynamic half-shark"). There was an entire life on that wall, so much of it stolen from Emma before she could live it.

"Oh, good, I've found you," Lesley said, poking her head into the room. "Can you have His Highness return this to his father? Usually he makes sure to collect them all but this one had fallen on the floor."

She handed me a piece of paper, and then left as fast as she'd come. I turned it around in my hands, in wonderment. It was—or would be, if Richard ever finished it—a stunning watercolor of Emma as she faced out the window, a wisp of a smile playing on her face in a way I'd often seen on Nick's. She had been rendered more present than she actually was, as if Richard was imagining her in that other life, where she'd made other choices. The detail with which he'd captured the lines of her face and the way she propped up her chin on her palm . . . there were feelings in every brush stroke. Maybe this was the one way he felt he could express them. When Nick came back from his walk, I wordlessly handed the painting to him.

"Crikey," was all he said.

"This isn't the work of someone who doesn't care," I said. "For whatever that's worth. But I think it should be worth quite a lot."

He put down the paper and slid his hands around my waist. "*You* are worth quite a lot," he said. "And now that I'm going to live in the open where you're concerned, I want to do it with everything. Even Mum. It's time. It's decades past time."

Just saying that out loud seemed to release him from an invisible grip.

"I thought I couldn't face it. But now I know that I was just waiting for the right person to face it *with*," he explained. "I always thought the press was her worst enemy, but really, it was a perfect storm of the wrong husband, the wrong support system, the wrong life."

He backed away a step. "And I will not be the wrong husband, nor the wrong support system, nor will I give you the wrong life."

My head got very light as he dropped to one knee.

"I always told myself this could wait until I was older," Nick said with a nervous, crooked smile. "But it's stupid to pretend for another day that this isn't *it* for me. I love you, Bex. My soul married yours that first night at Windsor, and while I'll be the king of this country someday, *every* day I will be your servant."

And then he fished a ring box out of his pocket.

A tear slid down my cheek as he opened it to reveal a flamboyantly plastic affair, with a red stone whittled faintly into a heart shape and clamped atop a muted olive-gold band.

"It's from the first Cracker Jack box we ate in Oxford," he said. "Somehow I ended up with it. I thought... I thought your father would approve."

"He does," I said thickly. "Wherever he is."

"There would be a real ring eventually, of course," he said, slipping the cartoonish bauble on my finger. It fit horribly. It was perfect. "But if you'll kindly agree to marry me, I will drive us home so fast to celebrate that Popeye will have to bribe some policemen. Please, love. Say yes."

Nick looked up at me, his eyes wet with more love than I ever thought I would be allotted in this lifetime.

It was the easiest answer I have ever given.

He wrapped me in his arms, and time was briefly lost to us as we shared, if not the most passionate kiss of the weekend, undoubtedly the sweetest. And then we joined hands, wordlessly, and walked out into the sun, blithely unaware that there could ever again be darkness.

# PART FOUR

# AUTUMN 2013

*"To be a king and wear a crown is a thing more glorious to them that see it than it is pleasant to them that bear it."*

—Queen Elizabeth, 1601

# CHAPTER ONE

The Whispering Espresso paint job in Marj's Clarence House office was still fresh when we returned from Cornwall, faint fumes lingering stubbornly underneath the scent of her Woods of Windsor potpourri. And that's almost the last we saw of her new walls: In the ensuing months, they slowly vanished behind a garish collage of color-coded notecards, thumbtacked lists of stylists and waxers and trainers and facialists with a reputation for discretion, and a note from Freddie telling her, and I quote, *sod it all and go have a shag*, which I doubt Marj even noticed, much less did. And at the center of the chaos was a meticulous timeline plotting the days between Nick's and my private betrothal straight through to a date underlined, starred, and circled in red. To most of the world, it was Christmas. To Marj, it was E-Day.

Every moment leading up to the big announcement—that the United Kingdom's most eligible bachelor (and Number Two on *Vanity Fair*'s "World's Dishiest Nicks" list) was off the market—was choreographed as tightly as a ballet. I had to be slid carefully back into public view, with purpose but not presumption; it was too soon for me to pop up at official events, but neither could Nick haul up from his Naval base just to push a shopping cart with me, nor lie out in Kensington Gardens feeding me cheese. Because Marj was a puppet master par excellence, she found the perfect solution. Polo matches carried the right amount of high-class cachet, while still being an ostensibly platonic place for me to be seen socializing anew with the Brothers Wales. So Nick stocked up on antihistamine, and I loaded up on tweedy blazers and horsy boots.

"Now, Bex, Knickers'll need nurturing through this," Freddie said over pints the night before Operation Polo began. "The last time a great hairy hooved beast thundered toward him, he cried."

"From the *dander*," Nick said.

Freddie cupped his ear. "The *danger*, you say?"

"Well, now that you mention it," Nick said. "That same day, some bloody great pillock whacked my leg with a polo mallet to see if I felt it. I had a bruise for weeks."

"Oh, *mortal* danger, then," I said.

"He must really love you, Killer," Freddie said.

"Can't think why at the moment," Nick grumbled, but he squeezed my hand.

Marj let Clive print a rumor in the *Recorder* that I would be attending Nick's first match, as a thank-you for his discretion regarding Richard and India. Smelling his big break, he broke up with Davinia—"a good investigative reporter must be unencumbered"—broke the story, and broke the proverbial seal. The game was afoot. For three months I was documented as Nick's loyal yet restrained public supporter. I gave him chaste hellos; I pet his horse, Elton John, so named because he'd lost a bet with Freddie; and I chuckled with Bea and Gemma, helping carefully rebrand the latter as Nick's unthreatening chum. The gossip kindling piled up all summer, and in the fall, Marj dropped in the match: Nick and I arrived together at the union of recent *Strictly Come Dancing* runner-up Penelope Six-Names and Maxwell, son of Baron Something-Something.

Ostensibly, we went as old Oxford chums of Penelope's, but really, it was the only sufficiently upmarket society wedding on the docket. (Six-Names was beside herself; I think she was more excited that Nick was attending her wedding than she was about attending it herself.) I wore a dusty rose suit with my very first fascinator, a soaring pink and gold confection, and it was so hard to wrangle that I kept knocking it asunder on the car door, or inadvertently poking Nick in the face. We had to hustle me out of the car around a hidden corner.

"Fascinators are impossible," I said, wiggling it back in place before we walked into the paparazzi's eyeline. "I hope I didn't scar you for life. Six-Names would never get over it if her wedding ruined your face."

"That can't be right," Nick said.

"It's true. I think I scratched you." I checked my reflection in the car's glossy exterior. "Oh, man. I actually bent it."

"No. Her name," he said. "She's Penelope Eight-Names, now, isn't she?"

I paused. "I was going to guess Penelope Six-Names Something-Something."

"We'll have to consult Gran on what's more proper," he said. "I'd hate to get it wrong on our wedding invitations."

The photo of us laughing together on our walk up the hill to the church was as good as gold. PLACE YOUR BEX, ordered the *Mirror*; the *Mail*'s Xandra Deane went with DAMN YANKEE. I'd been allowed to tell my mother, Lacey, and our closest friends that a betrothal was imminent, as much to employ their aid as anything, but I didn't let on that Nick had already asked and been accepted. With our lives becoming public fodder, I wanted one secret that belonged only to us, and for similar reasons, Nick had insisted that the presentation of a ring—one that didn't come out of a box of American snack food—should unfurl without first being scripted by Marj. And to that end, he'd been thoroughly irritating. He fished through his pocket during pregnant conversational pauses. He hid things in his clenched fist, only to reveal that they were coins or paper clips or, once, a dead bug. He even pulled a jewelry box from under his pillow one morning, then opened it to reveal his favorite cufflinks with a bemused, "How did *those* get there?"

By the time my birthday rolled around, Nick had told me very seriously that Marj realized a formal proposal was impractical until after his Navy deployment, and that she had Eleanor's authorization to push E-Day to the following year. So I thought nothing of it when he presented me with a large rectangular box swathed three times over in a crumply surplus of Thomas the Tank Engine paper. (As with every guy I've ever known, including my father, Nick is the worst at wrapping presents.) I ripped off the blue bow and stuck it to my forehead, then tore into the gift and laughed when it turned out to be a dented Cracker Jack box.

"Yes!" I crowed. "I just finished my last one. How did you know?"

I blithely pulled open the top, which I do remember thinking had been glued extra messily by the assembly line, and shared a few handfuls before I fished around for my toy.

"Aha!" I brandished a ring. "Man, it's heavier than the usual cheap crap."

Nick's lip twitched. "I'll be sure to give Gran your glowing review."

It was in that second that I actually looked at the ring. I had seen it before. The whole world had, on the finger of a certain prince's mother, and I nearly dropped it when I realized I was holding something very old, very significant, and very, very *not* cheap.

"Holy shit" was my regal reaction.

"Happy birthday," Nick said proudly.

The twelve-carat Lyons Emerald was a flawless, classically square stone, ringed twice with tiny diamonds and set in antique Welsh gold. It originally belonged to Queen Victoria II, and when her daughter Princess Mary inherited it, she stuffed it in a drawer because she insisted baubles like that were for *shallow, selfish, silly little girls*, to which her sister-in-law Marta allegedly retorted, "If you'd been a little sillier and a little more shallow, you might not die a virgin." (Richard did not fall far from his grandmother's tree.) This feud frothed until Mary did die at age seventy-two, virginity status unknown, while watching the competitive sheepdog trial show *One Man and His Dog*—at which point the ring went to Eleanor, who gave it to her son, who slipped it onto the finger of one Lady Emma Somers. I have never been much for jewelry, beyond my flag pin and diamond pendant from Nick, but even I always thought the Lyons Emerald was magnificent. And though I hated to admit it, for fear of sounding like the avaricious Ivy League climber I'd been reputed to be, I loved the sight of it sparkling at the end of my arm.

I must have given Nick quite a look, because he jumped out of his seat. "Though it pains me to say this, you are going to have to hold that thought," he said, opening the front door.

"Goodness, you're punctual," said my mother, whom I'd thought was in Iowa, as she breezed inside holding a cake box. "It *is* Bex we're talking about here."

Lacey ran in after her, squealing and wielding Champagne, and Nick suddenly found himself in the middle of a high-volume group hug as the three of us wept and hugged and cooed over my ring—our joy mixed with regret for the thing that none of us wanted to say out loud, which was the unfairness of Dad not being there to see it, too.

The Lyons Emerald was only on my finger until the following day, after our official engagement shoot, at which point it went back into safekeeping until E-Day arrived. The photographer, a distinguished sir named Alistair Luddington, had snapped all the royal portraits of recent history, including the famous Richard and Emma photo outside Balmoral in which she delights at his kilt misbehaving in the wind. The theatrically cranky Sir Alistair would have been horrified if he'd realized my mother hovered behind him the entire time he worked, making manic smiley faces as if I were four and we were in the Sears Portrait Studio, and he was prone to byzantine, contradictory advice every time Nick's pose got as stiff as the breeze that nearly stole Richard's mystery.

"If that's your best move, you have no hope of ever producing an heir," he sighed as we tried to cuddle naturally in a complicated setup that was, of course, meticulously controlled merely to look natural. "I told you before. Hold her. Really *take* her. But gently. I want *heat.* But not sex. Grab her. But not hard. With *love.* But not lust. It could not be simpler. And for God's sake, don't block that ring."

"Well, if that's all," Nick had said, planting my bejeweled hand firmly on his backside.

Alistair's camera clicked. "One for Her Majesty's pianoforte," he said.

My newly hired makeup specialist, a fellow American named Kira with a divine cloud of an afro, insisted on putting a microfiber cloth over my hand so she wouldn't cloud the ring with powder residue. She'd converted a corner of the Clarence House drawing room into Bex Central, likewise draping the antiques in towels—one of them had a shark on it, so incongruous with the portrait of Arthur I in plump repose—and pulled me away every ten minutes to thwack my face with a giant brush, spritz my flyaways, and apply another layer of the coat of varnish I have come to realize will now be in place almost all the time.

During our first break, Lacey wandered over to ogle the array of cosmetics, and reached for a bold orange-red lipstick that must have been there by accident, because Eleanor would cry harlot if it ever touched my mouth (it is all neutral glosses for me now).

"Hands off, Lacey," Kira said politely.

"I wasn't going to *keep* it," Lacey said, chastened. "Your hair is crazy shiny, Bex. Is that the new conditioner I got you?"

"Hell no," Kira said. "It's a mask from Leonor Greyl. She's in the big leagues now."

"Your stuff smells way better," I whispered when Kira bent over to dig in her massive bag. Lacey grinned, then reached out to flick a lock of hair behind my shoulder.

"I said no touching," Kira said, still pleasant, emerging with a handful of Q-tips. "If the Palace doesn't like my art, then I lose my work visa, and believe me, I do not want to go back to doing teen soaps in Wilmington."

Lacey waved off my apologetic face, but she was clearly disappointed. When we'd first come back after Dad's funeral, we'd done a pretty good job keeping each other almost as close as we had in Iowa. For the first month or two, we'd even slept over at each other's places a few times. It was strange having the minutiae of our day-to-day lives feel so similar after such a huge catastrophic change—like we had to stop and remind ourselves every day what was missing—and we understood that struggle in each other without having to say it out loud. But then the slow burn of going public had begun. The run-up to E-Day meant Marj was calling me to Clarence House on a moment's notice, and because she'd told me repeatedly, in her words, *rain checks are not on my menu*, this had resulted in several incidents of plans being postponed or canceled, until Lacey and I had fallen out of one another's loops.

"How's Freddie?" I asked. "I haven't seen him since Elton John tried to kick me."

"Me neither." She pouted. "The last time we, um, *saw* each other"—she glanced at Kira, who was doing a heroic job pretending not to listen—"we made a date to go to Tony's new club. But he canceled and hasn't called me back."

"Maybe he's just busy," I said, losing some consonants as I spoke through Kira's lip-gloss wand. "Navy stuff."

"Mmm-hmm," Lacey said distantly, looking everywhere but at me. In the opposite corner of the drawing room, our mother and Agatha were studying a display of dueling pistols. I'm not sure which Lyons I thought was the most likely candidate to bond with my mother, but it wasn't Agatha, who, in terms of approachability, was Mom's polar opposite. But Mom had admired Agatha's fur-trimmed gloves that morning when we bumped into her in the foyer, and because praise-deprived Agatha soaks up compliments like a sponge, they now were nattering like old chums.

"Hope Agatha doesn't get too attached," Lacey said. "That family is only allowed to love one Porter at a time."

"Nick swears that's not a rule anymore," I said. "Freddie will turn up. He always does."

"I'm sure you're right," Lacey said. But she didn't believe me, and I knew it. It's both a testament to and an indictment of Freddie that he can keep someone on the hook with the merest scraps of attention; if he were anyone else, she'd have gotten breakup bangs and burned all her keepsakes by now, but he was Freddie and so he endured.

"Places!" Alistair called out, clapping his hands.

I turned to Lacey. "Are you okay?" I asked.

She waved me off with a smile, but it looked a little lonely. "Go. Nick is waiting."

Eleanor had decided the Royal Family's traditional Christmas Day walk to church would be a festive way to reveal Nick's proposal—her gift to the nation, along with confirmation that the future Defender of the Faith had chosen someone sufficiently devout (I was already an American; I could not also be an atheist). But protocol dictated that only those married into the family could spend the holidays at Sandringham, and, being generally as flexible as a lamppost, Her Majesty refused to accommodate me overnight. Instead, I woke up earlier on Christmas morning than I had since I was a child so that my car would arrive long before anyone thought to look for unusual activity at the house. I felt like a cat burglar: Go in, do the job, don't get caught, the stress of which was eclipsed only by the tiny matter of me finally meeting my future grandmother-in-law. It's not as if I really thought Eleanor would do something drastic, like throw a drink in my face or challenge me to a duel. But I would not have been her choice for Nick, not in a million years, not when she'd encouraged Agatha to marry a bounder like Julian just because, like a dog, he was pedigreed (and she hadn't thought Agatha—sturdy Agatha, best referred to as *a handsome woman*—could afford to wait for anyone nicer). As we wound north into Norfolk, I told myself that I should just be thankful she hadn't simply vetoed the engagement and deported me.

Unlike Buckingham Palace, Sandringham is not just a residence; it's also an immense working estate, encompassing everything from national parkland to a sawmill and an apple juice factory. But its jewel is the redbrick Sandringham House, paradoxically both sprawling and compressed to the eye, all narrow bay windows and vertical lines—like someone carved out a long cluster of row houses from one of London's ritzier boroughs, popped on pointier roofs, and plopped them in the middle of twenty thousand acres. Approaching it in the eerie predawn dark felt wildly like being the heroine in a Jane Austen novel, headed to Netherfield Park to check on my pneumonia-riddled sister, or dropping by Pemberley for haughty verbal foreplay with Mr. Darcy. But when I arrived, the vibe was more *Upstairs, Downstairs*. The ground level crawled only with people in the Queen's employ, because the rest were still in bed, presumably trying to stay warm. At the turn of the previous century, Sandringham was ahead of its time in adopting flushing toilets and modern showers, but hasn't led a technological charge since, including modern heating. Eleanor believes being cold is character-building, and won't coddle her guests with plush eiderdowns, so everyone ends up sleeping in as many layers as they wear to ski. Freddie once told me that he keeps a bottle of whiskey in bed. He calls it portable fire.

I was ushered with quiet efficiency to a high-ceilinged chamber with a canopy bed smack in the middle, a thin, itchy-looking blanket tucked in with military precision. The door had barely clicked shut before I took a running leap and flopped on that tall mattress. I had to take my unscheduled pleasures where I could get them.

The door opened again sneakily, and there was Nick, bundled up like an arctic explorer. He did an adorable fist-pump with the hand that clutched the ring box.

"You get to keep it this time!" he said, padding over and handing me the emerald. "And look, I had it engraved. It's a Lyons tradition."

I peered inside at the century-old gold band. I saw, ever so slightly rubbing out from age, the *VRII*; a much clearer script *M*; an *R* and *E* for Nick's parents, and an interlocking *N* and *B*, officially making me a link in this chain.

"I went with *B* for Bex so that even when we have to be Nicholas and Rebecca in public, you can look at this and remember who we are at home," Nick said. "Although Freddie's suggestion was a pair of *K*s for 'Knickers' and 'Killer.'"

I grinned. "That might have been hard to explain to history."

Nick slid the ring gracefully onto my finger. "It's all changing," he said. "In mere hours, everything will be different."

I rolled over and welcomed him on the bed next to me. "Any second thoughts?"

"Yes, actually. Be a love and pop the ring back in my sock drawer."

"No way," I said. "You do whatever you want, but I will smuggle this sucker back to Iowa if I have to."

Nick grew serious. "I am certainly not having second thoughts about you," he said. "As for the rest of it..."

His voice dropped off. Today wasn't just about us. It was about everything. It was about Emma.

Nick had spent months advocating telling the truth about his mother, but it wasn't until he realized that our engagement had turned the lie into a time bomb that he got anyone's attention: While nobody was suspicious now, Nick pointed out, *everyone* would side-eye Emma missing her firstborn's wedding, especially with her ring winking at them from the bride's finger. Like magic, the matter appeared on the agenda of our next Team Wales confab at Clarence House. Nick arrived with the jittery relief of someone who'd sealed a big deal but forgotten to ask the price; Richard refused to meet anyone's eyes, and Freddie seemed tense-jawed and moody.

"Here is how it will work," Marj announced. "Nicholas and Rebecca will tape a television interview discussing their courtship, which will air a few weeks after the Christmas reveal. During the course of this chat, Nicholas will explain that there is a particular truth he must share to ensure that Emma can be part of his festive day."

Freddie whistled. "Very tricky, Marjie," he said. "Burying the lede, as they say."

"Except it makes *me* look like the liar," Nick said, his triumph turning to irritation.

"Technically, we all are," Freddie said. "We went on with Katie Kenneth and made up stuff about Mum just the same as everyone else."

"It's not too late to call it off, Your Highnesses," Barnes intoned. "Once this cat is out of the bag, it's never going back in."

"I am not calling it off," Nick said tightly. "I'm not the one who put the cat *in* the bag."

"Yes, best watch out for those animal cruelty people you fundraise for, *Richard*," Freddie said, tapping a staccato on the glossy dining room table. "Once they find out you've been shoving cats in bags, they'll be so put out."

"Shush," Richard snapped. "If you can't be serious, you can be excused."

"You are the one who pushed for this," Marj reminded Nick.

"But surely there's another way." Nick turned to his brother. "What do you think?"

"Doesn't matter," Freddie said. "I've been shushed."

"You're being treated like a child because you are acting like one," barked Richard.

"This is Her Majesty's plan, and I'll box *everyone's* ears if you don't put a plug in it. With all due respect," Marj added grudgingly. Reflexively, I glanced over her head at a famously unfinished portrait of Eleanor, her gown disappearing into tentative pencil scratchings, and knew why Marj had chosen that seat: to remind us who was really in charge.

"Thank you," Marj said when everyone fell silent. "Nicholas, you were objecting?"

"It's far too transparent," he argued. "And I don't like dragging Bex into it. I'm supposed to be introducing her to Great Britain, not asking her to smile quietly while I say, 'Surprise! We all lied, and Mum's bonkers! But won't this wedding be a treat?' "

I said nothing. I would've reassured Nick I could handle it, but that would be siding with Marj, and I refused to leave him on an island.

"Nick," Marj said softly. "I should hope you'd know that I am on your team. And this *does* make sense. Taking advantage of the goodwill from your wedding is our best shot at coming out unscathed, but for that to work, the truth must come from you."

"But why?" he wondered, softening slightly.

"Because they will hate me," Richard said.

The room fell thickly silent. This sliver of his soul caught us all off guard.

"They will hate me, but they will forgive you," he continued. "From me all they will hear is the lie, and none of the tragedy. But if it comes from you..." He pursed his lips. "They love you. They simply tolerate me."

Nick swallowed hard, then walked to the window and banged the wooden sill with the heel of his hand. Across the park, the imperious façade of Buckingham Palace glared back at us, as if to underscore that we could never hide from it or anything else.

"All right," he said. "I'll do it."

But as Nick and I lay in that freezing Sandringham bedroom, enjoying our last moment of peace before the news cameras and the rest of the world intruded, I could see his innate desire for privacy had him still wrestling with ripping open this wound.

"You made the right choice," I said, gently touching his cheek. "And you're not saying anything that isn't true. These are your feelings. That's all they need to hear."

On the mantel, one of Sandringham's one hundred and eighty-three clocks started to chime six a.m.

"That's our cue," I said, kissing his arm and getting a mouthful of parka. "Merry Christmas."

"*Happy* Christmas," he said, kissing me back. "Aren't Marj and Barnes teaching you anything?"

Barnes and Marj had, in fact, spent hours training me to avoid *um* and *uh*, and any déclassé colloquialisms or minor swear words, via an incredibly high-tech system of engaging me in conversation and then poking me if I screwed up. It was primitive, but it was working. So was the teeth-whitening, and the frequent visits from Kira to check on my eyebrows. (I'd gotten tipsy on an uncharacteristically pricey Pinot Noir during the breakup and done some regrettable tweezing, which Kira was trying to fix so gradually that nobody would remember they'd ever looked any other way.) Barnes and Marj constantly reminded me that the real work had not yet begun, but I'd been buffed and styled into enough of a patina of elegance that by the time we found ourselves back downstairs, it had done the work of the armor it kind of was. The real, vulnerable me felt shielded, even from the prospect of international scrutiny.

Nick and I found Agatha lurking outside the room where we'd be blowing open Britain's best-kept secret, working a groove into the Persian rug, seemingly waiting for us.

"This is so extreme. Are you certain about this, Nicky?" Agatha wondered, as her greeting.

"Leave it out, Ags. You're always so serious," said Prince Edwin, bouncing down the stairs. He whacked me on the behind with a rolled-up magazine. "Pleased to meet you, Bexy."

Agatha's mouth pursed so tightly it looked like a raisin. "*Well*," she said, curling her lip at Edwin. "Nicky, if you're certain, about Emma . . . I suppose you're very brave, dear."

Kira gave my hunter-green V-neck dress a final tug, then clucked approvingly. Nick put his game face on, and I saw, like the tipping of an hourglass, the fatigued and nervous expression of the boy I loved shifting like sand into the friendly public reserve of the prince I was marrying. And then Barnes poked his head through the drawing room door and nodded to us.

"It's time," Nick said. "No going back now."

# CHAPTER TWO

If anyone in the White Drawing Room was bitter about sacrificing Christmas to get this scoop, they were professional enough not to let it show. In order to create the illusion of an intimate fireside chat, the place was clogged with producers in headsets, sound guys toting fluffy boom mics, three very caffeinated cameramen, and more empty-handed yet apparently essential technical personnel than I could have imagined you'd need for a three-person interview. The holiday was over; the production had begun.

Nick and I got a quick handshake from our interviewer—Katie Kenneth, whose *On Heir* on Freddie's birthday had been a raging success—before being hustled into our armchairs. Mine was lower than I expected, so I sat down with an awkward jolt, and then winced when someone turned on a light aimed right at my face. It was at least ten degrees warmer in front of them, and I could feel my nerves frothing again under their heat.

Nick leaned over to me. "Don't forget to mention the syphilis," he whispered.

I stifled a laugh as the cameraman counted us in and then pointed right at Katie, who slid on a smile and launched into a smooth, stately introduction before turning her warm gaze on us.

"So how did the fairy tale begin?" she asked with a twinkle. "When did you first meet?"

Somehow she was looking right at both of us. Nick and I simultaneously went to speak, then glanced each other, clamped our mouths shut, and blushed.

"Don't fret. I spent the last month in Maui eating macadamia nuts and drinking mai tais, so I'll be well off my game," Katie said with a wink. Nick and I burst out laughing, and her well-timed self-deprecation cleared whatever fog had set in on us. "We'll polish it up in the edit. Why don't you take it, Rebecca?"

The giggles subsided, but I still felt their residual cheer. Without hesitation I spoke my first words to be heard by the world at large.

"He opened the door for me the day I arrived at Oxford," I said. "In fact, he might've been the first person in England that I spoke to, except for my taxi driver."

"And I owe him a debt of gratitude," Nick said. "If he had been gallant enough to walk Rebecca's luggage up the road to the door on a rainy afternoon, she might not have been as impressed by my brute strength when I brought them to her room."

"You carried her suitcases?" Katie asked delightedly.

"Well, one of them was very small," I teased. "More of a glorified purse."

"One humble servant can only do so much," Nick said. "Although I'm still waiting for my tip."

This proved an outstanding jumping-off point, because it allowed us to slide into our natural rapport, and because it had the benefit of being true—which the answer to the next query, "When did you know it was love," was not. We couldn't very well discuss *Devour*, nor Nick's karaoke binge, nor the time I dropped tampons on him. Nick kept it vague but charming, claiming it swept us up so quickly that he couldn't remember *not* loving me, and blamed our years apart on his having some growing up to do. He also elicited more laughs when he revealed he'd proposed via Cracker Jack (Marj had hoped to recast this with *He carved my name into a glacier*, but Nick refused to tell a new lie right before unraveling the old one), and I was careful to chime in only when appropriate, so that I didn't look pushy. Katie called on me largely to ask about my passions for my adopted country, and steered clear of my parade of bikinis.

It was lovely—a well-executed preamble to the moment she'd been instructed to open Pandora's box.

"Rebecca," she said, her rich alto as smooth as double cream. "It must be bittersweet for you to experience this without your father."

Nick and I each reached for the other's hand. It wasn't planned; he took mine because he always did that when my father came up, and I took his because I knew what was coming.

"It's the only shadow on the day. My father loved Nick...olas." I kept forgetting to use his full name. "Part of me still can't believe Dad won't walk in here in five minutes and tease him about whether he properly asked for permission," I added, my eyes prickling. "But the Royal Family has been so welcoming. Nicholas even made sure Mom was here when he proposed. We feel very, very embraced."

Katie turned to Nick. "And Nicholas, all of Britain misses your mother. Hers was our last iconic wedding. Will she emerge for yours?"

"We hope so," Nick said. "But that depends on something I must say to the British people. The sad facts of my mother's condition are not what they have been led to believe, and I hope very much they'll understand the secrecy."

I can still feel how airless that room became, as everyone braced for a quarter-century's worth of spin to be unwound. And then Nick just let it all out, sincerely, emotionally, wholly. He begged forgiveness for what he called *a well-meaning but still misguided deception*, spoke eloquently about Emma's confusing non-diagnosis and making mental illness a personal cause of his, and promised the people that their beloved Princess of Wales was safe, cared for, and still loved, even if she was no longer the vibrant woman they once knew.

"You've kept this secret nearly your entire life, with no one the wiser," Katie Kenneth said. "Why reveal it now?"

"Because of this," Nick said, lifting my ring hand. "Because I still believe a piece of my mum is there, however deep it might be buried, and that piece of her needs to see that she raised someone who can love another person as completely as she loved us. And to be warmed with joy and hope, which might be our only weapons left against the darkness that took her from us."

He sucked on his lip briefly. "And because I miss my mum," he said frankly, his voice threatening to break. "I'm getting married, and it would break my heart on its happiest day not to see her face in that church."

Nearby, Marj shone with pride. Past the glare of the TV lights, I spied Freddie, red-cheeked, staring at a fixed point on the floor. And then I caught Richard rubbing at his eyes, and I realized he was fighting crying, too. With dawning horror, I felt my own tear ducts flood.

The next clip played over and over again on news channels all over the world. Katie handed me a Kleenex as Nick spontaneously kissed my hand and murmured, "Oh, love, don't cry. Everything's going to come out all right."

I blotted my eyes as delicately as possible. "I'm sorry," I said to Katie, with an awkward smile. "I haven't gotten my stiff upper lip yet."

Cut and print.

The interview left us with an hour before church to dry our tears and eat. I still hadn't met the Queen—the suspense would have killed me if I hadn't been too busy to die—so I was kicked upstairs to the junior dining room, meaning I took my meal in a fluffy bathrobe at a *less*-favored centuries-old mahogany table (Eleanor has a furniture hierarchy, to go along with her other rules) next to Lady Elizabeth feeding Henry in his high chair. Agatha's son Nigel sat at the other end, legally an adult, old enough to buy the nudie magazine he was crudely leafing through over breakfast, yet still unwelcome at the proper table.

"Because nothing says Happy Christmas like the newest issue of *Escort*," Elizabeth sang, as Nigel thoughtfully unfurled a vertical centerfold.

I love Elizabeth. She is a beam of sunshine even when sarcastic—my mother's bubbly gossipy streak shot through with Freddie's sense of mischief. Once married, she and Edwin became the Duke and Duchess of Cleveland, reviving his late father's dukedom, but the press still calls her Elizabeth or Lady Liz; she likes it that way, claiming hanging onto your name is like keeping a piece of home. (I love this theory, knowing I will be Bex to the world for longer than I hold any other title.) And as improbable as it seems, she deliriously adores Edwin. On this Christmas, the two of them sported matching five-months pregnant bellies—his a food baby; hers, another real one—and I'd twice caught them sucking face in the hallway like turbo Hoovers.

"Don't be embarrassed, Eddybear," she'd said. "Bex understands. *She* still has hormones."

While she fed baby Henry, Elizabeth filled me in on the Christmas Eve gift exchange. Nick had talked Freddie out of the cruel gag of giving Richard a World's Best Dad mug, so instead they got him a Whoopee cushion with Barnes's face on it. Eleanor had given all the men self-tanner in an abusive shade of bronze, and Elizabeth gave Edwin some men's bikini-style leopard-silk underpants that promised supernatural strength, luck, and genital potency. The ever-resourceful Freddie had procured for Eleanor a gag positive pregnancy test with a note that said, *Whoops*. And Nick had found Freddie a book called *Celibate? Celebrate!*, which apparently prompted an entire routine in which Freddie pretended it might be infectious. Elizabeth also reported that Agatha consumed the better part of a bottle of Burgundy and ate the lesser part of her roast, so that by the post-dinner brandy, she was loudly complaining that she never got any of the good jewels despite being "an actual blood Lyons," and that her ruby engagement ring was tiny and gauche—at which point Awful Julian called *her* tiny and gauche and passed out in front of the fire. Queen Mum Marta, ever the firecracker even in her eleventh decade of life, apparently rapped Agatha on the head with a candle snuffer and hissed, "A ruby is not a hardship and neither is a warm body."

"Amazing," I said to Elizabeth, sticking a fat piece of bacon into my mouth. "My family gatherings seem so sedate now. Even with the Easter Sunday arm wrestling."

"These *will* be your family gatherings soon enough," Elizabeth said in that perky voice that sounds delighted even when she's bitching. "Aggie's *so* bitter. You'll see. About Julian, about the succession laws..." She lowered her voice. "I can't blame her, but honestly, that old rule saved us from him being the heir." She nodded toward Nigel, who was using his reflection in the table to squeeze a juicy zit. "We'd have to sink the island and start over."

Soon enough, the calm ceded to the storm once more. My TV makeup was chipped off and replaced with something equally spackled but less intense. I carefully buttoned my sumptuous Black Watch tartan Alexander McQueen coat, weighted at the hem so no winter breezes would kick it above my knees. And Kira secured my navy cocktail hat with an elastic band matched to my hair, then styled a soft half updo that hid the evidence while maintaining a little youthful swing. The effect was as seamless as if I'd been baptized at Buckingham Palace myself. When Nick met me at the top of the stairs, he stopped short for a moment, then cleared his throat.

"Pardon me, have you seen Bex Porter?" he asked. "Tall, ponytail, sporty. Very loud."

"She can't come to the phone right now," I said, and it felt true, like the girl who used to live inside me was being elbowed aside to make room.

We'd been told to congregate in the Saloon, which is the largest room in the house but also one of the most informal, with clusters of overstuffed chairs, family photos atop the piano, and a giant jigsaw puzzle on a low baize-covered table. When we appeared at the door, Richard abandoned Edwin mid-sentence and came over to shake Nick's hand as I curtsied.

"Well played today," he said gruffly, almost as if it caused him pain. "Both of you."

Then he turned and left. It was polite to the point of being historic, where Richard and I were concerned. I gave Nick a quizzical look.

"He's been trying," Nick said. "I thought it was because of Mum, but actually, I think getting rumbled with India Bolingbroke embarrassed him and he's grateful I didn't tell anyone. So he's being... marginally pleasant, at times."

"I'll take anything I can get from him that isn't pure cold rage," I said.

"Yes, we must aim high," he agreed. "All right, you, no more stalling."

Nick escorted me toward a slight woman with immaculate posture and an unmistakable profile, perched at a refined oak desk. She took a beat to finish writing—Eleanor is the master of finding ways to make sure you know who's time you're on—and popped a Polo mint into her mouth before standing.

"Rebecca, I'd like to present you to Her Majesty the Queen," Nick said.

In my periphery, I saw the Queen Mum raise her tumbler.

"Well, it's about bloody time, isn't it?" she toasted us.

The first time I saw Eleanor, so iconic and impressive in her monarchial finest, was from a careful distance. Standing face-to-face was like nosing up to a Seurat and discerning the dots. At nearly eighty, she'd crossed into that age where makeup starts looking like the paint job it is, and her skin was thinner, the lines etched more prominently. Yet this hadn't robbed her of her elegance, nor entirely of her beauty, and I realized how Agatha must have suffered for inheriting neither.

The royal physician had already awarded me a clean bill of health—*no syphilis*, I wanted to blurt—but still Eleanor examined me as keenly as she would a horse at Tattersalls. Her gimlet eye was the same one I felt at Nick's birthday, only this time I had nowhere to hide. And she did not miss the flag pin proudly displayed on the lapel of my coat—public, too, now that we were.

"How do you do, Miss Porter," she finally said.

"Thank you very much for having me, Your Majesty."

She seized my left hand in her cool, papery one, holding it up as carefully as a scientist so the light bounced off every facet of my ring. "It suits you," she said as she let my hand drop. "Though I daresay that ring can work miracles on any hand."

I felt a light whacking at my legs.

"Sturdy calves. She'll carry a child nicely," said Marta, bringing her empty tumbler to the decanter on Eleanor's desk. "Sprog her up before I die, Nicky boy. I assume you know how."

Nick looked like *he* wanted to die. But before Marta could begin any kind of instruction, the Queen's equerry, a petite and balding man called Murray—I still am not clear whether this is his first name or his last—informed us that the time had come for us to leave for church. Eleanor paused as she went past me, and laid a hand on my arm.

"Once you walk out that door, you are one of us," she said. "Ready or not."

Nick and I would be last in the procession. The press release about our engagement had been out for almost an hour, with word spreading fast, and everyone else spilling out of Sandringham first was effectively a human drum roll (never let it be said that Eleanor lacks a sense of drama). My hand floated up to my pin and I rubbed it for luck as, one by one, Nick's family—my family, soon—passed through the door to cheers and the pop of flashbulbs.

People don't usually get to take stock of the exact second everything changes; by the time they catch up to it, like a breeze, it has passed. But as we reached the door, the world slowed down so my artist's mind could engrave upon itself every sight and smell and sound of what I was doing. The light spilling through the open doorway. The roar of the villagers. The clammy, nervous sweat starting to form under my arms. The tie Nick chose, the exact shade of his blue suit, the heaviness of his ring on my finger. For years we'd walked the razor's edge between public and private, together and apart, and as we stood there on the verge, I was struck hardest by the power of what it felt like to *decide*. To take an outstretched hand knowing it would lead me on a journey I could not reverse. And when I let out that breath and followed Nick into the glare, I left a part of myself behind.

# CHAPTER THREE

Practically overnight, I went from being vaguely recognizable outside Great Britain—like an itch you can't quite scratch—to being very famous. Aggressively famous. The kind of famous where I looked so glossy on the covers of *People* and *OK!* and *Hello!* that I found myself abstractedly intrigued by that shiny celebrity with the friendly face and the well-groomed eyebrows. *Vogue* featured a lengthy but still only half-accurate piece about my background; lesser magazines dissected The Mysteries of Bex abetted by people I barely knew who crawled out of the woodwork with old yearbooks and apocryphal stories and colorful descriptors like *brash* and *ballsy*, and *giant raging bitch*. SHE WASN'T EVEN QUEEN OF HER PROM, shrieked Xandra Deane, as worked up about our impending matrimony as if I'd been dispatched specifically to seduce Nick and then take down the monarchy as the final and very delayed parting blow of the American Revolution.

My mother archived all the clippings—good and bad—in alphabetized acid-free boxes. One night she fell asleep with them on Dad's side of the bed, and told me he'd appeared in her dream to warn her that I shouldn't wear pink on my wedding weekend. Mom seemed to derive peace from the notion that he'd weighed in from the Beyond (even if we both knew it would've been more his style to duck in and leave a message about the Cubs' bullpen), and having something positive to concentrate on cut through her grief, which in turn cut through mine.

When Gaz heard the news, he burst into tears and offered our unborn children free legal counsel for life. Joss surfaced for some excited noises about who might design my wedding dress, and I texted Lady Bollocks a message that said, He WILL. Marry. An American. Her response was simply, Wrong number.

Clive was tougher. The bombshell interview with Katie Kenneth was picked up worldwide, along with Alistair's newest photo: Nick and Freddie crouched around Emma, smiling, while she stared dreamily off to the side, a freshly tended pixie cut giving her face a stark vulnerability. It was superb black-and-white portraiture, bathed in light and shadow, capturing the tragedy of the story without wallowing in it. Eleanor had conducted the orchestra flawlessly: After the initial media freak-out, the boys were praised for their silent bravery in the face of Emma's decay, the news cycle moved toward a discussion of the unnecessary stigma surrounding psychological issues, and then everyone got so distracted by the prospect of Richard wheeling Emma into the Abbey that the whole thing took on the air of an epic, tragic romance. Bonuses came fat and frequent at Clarence House, and Clive, an unofficial staffer in his own mind, felt left out in the cold.

"Two scoops," he sputtered. "*Two*, and no scraps for a friend?"

"This was over my head, mate," Nick said, handing him an apologetic lager across the dining table at Kensington.

"Not even a hint, *mate*?" he asked. "I thought we were scratching each other's backs."

"Marj gave you the polo bit, though," Nick said earnestly. "You broke that. Caused a total stir. That had to have helped, yeah?"

"That was ages ago, Nick, and a trifle compared to this," Clive said. "I've done nothing but support you. I buried India sneaking out of Clarence House. I could've dined out on that, but I didn't want to, not at your expense. I've never once said any of what I know. About anything. Or *anyone*." He gave me a very brief but pointed look. "But no one will take me seriously if they think you lot don't, and by freezing me out, that's exactly what you're suggesting."

"I'm so sorry, Clive," Nick said, distressed. "These were bigger than I am. It comes from the top."

"What about going forward? A wedding date, the honeymoon, the dress designer?" Clive asked, his face taking on a desperate sheen.

Nick spread his hand helplessly. "I can ask, but I can't promise," he said. "It's a delicate balance with the various papers, and there's a protocol Marj follows. I know it's my wedding, but it simply isn't my show."

"But someday it will be...?"

"Right, yeah," Nick said, and maybe he meant it, but to me it sounded like he wasn't completely comfortable with this negotiation.

I fretted about that to Cilla about a week later. We were in the airy dining room of her and Gaz's rented townhouse and home office, on a picturesque street called Hans Crescent that ran around the back side of Harrods—chosen because Gaz thought it made him look desirable if one could shop for his legal help and a diamond-encrusted nine-iron in the same block.

"I get worried that Clive is relying on us for big boosts that we can't give him, you know?" I said as Cilla bustled around her kitchen.

"Clive will get over it," Cilla promised, setting down a plate of tea sandwiches, the crusts neatly cut off. "The Fitzwilliams have been loyal friends to Nick's family longer than Clive's been alive." She slid me a cup of tea and a sugar dish. "How are *you*?"

"I'm not sure," I told her honestly. "Ever since Nick and I got back together it's been this rush of happiness and activity, but as soon as I slow down I get sad again. About Dad, about Emma..." I looked down at my ring. "I know she's still here, but not the way Nick wishes she was."

"I can't believe he kept that to himself for so long," Cilla said. "When did he finally tell you?"

"A few years ago," I said. "I don't think he'd ever said it out loud before. He went so pale."

"No wonder he was always so sensitive." Cilla sighed, dropping a sugar cube into her tea.

"He is a lot lighter now," I said. "I wish they'd done it years ago."

The film of sadness that covered Nick might never wholly disappear, but it did diminish. He talked about Emma more. His insomnia had ebbed. And, perhaps because he was finally rested, he even relaxed about the press. And then just as quickly as the tide turned in him, he rode it out of town: His Navy frigate, HMS *Cleveland*, deployed that January just two weeks after the Emma interview did. It was hard not having him around in those euphoric days when all we wanted was to be privately obnoxious about calling ourselves *affianced*, and it meant that I was left alone to find my footing.

I was telling a very sympathetic Cilla this when Joss blew into the flat like a tornado. She'd missed two buttons on her shirt, and mascara had run all over her face.

"It's over," she wailed, flinging herself into a chair with such force that Cilla's tea spilled. "The store. It's gone. It's all gone."

The bigger surprise was that Soj had lasted this long. But as foolhardy an enterprise as it seemed, Joss never saw it as a passing fad. In fact, her design aspirations may have been the only real constant in her life, especially because her impatient parents—whom she saw as faithless—had essentially closed her out of theirs.

"I knew we were losing money, but I didn't realize it was that bad." She sniffled. "I told Hunt we could still get a shirt on Bex, but—"

"I think your style is too edgy for Bex's new position," Cilla said tactfully.

"Doesn't have to be," Joss said. "People change. Hunt changed. Turned me out on the street and crawled back to his wife." She sniffled savagely. "Good luck having two hours of sex with a man who thinks he's so bloody innovative just because he likes nipple clamps. That's *so* three years ago, you stodgy old bastard. God, Viagra is the *worst*."

By the time Lacey joined us, looking elegant in a gray and black L.K.Bennett dress that I realized with a jolt was one of the finalists for my engagement shoot, the three of us had hammered out a plan for Joss to stay with me until her subletters moved out, and run Soj from her maisonette.

"And maybe we can collaborate on something for you," Joss said, brightening.

"I will try," I said. "I don't get a lot of..."

"You picked out what you're wearing today, didn't you?" Lacey asked, watching me as she poured cream into her tea.

"Well, sure. To go to Marks & Spencer, and then here," I said.

"Were you photographed?" Lacey pressed.

"I don't think so."

Wrong. The press would briefly dub me Princess Penny Pincher. I had just needed socks.

"So you have *some* freedom," Joss prompted.

"It depends," I hedged.

"On what?" Lacey asked.

I felt like she was increasing the target on my back rather than helping erase it.

"On whether my twin sister has already stolen what I was supposed to wear," I said as good-naturedly as I could manage.

Lacey looked at herself. "This? I thought you didn't want it."

"Yes, but Marj needs to return it," I said. "What's mine can't be yours if it isn't actually mine to begin with."

Lacey bit her lip. "I'll pay for it, then. It'll look great with the booties I got for when Tony takes me to Paris."

"Tony the Drug Dealer?" Joss asked, the thrill of gossip cutting through her depression.

"That was all extremely exaggerated," Lacey said smoothly.

When the New Year dawned without any sign of Freddie, Lacey had glommed onto Tony. He'd evaded jail time for Club Theme's alleged extracurricular activities, but I still thought he was crooked, and I'd hoped Lacey would figure that out and tire of him. But instead, they'd been in the paper with increasing frequency. The press now compared the members of the old Ivy League instead of coupling us; every time Lacey got dinged for her hair or her tan or the length of her skirt, she redoubled her efforts (and possibly her credit card bills) to look flawless the next time. Barnes and Marj were grumping about it to me, but I was not about to dive into Lacey's personal life.

"Mind that Tony," Cilla warned Lacey. "He's all about the game."

Lacey waved her off. "He's changed, Cilla," she said. "He's so driven, and he knows absolutely everyone. He wants to take Club Theme overseas, and wants me to help." She turned to me. "You and Nick can come to the opening! It would be great PR."

That made it the second time in under a minute that someone had traded on our relationship to ask me to do something for their own personal gain.

"Let's talk about happier things," Cilla interrupted smoothly. "I haven't had this much insider dish on a royal wedding since my fourth cousin Ramona objected to that obvious farce in Liechtenstein. When does the planning start?"

"I'm sure a binder for it was born the same day Nick was," I said. "He's on the ship until summer, so the ceremony probably won't be until next year. Marj started listing off all the details we need to lock in between now and then, but I blacked out somewhere around choosing which carriage we're going to ride in afterward." I grinned at Lacey. "My maid of honor will have her hands full with me."

"Of course," Lacey said. "When I can," she added, not entirely meeting my eyes. "I might be up for a promotion at Whistles, and this Paris trip—"

"Lacey," I said. "I can't pick out a dress and a tiara and wedding shoes without you. I can barely pick out my own jeans."

Lacey looked uncertain. "The Palace might not let me weigh in that much."

I thought back to everything Freddie said about feeling like the spare, and about how much Lacey and I had already lost this year. I would hold on tight if it killed me.

"I'll make them," I said wildly. "You're my sister. This is our adventure. Period."

"What is the difference between a baron and a baronet?" Lady Bollocks asked, pacing in front of me, tapping her riding crop in the palm of her hand.

"The last two letters," I joked.

Bea cracked the crop onto my coffee table. I pitied her horse.

"I am not doing this for my health," she said. "Who is the premier marquess in the peerage?"

"Um." I rubbed my forehead. "Hereford. No! Shoot. That's the viscount. Dammit."

"How do you pronounce this honorable surname?" she asked, handing me a piece of paper that read *Crespigny*.

"Wait, aren't you going to tell me any of the other answers?" I asked.

"No," Bea said, poking me with the crop. "Because you ought to know them like breathing. Figure it out. I am not here to coddle you. Now name the heraldic tinctures."

The first months of Nick's deployment were a learning curve whose slope rivaled the Alps we'd skied in Klosters. The business of renovating Bex into Duchess Rebecca had kicked into high gear, and the Palace made it clear that, like a puppy, I couldn't be taken out in public until I was properly trained.

"Her Majesty knows that the Soane museum and Paint Britain value your contributions," Marj had told me at my first private meeting with her without Nick by my side. "But perhaps the time has come for your positions to become opportunities for a person who does not have so many new responsibilities."

Translation: resign, and begin the uphill journey to ladyhood that Eleanor clearly thought would be an even more demanding full-time job. Marj's desk was stacked so high with binders and agendas, and revisions to the binders and agendas, that I once walked in to see her and walked right out again because I thought she wasn't there. Everything had a painstaking timetable; I wouldn't be surprised to learn Marj was charting my ovulation. She micromanaged my appearance and comportment, assessed the curve of my back in my natural stance, weighed and measured me weekly, drafted nutrition plans, and diagrammed what about my personal grooming needed to change and how fast. My eyebrows were filling in, and now it was my head's turn: a nominal number of extensions were bonded to my insufficient hair, with more added every two or three weeks for maximum subtlety, until we reached the desired level of luxuriousness.

Most of that I'd known was coming, at least in the abstract, although I admit I'd assumed the contents of my stomach were my own business. But the raft of reading, tutoring, and tests, like some kind of High Society High School, were a surprise. I thought Lacey might get a kick out of helping—she was always better at making flash cards; she even color-coded them—but it was Cilla who pointed out that Bea, as the actual titled lady in our circle, was the perfect candidate: a ruthless taskmaster who never pulled a punch and loved dining out on her superior breeding.

I tried folding Lacey into Project Bex in other ways. I arranged best man and maid of honor confabs for her and Freddie, figuring she would appreciate a sanctioned excuse to be in his orbit, but each time he produced a reason to beg off, ranging from legitimate (a Navy search-and-rescue) to slender (planning a garden for the Chelsea Flower Show) to apocryphal.

"I can't right now, Killer," he'd told me on my last attempt. "I'm in the middle of the Master Cleanse."

I had been unable to suppress a very loud snort.

"The Master Cleanse is no snorting matter," Freddie said very seriously.

I knew Lacey was taking this personally, beyond her general disappointment at Freddie having given her tractor beam the slip—how could she not, when she'd allegedly been bumped below *bloat* and *bowels* on Freddie's priority list. So I sought out the next best thing for her: shopping. Marj handed down an edict to spiff myself up even if I was just dashing out to the drugstore, along with a monthly wardrobe budget triple the size of my rent, and when I invited Lacey to help me spend it I got the first hug she'd initiated in months. But Marj had other ideas, assigning me a facilitator—Eleanor loathed the Hollywood air of *stylist*—and my own concierges at Harrods, Harvey Nichols, and Selfridges (the Queen also thought *personal shopper* sounded too spendthrift). That long-ago day trying on gowns in Harrods's private utopia became my normal shopping experience, thanks to Donna, a smartly suited brunette who'd guided eight starlets into adulthood without once falling into a vortex of transparency and tube tops. She adeptly meted out the budget and had a knack for suggesting alterations that gave an expressive pop to something I'd never have glanced at twice. She knew to strategize sewing weights into any hem, if a dress inhibited the way

I had to sit or stand, could weather a traffic jam, or would look discordant with any of Nick's blue suits. And she didn't need any help.

Lacey responded with that dog-with-a-bone mentality that helped her pass algebra when we were in middle school and got her to med school (if apparently not through it) and even into Freddie's bed. As we slowly stockpiled outfits for any occasion that might arise, Donna bumped up against Lacey at every turn, pushing the boundaries, desperate to make her mark.

"I like this one for an evening event," Lacey said, pulling out a sexy gold strapless dress.

Donna made a polite noise and put it back on the rack. Lacey turned to me and examined the suit I was trying on, for my eventual first meeting with the Archbishop of Canterbury.

"That skirt could be a bit shorter," she said. "You're not eighty."

"The Palace prefers to abide by certain rules," Donna said pleasantly. "Rebecca's nice long legs make any length work."

"But it's so off-trend," Lacey complained.

"The Palace prefers not to bow to trends," Donna said. "Rebecca has to look timeless."

"But look at this day dress," Lacey said, pulling one off the rack. "It's so mumsy. That *neckline*. Bex is flat-chested so she can wear something low-cut without it looking vulgar."

"The Palace prefers not to involve a lady's sternum," Donna said, calm but firm. I wondered if Marj had handed her a list to memorize.

"Well, fortunately, I have some accessories that will help," Lacey said.

"The Palace prefers a minimum of fuss," Donna said.

"The Palace prefers a minimum of *fun*," Lacey groused.

I tried to make whatever concessions and conciliatory gestures I could, but I caught myself deferring to Donna more and more because, frankly, she was right. There were certain parameters I was not free to wiggle around, or at least, not during what was essentially my rookie year. After two full days of push-pull, Lacey retreated to the couch, giving only one-word answers and perfunctory smiles. Then she bailed and never returned. I tried tempting her with outings that had nothing at all to do with me or the wedding, but Lacey found conflicts with them all.

By May, our conversations were just laundry lists of items she'd bought, restaurants she'd gone to, or men who were secretly in love with her, and she never, ever asked *me* anything. Not about how I was doing, or how Nick was, and not even razzing me about my thickening hair. Lacey was as finely attuned to my scalp as musicians are to their instruments, and she was the one person I'd counted on to tease me about the six hours I would spend letting Kira fuse bundles of a vegetarian Indian girl's hair to my own inferior head. It was tedious and weird—before they were trimmed, they came down to my elbows, making me look like a cut-rate reality-TV star—but I didn't want to bring it up for fear of looking like I was all me, me, me.

And yet, even without its emotional stalwarts, Team Bex was bigger than ever. Marj drafted a phalanx of expert strangers who diagnosed me as a Neanderthal hunchback with Clydesdale tendencies, and began shepherding my way through Duchessing for Dummies. No longer could I clomp from point A to point B. I had to glide, each leg crossing slightly in front of the other, my foot going heel-sole-toe at exactly the right smooth pace. I was taught to don and doff coats without them hitting the floor; to use only my left hand to hold drinks at official events so that my right would never be damp or clammy for handshakes; and accordingly, that I'd be better off never taking an hors d'oeuvre, lest I be forced to shovel it into my mouth. Before sitting, I learned to bump the chair ever so gently with my calves to be sure of where it was without glancing behind me. I must only cross my ankles, never my legs, and when getting up from that position, it is a discreet ballet of scooting to the edge of the chair and then standing quickly *while* uncrossing things. I am not uncoordinated, but that tripped me up six times the first day. In flats. Marj made my instructor sign a second confidentiality agreement on the spot, and then suggested some off-hours practicing. It's a wonder it took me as long as it did to hire Cilla permanently, because her suggestion to bring Lady Bollocks into my Duchess for Dummies training was a masterstroke. There was a reason Bea was so successful in Thoroughbred competitions that rewarded obedience.

"*No*, Bex," groaned Bea on a hot May afternoon. "You look like you're sitting on the loo."

I tried again.

"Rebecca, we cannot literally glue your knees together," she scolded me.

"They barely came apart," I protested. "It was a sliver."

"A sliver is all they need."

I groaned, smacking the car, then ducking back into it. "This is way harder than it looks. *Ow.*" I had forgotten to, per my crib sheet, *place a gentle hand on the doorframe so as not to crack one's head.*

Barnes had implied that the only transgression that would rain down greater hellfire than a photo of my underwear would be getting pregnant, especially now that there was at least one paparazzo on Crotch Patrol trying to nab the upskirt shot that would set him up for life, and an entire website called The American't dedicated to shots of me embarrassing myself. And so, in the privacy of the Larchmont-Kent-Smythe manor's gated driveway, I practiced Remedial Vehicular Entrance and Egress with the dedication I once applied to practicing fastballs.

"Brilliant. Does that one come with a complimentary Pap test swab?" Bea crabbed after my umpteenth try.

"It could not have been that bad," I said, sinking back into her parents' Bentley. "There is no way I've spent my entire life flashing people every time I've gotten out of a car."

"Believe whatever you like. Go again," she said. "Oh yes, marvelous. Now you'll go down in history as the American who can't keep her bits to herself."

"When will people stop caring that I'm American?" I grumbled, sliding back into the car.

"When you give them something else to talk about," Bea said blithely. "Which had better not be your cervix. Come on, go again."

"Can I at least have a glass of water first?" I fanned myself.

She checked her watch. "It has to be quick. I have a date with my mount in an hour."

"You can just call her Gemma." I couldn't resist.

"I assume that is your concussion talking."

"I'm just teasing, Bea," I said. "Cheer up."

"I will do no such thing," Bea said, stomping toward the front door, her riding boots aggravating the gravel into crunching protest.

All complaining aside, there was something perversely soothing about Bea cracking the whip on me, as if she believed I was perfectly capable of being correct the first time and was simply pretending to be inept. But that it took so much work to make me presentable in the first place felt like another item on The Firm's long list of my flaws, right above "pre-cellulite on the upper rear thighs"—never mind that the only person who ever saw my upper rear thighs had already agreed to marry me—and "inability to distinguish fish fork and oyster fork."

"What's got you frowning?" Bea asked, steering me into a seat in her parents' rustic country kitchen, and passing me a depressingly sensible snack of fruit, crudité, and raw almonds.

"That," I said, nodding to my plate. "I was hoping for scones."

"No cheating," Bea said. "There will be no royal muffin top, and you cannot get spots."

"Fine." I grudgingly bit into a carrot. "I'm doing all right, I think. I hate that Eleanor made me quit the Soane. I miss it. My boss actually cried. I think I'm the only person who listened when she explained why ecru tissue paper is better than eggshell."

"I did warn you that being with Nick is a job in and of itself," Bea said.

"Yes, Bea, you were right, as always," I said, and she very nearly smiled. "Honestly, I don't begrudge it, but it's a real mindfuck to give up a job that made me feel like *me* in order to take a job that's all about making me into someone *else*." I scrunched up my face. "And I miss having somewhere to go that isn't my living room, or Marj's office."

"*Wrinkles*," Bea said, smacking me on the hand.

"I am allowed to have facial expressions!"

"Debatable," she said. "When is Nick back?"

"Next month," I said. "Finally. I can't wait."

"Excellent. Then Joss can push off back to Fulham and stop trying to guilt you into letting her design something for you."

"Yeah, I don't know what I'm going to do about her," I said. "I got home the other day and found her wearing my clothes. She said she was studying them. Do I just give in? I'm worried she's losing it."

"Stop talking nonsense," Bea said. "You cannot give everyone the pleasure of your patronage, Bex."

"It's stressing me out, though," I said. "I don't want to hurt her."

Bea leaned back in her seat. "Why isn't Lacey helping you with this? The least she could do is take Joss off your hands."

"They barely know each other. And it's been weeks since we really talked," I said glumly. "If she even knows I quit working, it's because she read it in the *Mail*. Sometimes I think she's avoiding me."

I'd called Lacey the minute I'd taken that large, sobering step away from what I still thought of as my real life, but I'd hung up on her voice mail, and the window to tell her unprompted slammed shut. She'd have to ask. And she hadn't.

"Snap out of it," Bea said, poking me with her nail. "You have too much on your plate to worry about Lacey."

"That's rich, coming from someone who spent years stressed about Pudge," I said.

"And did that work? No," Bea said. "In fact, it was once I stopped bothering about her that she pulled herself together, and now look at her. Norway is obsessed."

"Lacey and Pudge aren't the same, though," I said. "Pudge had an addiction."

"I'd argue Lacey does, too."

"To what?" I asked.

Bea bit into a slice of apple. "To attention. To you. To *your* attention."

"That's not fair," I said automatically. "Our relationship is different. Twins are—"

"Yes, yes. You're bonded. It's special. Etcetera," Bea said. "I may not be a twin, but that doesn't mean I can't read one. Lacey is trying to get your attention by giving you none, and you are so desperate to make her happy that you're going to ruin everything for yourself."

"I can fix this, Bea," I insisted. "She's invited to Royal Ascot with me. It'll be a great way to remind her that we can still be the Porter twins even when I'm the Duchess of Wherever."

"Doubtful," Bea said, snagging the last piece of celery. "But I have said my piece. Now, back to work. And if you flash me any of your knickers at all this time, I will call the *Daily Mail* and tell them you've never worn any."

# CHAPTER FOUR

By summer, unbeknownst to us, *The Bexicon* was rushing toward its conclusion so it could hit bookstores in time to stuff people's Christmas stockings. Aurelia Maupassant chose to close her trove of flattering fallacies with this interpretation of my debut at Royal Ascot:

> It was a triumphant appearance. As the young prince and his future wife stood on the balcony of the Royal Box, their faces showed it all: happiness, contentment, and commitment to each other and to the people amassed below them. Porter was the very picture of perfection, a living dream, an aspirational totem for those who cleave to the most hopeless and hopeful of romantic beliefs that someday, too, their princes will come.

If that's what she saw, then I'll take it.

The five-day, multimillion-pound Royal Ascot race meet every June is characterized by crazy hats, extremely rich purses—both in terms of prizes, and handbags—and the prestige of Eleanor's daily attendance. This year, Nick's ship would arrive in port in time for him to join the Queen's procession, a prime opportunity for The Firm's PR machine to capitalize on the mounting yen for a Posh and Bex sighting. The world seemed to feel that being given royal lovebirds, only to have them ripped away for half a year while one of them shipped out to the Indian Ocean, was voyeuristically unfair. So when word got out that we'd be there on Ladies' Day, the *Guardian* ran the headline AND THEY'RE OFF, and the best of the Bex-themed fashion blogs, Bex-a-Porter, put a countdown to Ascot on the homepage along with a poll in which 73 percent of voters wanted me to wear a hat that made me taller than Nick.

Royal Ascot's dress code already falls in line with the litany of rules I have to obey: Sleeves are mandatory, or at least straps wider than an inch. Skirts must fall no higher than the vaguely defined *just above the knee*, and hats must have a base of four inches or larger (I wish I'd been present when they decided three inches was too trashy to bear). Lacey was still allergic to Donna—it was mutual—so it was Cilla, at loose ends now that she'd quit nannying and moved in with Gaz, who acted as my wingman during the flurry of emergency fittings.

"You'll want something bright, I think, Rebecca," Donna theorized.

"You've pulled some ripping patterns," Cilla observed. "In the right spots, they'll hide any wrinkles from the car ride."

"I was thinking a floral," Donna said, impressed.

"But just a touch of it. She can't look like a throw pillow."

Donna pulled from the rack a summery white dress with a fiery cluster of poppies at the waist, a few wafting petals sprinkled in both directions.

"My first pick," she said. "You've got a keen instinct."

"You did the hard part." Cilla beamed. She was the anti-Lacey. A love match was born.

The day of the races did not dawn fortuitously. We had to be in place well before the royal procession at two o'clock, but Bex Standard Time didn't exist yet, so my usual well-intentioned struggles with punctuality resulted in Kira nagging me to tears. And then Lacey made Mom and me wait an additional half hour before texting that she'd have to meet us there. It was only thanks to PPO Stout's lead foot that we were almost back on schedule when we drove in through the pack of wobbly race-goers spilling toward the grandstand. The racetrack has tried curtailing the party atmosphere, even adding an amnesty box inviting you to deposit any drugs you might have planned to sneak inside. (Freddie told me very seriously, in front of a stone-faced Twiggy, that they are doled out as Christmas bonuses to the PPOs.) I wish I'd attended just once when I could still anonymously people-watch, but instead we took an elevator above the fray to the curved, blue-carpeted Royal Box, jutting out like a flying saucer from the rest of Ascot's grandstands. Clive and the rest of the Fitzwilliams had beaten us there, with his father, Edgeware, holding court among the other toffs about a recent rugby match in which his fourth son Tim majestically shattered his nose. Dim Tim himself stood by, listening, and offering little other than a vacuous smile and a wonderful view of his new Picasso of a face: flat where it should be strong, his nostrils too close to his eyes. His brothers' buffet of distortions, to go with their matching hulking blondness, made Clive even more of an anomaly in the family than he already was.

"Clive!" I called out, spying him from behind.

He turned around, and with him, Paddington Larchmont-Kent-Smythe, in a yellow chiffon day dress straight out of a Fred Astaire movie.

"Rebecca!" Paddington said, gliding over to embrace me. "It's so fulfilling to be reunited."

"Um, yes, with you, too, Pud—er, Padding...Larchmont...?" I fumbled.

"You may use whichever name speaks to you," she said, warm but still somehow remote, like she was communicating from a dimension a half step out of sync with my own. Per *Tatler*, she was spending every third week in an ashram.

"Bex." Clive ducked in to kiss my cheek, dashing in his tailcoat. "It's been ages."

"Got any sure winners?" I asked.

"He'd better," said Thick Trevor as he passed, yanking painfully on his brother's earlobe. "Horse racing's the only kind of sport he plays: one where you don't actually do anything."

Clive shot him a disgusted expression as Pudge waved at the throngs outside.

"I was trying to absorb psychic energies from the people, because it's so *fucking* electric down there." Her new-age veneer made her old favorite word sound like a spiritual orgasm. "But nothing came to me. I shall meditate on it."

She kissed Clive on the mouth and then floated away.

"You two? I never would have called that," I said. "Hard to believe she's the same Pudge who could barely sit up at Klosters."

"Hard to believe you're the same Bex," he said, giving me the once-over, then pulling me to the window. "Have you taken in the view yet? Pretty impressive stuff."

The racecourse was set in countryside as green as my emerald. The crowd hummed with excitement as the bookmakers began taking punters' money for the day's races under their colorful umbrellas, and every ten seconds another wonderful, ridiculous hat wandered into view: a bust of David Beckham; a Mad Hatter's tea party recreated in elaborate clay sculptures, the Cheshire Cat's tail flicking the wearer's ear; even a tiny topiary trimmed in the image of Nick's face. And directly beneath us, a drunk woman was being escorted out under great protest—possibly because *her* hat, while chaste looking at eye level, from above was clearly a graphic depiction of a vagina. In her defense, it *was* Ladies' Day.

"Amazing," I said. "I never thought I'd be standing here."

"Nor did I," Clive said frankly.

I cast him a sidelong glance. "Yes, I know."

"How are you doing with all of this?" he asked. "You look smart, but if I know anything about The Firm, it's that appearances are deceiving when they need to be."

"Yes, no one ever accused me of being smart by any definition," I quipped, though his remark needled me. "I'm... so-so. It's hard without Nick. Marj is throwing stuff at me faster than I can keep up, and every day I find out I'm supposed to have a stance on, like, monograms, or something. And, man, the press is weird—no offense."

"None taken, *man*," he said.

"The other day, Xandra Deane said Nick and I are fighting because I want our children to be born in America." I shook my head. "Nick was at sea, and the last thing I want to discuss when I finally see him is childbirth."

"Xandra Deane is a professional royals hater," Clive said. "No one knows why—maybe because vitriol sells papers. But she's mysterious in general. Loads of people claim they know someone who's met her, but it's never a firsthand story."

"Maybe you can hunt her down," I said. "Weren't you applying for stuff at the *Mail*?"

He stiffened. "No takers," he said. "I missed the two biggest Lyons stories to come out in years, so I lost my momentum. But I'm making my way. Human interest profiles are very enriching. It's a real way to touch people."

I saw through him. His recent *Recorder* piece on an ancient male MP, who writes raunchy mysteries under the pseudonym Petunia Cortlandt, had read like Clive found it beneath him after the heady rush of the polo scoop from a year ago, and I think he regretted discarding the supremely socially connected Davinia Cathcart-Hanson before his ascent had been assured. I felt responsible. Bea said I didn't owe everyone my patronage, but no one taught me the distinction between that and loyalty.

"I'll talk to Marj," I said. "I know it's a delicate balance between being our friend and..."

"...and my career?" Clive supplied. He smiled absently, staring out the window. "It is hard," he said. "Nick only knows the half of how discreet I've been over the years."

"If it's Paris you're alluding to," I said with a slight edge, "neither of us did anything wrong that night, so maybe I'll just tell Nick and be done with it."

"No, Bex. No," Clive said. "Don't tell him. My point is only that it's hard to make it clear to him just how loyal I am, when I can't do it without...you know."

"You've been great," I said. "I bet we can work something out."

Clive lit up, which made me wonder fleetingly if I'd overpromised. I was saved by Gaz and Cilla, with Bea in tow, looking impeccable in blue.

"Incoming," Cilla breathed.

I glanced past her and saw Lacey heading over from near the elevator, smart in a red suit and a striking black hat, albeit one that looked hastily affixed.

"Sorry I'm late," she said, and I detected a distinct whiff of alcohol on her breath. "I came with Tony's friends, and they had to make a stop." She gestured at the small purple button attached to my dress. "Where can I get those little passes for them to come up?"

I froze. Did she really think I could invite random guests? This wasn't even my party.

"This isn't a nightclub, Lacey, it's the Royal Box at Ascot," our good old Lady Bollocks said, and I shot her a grateful look. "You can't just have the bouncer lift the rope."

"Why not?" Lacey asked. "This place is huge, and they're with me, and I'm with her, and she's with the heir." She looped an arm through mine, wobbling in her heels. I wondered what all had been consumed in that limo.

"If you don't understand, then I am not wasting my breath explaining," Bea snapped.

Nigel sidled up, white as a sheet. "Er, did you say Tony is coming?" he asked quietly, tugging at his waistcoat. "Bloody hell, I owe him a hundred... never mind. Just tell him to, er, be cool." He scampered away.

"An excellent demonstration of why your drug runner can't come up here," Bea said.

Lacey looked crestfallen. "But I can't tell them I couldn't get them in," she said.

"Why ever not?" Bea said, then glanced down at her racing form as if the subject were closed. "Great Scott, ten-to-one odds on Jolly Roger in the first? He's a brute. Can't pass that up."

Lacey bit her lip. "Shit," she said, loudly enough that I saw Pansy Larchmont-Kent-Smythe swing around and glare at us. "Fine. But when I get back, I have some news," she said, steadying herself ever so briefly before leaving.

"It never ends," Cilla said under her breath.

As I watched Lacey go, my mother and I met eyes across the room. I didn't want to ruin her day, so I gave her a sprightly thumbs-up, then turned back to my friends and sighed with what amounted to my whole being.

George IV was, by all accounts, a fatuous king and a worse husband, but he had an undeniable knack for pageantry: A lot of the things that are now hallmarks of the monarchy were his initiatives, including the redesign of Buckingham Palace that yielded its current famous façade, at least half the sparkle of its interior, and the Royal Procession at Ascot. The carriage parade begins at Windsor Great Park and winds around onto the racecourse past the grandstand, where a band strikes up "God Save the Queen." There's something magical about the rousing, carousing sound of sauced, exultant male and female voices shout-singing that anthem. If I'm around to hear "God Save the King" sung to Nick, I will cry every time. I got misty enough seeing through my binoculars how enthused he was by his first time in the procession with Eleanor. Her famous halting, semicircular wave had over the years become a flick, like she was halfheartedly shooing a gnat, but Nick's was so hearty he almost banged into Her Majesty's hat.

"Honey, he's so handsome," Mom said, squeezing my arm.

"He's always been a dish," agreed Gaz. "Can you imagine Nigel's ugly mug on our money? If I'm going to make a fat pile of dosh at the track, I want it to be attractive."

When Nick finally came up the elevator, and I saw him for the first time since January, I practiced my very best Barnes-approved walk and gave him a demure (if tight) hug and a kiss on both cheeks. Eleanor is lucky we didn't tear into each other like some kind of Animal Planet show.

"Welcome home, sailor," I said.

"You've no idea how good it is to see you," Nick said, flicking my flag pin, which I'd put on the brim of my hat. "And also agonizing, because there are no hidey-holes in here for acting on these extremely inappropriate thoughts I'm having, *oh, hello*, Gran. Didn't see you there."

Eleanor's face betrayed nothing—a lifetime of living behind a mask means hers very rarely slips, even in private—as she came around and laid an affectionate hand on Nick's arm.

I curtsied. "Your Majesty. I was just telling Nick that I hope he can give me some insider tips on how to read a racing form."

Nick shook his head. "I'm useless. I go by the jockey's colors."

"And I go by horse names," Freddie said, joining us. "There's some revolting nag in the Gold Cup called Dynastic that I hear is a lock to come in last. Know anything about that, Gran?"

The mask dropped and Eleanor all but vibrated with competitive fire. An inveterate horsewoman and Thoroughbred owner, she'd won some hardware over the years, but the Gold Cup—the most prestigious in British distance racing and the first leg of its own Triple Crown—cruelly eluded her. Bookmakers said Dynastic was her best shot at it in twenty years.

"Bite your tongue," she said to Freddie. "I'll expect your support in the form of a very generous bet."

"Only if you let me have a tipple of brandy out of the Cup when you win," he teased, poking cheekily at her hat. She swatted his hand away, with the kind of smile you give the overgrown imp you adore in spite of yourself, and headed off to her table. Lacey, across the room nursing a cocktail, waved awkwardly, and Freddie tipped his hat to her before pretending he was thrilled to see Thick Trevor and Dim Tim on the complete opposite side of the room.

"What's that about?" Nick wondered, watching Freddie go. Before I could answer, Mom stopped over to give Nick a squeeze before making a beeline for Agatha. The two of them set to chatting like a couple of old ladies in their rocking chairs.

"And what's *that*?" Nick asked.

"That is either a match made in heaven or an unholy alliance," I said.

"Speaking of which," Nick said, nudging me flirtatiously, "you would not believe the unholy things I'm thinking."

"Can you get your mind out of the sack for a second?" I grinned.

"Not a chance," he said. "I've been on the high seas, Rebecca. It makes a man thirsty."

I laughed. "Settle down, Sub-Lieutenant. I'm a sure thing," I said. "But first I have so much to tell you."

"Nicholas!" said Paddington, breezing back from wherever she'd found her meditative bliss. "What a fucking pleasure!" She wetly pecked both his cheeks. "I haven't seen you since that night we... well. You know."

"Er," Nick said, the tips of ears beginning to vibrate.

"He's such a spiritual lover," Paddington said to me.

"He...yes?" The implied question mark at the end was unintentional.

"The plane we were on was exquisite. I am so fucking delighted he's found the right soul to unite with in carnal Nirvana," Paddington said, and she seemed profoundly earnest about it. "Now if you'll excuse me, my sex partner is waiting for me over there."

During the ensuing seconds of silence, I must have burned a thousand calories just keeping my face impassive.

"We were split up. It was just one time," he said.

"One very *spiritual* time."

"And it only happened because I didn't actually recognize her until after. Well, during." He rubbed his head. "Wait, I'm making it worse. This is why I didn't want to get into everything that happened during the Dark Period. It was just...you know...things happen over the course of two years and...*two years*, Bex."

"Relax, I think it's funny," I said. "Things happened with me, too. Want me to spill one to even the score?"

I was teasing, but my eyes drifted to Clive. And then, against my will, toward Freddie. Maybe it was time to clear the ledger.

"Emphatically not," Nick said. "Honestly, I prefer pretending those two years never happened." He shook his head, as if evicting the thought. "How is everything else? How's Lacey? How is your mother? Are you eloping with Barnes?" He took my hand. "Are you *really* okay?"

My eyes met his, that cornflower blue I would be able to recreate in oils from memory even if I never saw him again. I felt my jagged edges begin to realign.

"I am now," I said.

Royal Ascot was awesome, even if Freddie would have poked fun at that very American turn of phrase. Gaz had the first three winners, and every single horse I backed came in dead last, which we agreed was, in its way, also a highly specialized achievement. The din of the spectators was infectious, but when the Gold Cup came around, the Royal Box fell silent. Everyone there had some sum of money—nominal or otherwise—on Dynastic, including Gaz, whose pick six Jackpot ticket now depended on the filly. When the gates flew open the tension was palpable, and Dynastic, stuck in fifth place, wasn't helping.

"Come on, get 'er going," Gaz urged. "That's the ticket."

"She's gaining," Freddie said excitedly. "Must've eaten her Weetabix this morning."

"Come on Dynastic." Gaz again, bathed in sweat.

"Come on, Perpetual Ocean," whispered Bea. "Oh, leave it out," she said when I gave her a mock-scandalized expression.

And then, right out of *My Fair Lady*: "GO ON, MY GIRL. MOVE YOUR ARSE."

It was Eleanor.

And it unlocked the room. Everyone began roaring and jumping in place, and when Dynastic galloped across the finish line a nose in first, Eleanor lit up so brightly that she may have emitted UV rays. Spectators below the Royal Enclosure looked up, cheering, the men tossing their toppers into the air to celebrate the Queen's win. When an impromptu chorus of the anthem rang out, Eleanor waved with more vigor than I'd ever seen, before throwing her arms around a bemused Richard and knocking his top hat askew.

Gaz whooped and twirled Cilla. "My love, that's four in a row. I've never had this kind of luck. It's all down to you. *You're* the Gold Cup," he said, dropping on one knee. "Marry me, you distressingly foxy goddess."

Cilla blinked. "What? Are you drunk? You've got two to go before your bet pays out."

"If you say yes, then I've already won," Gaz said. "Look, I'll rip up the ticket right now to prove I don't care—"

"No!" Nick and I shouted in unison.

"No, you clod, don't rip up your bloody Jackpot," Cilla said, though she had tears shining in her eyes. "I believe you. Of course I'll marry you. Who else would be mad enough to do it?"

Gaz jumped up, grabbed Cilla, dipped her, and then planted a heroic kiss on her. Nick fairly clutched at me with delight. He's such a sucker for this stuff.

"One condition," Cilla sniffled through a joyful smile. "We are not naming our child after any of your grandfather's fonts."

"I wouldn't dream of it," Gaz said. "The only other one that crackpot invented was called the Serif of Nottingham."

Once Eleanor relaxed, the level of carousing ticked up a notch. Gaz's Jackpot ticket did indeed win; Dim Tim started flirting vapidly with Lacey, prompting Freddie to inform him that with his nose's new location, he'd need to stand six inches further to the right in order to sniff around her with more accuracy; and right before the fifth race, my mother told me she and Agatha had bonded over *Orange Is the New Black* and that Agatha promised to teach her to ride.

"She's truly suffered at the hands of that dreadful Julian," Mom said. "She can't keep blowing out her own candle."

"Please tell me that's not a euphemism."

"It's from my therapy group," Mom said. "It means that she's not letting herself shine. I told her she should leave him."

And as if my family fomenting Lyons marital rebellion wasn't enough, I had Lacey to deal with when she corralled me before the sixth race.

"Bex, help me pick a horse," she said, dragging me over to a quiet corner.

"Well, I heard David Beckham's Left Foot and IWantItThatWay are hot favorites, but Gaz was talking up Who's Your Monkey, and he hasn't lost a race all day," I said.

"I don't actually care," Lacey said. "I just want to tell you my news. I was late today because I had a meeting with a publisher." She flushed excitedly. "I'm going to write a book!"

"Lace, that's amazing!" I gasped. "I didn't know you wanted to be a writer."

"Neither did I." She beamed. "But this editor contacted me, and it turns out she thinks I'd be perfect for writing a style book."

"I'm so proud of you, Lace," I said. "My sister, the author!"

"It feels really good. Like I finally have a purpose," she said. "Whistles has been so unchallenging lately. I think my brain is getting flabby."

I was delighted by the sight of her so thrilled about something genuinely great. All our lives, Lacey was happiest when she had a concrete project—and I hoped maybe her being at loose ends was the cause of whatever had started to curdle between us.

"It's not a done deal," she added. "I still need sample chapters, and all that. So when you have a sec, we should sit down and figure out how this might work."

"We?" My heart started to sink.

"Well, yeah," she said. "Your transformation from regular to royalty. I mean, honestly, before they made you use that Donna person, I was the driving force behind getting you out of bad pants. I think people will be really interested in how we—Bex, why are you looking at me like that?"

"Lacey, I don't think...I *really* don't think they'll let me do that."

"Why not?" Her face started to harden. "It's positive press for you, and people love a sister act. It'll be the Ivy League all over again."

"For the hundredth time, that wasn't a compliment," I said, hearing Bea.

"You cannot be serious," she said. "You are not honestly going to ruin this for me."

I made a helpless gesture. "The Palace is never going to authorize that. I don't even know how I would begin to convince Eleanor. We've only ever spoken twice."

"Don't know how?" she asked. "Or don't want to try?"

"I would love to see you write a book. It just..."

"Sure. Got it," Lacey said harshly. "Well, excuse me. I need to go place a bet. I hear My Sister's A Bitch is running in the seventh and suddenly I think it's a lock to win."

She stomped away, right past Nick.

"Trouble?" he asked.

I wanted to tell him, but once I started, I doubted I'd stop, and this wasn't the place. "Let's just say it's beyond good to have you back," I said. "And you seem so happy."

"I am," he said, casting a surreptitious glance around the room and then giving me a quick kiss. "Other than missing you, I really love it out there. It's the first time I've had such a tangible sense of purpose. Or that I've been confident any accolades I've gotten have been merit-based and not just because of...you know." He waved his arm around the room. "I feel like I've been waiting for this my whole life."

He took a long beat. "In fact, they might want me to go out again right away."

"Okay," I said uncertainly.

"It's unorthodox, but it'd be brilliant for me," he said. "See, they're recommissioning an HMS *Pembroke* frigate, and they thought I'd like being on its inaugural crew. The *Cleveland* is being benched for an upgrade that'll take a year, or even longer, so a transfer gives me more practical experience much faster than I'd get it otherwise." His face was alight. "I'd be back well in time for the wedding. That's doable, yes?"

I wasn't sure how to respond. I desperately didn't want him to leave again, not having just gotten him back, not with the other sands shifting beneath me.

Nick must have seen this play across my face. "I know," he said softly. "Two deployments in a row is a lot. If you need me, just say the word."

I wanted to, so badly. But when I looked up at him, I saw every crestfallen face when he told me Richard had denied his requests to join up, and every hurt expression when the media made fun of him for it.

"No," I said. "You should go."

"It might not happen," he hedged.

"Nicholas." It was Eleanor, calling to us from across the room. "They've waited long enough," she said, pointing toward the public. "Time to give them what they want."

Nick turned to me, a question on his face. I thought of Lacey storming away. I thought of my father, gone, and my mother, moving on; I thought of the Bex who'd climbed fences and never wanted to answer to anyone, and I thought of the Bex who'd lain in bed with Nick and daydreamed about living as a public couple, loving each other loudly, planning a wedding that would be wholly ours. I wanted to feel *engaged*, and not just like a girl wearing a very big ring. I wanted my best friend back. But there were two people I loved more than anything who'd been scrambling for a purpose. I couldn't satisfy one of them, but I could help the other.

"I'm fine." I took his hand. "I'll be fine."

I put the brightest smile I could conjure onto my face, and apparently I nailed it, because the pictures of us waving at the window convinced Aurelia Maupassant and most of the world that we were as deliriously untroubled as they wanted us to be. And as I gazed upon thousands of racegoers holding up cameraphones, shouting at us joyously, I floated outside myself and saw a person who was learning for the first time what it was like to belong, not just to someone else, but to something much bigger than herself.

# CHAPTER FIVE

## TROUBLE IN PORTERDISE?

**Bexzilla Wants Nicky to Love Her More Than Britain, worries XANDRA DEANE**

Posh and Bex are having problems: Our exclusive sources reveal Prince Nicholas now regrets his impetuous proposal to his brash Yankee bride.

In addition to helping her sister cash in with a book deal, Rebecca Porter, 26, apparently tried to disrupt Nicholas's career. The Prince, 27, may report for a second tour of duty aboard a Royal Navy frigate, and allegedly the American Porter is enraged that he, unlike she, sees the value in an honest day's work.

"He tried to explain that it's for his country, and she screamed, 'Well, it's not *my* country,'" says an insider. "She was furious. Thought tasting wedding cakes was more important. Nick was appalled. I should think he *wants* to get away."

At least the tantrum rumours explain what it is that Rebecca does all day.

There are few things as horrifying as realizing the *Daily Mail* is even marginally correct about your personal life. Lacey's book was not, to my knowledge, still in play; then again, after Ascot, we were barely in contact. The press had stopped photographing her walking to Whistles, so the only proof I had that she was even still in England was when I would come home and find she'd used her spare key to raid my closet. But when it came to Nick, though Xandra Deane had turned the volume up to eleven and had pertinent facts wrong, emotionally she was on the correct frequency.

A bare ten days after Ascot, with not nearly enough nights together in between, Nick went off on the HMS *Pembroke* until the New Year. It felt cruelly ironic that a frigate sharing a name with the place that brought him into my life was now sailing him right out of it. I'd wanted to be strong, but when I found out how fast he'd be leaving, my tear ducts overruled me.

"Shit, I'm sorry," Nick said, searching for a Kleenex, then giving up and handing me a napkin that had been on the coffee table. "You did say you were all right with this, Bex."

"I know. I hate that I'm crying." I curled my legs under me on the couch and hugged a throw pillow to my chest. "It just hit me how much I miss having you here. You and Paint Britain are the two things that make me feel the most like myself, and you're both gone."

"Then go back there," he said.

I blinked. "But Marj and Eleanor said I had to stop working."

Nick shrugged. "Don't listen," he said. "I wouldn't."

"Since when am I allowed to say no?" I said. "Where were you with that advice a couple of months ago?"

"If you recall, I didn't know about it until after you'd already resigned," he said. "I agree it's not ideal that I can't be here all the time, and I wish I could, but it's a fact of life in the Navy. Someday, I'll be in your hair constantly. But I must serve the country if I'm meant to lead it, and if I quit now, everyone will say I'm no better than Edwin, hoovering up taxpayer money."

"I know," I told him. "I do know. I just keep imagining you off on a ship, and me at home juggling babies you only see three times a year. I wish I'd thought everything through, is all."

He sat back a little. "Or what?" he said. "You wouldn't have agreed to marry me?"

"No, of course not. I just..." I blew out my cheeks. "I don't know what I mean."

I'm not sure why I didn't just tell him point-blank that I felt stranded. And in the wake of Nick's departure, it started nibbling at me that maybe we had been as impetuous as Xandra Deane claimed. We'd careened into each other's arms after my father died, and the ensuing tide of emotion had carried us here and dumped us and ebbed. Nick's sense of duty is part of what I love about him, but I should have fought for more time by his side to get assimilated before I lost him to it, and communications to the HMS *Pembroke* were too irregular to talk through the questions that tortured me in the middle of the night. When *could* I say no to The Firm? Did I have the leverage to fight for myself? When was he going to take this promised desk job? Where would we live? What *about* our theoretical children? When was I expected to have one? And how would it make friends, if we were boxed in by a gated-off palace? Cruelly, the person who really could've understood was Nick's mother, physically sitting alone in Cornwall but mentally out of reach.

Planning the Wedding of the Century only exacerbated my unsteadiness, even though all the ingredients were there for it to be a giddy delight: financial carte blanche and the heft of a royal decree. Church closed for cleaning? Finish it early. A groom at sea? Recall the ship. But I myself had very little say. The date was chosen because late April fit Eleanor's calendar. It had been Marj who'd made the list of designers who could bid for my wedding dress, and selected meaningful flowers for my bouquet. I was told to pick an organist, and flower girls and pages from distantly related blue-blood families I'd never met, and even to pare down the existing guest list to make room for our friends. All of which I did, dutifully, before learning they were perfunctory offers, and Eleanor had already made all those decisions.

Even the autonomy I *thought* I had was illusory. The Palace didn't want me photographed anywhere unauthorized, which meant Stout had to phone in a request any time I wanted to so much as pop out for an ice cream cone, which was such a pain that I stopped going anywhere at all. Shopping, if you could call it that, now took place in a converted room at Clarence House, where I was expected to stand still and silent so that everyone else's opinions could be heard. Donna and her team bustled around me, dissecting my body with scientific detachment as they whipped outfits on and off my frame, before bagging and tagging clothes with color-coded notes marking what should be mixed and matched, reworn or archived, auctioned or donated. It was busywork, but busywork that required my presence and attention, even though nobody there ever paused to acknowledge that I was *me* and not just a mannequin. As the months stretched on, I used all my energies to look sparkling during those fifteen-second windows when I was publicly visible, and the rest of the time I diligently obeyed my schedule and studied trivia about our potential guests and jogged on the treadmill Marj sent to my flat (along with an industrial-strength juicer that was louder than my dishwasher). I felt like little more than a prop in a very complicated play—as if I could be anyone, and events would still roll on unchanged.

Unfortunately, the longer I went without another major public appearance, the more screeds Xandra Deane fired off painting me as an unemployed drain on the taxpayers, shirking my official duties in favor of staying home and polishing the Lyons Emerald. Like Nick in his first years out of Oxford, I couldn't defend myself—there is nothing less sympathetic than blubbering that your self-care regimen has made it impossible to hold down an outside job—so the rumors picked up steam. I understood it. I would have believed them, too. Because even I'd lost sight of myself.

So I did something about it.

I'm not sure why I didn't act sooner. I think that when the daily grind of my duchess training began, it had provided a welcome distraction from the loss of my dad, and then kept me occupied in Nick's absence. And because failure at it was not an option, I let it consume me without realizing that *occupied* and *satisfied* are not the same thing. In the end, oddly, it was Prince Edwin who galvanized me (albeit indirectly). One random Thursday in August, I was sitting in Marj's office, preparing for our regular confab, when two things happened at once: I heard Barnes spitting nails at Edwin's new press secretary because Edwin went on *Sunrise* to announce he was starting his own experimental theater company—against Eleanor's specific wishes—and I got an email from Maud at the Soane. The two things started to coalesce in my mind, along with the memory of my dad sending me back here long ago to *go be Bex*. I wondered if he was watching from his Coucherator in the sky, sad that I'd found myself in a situation where me being Bex was considered a hindrance. By the time Marj returned from bullying the old Xerox machine, my spine had returned to me and I had a speech ready. Sort of.

"Right," Marj said, sweeping in and dropping an iPod in my lap. "In there you'll find preapproved music for which you are allowed to express a public affinity. Some classical, some pop, some dance, and nobody who's ever eaten meat in front of Paul McCartney." She sighed. "That ruled out rather a lot of them."

I scrolled through it. "Oh, good, I get the Spice Girls?"

"Eleanor enjoys the frightening one," Marj said. "Now, about your—"

"Excuse me, Marj, if I may," I said. "I have something for the agenda. I mean, to put on my schedule." I showed her Maud's message. "My old boss Maud runs Paint Britain now, and she offered me a spot on the board, and wants to seal it with an event. I'm going to do it."

"Are you?" Marj fastidiously removed her glasses and placed them, folded, on the desk.

"I am." I hoped she didn't catch the waver in my voice. "I think I've been a pretty good pupil over the last several months, and I appreciate the time and care everyone is putting into me, but I'm starting to lose my mind a little. I need to produce something other than myself. And I need to show people what I bring to this family other than reformed hair and well-chosen coats. If Edwin can go off-book and mount some weird interpretive Shakespeare in Hay-on-Wye, or whatever Barnes was yelling about, then I think I should be allowed to take on some public philanthropy. Especially for a charity *I* started, of which Richard is a patron. It would be good for everyone."

Marj stared at me for a full minute.

"We will finalize the details," she said simply.

Adrenaline shot though me. "And I'd like our friend Joss to pitch a dress for me to wear," I blurted. Marj raised an eyebrow. "Please. Donna was just saying we should try to boost some smaller British designers. If it's a mess, I promise I won't ask again."

Marj closed her eyes, as if praying for deliverance.

"Have her sketches to me tomorrow," she said, and then handed me a folder about the history of indoor cycling in Britain.

I opened my mouth.

"Do not press your luck," Marj said. "Now, velodromes. Let's begin."

The Paint Britain event coincided with Nick's twenty-eighth birthday (Marj loves a mushy PR spin), which he was spending on the waters of Someplace, presumably looking sexy doing whatever he did with weapons. Paint Britain had been my refuge from missing Nick before, and the prospect of a day doing what I loved bolstered my spirits again. Unfortunately, it was not as giddy an occasion for my old friend. A confident Joss had presented Marj with a sketch for a white dress in a cheerful paint-splatter pattern. It was lively, if a bit on the nose, but Donna instantly recognized it as a copy of a year-old dress from a high street store, which itself was questionably similar to a Chanel. If we had trumpeted plagiarism as a custom original, the press and the blogs would have had a field day—especially Bex-a-Porter, which noticed if I so much as repeated a bracelet.

"Please let me try again," Joss had begged me, tears running down her face.

"Maybe this is a sign you need a break," I said as kindly as I could. "We've all been there, where the pressure and stress makes your eyes cross."

"Right, like you know stress," she sobbed. "My father's jammed too far up the Royal Family's privates to support my company. The only cash I have coming in is from my subletters, so I can't tell them to leave. One word from you and I could have a dress that sells out all over the world, and you won't help me."

"I did help you. I *tried*. You set me up for a scandal," I said. "I know you didn't mean to, but come on. I can't ask the Palace to take that chance again."

"Oh yes, wouldn't want to make the Palace cross. What if they take back that big fat rock?" Joss snapped. "I knew you never liked me as much as the others, and now it's showing."

"Joss—"

"Piss off, Princess," she said savagely. "Clive said I can stay with him. *He's* a real friend."

I was miserable about how badly this had backfired. I'd been so sure Lacey's book wouldn't fly that I'd never even tried broaching the topic with the powers that be; this favor for Joss hadn't seemed so out of reach, and yet now we were on the outs, too. With my personal relationships looking as shaky as my mental state, I was even more grateful to be—in a sense—going back to the work that had held me together once before.

The Tate Modern had arranged for Paint Britain to set up creative stations outside on the South Bank, the London Eye looming picturesquely across the Thames in every photo. Part of the price of getting what I wanted had included co-billing with our lofty patron Richard, and I'd dreaded spending the day with him, but I've never seen him so alive and kind—getting dirty with the kids as they did spin art and dug into some sculptors' clay, and doing a lovely impromptu pencil sketch that he donated for our fundraising efforts. The two of us went head-to-head in a paint-balloon contest to see who could make a bigger splatter (he won), and one child did such a gorgeous watercolor that Richard and I got into a bidding war for the piece, and then each agreed to pay our highest offer if she would do another one and let us hang it in the Tate—an idea Richard had on the spot, which led to a permanent Paint Britain exhibition there.

"That was awesome," I said after we posed for one final photograph and were returning to our lounge. "You were amazing!"

"It's a lovely charity," he said stiffly.

"We should do this more often," I babbled, high on how far Paint Britain had come from its days in the Soane basement. "You're really talented. That watercolor you left at Cornwall—did you ever finish it?"

Richard turned so rapidly that I almost crashed into him. "We are not friends," he said evenly.

"Excuse me?"

"We both love art, and you are marrying my son, but we are not pals." He gave emphasis to the oh-so-American word. "Nor do we need to be."

His coldness touched a nerve in me that had first been tweaked years ago in Nick's room at Pembroke.

"You mean, we both love art, and we both love Nick," I said pointedly. "Right?"

"This conversation is over." He continued walking, brisker this time.

"I would like to get along, Rich—sir," I amended, as I trotted behind him, wobbling in my wedges. "And if we did, it might go a long way toward fixing your relationship with Nick."

"That is none of your concern."

"It is totally my concern," I said. "Because without Emma—"

"Joining this family does not give you the right to speak to me about it," Richard said. "Especially about Nicholas's mother."

"Fine, we don't have to talk about it, but please at least talk to him," I begged. "That lie was killing Nick. He needed you. He still does."

From a half step behind, I saw Richard's jaw tense, but I barreled on anyway. "A terrible thing happened to Emma, but now at least you can live out in the open with it, together," I said. "You're all free. Finally."

As we burst through the door of our private lounge, Richard wheeled on me. "That terrible thing did not just happen to her," he said. "My wife spent twenty-five years out of her mind, but very happy inside her own head. Whereas I spent twenty-five years hoping someday my mother would allow me to divorce Emma and say that we had drifted apart, so I could have a life that fulfilled me. But if I do that now, I will be despised for it, and any real feelings I have for another person will be irrelevant and wasted and impossible. So I am *not* free. *Nobody* is free."

I found my voice, but it was very soft. "That watercolor. It was so full of love."

"For a twenty-year-old girl I should never have married."

"But you did. And you got two wonderful sons out of the bargain. Which you'd know if you ever really looked at either of them."

I'd gone too far. He leaned into me, eyes crackling with anger, a gaze I'd long been afraid of having turned on me.

"You are here at the mercy of Her Majesty and me," he said quietly, but with ferocity. "Nicholas wanted to join the Navy, and we agreed, on the condition that he took finding a bride as seriously as he took his military service. He did not. We set a deadline. And there you were, right before the clock ran out, satisfying the letter of our decree if not the spirit." His lip curled. "You are wearing that ring today only because of our tolerance and your own good luck. Remember that the next time you think you understand anything."

And with that, he signaled to Barnes, collected his things, and left.

Marj poked her head into the room. "Rebecca," she said grimly.

*Right before the clock ran out* was still ringing in my ears.

"Just give me a sec."

"No," Marj said. "There's some news."

It was Lacey. Impeccable timing.

"Well, happy birthday to Prince Nicholas, eh?" the blond *Sunrise* host asked the next morning, crossing her tan legs and turning toward Katie Kenneth. "But the real question is how the Royal Family will handle this, isn't it?"

"It is, Holly, and it's a very complex situation," said calm, maternal Katie, who, by dint of having interviewed me and Nick, was the media expert of choice. "It's not immediately clear whether Lacey Porter herself broke any laws."

"And Lacey is of course due to stand up as Bex's maid of honor in just about eight months' time," said Holly, as photos of the two of us flashed up on the screen: in high school at the famed Dumpster Guy Prom; at my aunt Kitty's third wedding, Lacey looking like a goddess and me in some ill-advised pantsuit; and of course, a variety of paparazzi shots.

"They could've picked something where my hair looked better," I mumbled to myself, before realizing I sounded exactly like my sister.

"Any indication whether this is affecting the wedding plans, Katie?" Holly was asking.

"None at all, Holly. The Palace won't comment because Lacey is not a member of the Royal Family," Katie replied. "The good thing for Rebecca and Nicholas, but I suppose a bad thing for us, is that their friends are generally quite tight-lipped, and that has held true today. But safe to say nobody slept much in the palace last night. The Queen has a very low tolerance for misbehavior, which she's shown time and again with her own son Edwin."

"But Lacey Porter might be out of her jurisdiction," Holly speculated.

"I daren't suggest *anything* is outside the Queen's jurisdiction," Katie said.

I snorted from my perch on my living room sofa, where I was in pajama bottoms and a novelty London Underground T-shirt that read *Mind the Gap*. Dad had bought it for me when I moved back, as a way of bucking me up, and I tended to wear it whenever I needed extra Earl Porter go-get-'em mojo. Which I would require in spades, because Lacey had, metaphorically, definitely *not* minded the gap, and both tabloids and the more respectable broadsheets alike had leapt right on top of it. Even the London *Times* couldn't resist LACEY PORTER IN PARISIAN DRUG SCANDAL, although at least it was below the fold.

After months of guilt, confusion, and worry, being standard-issue pissed at Lacey was almost a relief, because it was so uncomplicated. Even now, my blood runs hot when I think about the whole idiotic mess. (I keep imagining Eleanor in her nightgown and curlers, crunching her morning toast over the paper, clucking, "Are young people just *stupider* now?") Tony's reputation preceded him, but the drug he hooked my sister on was status: all his flash, and the attendant flashbulbs, and so she chose to be blind to the rest. They were attending the opening of his pop-up, Versailles, which was located in a Parisian townhouse tarted up like one of Louis XIV's mistresses. Opening night encouraged regal fancy dress, so Tony had donned full Sun King regalia, and Lacey, drunk at best in the paparazzi shots and interior photos that eventually leaked, had gone as *me* in a brown wig, a fake emerald, and a green dress so similar to my engagement photos that I actually checked to see if mine was gone (it wasn't). And after that debauched all-nighter,

Tricky Tony, possibly the dumbest egomaniac alive, sped through Paris in a rented Maserati stuffed to the gills with cocaine and cash. When the gendarme booked him for speeding and got so much more, it was my sister in the front seat with him, my sister who got hauled off in cuffs, and my sister who spied the paparazzi and gave them an angry middle finger.

Paris might be out to get me. Porter women are zero-for-two there.

Marj broke the news once she hustled me safely into the car. My mother was already en route to Paris, and Marj ordered me to stay put in my flat, where the paparazzi had immediately descended in hopes of catching Lacey skulking to me in shame, or me leaving, either cocky and defensive or bathed in betrayed tears. I shut myself in, unable to sleep or relax or even eat, waiting for word about Lacey and hitting reload on my in-box, veering between being sure Nick was too busy—I imagined him shirtless and firing cannons, for fantasy's sake—and being afraid he was too mad to talk. As was I: Beyond Marj and, quickly, my mother, to confirm she was safely in France, I kicked every call to voice mail and ignored a novel-length text from Clive explaining that while he was a novice to television, he would gladly stave off his nerves and defend Lacey's honor and whitewash the situation in our favor. When I showed the text to Marj in the backseat of the car, she deleted it without a word.

"I have met Lacey Porter, of course. We went around town a bit," Maxwell, son of Baron Something-Something, was now saying on the TV. The network must've begged Penelope Eight-Names to fork him over as a character witness. "Lacey is a bright young woman who I believe was simply in the wrong place at the wrong time with the wrong people."

Holly frowned as best she could around her Botox. "That middle finger looked a bit defensive, though, wouldn't you say?"

The photo flashed up on the screen. Lacey's face was contorted with anger.

"Er. I really couldn't say. She's just, er, so bright..." Something-Something stammered, way out of his depth.

My cell phone rang.

"I've spoken to the embassies in Paris," was Marj's opening salvo.

"She may be called back to testify, but we've managed to get her out without being charged as an accessory."

I exhaled a breath I hadn't even realized I'd drawn. "Thank you, Marj. We don't deserve this. I can't tell you how grateful I am."

"We've told the press she's under house arrest in Paris for a week, so that we can sneak her home with your mother."

"Maybe we should leave her there," I muttered, feeling my blood boil again.

"The Palace will not be doing anything further on Lacey's behalf," Marj said. "You understand."

"I do."

"And to that end," she said delicately, "I've spoken to Her Majesty—"

I refreshed my email. Nothing.

"—and Her Majesty thinks it wise if your twin takes a much-diminished role in the wedding," Marj finished.

I had, in an early morning fit of fretting, predicted this to myself. "Does that mean she can't be my maid of honor?"

"Her Majesty believes a much-diminished role might be wise," Marj repeated.

"So, that's a no."

"If that is how you choose you interpret it."

"But if Eleanor says..."

"Her Majesty," Marj said firmly, "has simply offered a gentle suggestion."

Sometimes it was like we were all speaking in code.

"I'll take her *suggestion* under advisement, then," I said. "And do let her know I appreciate her, um, very reasoned counsel."

"One more thing," Marj said. "And you'll not like it, Bex."

My heart shuddered.

"No more Paint Britain for a while," she said, and by giving it to me plain, for once, it felt like she was sympathizing with me. "You'd be besieged with questions about Lacey. It would hurt the charity *and* drive you potty." She paused. "This is nonnegotiable."

And just like that, the scrap of myself I'd fought for was yanked away. We rang off and I looked back up at the television in time to see news footage of my sister leaving a Parisian police station, surrounded by photographers. For someone who craved the spotlight, she didn't seem to enjoy it much as she pushed through the melee, holding her purse in front of her face. *Be careful what you wish for* may be both of our epitaphs.

*Sunrise* ended after a discussion with the bloggers behind Bex-a-Porter and The American't about my style. The first, a lively blonde named Kelly appearing via satellite from Los Angeles, was complimentary, but The American't vehemently believed my jeans were tight enough to show a panty line. This shoved me into a nasty Internet wormhole. With little else to do but wait, I devoured the comments that said I was superficial and inept and embarrassing, and composed and deleted a dozen anonymous defenses of myself (Ms. Edwina Monet thought my jeans fit perfectly). The press was blaming me for Lacey's misbehavior—everyone from Xandra Deane to the fast-proliferating royal-watching blogs, one of which, The Royal Flush, claimed I had been specifically tasked with controlling my sister and failed. It was incorrect, but only technically. This felt like a botch job, and *I* felt a failure.

At midnight, ushering in the third day of this ridiculous drama, I still had not slept. Words from The Royal Flush's post floated before my eyes when they were open, and when they were closed, all I saw was the look on Richard's face when he told me I was Nick's last-ditch marital Hail Mary. I was overtired and overwhelmed and in an utterly shambolic mental state when the key turned in the front door of my flat.

"Bex?" Lacey stuck her head around my bedroom door. She looked rough: exhausted, puffy, her hair in a lank ponytail. "Are you alone?"

I sat up and clicked on my bedside lamp.

"Who the hell do you think would be here?" I asked.

"Well, Nick," she offered.

"Nick is at sea," I said. "You not knowing that speaks volumes."

Lacey hung back in the doorjamb. When we were kids, she would have climbed in bed with me, uninvited. Of course, when we were kids, the person likely to be caught in a prank gone wrong was me.

"How did you get past the paparazzi?" I asked.

"PPO Popeye," she said. "He dropped Mom at her hotel and started to take me home, but there were so many people waiting outside. I hid under a blanket like you used to do and he took me here. I snuck in the back." She bit her lip. "I couldn't make myself walk past them."

"Maybe you should have thought of that before you flipped off one of them." I rubbed my eyes. "I can't *believe* you stayed mixed up with that asshole Tony."

"I was just a passenger. How was I supposed to know what Tony was up to?"

"Maybe from years of us talking about it?" I said. "Did you not think? About any of it? This makes us look so trashy, Lace."

"I should have known the only thing you'd care about would be how *you* look," Lacey snapped. "Nobody got hurt. They weren't even his. He was holding the drugs for a friend."

"I cannot believe you are trying to feed me that old line," I said, cringing. "Why are you even defending him? It was a crime, Lacey. There were enough drugs in that car to light up half of London. You got *arrested*." I took a hot, impatient breath. "Have you even thanked anyone? Marj had to massage the US Embassy to get you out. But you'll have to go back and testify."

"Can't Marj call in a favor or something?" Lacey chewed on her thumbnail.

"The US Embassy *was* the favor," I said through gritted teeth.

"Then Nick, maybe?" Lacey wheedled.

I said nothing.

"This is so unfair," she said. "I'm getting blamed for someone else's mistake! If it were you, they'd move mountains."

"If it were me, I wouldn't have been in Tricky Tony's car," I said. "But I'm also the one engaged to Nick, so yeah, they would have to do more."

"But I'm your sister! It's so selfish of them!" she insisted. "And of you. After everything I've done for you, I can't believe you won't make this go away."

I felt all the blood in my body rush to my face. "I think you need to leave."

She reacted as if I had slapped her. "You're not serious."

Lacey looked around as if she expected someone to back her up, but the only company she had was on my dresser: a framed photo of our seventh birthday, me giving her rabbit ears, her missing a tooth, both of us sitting behind a vanilla sheet cake with rainbow frosting. She'd thrown a tantrum when I asked for chocolate, and I gave in because the histrionics weren't worth it. Cake was cake.

"You can't throw me out. I need you," she pleaded.

"Yeah, when you can use me," I said. "I take your calls. You never take *mine*."

"That's because you spend all your time talking about Nick," Lacey spat.

"That's funny, because I could tell you the last six places you ate dinner, but you didn't even know that Nick deployed again," I countered. "And Nick was not a problem for you two minutes ago when you wanted him to do you a solid with the French police, and he wasn't a problem when he was getting you into clubs, and he absolutely wasn't a problem when you wanted to meet Freddie."

"Nick was the *entire* problem with Freddie," she said with vitriol. "Have you completely forgotten how hysterical he was that we not date in case it made *you* look bad? I put what I wanted on hold to get you through years of dating and *not* dating Nick, and now you won't even do me the smallest favor, because you're saintly Princess Rebecca, with her perfect fake hair and her perfect life."

"You know that's not how it is!" I said, worked up enough that I threw off the covers and stood up. "You of all people know how weird and hard this has been."

Lacey rolled her eyes. "Yeah, poor you. Dad paid for your flat so you could land a guy. I gave up med school to be with you and you gave up... what, art classes? And all you got out of it was, hmm, let me think... *everything*. I feel *so sorry* for you."

"Are you kidding me?" I actually stomped my foot; nobody brought out my juvenile side like Lacey. "You gave up med school so you could sleep with Freddie. I am just the excuse you used to pull it off."

"You ditched me at Cornell!" she accused.

"I did not!" I protested. "I did something for myself."

"No, you ran off and left me in your dust," she said. "And I think you like it that way."

"Our lives aren't some kind of race, Lacey!"

"Then why do I always feel like I'm losing?" she said, almost crying now.

We had, without realizing it, moved toward each other so that we were yelling in each other's faces—our gravitational pull in its worst iteration. Abruptly she turned and stomped out, smacking the doorframe with her hand, then stomped back in again and set her jaw.

"I got fired," she says. "From Whistles. Before Ascot." At my dumbfounded face, Lacey sneered, "Now who's the one who doesn't know anything?"

"But I asked how work was, and you'd say it was great."

"What, and admit they didn't want me if I didn't come with you?" she said spitefully. "Once Donna shoved her way in and you stopped shopping in public, my manager decided he didn't need me anymore. Because everything revolves around *you*. The book deal fell apart because they only wanted me if it came with *you*. I don't get Freddie because of *you*." She clenched and unclenched her fists. "You are not the only person your relationship happened to. We all had to rewrite our lives. I had to change how I acted, who I dated, what I wore to work."

"I can't help what Nick's family is," I said, frustrated. "And you would have been in deep shit for this no matter who I was marrying. Probably deeper, because you'd still be there."

"But the paparazzi wouldn't have been there," Lacey countered. "I get all of the crap from Hurricane Posh and Bex, and none of the benefits. We used to be the Porter twins, and now we're just Rebecca Porter and the other one." She was crying now, which only added to her anger. "I don't know who I am now or why I'm even still here, and all anyone wants to ask about is you. Nick and Bex, Nick and Bex, Bex, Bex, Bex. Who. Cares. I'm over it. I'm over *you*."

"Well, then, you made this really easy for me," I said. "Consider yourself officially relieved of your wedding duties."

Lacey's jaw actually dropped. "What?"

"You just said you're over me. I figured you'd be relieved," I said, but my lips were quivering. Her words had hit me like a physical blow.

"Great. You're right. I don't want to be in your ridiculous wedding," Lacey said, pivoting and marching into the hallway.

"Then you did finally get something you wanted," I called after her, hearing myself on the verge of tears. "Maybe you should get arrested more often."

"Maybe I shouldn't even *come*," she shouted, punctuating this with a slam of the door.

"Dammit," I whispered.

I should have gone after her. I should have told her we needed to help each other. But instead, I collapsed in tears on the corner of the bed, and felt the invisible tie between us snap.

# CHAPTER SIX

The details of my wedding gown have been protected like the state secret they are. With eight months to go, Donna, Marj, and I had whittled the list of design candidates to three, each of whom signed confidentiality agreements longer than a novel, and took a circuitous route to our fittings that added forty-five minutes to the trip and required three car changes. One of the interns buzzing around Clarence House politely asked me in passing how it was going, and I'd cracked, "I'm leaning toward something in British racing green." When it made the papers the next day, the poor trembling girl was dispatched to purgatory (Edwin's offices) and I was instructed to respond to all queries, even from insiders, with the antiseptic, "It'll be lovely."

Eventually, my opinion was sought—Eleanor was human enough to realize that a bride should get a vote on her own gown—but she strongly expressed a preference for covered shoulders, and luckily, I agreed. Sleeves seemed more regal, despite the ensuing need for armpit Botox. Beyond that, I had no interest in trying to make a fashion statement, and the mere concept of a poufy affair with bows and ruffles and fringe made me itch. I think my missing Disney gene disappointed Fancy Nancy, because she worried several times that all my stipulations would lead to something that wasn't fairy-tale-princess enough.

Eventually, I had to remind her, "Neither am I." Marj guffawed before she could help herself.

The first designer had barely wrapped one piece of white fabric around me, looking more like a towel than anything, before my mother burst into tears. By the third, she had plowed through an entire tissue box, while I stood there and tried not to feel anything that might cause me to move and make one of the seamstress's long pins miss its mark. It reminded me of some of the letters between King Albert and his wife, Georgina Lyons-Bowes, from before they were married—specifically, a chunk Nick calls Too Hot for History that did not end up in the Ashmolean, but which he had bound for me as a gift: *My dearest, Mother thinks I am entirely too plump, but you must have something to grip onto! These tiresome gown fittings will only be worth it the moment you remove it from me on our wedding night. You cannot imagine how I long for the naughty tickle of your mustache.* (The answer: a great deal, judging by the number of creative ways she expressed it.) Comparatively, though I shared with Georgina a waistline being monitored with obsessive fervor, Nick's sporadic correspondence was harried and rambling, thanks to his habit of typing everything he thought the exact second he thought it. Like, I don't have much time to write but I can't believe Lacey would ooooh hurrah, it's fish fingers for supper, must dash. And this morning's read, I don't have much time to write but please tell Marj my top choice is the Navy uniform but if Gran insists then I'll wear the Irish Guards one IF it includes the sword, because oh bollocks now what? I just cleaned that bloody thing. Hardly museum-worthy.

By October, the Bex Brigade had its dress. Somewhere in our discussions with the Alexander McQueen team about lacework—handmade, intricate, full of custom symbolism—I'd realized that this was inspiring the kind of artistic satisfaction I'd been missing in my daily life. And the design itself just felt right: a simple ivory gown, the long-sleeved bodice rising slightly up the back of my neck and splitting down into a narrow V that would flatter my smaller chest. It would nip at the waist and fall in graceful, clean lines to the floor, the skirt embroidered with microscopic, meaningful surprises—all very romantic and royal and unusually modest, with shades of both Grace Kelly's and Georgina's iconic gowns, both of them unexpected princesses themselves (as was Maria from *The Sound of Music*, in a sense, whose dress this also resembled—Nick gets choked up at that scene every time, so I suspect it will go over well). When I'd thanked the designer for sketching me a masterpiece, Mom had burst into a fresh waterfall of tears.

We did the fittings at Buckingham Palace, because the halls could best approximate the square footage of Westminster Abbey when considering how my train flowed, and whether Nick could escort me without trampling it. On this particular day, the peanut gallery took notes and whispered while I did laps of the long Marble Hall, kneeling at the statue of Mars and Venus as if it were the altar, with Cilla playing the role of Nick. Marj and Donna had been so impressed with her Bex-wrangling skills after Ascot that they'd fought for, and finally gotten, a salary and benefits to keep her around full-time. It helped my mental state to have an ally on the Bex Brigade who'd known me since the beginning.

"Remember the night we met, and you didn't even recognize him?" Cilla asked, reading my mind as we practiced. "Now look where you are." She grinned. "Nick hardly ever sat in for the porter, actually, because visitors would go all squidgy on him. I'll wager he saw your photo in the dossier and was after you from the start."

I burst out laughing as we straightened. "Let's tell *that* to everyone who thinks I came to Oxford to seduce him," I said.

"I just might," Cilla said. "It's possible!"

"Nick dated physically perfect blue bloods before me," I said. "I am *so* sure he saw my picture and said, 'Ooh, push off, India, we've got a really average-looking one coming in.' Frankly, I'd have thought Lacey was more his type."

"Oh, you hush," Cilla said. Then she chanced a peek at me. "How *is* Lacey? Any movement on that front?"

I glanced over my shoulder at Mom, who was covering a yawn with the sleeve of her tweedy Chanel suit, the frequency of her transatlantic flights taking its toll. She knew Lacey and I had exchanged words the night she returned from Paris, but clearly neither of us had confessed that we hadn't exchanged any at all in the two months since then. Like the rest of England, I now tracked my sister's comings and goings only in the papers. The press had been merciless to her (and per Mom's retelling, she'd incurred a fair bit of The Wrath of Lady Porter as well), so Lacey was fighting them with the exact weapon that had been turned on her: the lens. She baited them with shots of her beaming through deliriously respectable lunches with squeaky-clean finance types, guys with important Nordic names like Harald and Uli, and she wore businesslike specs so that she looked supremely respectable when she was photographed walking to her new party-planning job. It was a sign of how much our relationship had deteriorated that I couldn't tell if she was faking it. With the guys *or* the glasses.

"No movement. We haven't talked," I said. "I think Lacey's expecting me to budge first, but I'm not going to this time. I don't think I should have to throw myself on my sword."

Cilla frowned. "I cannot believe I am about to say this, but I don't think I have any ancestors who did that literally," she said. "That seems impossible."

I loved her for trying to cheer me, but I must still have looked sad, because she made a concerned click and murmured, "I'm sorry, poppet. I know you miss her."

She squeezed my hand, then clamped down on it so hard I almost yelped. Eleanor had come gliding down the Ministers' Staircase, in a plaid skirt and cashmere sweater and thick glasses, looking for all the world like she was sneaking down the back stairs in search of her knitting or a lost issue of some pheasant hunting magazine. *You are here at the mercy of Her Majesty and me*, the cold Prince of Wales had said, but as Eleanor's gaze fell upon me, I didn't see anything in her eyes to reflect that—not pity, not resentment, and in fact, not much mercy.

"Rebecca, good afternoon," the Queen said, her eyes traveling to Cilla, who looked sleekly professional with her wild auburn hair arranged in a knot. They had been in each other's orbit before, but never introduced, and I assumed the job fell to me now.

"Hello, Your Majesty," I said. "May I present my dear friend Cilla Sutcliffe."

We both dropped into a curtsy as Eleanor came down the last steps.

"My father sends his respectful best, Your Majesty," Cilla said.

"We do miss his skills around here," Eleanor said. "And if I'm not mistaken, one of the paintings upstairs came to us because your ancestor lost it at the whist table."

"Indeed, ma'am," Cilla said. "Something tells me it looks rather nicer here than in her loo."

Eleanor let out a short bark of a laugh, which I think caught her by surprise as much as it did us. I felt a stab of pride that what my friend lacked in physical stature, she made up for in sheer will. Not even the Queen could make her blink.

Eleanor was still chuckling when she turned to me. "I presume Nicholas emails *you*, at least, Rebecca. How is he faring?"

I mentally scanned the contents of his emails. Oh bollocks, now what, did not seem like the best sentiment to pass along.

"He's loving the fish fingers," I said. "And he's willing to wear the Irish Guards uniform."

"But only with the sword," she intuited. "I thought as much. The men all fancy the blade. Predictable as whiskey." Then she straightened. "Miss Sutcliffe, I'll need the pleasure of Rebecca's company for a moment. She need not remove the curtain she's wearing." A smile played at her lips again. "Very Scarlett O'Hara," she added.

With a flick of a crooked finger, Eleanor commanded me to follow her upstairs. I trudged after her in my preponderance of muslin and makeshift train—like she'd caught me playing dress-up in her lobby and was marching me off for a scolding—and passed deep into parts of Buckingham Palace I had not seen and might never again. A bajillion questions ran through my head: *Where is the pool? What's playing in the movie theater? Have you even seen all seventy-eight bathrooms?* Footmen and maids moved seamlessly past, merely part of the décor but for their pauses to venerate Her Majesty. It struck me then, and may haunt me forever, that in the royal world the walls are rarely the only witnesses. Even your alone time can have a cast of hundreds.

The Queen's private sitting room was surprisingly normal, at least on her spectrum. The ceilings were high, the pale-mint walls adorned with plaster wedding-cake detail, but there was none of the gilt that characterized the rest of the palace, and the furnishings looked forty years old instead of a hundred and forty. It was a comfortingly cluttered mess: stacks of newspapers and magazines, a teacup leaving a stain on some old correspondence, a dog's chew toys on the carpet. The bedroom we passed into was considerably tidier, like it had been spruced up for company—which perhaps it had, because laid out on a velvet cloth on the Queen's curtained bed sat six dazzling tiaras, catching the light from the large windows and casting dancing beams onto a nightstand photo of Eleanor's long-dead husband, the Duke of Cleveland. Nick had his ears.

"I'm impressed that your eyes landed on the picture and not the jewels," Eleanor said.

"I see Nick in him," I said.

Eleanor crossed to the photo and picked it up, tapping it thoughtfully. "It's the ears," she said. "You know, in my day we had to marry. Henry was a nice man, and he would have been a good partner if he'd lived." She turned to me. "But I never quite got the fuss. There was a story on the news that Great Britain has more unmarried women over forty than ever before, and I thought, *Good for them*. You girls have it better today. You can do whatever you like."

She gave the duke one final look and then replaced the photo on her table carelessly. It fell over and slipped into the crack between the nightstand and the bed. She didn't notice.

"What did *you* want to do?" she asked.

"I thought it'd be something to do with art," I said. "Honestly, when I met Nick, I hadn't figured it out yet, ma'am. It felt like I had so much time."

"But I suppose you must *want* to get married," she said.

*We both do*, I remember wanting to say. I didn't believe Richard's implication, exactly, but I still kept hearing his words over and over again in my head: *There you were, right before the clock ran out.*

"Nick is special" is what I decided to tell Eleanor. "I can't imagine my life without him."

Her face brightened. "He *is* special. Even if he cannot complete a cryptic crossword to save his life," she said. "He has a heart as big as the crown he'll wear one day. You'll do well to remember that." She paused. "Both the heart and the crown."

Eleanor's almost transactional satisfaction with my nod made me wonder what precise promise—beyond love and loyalty—my assent had just made, as she walked to the half-dozen twinkling witnesses to the deal.

"In my time, a woman never wore a tiara before her wedding day, because it represented the crowning moment of committing oneself to another," she said. "Traditionally, the bride wears one from her own family that day and then one from her husband's thereafter, to signify her transference. But..." She twitched her hands slightly, as if to say, *No such luck here.* "It is also custom for the Queen to provide something borrowed, so without an ancestral diadem of your own, that is what I shall offer. Sit down at my dressing table and we'll see which flatters you best. If none of them suits..."

Her voice trailed off, implying that if none of them suited, I would damn well sit there until one of them did. But there was no fear of that. These tiaras sparkled in the light of that cloudy London day, glorious even to a girl who once called her Cubs hat her crown.

"I'm extremely touched, Your Majesty," I said, my hand fluttering to my heart in a way that actually did feel a little Scarlett O'Hara. Young Bex would've punched me in the arm if I could have gone back in time and told her she'd one day let the Queen plonk tiaras onto her half-fake hair, at a brass-and-glass dressing table next to a brush with a hairball brewing that was as majestic as its source.

"This one is called the Cambridge Lover's Knot," Eleanor said as she set one on my head. It was a stunning array of nineteen diamond arches, each bearing a swinging oblong pearl, and it was oppressively heavy. "I earmarked it for Emma, but it gave her an awful headache and it's terribly noisy, so she only ever wore it in her official portrait."

"Oxford might be ticked off if I'm endorsing anything named *Cambridge*," I said, intending it as joke.

Eleanor frowned. "Quite right," she said. "And with you wearing her ring, I suspect that might be too much Emma, don't you agree?"

I certainly did (although I suspect it wouldn't have mattered either way). No bride wants to glide toward her beloved dressed as his mother.

The second option was called the Surrey Fringe, a narrow piece of scrollwork more commonly turned upside down and worn as a necklace—and rightly, because we quickly assessed that it made my head looked like one end of a Christmas cracker. The third was an art deco jeweled floral wreath, best worn across the forehead, but which made me look like an unhinged *Great Gatsby* mega-fan, and the fourth barely stayed on my head for five seconds. It was the Girls of the Isles tiara—first given to Georgina Lyons-Bowes by a national women's group—and it was Eleanor's personal favorite.

"I would never actually let you wear this one," Eleanor said, replacing it on the bed with 60 percent more care than she showed the others. "I just thought you'd find it amusing to look like our money for a moment."

Number five was a princessy circlet of tall diamond curlicues. "This belonged to my sister," Eleanor said. "It fell off and got stuck in the loo at my coronation. They had to use forceps to retrieve it." I must have looked startled, because she added, "I believe we've had it cleaned."

The Loo Tiara was too large on me (and, I privately feared, tempting fate). The Queen removed it gently and replaced it with the simplest of the six.

"I suspect I've saved the best for last," she said.

This one was still chock full of diamonds, but more subtly—very streamlined, no dangling bits, nothing imposing about its height. If a tiara may be deemed sporty, this was the sportiest, and like the dress I'd chosen, it suited me to a tee.

The Queen smiled, but slowly, which was her way—like she wanted you on tenterhooks for as long as humanly possible.

"I shall inform Marj," she said.

Instead, she picked up her brush, hairball included, and began fussing with my extensions. Sometimes I wish that I could reassure my hair's original owner that it's being well looked after, and, in fact, getting the royal treatment in every way.

"It must be so challenging for you to have one foot here and one foot in America," the Queen said. "The United Kingdom and the United States have been brilliant allies, of course. I have visited five times, and met five different presidents. You're such an ebullient people."

"Thank you," I carefully replied, despite feeling she didn't wholly mean it as a compliment. "Both countries have been wonderful homes to me."

"One rarely ends up with one's first love, does one?" she mused. "We grow up, we change, we mature. We find new love." She fluffed my hair. "And sometimes one must make sacrifices for such love. Nicholas loves his country, and he will give himself up to it someday entirely, as I have. And you, of course, are giving yourself to him. Imagine how meaningful it might be to give yourself to his kingdom as well."

"You mean, by becoming a British citizen?" Every conversation with Eleanor was like an oral examination.

"I was simply ruminating on the complexities of the situation," Eleanor said, with a tug of the brush that verged on scary. "If you were marrying Freddie, a dual citizenship would be the cleanest approach. But Freddie does not share Nicholas's destiny. It is a conundrum."

It dawned on me right then what she meant.

"I have to give up my American citizenship," I said slowly.

"What an interesting suggestion," Eleanor said. She set down her brush and put her hands on my shoulders. "It *would* make a lovely wedding gift to Nicholas and Great Britain. I will be long gone when the time comes for you to be his queen consort, but indubitably I would rest easy in my grave if there were no confusion about where your loyalties lie."

I was flummoxed. Nick had never said a word to me about whether my Americanness was a stumbling block, but maybe the reason it wasn't a stumbling block that was he knew his grandmother would bulldoze it out of the way.

Eleanor snatched the tiara from my head and reached for a folder I hadn't noticed.

"I happen to have the paperwork here," she said. "I'm very touched you should want to consider such a momentous decision, but you must think it through. We wouldn't want you to rush into anything, would we?"

"No, we would not," I said, sounding hollow even to my own ears.

"Your clothes will be in the chamber across the hall. Murray will escort you back to your mother when you are dressed," she said, gesturing for me to leave.

Dazed, I bobbed into a curtsy, gathered my skirts, and exited the room, at which point Murray—eyes tactfully averted from my strange state of semi-undress—ushered me into another one that was identical except for its paint job and personal effects. When he closed the door, I sat hard into a stuffed peach armchair and gazed at the folder in my hands with blurring eyes. There, alone, the memory of Eleanor's hands pressing on my shoulders as she told me she could only die happy if I kicked the United States to the curb, I felt like a pawn lured into checkmate.

# CHAPTER SEVEN

I did not sign anything. Nor did I discuss it with anyone. Instead, the paperwork burned a hole on my table until I buried it under magazines and abandoned cryptic crosswords. I hadn't lived in the States for years, but renouncing my claim to it—and its claim to me—seemed tantamount to ripping myself in half. This was a test I could not pass: If I gave in, I displayed obedience, but zero mettle. My nationality was the only piece of me the Palace hadn't reshaped into something else, and I didn't want to let it go; though I knew Eleanor would not be ignored, I hoped that if I could just stall until Nick came home, he could help me protect myself.

The rest of the year became a confining, isolating waiting game. Marj gave no indication of when I'd get to come off the bench again, for Paint Britain or anything else. Clive was working long hours, still unable to get much career traction beyond his fluffy role at a paper no one read (I was beginning to suspect he wasn't very good at his job, but admired that he doggedly pursued it anyway). My mother was mostly in Iowa running Coucherator, Inc., at which she'd turned out to be an extremely dab hand. Joss wanted nothing to do with me. Cilla was trying to get her wedding off the docket before the final run-up to mine, which made me feel so guilty that I refused to lean on her, and in fact made her draw a few lines to protect her private life from her professional one. Gaz, usually religious with the diet-busting baked goods, was taking on extra work to pay for a May honeymoon to Bora Bora, and even Freddie was too busy for a box of wine and *Big Brother*.

"Sorry, Killer," he'd say. "I convinced Prince Dick that Great Ormond Street Hospital would accept me as a weak alternative to Knickers. I have to go snuggle some babies."

Or, "Bad luck, Bex, I'm out tonight—the Imperial War Museum asked me to open its RAF exhibit. Father's jaw dropped so far you could've stuffed in a pheasant." I could hear the grin. "I was tempted."

I heard the pride underneath his jokes; I knew how much he wanted to find a place in the Lyons den, as something other than the professional scalawag he'd fashioned himself. But I missed him. I missed the whole gang. Most people would handle that by joining a book club, or playing in a recreational sports league, but that is forbidden to me. So I stayed home and shopped online with the pseudonymous credit card I'd been issued—no one will bat an eyelash if a Ms. Prudence Cattermole orders too much saucy lingerie for her sailor fiancé's homecoming—and crumbled in private. By day, I had Marj feeding me carrots and water like a prize Thoroughbred; by night, where I once consumed booze to get over missing Nick, I now devoured the Internet. The American't analyzed my level of clavicle protrusion and the caloric value of my shopping cart, whenever Marj granted me passage to the supermarket. That nasty old crumpet Xandra Deane suggested that the ten pounds I'd shaved off was setting an outrageously poor example for girls all over the world (which was mostly frustrating because I privately agreed, and cheated on my diet at every opportunity), and The Royal Flush alleged I am a lifelong anorexic.

In fact, The Flush was giving Xandra stiff competition as my most persistently negative coverage. At first it mostly published bits and pieces with a whiff of truth, but as its traffic and reputation grew, so did its vitriol. That distaste swelled slowly, like a balloon, and then burst all over my birthday.

Lacey's and my Parting Shot that year consisted not of a midnight toast, but an exchange of obligatory, terse texts. That was bad enough. But the frosty November morning I officially turned twenty-seven, I woke up—still both lonely for my sister and upset with her—to find that The Royal Flush had gift-wrapped me something truly insidious: an investigative piece quoting several of Nick's alleged conquests from the Dark Period casting what can only politely be called aspersions on the solidity of our love.

> One billionaire mogul's daughter says that although he knew she was in a relationship at the time, the Prince still begged to rekindle their youthful romance. "He told me every day I was his dream girl, and that he always assumed we'd find our way back to each other," she says. "But I've seen that life, and no, thank you. I don't want to be a commodity. He was devastated."

I'd have bet money the next was Ceres Whitehall de Villency:

> "Nobody wants the job," agrees another aristocratic blonde, whom Nicholas squired both before and after Porter. "He's handsome, and he's nice, and attentive. He'd want to cuddle in bed, and talk about a future with me as his queen. But I couldn't do it. I want to be free. I'm not a dowdy-heels-and-hemlines girl, and I'm not the kind of doormat he'll need at his beck and call. If you ask me, he's not just chosen the safe bet, he's chosen the only bet."

Only India Bolingbroke went on the record, possibly because she was still cranky about losing out on both Nick and whatever she had with Richard.

> "I don't doubt Nicky thinks he wants to marry her," says the Prince's cuckolded ex. "But he's wanted to marry a lot of us. His father set him an ultimatum, you see, and she's just the only person who'd say yes. It's terribly awkward for them, and everyone, really. Perhaps that's why he's so committed to the Navy. Being at sea all the time makes it easier to settle."

This was The Flush's splashiest piece yet, and its cruelest. It got a lot of attention, and worse, traction; almost overnight, the website that hated me the most became uncomfortably high-profile. Alone in my flat, I went from dismissing the story as rubbish, to being unnerved that it echoed a sentiment Bea had expressed at Klosters, to complete paranoia. By the time Gaz and Cilla's wedding arrived, my despair had plumbed new depths, and I was drowning.

Cilla had always wanted an outdoor wedding, so she made it happen even in December in England—partly through sheer force of will, but also aided by Lady Bollocks, who lent them her family's sprawling seven-million-pound Richmond estate and helped procure a surfeit of heat lamps and outdoor fireplaces. I think I smiled my first genuine grin in weeks when I saw them blazing merrily in the back garden.

"I watched you get out of that car," Lady Bollocks said, coming from behind me and handing me a ginger-infused cocktail. "Full marks."

My Lady Training was also paying off in other ways. Donna had been coaching me on styling myself occasionally, and it finally clicked for me when I started to think about it like costuming a character. Here, I wasn't Bex; I was Rebecca, Artfully Uncontroversial Royal Fiancée Attending the Wedding of Old Friends. Donna had signed off proudly when I'd selected a delicately patterned silver day dress, with a neatly belted dove-gray wool coat, and—in an effort to be a real grown-up—four-inch heels.

"Thank you, but we have *got* to talk about the British and their sloped gravel driveways," I said. "It's like a trap. It was all I could do not to wipe out in these suckers."

"We like a challenge," Bea said airily. "Besides, it's marvelous for your calves."

I half snorted—I'm working on it—and then spotted Gemma, already seated on the bride's side of the aisle.

"I assume we're sitting over there?" I asked.

"Yes, and I have no further comment on that subject," Bea said.

"Bea, we're in modern times now," I said. "People will be happy for you two."

She just harrumphed, which is not something I'd ever heard before, and which sounds exactly like it is spelled.

"Bex! At last, you've come out of hiding," Clive said, strolling up with Paddington on his arm. "How is the wedding planning, or is it all terribly top secret?"

"What wedding?" I joked, rather than come up with a smoothly varnished lie.

"Isn't this the most glorious occasion?" Paddington said, spreading her arms wide and flashing an inordinate amount of side-boob in her slouchy tank dress. "The sacred union of two perfectly matched souls is just so fucking moving."

"*Pudge*," Bea hissed. "Language. This is a *wedding*. There is a *minister* here."

"Words only have the power we give them, Beatrix," Pudge said. "Open your spirit."

I could tell Bea wanted to inform Pudge exactly where she could stick her spirit, but the ushers began nudging us to our seats. Paddington glided with Clive over toward Joss, who clearly had not taken my advice to give herself a mental break. She was clad in a blue chiffon monstrosity with *I do* scribbled over and over, like a pattern, and her long, black, sleek hair evoked Pudge's.

"We're well shot of Joss, I think," Bea murmured, narrowing her eyes. "They make such a peculiar threesome."

The din settled into an excited thrum as Gaz took his place at the altar under a thatched canopy bedecked in holly and ivy and poinsettias. Freddie stood in for Nick as best man, both of them dapper in suits and ties (Gaz nixed morning dress because he believes top hats don't flatter his neck). Penelope Eight-Names, clutching Maxwell Something-Something's hand, caught my eye and pointed to her massively pregnant belly as if to say, *ta-da*. I smiled politely back at her, then turned back in time to see Freddie pretending to look stern and mouthing, *Pay attention, Killer*.

Cilla wore her grandmother's gown and a family-heirloom veil pinned to her glorious auburn hair, and looked so transcendent she might as well have been six feet tall. Gaz started weeping the moment she came out, and did not stop—not when the officiant asked if anyone objected and Freddie raised his hand, not even when they got to the bit Gaz himself put in the vows as a joke ("in sickness and in health, in serif and in sans"). They could not stop looking at each other, love and joy written on their faces like words on the pages of a book. When Cilla's *I will* and Gaz's *Too bloody right I will* rang out clear and pure, Gaz pulled her into an elated if rather salty kiss, and we all teared up, even Lady Bollocks. I knew I'd been lucky to witness their contentiously adoring courtship, not to mention their proposal, and now the beginning of their future. As much as I thought I could not live without Nick, Cilla and Gaz were irreplaceable family to me, too. I poured as much of this nostalgia as possible into the hug I gave Cilla after the ceremony.

"I'd have had you up there, if it wouldn't have been such a to-do for you," she whispered.

I shook my head and hugged harder. "Better to keep the focus on you," I said. "I am just thrilled to be here. I love you, and it was flawless."

She pulled back, her eyes shining. "And so will yours be."

"On that note," I said, turning to Gaz. "I have a favor to ask."

"Want to sue the knickers off The Royal Flush?" he asked. "I can look into it."

I grinned. "Tempting, but no." I drew a breath. "My mother isn't sure she can walk me down the aisle without totally losing it," I said. "My aunt Kitty's been divorced three times, so I'm not close with my uncles, and my grandfathers are both dead. You are the best extended family I could want anyway, so I wondered if you would mind giving me away."

Gaz blinked once, hard, then burst into the most spectacular wail.

"Don't play it so coy, darling," Cilla teased.

Gaz wiped his eyes on the kerchief that had been in his jacket pocket—it had gotten a lot of play already—and then looked at me, red and puffy and wonderful.

"That is the most magnificent favor that a person has ever been asked," he said. "I'm so honored I could cry."

"Bloody hell, if that wasn't crying, what *is*?" Freddie asked, thumping Gaz on the back. "Jolly good work here, Garamond. Bex, we're in the way of their fans. Let's go drink."

As he dragged me away, an elderly woman who'd made a beeline for Cilla stopped and grasped my arm. "You look lovely. We're so excited for you, dear. And aren't *you* a dish," she said to Freddie, whacking him lightly on the shoulder with her program. "You two make such a charming couple."

"He's the other one, Estelle," her equally elderly spouse hissed as they trundled past us. "She's marrying the main one."

"Fred, that isn't—" I began.

"Don't worry, I'm used to it. Hear it all the time," Freddie told me, but his gaiety was forced. "At least she thinks I'm dishy. But now I really need that drink."

The reception, like the wedding itself, was intimate, funny, unexpected. There were six toasts from Cilla's side of the family and one riotous speech from Gaz's father, the infamous disgraced finance minister, about how not to handle your joint bank accounts. Cilla danced a comedic tango with her new husband before a lively foxtrot with her dad, which made my heart ache for mine. I caught myself envying my friends. This wedding was deeply personal, with no artifice; Gaz and Cilla could just be Gaz and Cilla, the same in public and in private, a luxury that Nick and I never would have. This ceremony was for them. Ours was for the country, and for the Crown, and I felt a pang for what could have been if Nick had been born anything but what he was—a pang that was as much for him as for me. Instead of cheering me up, the cocktails pushed me deeper into the melancholy I had tried and failed to leave at home.

Freddie noticed. And he tried to help. He told gleefully atrocious rumors, including one about Dim Tim Fitzwilliam and a yak that I wasn't even sure I fully understood. He roped Gemma and Bea—the latter, in diametric opposition to me, rather more buoyant than usual—into a rousing game of Spot the Sutcliffes (we were tripped up when the man with the parrot turned out only to be the owner of Cilla's village pharmacy). And he coaxed me onto the dance floor, where I gave gaiety my best shot. But I was a husk out there. As the music slowed into a ballad, I glanced over and saw Bea and Gemma grind to a halt, awkwardly, before Bea drew her girlfriend in for a loving slow dance. It was a public spontaneity of emotion that had become absent from my own life, and it ground me to a wobbly, empty halt.

Freddie abruptly pulled me close, as if to dance. "Are you all right?" he whispered.

I could not speak. My emotional dam was poorly built, destined to burst, but I'd never thought it would happen here. BITCHY BEX'S BRIDAL BREAKDOWN would be the best day of Xandra Deane's life.

Freddie clearly sensed this, because he raised his voice and said, "I'm sure Bea has some allergy medication in the house."

He marched us past Bea and said, under his breath, "Mayday."

Out of the corner of my eye, I saw Clive begin to extricate himself from Paddington to join us. Bea waved him off with a very awkward thumbs-up—like she'd never done that before, which she probably hadn't—and he seemed surprised and reluctant, even as Paddington pulled him away. Then Bea leapt into action.

"Let's keep this as tight as possible," she said. "Freddie, you get her out of here and straighten her out."

"No." I shook them off. "This is Gaz and Cilla's wedding. It's important. I can't leave."

"You cannot *stay*," Bea countered. "Not catatonic. We'll tell Gaz you got far too drunk, which he'll think is an extreme compliment."

Gemma piped up, "There's a secret back road. Freddie, you leave alone, wave at the paparazzi, drive off, and then double back. I'll tell you where. Bea can take Bex."

Freddie saluted. "Aye, aye, Captain."

Bea then marched me out of the barn with loud commentary about the whereabouts of her antihistamine. I followed mutely, mentally adrift, as we completed our diversion and then crept to a well-hidden access road snaking through the foliage. I tried fervently to tamp down the feelings that wanted to come out in pure, unregulated Bex fashion, but when Bea propped me up on a gate and turned to leave, brushing off her hands as if her work was done, I met her with a sob. She sighed, then put an arm around my shoulders and let me heave it out all over her cashmere wrap, turning her head away as if feelings might be contagious.

"I told you this was a job, and it is," she said after I had burned through the first wave of tears. "But that doesn't mean you're not the right person for it."

She wiped my eye with a thumb. "You won't get many of these," she said. "Take full advantage of this one and get it all out."

"I can see why Nick loved Gemma. I'm super glad for both of us that she turned out to be a lesbian," I blurted.

Bea laughed. "Rebecca, so am I," she said.

"Why didn't you tell me back then?" I asked, snuffling. "About Gemma?"

Bea looked exasperated. "Because it wouldn't have mattered," she said. "She wasn't the problem. She was a symptom." She paused. "And I didn't bloody well want to. We're not all as blubbery about things as you are." She nudged me. "Here's Freddie."

He pulled over and she yanked open the door on his borrowed sports coupe—Freddie never met a sedan he didn't disdain—and hurled me into the passenger seat.

"Crikey," was all Freddie said when he saw my condition.

"I'm so sorry," I mumbled. "I ruined your night."

"Nonsense," he said. "I'm an officer, and occasionally I am a gentleman, and I am seeing you home. And then whatever this is, we'll fix it."

I spent the whole ride crying, but casually, helplessly, as if someone was ritualistically flushing my tear ducts. Freddie simply drove, companionably silent, and then hustled me back into the flat. He took one look at the lived-in mess, my laptop—still awake, with new comment alerts pinging fast and furious—open to The Royal Flush. He shook his head.

"Let's get you into bed," he said.

I barely blinked as he led me into my bedroom. As soon as he let me go, I flopped onto my mattress with extreme melodrama and a very satisfying thwack.

"Five stars. Great buildup to a satisfying climax," he said.

A fresh gallon of tears burst out of my face. Freddie sat next to me on the bed and patted my back awkwardly, silently, for what must have been twenty minutes.

"I'm going to get you some water and a snack," he finally said.

"I'm not drunk," I mumbled into my comforter.

"Aha, it speaks!" he said. "But you have to be dehydrated. Be right back."

The day's events swam in front of my swollen eyes. Gemma and Bea throwing their reservations to the wind. Cilla's father and Gaz's, leaning against the bar, watching their children slow dance. And Cilla, so beautiful in her wedding dress; Gaz, blooming with pride. They'd texted me during the drive home, seeing through the ruse and somehow loving me anyway. I loathed myself the more for not deserving it.

"You have no reasonable snacks," Freddie said. I opened my eyes to see two of him holding a bag of kale chips and a glass of water. He coalesced back into one.

"I've been put on a diet," I told him.

"What? That's absurd," he said, giving the bag a tentative, unimpressed sniff.

I shoved a joyless fistful into my mouth. "Takes a lot to upgrade me into duchess material."

"Is that what's bothering you?" Freddie asked, sitting back down on the bed. "Talk to me, Bex. Please. You can trust me."

I sat up, my head spinning, and chugged half the glass of water before wiping my lips ingloriously on my arm.

"Did you know we can't invite both the Duke of Albany and the Earl of Norwich because they've vowed to duel if they're ever in the same room again?" I hiccupped.

Freddie frowned. "Who?"

"Or that the Duke of Bridgewater proposed to Eleanor three times before she married your grandfather, and everyone thinks he's still hot for her?" I barreled on. "Or that I spent weeks memorizing five facts about each of the eight hundred people on the guest list for the Wedding of the Century, only to find out Eleanor had already cut two hundred of them and added fifty others and never told me?"

Freddie just shook his head. "Gran would be much easier to get along with if she let old Bridgie get a leg over," he said tastelessly, to get me to crack a smile. Instead my face crumpled.

"And did you know Barnes holds weekly meetings to discuss my facial expressions and what's wrong with them? And that The American't has a whole category devoted to my man hands?" I kept going. "Or that Marj weighs me every three days and has a folder called Nancy's Accent? And I had to kick Lacey out of the wedding? Oh, and Nick maybe settled for me because he had to, and Eleanor wants me to renounce my citizenship?"

"Wait. *What?*"

"And I can't talk to Nick about any of this because he's offline all the time, and it sounds whiny, and I can't freak him out while he's off fighting pirates or whatever," I said, my hysteria cresting. "I am an *idiot.* I told him to go on this extra deployment even though everything inside me was crying for him to stay home and save me."

"Save you? From what?" Freddie asked, still nonplussed.

"From everything!" I waved my arms around my bedroom. "From myself, from Eleanor, from Marj, from Lacey, even. From failure," I said, starting to cry again. "I'm an unsuitable American, and your family acts like I'm a defective model that needs refurbishing in a hurry before anyone notices I was the last-ditch option. But it's too late. *Everyone* knows it."

"Bex! I told you, The Royal Flush is—"

"You and I both know that where there's smoke, there's fire," I said.

Freddie was silent.

"I can't tell what's true about anything anymore. I don't even know what's true about *myself.* I am wearing fucking *pantyhose*, Freddie!" Another sob surged out of me. "I haven't felt like *me* in I don't know how long. I couldn't even keep it together at my best friends' wedding tonight. What kind of asshole does that? And now your grandmother is telling me that I have to give up the last piece of the person I used to be, the person I recognize, and without Nick here to bring me back to myself, I am losing. My. Mind."

"Bloody hell, Bex," Freddie said. "How did it get this bad before you talked to anyone?"

I gave him a helpless look. "Who am I supposed to I talk to? My mom is still grieving. I can't put this on her. Lacey and I aren't speaking. Cilla works for me. And everyone has other stuff going on that's just as important. I feel so weak and awful and embarrassed that I can't deal with this on my own." I took another quivering breath. "And the worst part is, I find myself getting angry with Nick about it. Like this is his fault. I was scared he'd resent me if I told him not to go, but now I'm resentful that he went. And I hate that. I hate feeling that way. But I do. And sometimes..."

I fought for what I wanted to say. Freddie was frowning, as if he were trying very hard to process everything I was dumping on him. My pressure valve had blown off and hit him squarely in the chest.

"...Sometimes I just want to *get out*," I said. "Which is something Nick said to me once, years ago, and I thought I understood him then, but I *really* do now. When most people get engaged, it's a love story, and I used to feel that way, too. But now it's more like a business transaction. I spend every day working for the good of a company that doesn't seem to like me very much, fighting for approval I will never get, dieting for a goal weight they will always lower, and sometimes I catch myself thinking, *Why the hell did I take this job?*"

Freddie put an arm around my shoulders, looking increasingly upset—not with me, but for me. "Bloody hell," he said again, to the wall.

I started crying again, in earnest. "How can I even feel that way? I love Nick. But I sometimes hate what loving Nick has led to, and I catch myself wondering what it would be like if I just got up and ran. And I hate those feelings most of all. Because I can't tell which of *them* are real, either, and it doesn't matter anyway, because I can't run, and I just...I just...I *can't*."

Freddie looked at me with nervous intensity. In the quickest of flashes, he tipped up my chin.

"What if I told you that it does matter?" he asked urgently. "What if I told you that you *can* run? And what if that was with me?"

"What are you doing, Fred?" I breathed.

"You once told me I'd never had my heart broken, but it's not true. Mine felt like it smashed the day I helped Nick make that bloody lasagna, because I knew I'd missed my chance," he said. "If I'd known when we kissed how much it would kill me not to do it again, I wouldn't have let you walk out of that bloody little room."

I could only blink.

"I tried staying away from you. I did stay away from Lacey, because I didn't trust myself not to make things worse." He inched closer. "But there's something here, Bex. You can't pretend there isn't. I'm not saying I know what it is, or what it means, but we jumped at each other that night when we only had *us* to think about, and I've been reliving it ever since."

He took my face in his hands. "Tell me you don't feel it," he whispered.

Then his lips were on mine. Unlike the fire and madness of a year and a half ago, this kiss was slow and powerful and tender, his hands stroking my jaw, my hair. There wasn't the hunger, but there was just as much need.

Freddie pulled away, then kissed me again, so lightly. "Maybe it's crazy, but it's not impossible. Not for us," he said, touching his forehead to mine. "You can be free, Bex, if that's what you want. Let *me* save you. Let's save each other."

Long ago, I reminded Nick that he had the power to turn a life of being in-waiting into a life he wanted to live—that he could still be in charge of himself. So could I, and so could Freddie, and running away was not taking charge; it was just running. Besides, if I'd ever really wanted to leave, I wouldn't have needed Freddie to open the door. I would have saved myself. My heart's decision was made and sealed in a nondescript love nest in Windsor Castle, where, surrounded by the trappings of Nick's station, he and I had found a way. The optimism we kindled that day had flickered, but it hadn't died.

Freddie saw it in my eyes without me saying a word.

"What have I done," he said to himself, looking almost seasick.

He shot to his feet, pacing and fretting, and I let him, because anything I said might sound patronizing or pitying, and I didn't want him to feel either one. He pulled out his silver cigarette case as he walked and idly flipped it open, then clicked it shut, over and over, before frowning sadly at it and tucking it away again. I simply waited.

Freddie paused near the window and fiddled with the shade. "Are those photographers out there?"

"Probably. There usually are a few, since the Lacey thing."

He peered through the glass. "Wait, no, one of your neighbors is having a party. Maybe I should go. Might meet someone."

He laughed mirthlessly and then let go of the shade. It snapped back just a bit askew, a metaphor if ever there was one.

"I did five engagements in the last two weeks, and I still heard Father grumbling to himself about when the first-string is coming back," he said, bitterness seeping into his tone.

"I know how much you hate the way Richard talks down to you," I said softly. "It's unfair. You don't deserve it."

"He and Gran only see me as the Ginger Gigolo, or whatever the news used to call it," Freddie said, kicking stubbornly at the carpet. "And I've been playing at that for so long that sometimes I forget it started out as an act. Even Lacey looks at me like a person with potential, who just needs a spot of repairs." He exhaled hard. "But you treat me like who I am is enough. Like you already see in me something nobody else has bothered to look for. That's important to me."

"Well, *you* are important to *me*," I told him.

"You sounded so broken tonight," he said. "Talking about running, and feeling erased. Thinking no one really ever sees you. Things I've said to myself a hundred times." He bit his lip. "For a second, the answer just seemed so simple. For both of us."

"It wouldn't be simple. It would be worse," I said. "You would never forgive yourself, and neither would I. We can't scorch the earth forever just because we're unhappy now."

Freddie blew out his cheeks and came around and sat next to me on the bed. "I know," he said. "I think I knew it before I even said it. I *shouldn't* have said it. *Any* of this." He scratched the back of his head in frustration. "I just thought... I felt something, and maybe you did, too, and this was the last chance to save both of us. And instead I've mucked up heroically. God, Bea told me to fix things and I've only made them worse."

"Well, I helped," I said. "I'm good at that."

"The worst of it is, somewhere in here I think I realized you're one of my best friends," he said, rubbing his eyes. "Unfortunately it was after that bit with all the kissing."

That sat between us for a second.

"Are you going to tell him?" he asked plainly.

"I should," I said. "He deserves the truth."

"I won't ask you to keep this secret," he said. "Not again, not when you're getting married and it matters. But part of me thinks it *doesn't* matter. Nothing much happened. Nothing is changing." He looked so sad. "I don't want to break his heart for nothing. Does that make me a coward?"

"No," I said. "It makes you his brother."

Our eyes met, and we nodded slowly, as if a decision had silently been made. Then Freddie looked at his watch. "It's an appalling hour of the morning," he said. "And I'm not sure how to take my leave after all of this. *Bye, thanks for listening, sorry about the tongue?*"

"How about just, *See you later, Killer,*" I offered.

"I know this is strange to say, after what I did," he said as he stood. "But I'm glad you truly do love him."

"Did you ever doubt it?"

"Did you?"

"No," I said.

"Neither did I," he said. Then his old mischievous gleam surfaced. "Well, maybe for ten very specific seconds."

I socked him in the arm. He took it as it was intended.

"And how about you talk to someone properly next time," he said. "I know Marj and Barnes and Prince Dick are always railing about whatever you've done wrong, but there are plenty of people who like you just as you are. You should remember that when you start feeling like you're being erased."

"I could say exactly the same to you," I told him.

Freddie gave me a lovely smile. "You know, I spent the last year telling myself I hadn't got the girl, but I think I was wrong. In the way I was meant to, perhaps I've had her all along."

My phone pierced the moment. I frowned at the jumble of numbers on the home screen, and got a prickly feeling in my chest.

"Bex? Thank God I caught you. I was sure you'd be passed out by now."

"Nick!" I gasped, glancing up at Freddie.

"I think that's my cue," Freddie said. I watched him disappear, and in the split second that I processed the melancholic end of whatever this night had been, the scale tipped back in the other direction with a heady rush.

"Bex? Are you there?" Nick asked. "Our bloody email is on the fritz. I've been stewing for weeks until I pulled rank and made them give me a phone."

"Is everything okay?" I asked, sensing urgency.

"It's about your citizenship," Nick said. "Did I get to you in time? Don't do it. Don't give it up."

My eyes fell on my coat, crumpled on the floor, my flag pin there on the lapel. "I can't believe your timing," I choked out. "I haven't done it. Not yet. I—"

"It isn't coming from me. And I'm furious with Gran for pulling that stunt while I'm gone," he said. "Rip up those papers and let her take it up with me on January third."

"Is she right, though?" I asked. "Nick, please be honest about that much. Don't tell me it's up to me and then have it turn out that it really wasn't."

"There's no moral superiority in citizenship. I didn't care that you were an American when I fell in love with you, and the Commonwealth won't care when it falls in love with you, either," he said. "If that's idealistic of me, then so be it."

"Wait. Did you say January third?" I asked. "That sounds almost soon."

"Twenty-one days," he said, and I heard a huskiness in his voice. "Bex, please use this against me for the rest of our lives as an example of how I am about as clever as a shed. It was too long to be gone, and at the worst possible time."

I closed my eyes. "I love you," I said. "I have never meant it more in my life."

"You know, nobody told me how long I could stay on this phone," he said. "We can talk until it dies, and Miss Porter, it is fully charged."

"That might be the sexiest thing you have ever said to me."

Nick laughed. "I'm going to consider that a homework assignment," he said.

The charge only had about fifteen minutes in it—Nick said the phones were bricks from the nineties—but those fifteen minutes rebuilt me as if they were fifteen days, and when we hung up, I was awash in love and guilt and a renewed strength. I don't know why it takes something monumentally destructive to remind you what you want to save. This was not the life I would have chosen, but Nick would always be the person. And if I couldn't take back the night that brought me to that epiphany, I would give him the greatest show of commitment I had at my fingertips. So I ran to the living room and shuffled through the magazines and the tabloids and the other detritus of my self-containment, until I found the oath of renunciation. Nick loved me enough to go up against Eleanor on this, but I loved him enough not to make him—to do the one thing I knew would mean the most to his grandmother and to his country. I wanted them all to know that as far as I was concerned, he, and we, were worth every sacrifice. I picked up a pen, muttered the Pledge of Allegiance one last time, and signed the papers. I was all in with Nick once more, and it was a gamble I might be about to lose.

# PART FIVE

# PRESENT DAY

*"In my end is my beginning."*

—Mary, Queen of Scots

# CHAPTER ONE

I did something."

Standing in my hotel room, one day before what's supposed to be the most exciting moment of my family's life, Lacey looks wan and haggard. Her normally bouncy blond hair is limp and brittle at the ends, as if the life has been sanded out of it by her thumb and forefinger—a telltale sign she's been freaking out. That makes two of us.

"I did something, too," I say. "But I think you already knew that."

I throw my phone onto the bed beside where she's standing.

TIME IS RUNNING OUT.

When she sees all the texts, her breath catches; clearly she'd hoped to get to me first. I try not to feel sympathy, even though her anguish looks genuine. I want to get through this without feeling anything at all, if possible. But the longer Lacey is silent, the angrier I am. I shouldn't have to go first, but she can't seem to muster the words—whereas I have a thousand of them right now, none of them polite, and I'm scared to open my mouth in case they all tumble out at the same time.

As usual, my mouth opens anyway.

"Do you hate me this much?"

"No," Lacey says emphatically.

"Then how could you?" This is supposed to sound coolly accusatory, but it comes out wounded.

"How could *you*?" she fires back.

"It isn't what you think," I insist.

"How do you know what I think?"

"Well, I guess I'll read all about it when Clive publishes your tell-all," I snap. "The Royal Flush himself, finally flushing me. How long have you been in on his sleazy little game?"

"I wasn't! He tricked me into it!" she said.

"Bullshit. He can't have pulled this off overnight," I said. "He's been going at us anonymously for nine months now. You haven't spoken to me in almost that long. You expect me to believe those two things aren't connected?"

Lacey closes her eyes. "They're not," she insists. "All I did was trust him. You can't expect me to have figured out he's a shithead if you never did."

"Even so," I say, "the only person you should have talked to about any of this was me. And you know that. Which makes me think you hit the self-destruct button on purpose." My voice cracks. "Why are you even here? To gloat? I saw the photo you left for me. Why didn't you give *that* to Clive, too?"

Her lip trembles. "I love that picture. It was a peace offering," she says.

"Funny," I say, pointing wildly at my phone, "because that feels like war."

We are both trying to keep our voices down so the Bex Brigade doesn't hear anything.

"Why does he say he's got proof, Lace?" I demand. "What kind of hard proof could he possibly have, of any of this? What don't I know?"

Lacey swallows hard. "I'm on tape," she says. "The proof is *me*."

"Don't worry, Cilla, they won't mind. We have no secrets," we hear, and then Mom charges through the door. "Ah, here we go. What a sight for sore eyes," she says, clicking it shut behind her. "I knew you two wouldn't let a little disagreement ruin the—"

Her voice trails off as she notices Lacey and me trying and failing to arrange our faces into casual expressions, all while barely looking at her and not at all looking at each other.

"So you're *not* hugging this out," she says, Fancy Nancy immediately back on the shelf. She looks so pretty in her green suit, some of the optimism not yet having drained from her face. "This cannot just be about Paris. What's really going on?"

Lacey and I turn away from each other. We are silent. Mom crosses her arms.

"Out with it, or I will get Barnes and Marj in here," she says.

Lacey looks at me, as if it's my job to run this show. This irritates me just enough that I do it—which of course is classic Lacey.

"Freddie and I kissed," I blurt. "And I gather Lacey saw it and told Clive, and now he's blackmailing me for insider information on the Royal Family. Like, indefinitely. Or else."

At the word *blackmail*, the color drains from my mother's face. At *or else*, she sways.

"If this is some kind of prank," she says thinly, "it's not funny."

"No, it's not funny," I say. "She stabbed me in the back."

"Look who's talking, *Killer*," Lacey says.

"I told you, it wasn't—"

"Oh, right, as if—"

"*Girls.*" Mom's tone makes us twelve years old again. She gropes like a blinded woman to the armchair in the corner and sits down, blinking. "When did this happen?"

"A couple of months ago."

"And Clive knows." Mom looks at Lacey. "And Clive is bad."

"Yesssss," Lacey says, stretching the word with dread.

Mom sighs. "Oh, Earl, give me strength."

This nearly ruins me. Dad would be so disappointed in both of us. Lacey and I scowl at each other in the manner of two people trying to transfer as much shame as possible onto the other person so that their own will sting less. It doesn't work; it never does.

"I think you'd better tell me everything. And I mean *everything*," Mom says.

I nod, although I'm scared of what Lacey is going to say. The situation is already really ugly, and I only know the half of it.

"I'll start this time," Lacey says, climbing up onto the bed and crossing her legs. She looks nervous, too. "The night of Gaz and Cilla's wedding, I was at a club, and I got a call from Clive. Actually, it was an S.O.S. text first, but then he called a bunch, and because I was a little tipsy, I was pretty sure this meant Bex was dead in a ditch."

"And that actually bothered you?" I say before I can stop myself. Mom glares at me. "Sorry," I mutter.

"I know we're in a fight, but it doesn't mean I don't miss you," Lacey says, wounded. "Anyway, I went outside and called him back, and he told me you left the wedding a total wreck, and that you obviously needed me but were too proud to ask for my help. And...I don't know, I felt something click, like I had a way to make this all magically okay after we'd been so pissed at each other. I just don't know how Clive knew what I was going to see once I let myself in."

"There is no way he could have known," I say. "Clive is a dick, apparently, but he's not magic."

"I think he played a hunch, and got lucky," she says. "He didn't have anything to lose. If nothing was going on, sending me there would just make him look thoughtful. But if he was right..." Lacey takes a deep breath. "At first, I only listened, but then I looked. I left when Freddie really went for it with you."

"You should've come in," I say lamely. "We could have explained."

"It seemed clear enough to me," she says. "The way he touched your face, and kissed you, saying it wasn't the first time...I was so angry. So jealous. I didn't think. I just ran."

"Straight to Clive," I guessed. "Who apparently hates me even more than you do."

"That's not how it happened, and I told you, I don't *hate* you," she insists. "I can't hate you, Bex. I wish I could. It would all hurt so much less."

"So instead of hating me, you hurt me back as hard as you could?" My resentment bubbles. "Newsflash, Lacey. These stories always have at least two sides. Not everything is only about you."

"No, it's too busy only being about *you*," she fires back, her tone escalating. "Do I need to remind you that you got mad at me for not toeing the line, when you're the one making out with your fiancé's brother? You already have Nick. Did you want to collect the complete set? Or just make sure you had it all so I had nothing?"

Lacey's vitriol catches me off guard, though I guess it shouldn't. "Wow," I say. "You may not hate me, but you do apparently think I'm a monster."

"I don't! It's just... You're getting me all worked up again," she flounders.

"*You're* worked up?" I say, hearing my voice turn shrill. "I have eight hundred guests picking up their dry cleaning today for a wedding that might not even happen if I don't agree to be Clive's mole." My eyes fill with tears. "I either betray Nick, or... betray Nick."

"Don't you think you already did that?" Lacey says harshly.

The wind ekes out of me.

"Lacey." My mother shakes her head.

"No. She's right. I did." I press the heels of my palms to my eyes. "And it wasn't the first time. The night that, um..." I can't say the words *Dad died.* "At that house party, Freddie and I kissed then, too."

Lacey closes her eyes. "I know," she says, pained. "I mean, I didn't, not for sure, but at one point Clive said he saw you both sneaking out of a closet that night, or something, and he always thought it was fishy."

"We'd been drinking," I said. "We didn't even know what we were doing. But, you know. Full disclosure."

Mom lets out a low whistle.

"You channeled Dad right there," I say, missing him fiercely.

"Earl Porter had a way with sound effects," Mom says with a sad expression. "Reminds me of you." She shakes her head as if to knock out a cobweb. "Don't get off-topic. When does Clive come back into this?"

"Clive told me he was still at the wedding, but I guess he followed you guys back to London and, like, staked the place out," Lacey says. "He saw me leave crying. But he didn't come find me until later. I guess he thought it was smarter to hang around, see if Freddie left, maybe get a time-stamped picture. Which he got. After what, I don't know."

"After nothing," I insist. "Do you really think I'd sleep with Freddie?"

"I didn't even think you'd kiss him, yet here we are," Lacey says plainly. "The guy I was in love with, the guy you told me I couldn't have because it would look bad. Do you know what it felt like, hearing him say things to you that I'd been dying for him to say to me? Honestly, my first instinct was to run in there and punch you both. Which is totally what you would've done before you were Princess Perfect, by the way."

"I know. And I swear, it caught me by surprise. Emotions were running high. I wish I had a better explanation than that," I say. "There's just a finite number of people who understand what it's like inside that family, and it turns out Freddie has been unhappier than anyone noticed, and he got carried away... I guess we both did."

"But from where I was standing, it looked like you'd spent all that time warning me away from him so you could have both Prince Charmings to yourself," Lacey says.

It stings that she ever could have thought this. And if she did, other people probably will, too.

"It was never like that," I tell her. "You have to believe that."

"This was all an accident," she counters. "*You* have to believe that."

We lock eyes. And then, just as it always does when my twin looks miserable, I feel my hardness start to smudge. What's the point of making our bad deeds a comparative science? We both messed up. For the first time, I keenly see that we are both each other's collateral damage.

Mom clears her throat subtly. "You two made quite a bed for yourselves," she says.

"Clive really got to me," Lacey admits. "He came over the next day, checking in, and found me all splotchy and puffy. Totally gross. I'd been crying for like twelve hours straight. He was so concerned, and *so* nice." She looks crushed. "Stupid, pathetic me, that's all it took. I played right into his hands. He must've been rejoicing inside when he realized what he had."

"You're not pathetic, or stupid. He's just good," I said. "And he must really hate me."

Lacey looks over at me. "He does," she says. "I went for drinks with him and Joss a lot over the last few months, and we'd always end up bitching about you and Nick like some bitter little support group. I'm not proud of it. But I thought I was safe with him. We were friends. He got every complicated feeling I had without ever judging any of them."

I rub my temples. How did Lacey and I get so far away from each other that we couldn't hear each other's complicated feelings as nonjudgmentally as other people did? But I can't say I don't understand her actions. Clive—and even Joss—had never been anything but kind to her, and once Freddie disappeared, she'd have had no other sounding board.

"There's more." Lacey looks queasy.

"How much more could there be?" Mom asks.

Lacey covers her face with her hands. "The thing is, even though he's still with Pudge, I was really into him after a while."

"Oh no," I say.

"There's something intoxicating about someone who has witnessed your nastiest impulses and likes you anyway," she says ruefully. "One night, we went out to dinner just the two of us, and we ended up at his place and one thing led to another..." She coughs. "We had sex. By the way, you were right, Bex. He's a weird kisser."

Mom grimaces. "You've *both*...?"

I look heavenward. "It's a long story."

Mom shifts uneasily. "There is a lot more sex in this than I anticipated," she says.

"Is it better if I call it something else?" Lacey asks.

"Pole-vaulting." I couldn't help it.

"Well, I'm sad to say, I was way into the pole-vaulting," Lacey says. "Whatever other problems he has, he's a talented pole-vaulter."

"No, go back to saying 'sex,'" Mom says, bodily cringing. "You're going to ruin the Summer Olympics for me."

"I'll skip ahead," Lacey offers. "We cracked a bottle of wine afterward, and then another one, just cuddling and talking. He started stroking my face, saying something about how he couldn't imagine how you could hurt me so badly. I thought we drifted off after that." She scrunches up her face. "I woke up thirsty at like five a.m., and he wasn't in bed, and I heard my own voice coming from the living room. Apparently we'd talked a whole lot longer, and he'd recorded me."

"How is that even possible?" Mom asks.

"I do remember him setting the alarm on his phone, at one point," Lacey replies. "He must have turned on the memo function. I don't know if he recorded me any other times, but he definitely got all our pillow talk, because I heard him playing it back."

My insides curl at how he used her. "What a sneaky bastard," I say.

"And a first-class asshole," pipes up Mom. She shrugs at our surprised expressions. "Sometimes the only appropriate word for a person is a rude one."

"The quality didn't seem like it was great, but it's unquestionably me," Lacey says. "I was saying that you're selfish, that you froze me out of the Royal Family so you could lord your status over me, that Nick shouldn't marry you." Her face is ashen. "I told him you and Freddie were having an affair. I may have called you a sex addict. It was hard to hear. I sound so bitter."

A loud knock comes at the door.

"Bex? Kira is here," Cilla says, opening it slightly and poking her head around it.

"Just a sec," Mom says, sounding very chipper. "Family bonding, dear. You understand."

Cilla clearly knows this is a lie. "Five minutes," she offers, then disappears.

Mom looks at Lacey. "So you're not in on the blackmail," Mom clarifies.

Lacey shakes her head vigorously. "No. God, no. It honestly took me a minute to even figure out what he was doing. He could've just been some weird fetishist, you know?" She looks over at me helplessly. "I swear, I never would have kept hanging out with him if I'd known he was The Royal Flush."

"I believe you," I tell her. And I do.

Lacey turns back to Mom. "I begged Clive not to do anything with what he had, so he asked what I could give him in return." She twitches. "I may have leaked the Agatha story."

"Ohhhhhh." I let out the word like air seeping out of a balloon. "Eleanor was pissed."

"Clearly I should not have repeated that to you." Mom looked abashed, then thoughtful. "Although Agatha was rather relieved to have it out there."

The story had run two days ago on The Royal Flush, and it alleged that Agatha and Awful Julian would be divorcing quietly during the nation's giddy afterglow from our wedding. I had wondered how the Flush scored such a scoop, in fact, and its total truth forced the Queen to let Agatha confirm everything—which in turn gave the site even more credibility.

"I figured giving up that info didn't really hurt anyone, and I thought I could buy us some time," Lacey explains. "Maybe until after the wedding. He seemed thrilled, but I guess he was just toying with me." Any cheer she has managed suddenly vanishes. "He called me this morning and told me...let's see if I can get it right...'I stand with Freddie and the rest of the world on this one. You're just the appetizer. She's the main course.'"

The strength of my gasp catches even me by surprise.

"Disgusting." A year's worth of anger at her dissolves. "It is amazing *how* disgusting."

"He is, as we'd say in my day, a cad," Mom says.

"I still can't believe Clive is The Royal Flush," I say. "Nick is not going to like this."

Nick is not going to like a lot of things. That particular thing, in fact, is just icing on the cake of Things Nick Won't Like.

"I just don't get where Clive is coming from," Lacey says. "Disliking you two is one thing, but this is beyond. What did he tell you?"

I heave a deep breath. Just thinking about the call makes me queasy.

"He just said he was sick of waiting for his turn, and that it was long past time for me to help him become a smash. And if I didn't, he'd do it himself by destroying me." Clive had sounded so calculating, so cool, that I instantly knew he'd practiced this threat a hundred times. "Basically, he freaked me out so badly that I hung up on him, so he started sending all these capsy texts."

As if on cue, my phone buzzes.

BEX. DO IT MY WAY AND WE BOTH WIN.

"This is a mess," I say, my voice catching. "Why the hell couldn't I just pull my shit together like a grown-up?"

"It's not your fault," Lacey attempts.

"It is completely my fault," I say. "I wish I could blame someone else, but the fact is that if I'd been smarter, or stronger, there would be nothing to tell."

"Bex," Mom says, getting up and coming to me, boring through me with her stare. "You have to be honest with me. If Nick isn't satisfying you as a lover, then—"

"*That's* where your head went?" Lacey squeaks.

"It's a fair question. If these Freddie incidents mean Bex needs satisfaction elsewhere, then she can't marry Nick," Mom says firmly. "I will put it in terms your father would have used. You can't just pick the best starting pitcher. You need middle relief *and* a closer."

I groan. "Dad would have left the room ages before that analogy was even necessary."

"Then *Cosmopolitan* will back me up. I've been reading a lot of it lately and it's quite enlightening," she says. "I even clipped some of those how-to guides. Mostly for Agatha, but—"

"*Stop*," Lacey and I say at the same time.

Mom rolls her eyes at us. "You two are the ones who brought up all the sex in the first place." She turns to me and gently runs a hand over my hair. "But it's not my only concern. Honey, remember at Nick's birthday party, when your father told you that you'd have to really love Nick to go through all of this? Earl was more right than he ever knew."

"He usually was," I say, tremulously.

"Please don't self-sacrifice here just because you feel like it's too late. Is all this worth it? The press, all the scrutiny, the rigid rules? Because if you don't really, really love him enough to put up with it, then I will call Eleanor myself and tell her the wedding is off and we can disappear someplace tropical and let the papers publish whatever they want. Speak now or forever hold your peace, baby. Is it too much?"

"It is a lot," I tell her. "But to me, he is worth everything."

A tear falls. Then another. Mom draws us both in and kisses the tops of our heads. Our last hug like this was the night Nick gave me the Lyons Emerald. And now I might have to give it back.

I pull away and look at them, beseeching. "What am I going to do?"

"*We,*" Lacey says.

"Thank you," I say, barely choking out the words. "But I think this one is on me alone."

"Well, you can't kill Clive without me," Lacey says. "You have to exsanguinate the body into mason jars so there's no blood trail. It's a two-person job."

"That is disturbingly specific," Mom says.

Lacey shrugs. "I was in med school for about five minutes, remember?" she says. "We had weird late-night discussions." She sounds wistful, which I take as a sign that another long-missed part of my sister may come back to me.

"Bex!" booms Cilla, banging on the door. "Get a move on, or I'll send Gaz in wearing nothing but a crumpet."

"Now what?" Lacey whispers.

"We get a move on," I say, wiping my face. "I don't want to know where Gaz would put the crumpet."

"But you haven't decided anything," she says. "We haven't helped yet."

"You have, actually," I say. "More than you know. I think..." I make sure it feels right; it does. "I'm going to tell Nick."

Lacey pales. "No. We can go to Clive. Surely he'll see sense. There has to be a way."

"Not this time," I say. "This all happened because I felt powerless. I can't take away Nick's power to decide. It's not fair. And I can't hide one lie by dumping other ones on top of it. I'd hate myself. It would kill whatever's left of me that still feels like me."

"She's right, sweetie," Mom says to Lacey. "Begin as you mean to continue, as they say."

"I have to tell Freddie, too." I rest my forehead on my bent knees. "It's going to ruin their relationship. I hate that the most. I've been without my sister, and it sucks."

"It will work out, Bex," Mom says. "Just be honest. Have faith."

I hear in this the same advice I gave Nick the day he told the truth about Emma. It had worked then; was there enough faith left to help me now? I feel Lacey's hand reach out and stroke my hair, and I luxuriate in the familiarity of this, like there was never a gulf between us.

"Your hair extensions seriously are fantastic," she murmurs. "I know there are no freebies, but would it kill you to hook a sister up?"

The door bursts open just as we both start to giggle.

"Time's up, Porters," Cilla says. "If Bex is late, we'll all be sent to the Tower."

"Are you ready?" Lacey asks me.

I shake my head, halfway between laughter and tears. "Do I have a choice?"

An elderly couple has draped the metal barricade outside Westminster Abbey with a banner claiming they've witnessed three generations of Lyons weddings. "Congratulations!" they cry out when my car door opens.

"Rebecca! Give us a wave!" shouts a younger woman. She is wearing Union Jack–printed novelty sunglasses and a light-up tiara.

"You look so pretty!" lisps a little girl at the front, no more than six or seven. She wiggles a bouquet of freesias at me.

I can get in and out of cars nearly as gracefully as Eleanor now, and as I glide to my feet, I am struck not only by the sheer number of people gathered to wish me well, but by their intensity. Once the calendar flipped into the year of our wedding, a switch congruently flipped in the hearts of the public and much of the media. I don't know why; maybe just the anticipation of the global spectacle, or the uptick in stories about Regular Girl Nabs Prince Charming (applications to Oxford from US exchange programs reportedly tripled, even without a prince in residence to lure them). Or, it's possible everybody decided that this was happening regardless, so they might as well get on board.

British and American flags bob vigorously as the teeming throng chants, sings, and cheers, at least a quarter of them wearing ghastly paper novelty masks of my face that will dance in the foreground of my nightmares for the rest of my life (matched for creepiness only by the time Nick put one on and danced around in his boxers, just to goad me). Nick and I have encountered friendly support at the few events we've done this year, but this is the first time it's been on such a massive scale—people who have waited all day for me to arrive at the rehearsal, and will stay overnight to see me come back tomorrow—and as I look back at them, I know the expression on my face is of unladylike shock and delight.

The little girl bounces and shouts, "Daddy, she sees me!"

I'm not supposed to engage people yet, but she is darling, missing two front teeth, with golden pigtails and a fluffy pink party dress. She reminds me of Lacey, an eternity ago.

I scoot over to where she stands. "Freesias are my favorite," I say, squatting and accepting the bouquet. "How did you know?"

"I read it in *heat* magazine. Mummy keeps it in the loo and says I'm not to touch it because it's for grown-up ladies." She beams proudly at me. "I was naughty."

"I'll never tell." I grin back. "What's your name?"

"Adelaide."

"Can I tell you a secret, Adelaide?" I ask. She leans eagerly into me. "I'm a little nervous," I confess.

"Mummy bet Daddy ten pounds that you'll mix up his names," she says.

"Nah, I'll be fine," I say. "His name's Harold, right?"

She giggles. "No!"

"Yes, Prince Harold Tiddlywinks Cadbury, I'm sure of it," I say.

She giggles harder. "You're very silly. Are you allowed to be silly?"

I grin. "I hope so, Adelaide."

PPO Stout puts gentle pressure on my arm. My impromptu sojourn has to end. I split the bouquet in half and hand part of it back to her.

"Here, you keep half, and I'll carry the rest tomorrow," I say as I stand. "For good luck."

Camera flashes go off like crazy. I've just unintentionally given The Firm its banner pre-wedding publicity moment, and almost laugh at the irony of providing the very best headline right before the very worst. As Stout pulls me away, I pause to take in the immensity of this, that rare species of mob that is entirely loving and positive. *I'm so sorry*, I say silently, before waving what might be my final good-bye and riding the swell of their good cheer through the doors.

Westminster Abbey is a transcendent, transporting place, all soaring stone arches and marble columns, capped with fan vaulting a distant hundred feet above our heads (which is, somehow, still only a fraction of the aisle that I'll walk). Right now, men in bright yellow work vests lug flowering shrubs inside, which will be blessed and replanted in public parks on Sunday, and the juxtaposition is so unexpected that it looks like a movie set. The greenery was Nick's suggestion. In fact, his return had given the entire creative team a jolt of inspiration, like finally finding the missing piece to our jigsaw puzzle and tapping it in place with glee. After a desperate and lonely year, the last four months passed in a giddy breeze.

Until this morning.

I hear a loud sniffle. Gaz is walking toward me, blotting his face with a hanky.

"Just a little emotional. Nothing I can't handle tomorrow," he says, patting my arm in a fatherly way, as if getting into the spirit of his role. "You look lovely, Future Duchess, but no offense, you cannot hold a candle to your sexy matron of honor."

"I reckon the words *sexy* and *matron* don't get paired up often," Cilla says from behind me, taking Adelaide's freesias and giving her husband a peck.

"They will now," he says. "Can't I be called man of honor in the program, if I'm giving away the bride and married to the matron?"

"We printed it up in Garamond, isn't that enough?" she teases.

Suddenly, the roar of the crowd trickles in again as the Abbey doors open.

"Right, everyone's here, let's get on with it," Marj says.

I swivel around to see her and Nick and Freddie. We are only rehearsing our part, as the rest of our families have roles that mostly come down to their drivers and styling teams staying on schedule. Nick looks flushed and self-conscious, even tense, as he always does after the dog-and-pony-show part of his job. He's in rolled-up shirtsleeves and navy pants—his frequent uniform, approachably debonair—and after all these years, even knowing that I'm going to have a catastrophic conversation with him later, the sight of Nick still makes my heart swell against my ribs. Slipping back into our cozy trio with Freddie has been both easier and harder than I thought—easier because Freddie and I love Nick, and don't love each other; harder because we feel the burden of proving, even to an unknowing Nick, that everything is normal.

"The bride and groom! What an honor," says the Dean of Westminster, approaching in my periphery. As he crosses the nave, he and Nick reach me simultaneously.

"Hi," I whisper.

Nick gives me what can only be described as a perfunctory bump that involves less lip than it does his own cheek grazing mine. When we break away, he is staring elsewhere, and a glance behind me shows that Freddie's own jaw is clenched and his gaze is locked straight ahead of him. I realize with a sinking feeling that I have misread Nick's expression. He is not tense from the crowd, nor his shyness, nor nerves.

He knows.

# CHAPTER TWO

"Your Highness, sir, are you in place at the altar?" the Dean of Westminster shouts.

We hear Nick's faint call of assent.

"Need a walkie-talkie in this old heap, eh?" the dean says, winking and clapping merrily. "Right! Let's get cracking. Rebecca, you'll be greeted here by me and the Archbishop of Canterbury for a little chitchat, *how'd you sleep, did you eat your brekkie*, while everyone gets your skirts in order. The archbish loves a spot of marmalade in the a.m. so file *that* away for easy small talk. And then you and your, er..."

He cocks his head at Gaz.

"Her man of honor," Gaz says hopefully.

"Her distinguished escort," Cilla corrects him.

"Quite right. The distinguished Mr. Bates will take Miss Porter around the Tomb of the Unknown Soldier, like so, careful not to molest the poppies, and then bang on up the aisle for a bit past the cheap seats. Steady, that's right. We'll be at this for about five minutes so I hope you wear your trainers tomorrow, eh?"

He chuckles, thrilling to this. We stare at the dean's back, following diligently and practicing the walking cadence, as he drones on about the history of the Abbey and the "O Rare Ben Jonson" stone on the floor. (Legend has it that when the poet qualified for burial there, he couldn't afford the square footage of a proper plot, so he bought one tile and had himself interred standing up.) After a minute of holding our joined hands at chest height, Gaz's arm trembles.

"A bit achy on the muscles, this," he says. "I should make man of honor exercise routines. I'll make a fortune."

"Right," I say absently.

"Oi, what's the matter?" he whispers. "Nick was as grim as a reaper when he came in."

"I messed up, Gaz."

"How bad?"

"Really bad."

"Cancel-the-wedding bad?" he asks jovially. "Shag-the-groom's-brother bad?"

I stiffen. Gaz grips my hand so tight I want to yelp. "I will neuter that git," he hisses as we reach the gilded, semi-enclosed Quire.

"Children's voices raised in song, the swell of anticipation of seeing His Highness, magical feelings, you get the idea," the dean calls to us, waving his hands as if he's conducting the choir himself.

"No! No shagging," I insist. "But it's complicated."

I can see Nick ahead, over the dean's shoulder, and feel my throat threatening to close.

"Just please don't hate me later," I plead. "And, please, *do not trust Clive.*"

Gaz side-eyes me with surprise. The rest of the way, I try that old trick of floating above myself to take in as much of this as possible, in case the dry run is the only run. But fear and dread root me to the ground, small and scared in this towering place where countless reigns and love stories have begun and ended. Gaz deposits me next to Nick. The air is thick.

"Right, then the archbish and I get to go all scold-y on you about marriage being a Holy Estate, don't be wanton, blah blah blah," the dean says, turning to face me and Nick with a dramatic swoosh. "Then we dish out some pressure to sprog up with some heirs, and then it's my favorite bit, *ye will answer at the dreadful day of judgment when the secrets of all hearts shall be disclosed,* where we look jolly mean and ask if anyone thinks you should call it off, and everyone hopes nobody's exes had a tipple before the ceremony."

When Nick and I don't laugh immediately, Gaz offers a loud guffaw, which kicks everyone else into gear. The dean looks elated, until he spies the tear escaping down my cheek.

"That's right, dear, let yourself be moved, that's why we rehearse," he says kindly.

Nick does not even look at me.

I have been inside Westminster Abbey several times since I moved to England, most often to draw, and invariably it would be packed with throngs of gawkers glued to their audio guides—or, at the very least, some docents and a school field trip. But I can probably count on two hands the number of people in history who've seen the Abbey completely empty, and now Nick and I are among them. After our rehearsal, Nick had asked the dean for a moment alone for us to reflect on our big day, and the dean had been only too thrilled to escort everyone else around the Cloisters so that we could be properly reverent of our forthcoming sacrament. While Nick lights a candle that I assume is for Emma—he does this in every church he enters—I wait for him in the Henry VII Lady Chapel, a large, rounded marvel behind the altar where a bunch of kings and queens and other mighty personages lie in eternal state. It's just me and the ghosts, all of whom I'm sure have a variety of notes, largely hypocritical, about my behavior. In the distance I hear Nick's footsteps click across the marble floor. My skin crawls. I am afraid.

And then he's there. Nick makes for me briefly, instinctively, and then catches himself and clenches his entire body.

"I've heard the most ridiculous story," he says, his voice pitched high and tight. "About my brother snogging the woman I'm supposed to marry."

"Nick—"

"I know, it's mental, I didn't believe it at first, either," he says, his tone veering slightly hysterical. "Real forbidden passion stuff. Quite juicy. Can't wait for the next installment."

"Nick, I'm sorry, and I love you," I say, as fervently as I can. "I could say both of those things a thousand times every day for the rest of our lives and it wouldn't come close to how much I mean them."

"You've an odd way of showing it."

"I know it looks that way," I say, "but Nick, I promise you, we're not in love, he's not in love—"

"Oh, good, then you were just pawing at each other for sport, that's much better."

"I just mean that he's mixed up. We both were. And it wasn't pawing." I try again. "Please don't be angry at him, he was—"

"Angry at Freddie?" he spits. "You're worried about me being angry at *Freddie*? I'm angry at Freddie every other day. I can deal with being angry at Freddie. I'm *not* used to being angry at you. And I am *so angry*, Bex. I can't fathom where I'm going to put all this anger so it won't explode out of me." He puffs out a breath. "I don't even care about the press stuff. I could live with that. It's the fact that it's *true*. And now your first concern is for *him*—"

"It isn't, Nick. It's for you. I'm just..." I can barely say it. "I'm scared that this is the end for you and me, and I don't want you to lose us both on the same day."

Nick purses his lips and fights to keep from crying. My hands are shaking.

"I almost wish Clive had told me," he says. "Because I never have to see him again to relive that memory. But Lacey apparently gave Freddie a heads-up, and he thought he'd be considerate and tell me so that you didn't have to. And it was so thoughtful. Really aces of him to break my heart right before my wedding rehearsal so I don't have any happy memories of this whole experience at all, if it even happens."

And there it is.

Nick flicks his eyes at me, then drops his head. "I can't even look at you," he whispers. "It used to be my favorite thing to do. And now..."

"Can I explain?" I ask.

"I've heard it."

"Not my side," I say. "It didn't happen without context, Nick, and maybe it won't help, but please. Let me try."

Nick is vibrating from anger or sadness, possibly both. He climbs into one of the benches and sits down, facing me, arms resting on the wood rail.

"All right," he says. "Tell me how you kissed my brother and never told me. Twice. Shall we have the dean take your confession?"

I absorb that one. I owe him that much. I don't know how to defend myself against this, exactly, but maybe I don't have to; maybe I just lay it all out there and let him accept me or not. I sit down on the opposite side of the chapel. The gulf between us is chilly, and it is horrible.

"The first time, you and I were broken up, and Freddie and I were drunk, and lonely, and probably horny, and it was pitch black and we bumped into each other. It could have been anyone, and once our senses caught up with us, we freaked out," I say. "I didn't tell you because you specifically said, twice, that you didn't want to know what happened while we were apart."

"I didn't mean that with regards to my own brother."

"You're totally right. I shouldn't have listened to you. I thought it would stir the pot for no good reason, so when you offered me a way out, I took it," I say. "Remember, though, you practically turned green when we talked about you and Pudge, and *this* was just a kiss."

"Was there another time that wasn't?"

"Not with Freddie," I say. If Nick and I have any chance, there needs to be nothing else left to catch him by surprise. "But I did sleep with Clive during that time. And yeah, I'm pretty skeeved out about it right now."

"There, we are in agreement," Nick mutters.

"I hadn't seen you or talked to you since the breakup, and I swear, Nick, *you* try standing anywhere near Ceres de Whatever in fucking foot pants while she looks so perfect and perfect *for* you. I just could not," I recall. "Clive rescued me and we got super-crazy drunk in Paris. I wanted to take it back right after it happened, and that was before he turned out to be a sleaze."

Nick rests his forehead on the rail of the choir pew. "Is there anyone else you shagged that I should know about?"

I smack my bench with both palms. "No," I say. "*No.* There are plenty of high horses you can climb up on right now, but not that one. We were broken up. For good, as far as I knew. And if the papers are right, you used that time to screw every ex-girlfriend you had and more people besides. Don't you dare shame me for anything I did."

His eyes flick up at me apologetically before returning to the floor.

"You said the first time didn't mean anything," he says. "With Freddie. That implies the second time did."

"It did," I say. "But not in the way you think."

"Do enlighten me," he says, his cheeks bright with anger. "I'm on the edge of my pew."

"I was upset," I say. "More than upset. I was *wrecked.* I was lonely, and I was overwhelmed, and you'd been gone for almost a year. I got scared that I was in over my head with all this."

"So you're punishing me for being in the Navy?" he asks curtly.

"I'm not punishing you for anything!" I spit back. "Do you really think that's who I am?"

He waits a beat before shaking his head.

"But yeah, you know what, I was angry with you," I continue. "Your first deployment was hard enough, but the second one did me in. I was mad at myself for telling you to go, but I might've been madder at you for letting me."

"How could I have known you didn't mean it? I'm not psychic," he points out.

"Be fair, Nick. You knew it was crazy. But you wanted to go, so you believed whatever would justify it," I say. "You didn't want the facts to get in the way of your decision."

"The Navy isn't just a lark to me!" he says. "I am useful out there. I am not useful here."

"You would have been useful to me." The sheer need in my voice almost hurts my feelings, I hate it so much. "Look, I'm just trying to explain how jumbled my head was. I'm proud of your commitment. That's why I never asked you to say no to the *Pembroke.* But you knew you were leaving me in shark-infested waters. How many times did you tell me you were afraid of bringing me into this life?

We almost lost each other over that once. And we might lose each other over it again."

"No, I think that'll be because you kissed my brother."

"That's what I mean about context, Nick." I breathe out hard through my nose. "I was spiraling. Freddie, too. We both felt lost in your family. Things got really emotional, and intense, and for a split second Freddie thought he was offering us both a way out."

"And that was a better plan than talking to Marj?"

"I'm Marj's *job,* Nick. I'm an equation she has to solve," I say. "You are the only person who chose me. Everyone else on your side just has to make the best of the fact that I was the one person still standing when Daddy forced you to pick a bride."

Nick looks up at me. "I never intended to keep my side of that deal," he says. "What was he going to do, remove me from the military under great public scrutiny? Crack me over the head and wake me up in Gretna Green? I just agreed so he'd let me join up."

"You never told me that. You never told me anything," I said. "All I was hearing was that I was a desperate guy's default option. And the way you charged off into the Navy and never looked back, it started to feel like maybe it was true."

"I don't understand why it's so easy for you to believe the worst," he says.

"It's never easy, Nick, it's *agony,*" I say, a sob rising in my throat.

We're quiet while he chews on the inside of his cheek.

"I did not handle our breakup as well as I wanted to," he says. "The longer we were apart, the more I missed..." He searches for the right phrase. "The feeling of family that you and I had. I wanted it again. I'd never had it with anyone except Freddie."

His voice catches on his brother's name, but he keeps going. "So yes, I slept with old girlfriends, and some new ones, and yes, I imagined whether we could have a life together. All those girls would have been easy and palatable choices if any of us had loved each other, but we didn't, and I realized I'd already had my choice and lost her." His eyes are moist. "And then suddenly you and I were together again. I couldn't waste it. The timing was ghastly with the Navy, but I was afraid if I waited, something might get in between us and screw it up again."

"And it did anyway. Again," I say, feeling drained.

"Maybe *that's* our destiny," he says. "Screwing up. Maybe we misread this all along."

The words echo off the walls, even though we are speaking quietly. Neither of us has moved, an aisle apart in fact but much further away in spirit. Nick gets up, as if to leave.

"Wait," I say, sliding out and crossing to where he is standing. This conversation is not finished yet. "I told you the Freddie kiss meant something to me, but I didn't tell you why."

He half turns to listen to me, his head still down. "The first time, I learned I wasn't over you," I say. "And the second time, I learned I never will be. That's why it mattered. I shouldn't have let it happen, but when it did, it killed any doubt or fear I felt, and filled me up with you instead. I'm not marrying the monarchy. I'm marrying *you*. And however bad it gets with the press, or your family, or even mine, I will always choose you. I'm yours for life. Whether you want me or not."

Nick jams his hands in his pockets and spends what feels like forever rattling the change in there.

"It's not your fault he wanted you," he finally whispers to the ground. "God knows I understand it. But it's all I can see when I close my eyes." His voice breaks. "*Twice*, Bex. Once before we were even engaged. If I'd known then..."

"Okay, let's play that." I feel like I'm negotiating for the rest of my life. "You once asked if I'd have turned down your proposal if I'd thought twice about your Naval deployments. The answer is no. Even knowing that this is the way it played out, even if this is the end, I would do it again a hundred times." I am crying in earnest now. "If I'd told you about Freddie then, would you still have chosen me? Do you still choose me now?"

Nick does look at me this time, long and hard and sad.

"I don't know," he says, and he walks out of the chapel, leaving me alone with the ghosts.

# CHAPTER THREE

Kira steps back and gives a triumphant hoot. "Nailed it," she says. "You can barely tell."

She hands me a mirror. An hour and a half ago, I looked like what's under the bandages after plastic surgery: splotchy and crimson, with eyelids like cocktail sausages. I'd retreated to The Goring and thrown myself into my mother's arms, sobbing out to her and Lacey everything I'd had to hold in during the drive; then I bled myself to Gaz and Cilla and haltingly released them to process it in private, telling them that I would respect their choice if they could no longer support me. I pulled myself together a hundred times, only to pop the seams again five minutes later, and hid behind sunglasses on the ride to Buckingham Palace to prepare for tonight's reception. When I took them off inside the Spartan, utilitarian room earmarked for my styling team, Kira whispered, "Take me now, Lord."

But she has worked a miracle. She shrank my eyelids with a mixture of compresses, witch hazel, and Preparation H, giving me the faint perfume of hemorrhoid cream of which every young bride dreams. She flushed me out with a gallon of Visine and filled me up with a gallon of water; with all that, some thin white eyeliner on my lower lids, and some artful highlighter, you can't even tell I spent the day running my heart through a meat grinder. Even I nearly believe the illusion. Apply enough spackle, and you can sell anything.

Kira makes me blot my lips one more time, then holds up her hand for a high five, which Cilla obligingly attempts and bungles.

"Watch the elbow and you'll never miss," I say.

They try again. It's perfect.

"I can't believe that works. Where did you learn that?" Kira asks, amazed.

My throat constricts as I remember the day Nick taught me, after The Glug. "State secret," I manage, feeling myself unspool.

Kira stomps her foot. "No. You will not get all weepy on me. Aren't you an artist? Do not spoil my masterpiece."

This makes me smile, which is its intent. Cilla hands me a bottle of water with a straw poking out so I won't disrupt my lipstick.

"Thank you," I tell her. "For everything. No one would blame you if you weren't here."

"I would blame me," Cilla says. "And not just because I'd be shirking my job. Although perhaps all this happening means I *did* shirk my job."

"Don't even say that. Your job isn't to babysit me, Cil."

"It is, a bit, but you're also my friend," Cilla points out. "I should have noticed on both ends how bad it had gotten."

"There has been a lot of *why didn't you tell me* and *I'm not psychic* today, all of it earned," I say. "Reminds me of when Nick and I broke up the first time." I catch myself. "Hopefully the only time."

"Has he said anything since the Abbey?" Cilla looks concerned.

"He's probably said a lot of things, but none of them to me," I say. "Which is kind of the crux of the problem. All along, if we'd just told each other everything right away, straight up, it might have been fine. Everyone thinks Americans are so in-your-face, but I was too scared to be a pain in the ass."

"I am married to Gaz," she says. "My arse is immune to pain. Remember that next time."

"You are a better friend than I deserve."

"Oh, shove it, love," she says good-naturedly. "This is not the Premier League. There's no rankings or win-loss records in our friendship. Whatever happens, you and Nick will need us, and we'd be daft as a brush not to be there for both of you."

She senses danger from my tear ducts, so she shoves the straw into my mouth and turns me to the long mirror.

"You're a picture, Bex," she says softly. "He'll melt."

Donna had procured a plum gossamer Jenny Packham with elbow-length sleeves and a chic, slouchy neckline. My hair is swept into a glamorous, bouncy ponytail, Kira's clever nod to the Bex from Oxford whom Nick rarely saw any other way, and Eleanor had proffered the Surrey Fringe as a choker but I opted instead for my diamond pendant. Even through my haze, I love how I look. I hope Nick will, too. If he shows. Intellectually I know it's unlikely he'll stand me up tonight—I'd have heard by now; he has too much respect for duty to jilt three hundred guests without a word—but given how we left things...well, it's little wonder we fell in love over a show specializing in cliffhangers.

"Right, go in, mingle, get out," Cilla says, checking her clipboard. "Early to bed tonight. We are going to proceed as if this wedding is happening."

"If this wedding doesn't happen, then he is dumb as the box of hair I put on your head every month," Kira says, clicking shut her giant toolbox of makeup. "I don't care who started it, or who slept with what, or whatever went on with you kids, but shit happens and when it's people who matter, we deal with it. You, Rebecca Porter, are a catch. You're the only person I've ever worked for who knows when my birthday is and asks about my family. If HRH can't get over whatever his problem is, then you go be a goddess someplace else."

We are silent.

"That was a better speech than mine," Cilla observes.

"You're both going to make me cry again," I say.

"Don't you dare." Kira smudges my blush one last time. "Blot your lippie if you reapply. It kills me that you never do that. Now go slay him."

Sure enough, Nick is exactly where he is supposed to be, in a small space off the gardens. I hang back to take in the sight: Prince Nicholas, dressed for ceremony in a devastating tux, washing down a granola bar with a Coke and nose-deep in a binder labeled *The Lesser Royals of Southeast Asia*. My mouth goes dry. We used to pretend we weren't madly in love before tearing into one another in private; now, everyone believes we've never been happier, yet I have no idea if we're even speaking. Out of all the illusions we have created, from my hair to my walk to the color of my teeth, pretending we are fine will be the biggest, and the flimsiest. The Lyons Emerald has never felt heavier on my finger. I wonder what they'll do to the engraving if I have to give it back. Maybe Nick can replace me with another *B*.

"There you are, Rebecca," says Marj, whom I hadn't even noticed in the corner of the room. Nick jerks up his head, then gives me a long, appraising gaze that I can't read. I shift under the weight of it, and feel the prick of my secret talisman, the flag pin, tacked covertly to my bra.

"Come in," Marj says. "Do you need one last look at the cheat books?"

I shake my head. "If I don't know it now, I never will."

"Is any of this lot even coming?" Nick asks.

"One must always prepare," Marj says, taking his binder and heaving it over to a folding table next to ten other ones like it, plus three volumes clearly for Freddie labeled *Comfortably Distant Relatives*, *Potentially Awkward*, and finally, *Seriously Do Not Touch*. I wonder if she has a *Let's Call the Whole Thing Off* binder. Knowing Marj, the answer is yes.

This is the first time I've seen Marj not wearing a cardigan, even in summer, and cocktail wear suits her. From the frock's silvery color and matching cropped jacket to the low, chunky heels, it all could as easily have come from the Queen's own armoire—apt, as she's effectively as much Nick's grandmother as Eleanor is. But there's fatigue around her edges. Should tomorrow go smoothly, her husband will ply her with cocktails on a hard-earned Carnival Cruise and hopefully toss her mobile overboard. When Nick does not greet me, much less kiss me hello, Marj betrays no reaction. If anyone deserves to live in crisis denial right now, it's her.

"You look marvelous," she says, giving me a kiss on both cheeks. "Like a right royal highness yourself. It's been quite a year, but you've come out of it brilliantly, Rebecca."

I flush, from shame, not pleasure, but she won't discern the difference.

"Thank you," I say. "If I ever seemed ungrateful, or cranky, I really am sorry. I know how hard you and Barnes worked to get me here."

Marj barks out a laugh. "When I started here, my equivalent on Emma's staff was a woman named Elaine who seemed like as much of an old battle-ax to me then as I seem to you now," she says. "One day Emma marched into her office, slammed a pile of these sorts of binders on the desk, and said, 'Shove it with knobs on, you stroppy old cow.' "

Nick looks astonished. I laugh in spite of myself.

"Your mother had a lot more spirit in her than anyone remembers," Marj says to Nick. "Whatever went wrong, mark my words, it was fated that way. She had an iron streak, from what I saw." Then she turns to me. "We put you through a wringer of the sort Emma never had to endure. I'd not have blamed you if you had a tantrum in my office. You probably ought to have."

"I am terrified of Barnes," I admit.

"That man has a Bunny-A-Day calendar in his desk drawer, and if you ever breathe a word of that, I will make up an outrageous lie about your medical history." She pauses. "Rebecca, I have no doubt you're ready, but if you ever need bucking up, I'm here."

Her eyes are misty. It's so bittersweet to hear this now, long after it's needed, and I think the only reason I am not crying is that my peripheral vision is trained on Nick, and the way he is listening, and whether this is changing anything. His face betrays no answers.

Marj collects herself and ushers us toward the terrace doors. Eleanor isn't coming, preferring to save her grand entrance for tomorrow, which means that tonight Richard is the Head Bastard In Charge—a free preview of a movie that won't come out for another decade—and he is being very formal about it, right down to making a footman bang a gold-and-black-striped stick on the ground and announce the guests as they enter down the terrace steps. Marj whispers in his ear and he gives the instructed five poundings before booming our arrival. Our smiles snap into place. Nick is much faster at this than I am. He has had a lifetime of practice.

"May I present the guests of honor, His Royal Highness Prince Nicholas of Wales, and his bride, Miss Rebecca Porter," he booms in a perfect voice for radio. "Who shall tomorrow become Duke and Duchess of Clarence, Earl and Countess of Athlone, and Baron and Baroness of Inverclyde, by the grace of Her Majesty the Queen."

"It was decided an hour ago," Nick mutters through his teeth. "Surprise." He does not sound excited.

Nick and I are separated by well-wishers as soon as we reach the bottom of the stairs. I wish I could appreciate the romance of the garden's landscaping and soft amber lights, but for the next ninety minutes, I am too busy cycling through every etiquette lesson Barnes and Marj drilled into me. I hold my Champagne in my left hand and sip it openly, leaving my right empty and dry; I do not eat; I ask people with children about their children, and people with dogs about their dogs. I remember that our pageboy's mother is called Kristen, and our flower girl's mother is Kirsten. I recognize Gregor of Hanover, whose calling cards dub him a sock baron; the trio of temptresses from Marta's family in Sweden, all most likely in the binders meant to warn Freddie away; and two of Nick's toff godparents for whom my notecards had read only, *Don't mention Transylvania* (which might be too tempting to resist, if I need to create a diversion later). I introduce Cilla to anyone of whose name I am not certain, forcing them to repeat it when they shake her hand so I can sort through my mental Rolodex and pull out helpful conversational tips—like that the Bulgarian Tsarina owns an original prop from every Harry Potter film, or that the Margrave of Baden prefers not to explain what a Margrave is but that the Landgrave of Hesse will wax for hours on the derivation of Landgrave, so it's best to avoid both topics.

"Aren't you exhausted?" Lady Elizabeth asks, as two Comfortably Distant Relatives from Norway wander away in search of more caviar. "All this palaver is why we didn't have a whole to-do. Well, one of the reasons."

She rests a hand on her pregnant belly; a third baby is coming in four months' time. "This one is going to be big," she groans. "It was a bit soon, really. The Maldives are just such an aphrodisiac. You should see Eddybear in his Speedo."

I try not to imagine this, and fail, and genially tune out while Lady Elizabeth rhapsodizes about pregnancy sex (by the look on her face, the Thai princess nearby understands more English than she's let on). Lacey keeps shooting me glances that say, alternately, *are you okay*, *what is up with Nick*, and *that dude with the tray of lollipop lamb chops never comes over here*. It's a comfort that I can read her mind again, but the catharses we've had are not the same thing as fixing what went wrong. I can't get complacent and forget that we still have so much work to do.

"Listen to me, blathering on about episiotomies when you've got a wedding night ahead of you," Lady Elizabeth says airily, giving me a sideways hug. "We have our whole lives to talk about these things. Go have fun. I need more olives for my orange juice." She makes a face. "It tastes like Agatha's hairspray smells, but I can't get enough right now."

She sails off and I feel a pang, because if the worst happens I will miss her. I can't wallow, though, because I have to chat up the King of Bhutan about land reform, and Christiane of Greece about wrestling (she is a lifelong fan of The Rock). Richard, right in my eyeline, pretends not to watch Christiane as she laughs. There is a lovely what-if quality to his face before he thinks to erase it, underlining a long-ago revelation made in the heat of rage. Richard can't ever reach for what he wants. I hope I still can.

"But it *wasn't* de Pluvinel who first used pillars to train his mount," Agatha says as she walks past me. "There's clear evidence Eumenes was doing it first."

"How did I never notice how bloody sexy your horse talk is?" purrs none other than Edgeware Fitzwilliam.

I have never worked harder to keep a neutral expression on my face.

"You're doing wonderfully," Marj whispers, suddenly at my shoulder. "Clarence is a good title, too. It was King Albert's, as a lad. Very historically meaningful."

She steers me to the foot of the terrace stairs, where Freddie and Nick are waiting in silence. I recognize the look on Nick's face. Aggressively Pleasant. Bad sign.

"Prince Frederick has asked to give a toast in lieu of your father, and then you and His Royal Highness can sneak out and get some sleep," she says. "Freddie, if you make any inappropriate jokes about genitals I will neuter you with a toast point, do you hear me?"

"Yes, Your Marjesty." He salutes her.

"Is this honestly necessary?" Nick hisses, but his brother is already off up the stairs, and we are forced to follow and stand together and wait for Freddie, of all people, to raise a glass to our future. I glue on my smile and search for friendly faces—Cilla, making a delicate gesture to remind me to stand up straight, and Mom, standing next to her wedding date, my aunt Kitty, who arrived in London two hours ago and looks simultaneously jet-legged and wowed. And a few feet away, there's Pansy Larchmont-Kent-Smythe grilling Gemma Sands about something Gemma clearly finds tiresome, and Bea with Clive and Paddington.

I gasp so loudly that Nick actually turns to me.

"Clive is here," I tell him through clenched teeth. "Don't look. *Nick.* You looked."

Nick draws himself up to his full height. "That's a lot of cheek, him coming here."

"He must not think I've told you," I say slowly. "He probably banked on me not knowing how to get him disinvited, and he's trying to scare me."

Clive gives us both a carefree wave as Freddie gets the masses to quiet their chatter. Freddie objectively looks handsome, but his face is drawn. I wonder what he and Nick did all afternoon while I had people meticulously combing my brows and zapping my tearstains.

"Welcome, all, to what promises to be a ripping weekend," Freddie says. "I shall keep this brisk and save the saucy bits for tomorrow. Gran won't want to miss the visual aids."

A titter travels through the crowd.

"As the elder brother, Nick got to do everything before I did," Freddie says. "Or so he thought. He officially learnt to drive first, but I banged around Balmoral in Father's car two weeks before Nick's first lesson. He was allowed to drink at family dinners before I was, but I'd already spent ages stealing the glasses people would set down and then quaffing them under the table. And he thinks he was the first to—wait, hang about, can't say that one out loud."

The group chuckles en masse.

"But tomorrow, he really will reach one milestone ahead of me," Freddie continued. "Not that I'm in any kind of hurry to catch him. I'm having rather too much fun with the, er, bridal interview process." Freddie is playing the playboy prince to the hilt. Even his bow tie is slightly askew. "But as far as that goes, I've been bravely doing the work of two. Because Nick was hit with a bolt of lightning eight years ago and he's been lost to the ladies of the realm ever since."

Nick twitches, imperceptible to anyone but me.

"I've had a front-row seat for this entire courtship. In fact, remind me to tell you all why Bex punched me the first day we met, although I assure you, I deserved it," Freddie says. "'Course, you lot hide the *Daily Mail* behind those copies of the *Financial Times*, so you know quite a bit's happened between now and then. But I started writing this speech in my head after that very first bashing—and there have been others, don't you worry—because I saw then exactly what I've seen every single day since, in good times and rough. Together or apart, Bex and Nick have quite simply always belonged to each other."

The crowd gives an appreciative sigh; there is a smattering of applause. I am in torment.

Freddie clears his throat. "And that's what everyone's really looking for, isn't it? The kind of love that makes clichés ring true. It's a jackpot that is nearly impossible to hit." His voice is getting shaky. "So what's truly special about tomorrow's milestone is that it's once-in-a-lifetime stuff. Nick may be useless at the *Times* cryptic, but that's just letters on a piece of paper. He already solved the only riddle that counts. He found something I didn't fully believe existed until I saw it with my own eyes, and I will be forever in his debt for giving me yet another reason to strive for more. To be the man that he is."

Freddie is now struggling. Beside me, I see a tear snake out of Nick's eye. I take his hand and we cling to each other so tightly that our knuckles turn white.

"By this time tomorrow, my dear friend Rebecca will be a full-fledged member of The Firm. We will teach her the handshake, and she will be stuck with us," Freddie says, composing himself. "And thank

God, because there is no better person to entrust with the care and keeping of my very best friend, my brother, and our future king. Please raise your glass and drink with me to Nicholas and Rebecca."

"To Nicholas and Rebecca!" the crowd echoes, and then there is warm-hearted applause. Freddie and I make eye contact as we each hug him in what I hope is not too stiff a manner. *I did my best, Killer*, his face seems to say.

"Nick." I reach for him.

Nick places his hand on the curve of my waist and leans into me. "Not now, Bex," he whispers. "Just... not now."

And then Advanced Pleasantness is back, and he's off to accept a firm handshake from his father—it is damning that, between the two of us, Richard is the more soothing option—and I know that Nick is right. However much time he needs is what I have to give him.

"Wonderfully touching," beams the Crown Prince of Sweden as I reach the lawn again. "The three of you seem so close."

Over his shoulder, Clive gives the most epically false look of affection and wiggles his mobile phone at me. I feel the world spin a little.

"Thank you, Your Highness," I tell him. "In fact, I need to take a private moment. To collect myself."

I make my way inside the palace and into a cool hallway that is deserted except for footmen with trays of cocktails and platters of appetizers and giant piles of homemade Cracker Jack. I had intended to locate a quiet bathroom, just to be alone, but suddenly I find myself walking down the Marble Hall and past PPOs Stout and Furrow, who are guarding the Ministers' Staircase, and up through the silent, dimly lit palace, past the public rooms, back toward the private living quarters. I don't even register exactly where I'm going until I get there.

Emma, clad in a floral silk bathrobe, is in her chambers—cozier than the Queen's, and neat as a pin—playing solitaire on a folding TV tray. Doctors deemed her too fragile for tonight's party, but she's been getting a fair amount of visitors since she arrived from Cornwall on Tuesday. Nick has come every day; so has Pansy Larchmont-Kent Smythe. Lesley is sitting in a wing chair, working on some knitting, and stands when I open the door.

"I didn't expect to see you until tomorrow, Your Grace!" she says.

"Trust me, I am so not anyone's Grace."

"Soon enough, soon enough," Lesley says. "Is the party over? Can I get you a cuppa?"

"No, thank you, Lesley. I just wanted to say hello."

"Well, I'll leave the two of you in peace for a bit, then," Lesley says, bustling into the next room. "I've got ever so much to do if I want to finish this blanket before Prince Edwin's new baby gets here. And you'll be next!" She waggles a motherly finger at me as she pulls the adjacent bedroom door closed behind her.

I take a seat on the sofa next to Emma, who doesn't acknowledge me, but neatly places a red jack on top of a black queen. I'm not even sure why I'm here, except that somehow this seemed like the only place I could tolerate.

"We all miss you downstairs," I babble. "Especially Nick. And even though we don't actually know each other, I think *I* miss you, too, because you're the only other person who could possibly understand how I got myself in this position." I put my face in my hands. "Although you would be so mad at me right now, and you would be right. I've ruined everything. I didn't mean to. I was trying to protect him from worrying about me the way he worried about you, and instead I made everything worse. I should have just been honest with him. That's how we ended up together in the first place."

I let out a sob. Emma looks up abruptly and peers at me, in what feels like a moment of actual, present eye contact.

"Do you think *forgive and forget* is a real thing?" I ask. "Because I did, until today. I've made the biggest mess, Emma, and the worst of it is that I could always see so clearly *why* this happened but I just now realized it doesn't matter. Everyone has reasons. *Murderers* have reasons. But the people they killed still stay dead. You can't just erase an action. Once it's done, it's written into your history. It's always there. And I think what I did is carved into Nick and I can't ever replace the piece of him I cut out. I let this break me, and then I broke him, too."

Emma studies me again, longer this time, then flips over a card that proves to be useless. I wish that she would turn to me and say something apt or comforting, but she doesn't. She is not miraculously cured at exactly the moment that I need her to be. She does not win her solitaire game. Emma is lost, and chances are she always will be.

But seeing what that looks like reminds me that I am not lost. Not yet.

"I may never see you again after tonight," I tell her. "But I want you to know, wherever you are in there, that Nick is the best thing that ever happened to me. I regret a lot of things, but I will never regret him."

Something moves in my periphery, and I look up to see Nick standing in the doorway. I still sometimes forget how gorgeous he is, and then it will hit me hard, like a wave breaking against you when your back is turned. I don't know what, if anything, he heard. I lean over to kiss Emma's cheek, then cross the room to face whatever it is that Nick is going to say. Which, for a bit, is nothing. Ten seconds are an eternity when they're full of dread.

"You look beautiful," he says, his voice catching. "The whole time we were downstairs, that's all that was in my head. That's the worst part, I think. Even now, you are perfect to me."

"I was never perfect, Nick," I say. "And not for nothing, I'm wearing like ten pounds of fake hair."

His face is so sad that it wrenches me. "Would you have told me?" he asks softly.

"Yes," I say, emphatically. "*Yes.*"

"I don't mean today," he says. "I mean ever."

I am not sure what to say. Mostly because I'm not sure, period.

"I like to think I would have," I begin slowly. "If I'd come out of that night with any lingering doubt, then of course, but..." I shrug. "I would have struggled with it, and I might have hated myself for it, but I genuinely might not have told you. Because I would have been scared of losing you over something that ultimately meant nothing, and I probably would have been right." I stretch my hands wide. "That's the truth. It's unflattering, but I owe you nothing less."

Nick studies me for a second. "Thank you," he says. He picks at a spot of peeling paint on the doorframe. "It's hard not having anyone to talk to about this. You and Freddie..." His voice trails off. "Do you think Freddie and I will ever be the same?"

"I don't know," I say. "But it's what he wants, more than anything."

He closes his eyes. "We've spent so much time together, the three of us, the same as always. At home. In Spain, at Father's birthday party," he says. "All I can think of is whether he was looking at you in your bikini the same way I was."

"But *I* was looking at *you*." I want to reach out and touch him, but I cannot until he is ready. "Look, I fucked up, Nick. There's no way around it. If I gave you the impression today that I was trying to wriggle out of anything, I'm sorry. I just wanted to explain what I was feeling when the whole thing happened, so you could understand how it's possible that I could love you so much and still get caught in a moment like that. But maybe I should have just thrown myself on your mercy. Maybe trying to explain it made it worse."

"I don't want you to beg, Bex," he says. "I just feel like I don't have enough time. Like I'm being forced to make a choice about something I haven't even begun to process."

"Then don't choose. Not now," I say. "Take until the last minute if you want."

"I need about a year," he says dryly.

"I wish we could *rewind* a year."

"I wish we could rewind *eight* years and never leave Oxford," he says. "Just you and me and *Devour*."

I look at him for a second. "I think that's our problem," I say. "When things got tough, we never figured out how to fix it without retreating into our Oxford bubble. We need to figure out a better strategy. We're not the same people we were then. This isn't the same world."

"I know that's probably true," he says. "But I liked us then. I hope we'll always have bits of who we used to be."

"We will, Nick," I promise. "I mean, *some* of this is still my own hair."

With a wry smile Nick reaches out and touches it, then lets it slip through his fingers. "Well, I sincerely hope the people we are now can do this next bit together." My heart soars for a second until he adds, "We have to talk to Clive. Present a united front, and all that."

Thud.

"Do you think that'll help?" I ask, trying to cover my disappointment.

"It might not, in the grander scheme," he says. "But on a personal level, for how I feel right this second, it might do me a world of good."

"I do have a few choice words for that asswad," I say thoughtfully.

Nick grins before he can stop himself. "Now there is the Bex I remember from Oxford." He cocks his head toward the hallway. "Let's go grill that bastard."

It is a stay of execution. I'll take it.

# CHAPTER FOUR

We don't have to wait long for our confrontation. When we reach the hallway between the private living quarters and the staterooms, Clive is arguing with an unmoved PPO Twiggy, as Stout rounds the corner. Twiggy is, in fact, trying to direct Clive back to the party with rather more force than is strictly necessary, and that's how I know that while Nick probably couldn't to take Clive off the guest list, he'd wasted no time putting him on the Shit List.

"Oi, there he is—Nick!" Clive says, smoothing the hair that had been shaken out of place. "I've got to dash, but I wanted to, er, wish you two well."

"Capital idea," Nick says, with warmth so convincing that it surprises me for a second. "Sorry, with so many high-profile guests staying here, we've really tightened security. Let him through, lads. He's family."

A wordless current passes between Nick and his PPOs, before they nod curtly and turn their backs to us, blocking the hallway from other comers. Knowing what I know, this feels so much like a scene from a TV show—where the uniformed officers walk away to let the rogue detective deliver renegade justice—that I wonder if we are heading for a beat-down.

"Hope nobody sleepwalks out of their guest rooms tonight. Might end up with a black eye," Clive natters nervously, nodding his jaw at Twiggy. "Actually, Nick, mind if I have a word with Bex? Sentimental reasons. Eve of the wedding, old friends. You understand."

"We've come a long way together, eh?" Nick says, dripping kindness.

"Let's find a quiet spot." He leads us back down the private hall. "Why don't we step in here?"

Then, in a flash, Nick grabs him by the lapels of his tuxedo jacket and all but hurls him into a small, wooden-paneled study. He shoves Clive so hard that Clive crashes into a sweating ice bucket that's clearly been there a while, knocking its contents—including an open wine bottle—onto a round wooden coffee table, soaking a copy of the *International Herald Tribune.* There's a huge portrait of Prince Richard hung over the fireplace, and beneath it on the mantel is a framed shot of him with Christiane of Greece, which is what clues me in that this is his private study. I avert my gaze; I feel like I'm riffling through his underwear drawer.

Clive mops at his leg, trying to regain his composure. His eyes flick from a heavily breathing Nick to me, and back again. He looks shaken, as if he'd only expected capitulation. He'd thought he had me.

"So Bex came running to you for help," he says, tugging at his collar, failing to cover his unease. "I'll grant you, I was fooled out there. I didn't think you had it in you."

"Of course I did," I say. "You're an idiot if you thought I'd do anything else."

"You've got some brass, calling me an idiot," Clive says. "You lot never believed I was any good at my job, and look at us now. I own you." His cheeks are flushed a desperate red.

"Clive, this is madness," Nick says. "I don't understand. What's this about? Are you punishing us for Oxford? That was years ago, and Bex never meant to—"

"Of course. You would assume this is about Bex." Clive almost chokes. "As if any woman you deign to touch must be so irresistible to the rest of us. Honestly, do you really think I'd waste my time pining over someone who was such a pathetic mess when you left that she actually let your lecherous brother have a taste? You Lyons men may have a taste for the fragile ones, but I do not."

Nick does not take the bait. "Then what is it, if it's not Bex?"

"Certainly couldn't be to do with *you*, could it?" Clive is vibrating with something I can only classify as the beginnings of a tantrum. "God, you're arrogant. You can't even fathom that you might've put a foot wrong. I'm sick of being the only person who isn't in your thrall. Sick of people wetting themselves just to stand six feet from you. What did you do to deserve that? What makes you any better than the rest of us?"

"Nothing," Nick says. "And I'm the first to admit that."

"Obviously the huge emotional strain of being Nick's friend didn't keep you from enjoying the perks. Vacations, parties, free drinks." I ticked them off on my fingers. "If you hated him so much, why didn't you just leave us all alone?"

"I'm not thick enough to give up my access," Clive says snidely. "Besides, Nick's not the only person whose father has expectations for his behavior, not that either of you gives a damn about what it's like in my family."

"I do give a damn. We were mates, Clive," Nick says. His face looks very sad. "We were in it together."

"No, *you* were in it. And the rest of us had to march along, and got nothing in return," he says. "Nick wants to go out? Everyone stand around him. Nick needs to leave a bar drunk? Cut your night short and get him out. Nick wants a girl? Everyone stand aside, even if you're already dating her. And I did. I kept quiet. I waited, and gave you chances to help me, but evidently my loyalty wasn't worth a favor."

"I didn't realize you saw friendship as a transaction," Nick says coldly.

"I'm a journalist," Clive says. "And you knew that. You knew how I could have benefited from your help. But I didn't matter to you, did I? You thought I was just another brainwashed Lyons foot soldier who didn't have the bollocks to stand up for himself. But I do."

"Not enough bollocks to do it out in the open, without a pen name," I point out.

"What you're doing isn't journalism, Clive," Nick says. "And you know that."

"What I know is that you never took me seriously, and once you made that clear, I looked after myself. I bided my time. And eventually I landed on the gossip scoop of the century." Clive looks proud of himself. "Britain's Golden Boy, cuckolded by his own brother. I did the digging, I manipulated the sources, I got the story, all by myself. The Royal Flush is going to be bigger than Xandra Deane. And you're at *my* mercy now."

*You are here at the mercy of Her Majesty and me.* It is a coincidence that Clive echoed Richard, and only I know he's done it, but the parallel it draws between the chilly, damaged Prince of Wales and the conniving, broken Clive Fitzwilliam is scary and enlightening to me.

And then it's Lacey's face I see. Everything Clive has said—about feeling overshadowed, overlooked, underestimated—are the things my sister has felt, to some degree, for the last couple of years. And I didn't hear her, either, or else didn't want to, until she was pushed to the brink.

At the anger on Nick's face, Clive adds, "Oh, and don't get any juvenile ideas about having your hired thugs lock me in a closet, or something. Joss has very specific instructions to follow if I don't check in tonight."

"I can't believe you've dragged her into this, too," I say.

"I didn't have to drag her into anything. She hates you," Clive says. "You shoved her right into my lap. Lacey, too, really. It's the sad little rejects that make it the easiest."

Clive has twisted into something unrecognizable. I can't believe I ever thought he was handsome; he is so ugly to me now.

"You think you have all this power," I tell him. "But you don't. Because we won't give it to you. I don't care what you say about me. I am not informing on my own family."

"But that's the rub. If you don't, they won't *be* your family," Clive points out. "You're actually doing more harm than if you just worked with me. I could write such lovely things about you. Then maybe everyone would finally forget that you and that sister of yours are such social-climbing slappers."

"You know, if I weren't getting married tomorrow, I would punch you," Nick says, flexing his left hand. "But Bex needs to be able to fit my ring on my finger."

I step up. "Luckily, I'm right-handed," I say. "You want a slapper? You got it."

I smack his cheek so hard that my whole hand turns bright red and throbs. I hit him again anyway

Clive struggles to keep his balance, panting slightly. "You bitch," he curses, grabbing his face.

"Shut your disgusting mouth," Nick snaps, finally loosening his grip on himself a bit. "The pathetic thing is, if you'd hung in there until we were all a bit older, a bit further along, who knows what might've happened. But you couldn't wait. And so you blew your own cover."

Then Nick raises my hand to his mouth and kisses it. "Fifty years from now, Bex and I will still be married, and you will be nothing more than a sad footnote in history," he says. "So run whatever tawdry story you like. I really don't give a damn."

Clive looks gobsmacked.

"Now, would you like to walk out, or shall I call Stout and Twiggy for an escort?" Nick asks, with such tremendous Advanced Pleasantness that I will never look at that expression the same way again. "*They* are not getting married tomorrow, to my knowledge, and I think they're in the mood for a bit of a scuffle."

Clive blots at his mouth with his sleeve; his teeth cut his lip when I cracked him.

"Right, then," he says. "I guess all that's left to decide is when to publish. Perhaps just before the bride leaves for the Abbey. All those cheers turning to boos. It'll be poetic."

"Oh, piss off, you miserable..." Nick turns to me. "What was the word?"

"Asswad," I supply.

Clive is openly astonished that we're standing our ground, and his bottom teeth are smeared with red. "Fine, dig your own graves," he says. "I look forward to throwing you in them."

And he storms out and slams the door.

"Is it inappropriate if I say that you were really—"

Suddenly Nick's hands are in my hair, and he is kissing me firmly, like an exorcism.

"—hot just now," I say, when he pulls away. "I guess not."

"That bastard," Nick fumes. "It's a good job you slapped him or I'd have thrown him out the window."

He sits down on the arm of the sofa, rubbing his tensed hand, as if he can feel the effects of the punch he didn't let himself throw.

"Nick," I say, taking his hands. "Thank you for defending me, but I won't hold you to it. We don't have to get married just to stick it to him."

Nick looks down at our entwined fingers. My ring sparkles up at us.

"I heard you," he says. "With Mum, and at the Abbey. I heard Freddie in his speech." He lets out a laugh. "In an odd way, Clive argued your case, too. He was trying to insult you. But if the guy who hates us most in the world points out how at sea you were, it must have been true."

I do not speak. I don't want to interrupt what seems to be him coming back to me.

"I was so hurt, Bex. I still am hurt. I'm still sad. I don't know what to do about it. But I do know the answer isn't losing you," he says. "Freddie is right. Whatever this is... it doesn't happen twice in a lifetime. I'd rather work at this with you than settle for less with anyone else."

He stands up and draws me close. "You know what you said to me at the Abbey today?" he murmurs. "That you're mine for life?"

I nod, mutely.

"Thank you for that," he says. "Because I'm yours, too."

He pulls me in and kisses me, less of a passionate outburst and more of a rebirth, and it feels as if something heavy that had been sitting on my heart finally falls away.

"I'm sorry," I begin when we part, and he holds up his hand.

"No more apologies," he says. "I don't want you to think I'm holding something over you. I'm not. This isn't a favor. This is just love."

"I love you, too," I say, fervently, my eyes filling with tears. "Which is why I hate to bring this up, but..."

"The wedding," Nick says, leaning back against the couch.

"The PR disaster."

"Reality sets in." He sighs. "I'm too wrung out from all this to think clearly right now."

"Listen," I say, "if I've learned one thing from this entire nightmare, it's that we need to tell our friends when we need their help." I link my hands behind his neck, then kiss him one more time, mostly to revel in being able to do it again. "Time to call in the reinforcements."

Twenty minutes later, the study looks like an Oxford night of yore, with one glaring absence.

"CLIVE," Bea thunders. "I could murder him."

"Has anyone tried Joss?" Nick asks.

"Voice mail," Cilla says.

"Well, she can't hide forever," Bea spits. "Certainly not from her father. When Eleanor finds out what Joss is up to she'll probably make him hang up his speculum."

Our other friends had still been in the garden, and responded to my mayday text within ten minutes—except for Lacey, who hasn't answered her phone, and Gaz, who stopped by the kitchen on the way up, making the argument that crisis management of any sort required snacks. He is now pacing in front of the fireplace, gnawing on a mushroom tart.

"I've been thinking about this all day," he muses. "I can't seem to crack it. I wonder if I could get an injunction against him. It's the middle of the night. But it is for the Royal Family. But I don't know what the injunction would be for."

"Stalking?" Cilla suggests.

"Treason? Kind of?" Gemma Sands offers, sprawled out in an armchair.

"Invasion of privacy?" Nick asks.

"Unlawful scum-sucking and general psychosexual asshattery?" I offer from my perch next to him, as close as I can be without sitting in his lap. I think we're subconsciously so relieved to be on the same side again that we're loath to give each other any space.

"I don't think we have to reach that hard," says Gaz. "Blackmail itself is illegal. But we've not got any proof of any of it."

A fly buzzes past and Bea swipes at it, irritated, then puts her hand on her hip and stops pacing and points at me. "You," she says. "For God's sake, Bex, I told you years ago that if you couldn't hack it you bloody well ought to—"

Nick clears his throat pointedly. Bea closes her mouth and tugs on her long sleeve, trying to look composed.

"—have spoken to someone about your feelings," she finishes, head high.

"I know," I say. "Trust me. But I was afraid of what you'd say."

"Me?" Bea places her hand on her chest. "I am supportive. Look how well I trained you to get in and out of a car."

"Pet, you'd have horsewhipped her, and you know it," Gemma says pleasantly.

"Speaking of, where is your sister?" Bea says. "I've a verbal horsewhipping for *that* girl that she's had coming for years."

I put up my hand and start to speak but Freddie beats me to it.

"Leave it out, Bea," he says flatly, his voice stripped of its usual exuberance. "Trust me, Lacey could not feel any worse right now. She'll have gutted herself enough already."

Bea takes a look at his wretched visage, as he leans against a dark corner of the room staring moodily into a scotch, and her features soften in a way that I have never seen on her. She walks up to Freddie and takes his face in her hands.

"My darling boy," she says simply. She stands there for a second until he reddens, and then she clears her throat. "Yes, well, if you'd asked me which of us was going to end up blackmailing another, I'd have always said Clive." She turns on Gemma. "Bex's judgment is obviously questionable, but I can't believe *you* were ever with him."

Gemma wrinkles her nose. "You and I were in a fight! And it was barely dating," she says. "If it makes you feel better, he's a terrible kisser. If that's what you even want to call it."

Bea frowns. "I have to tell Pudge. She's still not answering her phone."

"What if Pudge is in cahoots with him, too?" Gaz says.

Bea folds her arms across her chest. "Have you forgotten how brutal the *Mail* and *The Sun* and the rest of them were to her during her five-year bender? Pudge hates the gossip press. She's only with him because she thinks he's writing fluff, like that moronic piece about the county councillor who also sells personalized cheese wheels."

"She told *me* Clive is mainly her tantric pupil," Gemma pipes up.

Bea flicks her hand. "The point is, who knows what he's got on her.

My sister is a celebrity, too, of a sort." She takes her phone out of her clutch. "I'm calling her again."

"And where is Lacey?" I say, frowning at my own phone. Nick squeezes my leg.

"She'll turn up, Bex," Freddie says. "She's probably with your mother."

"Paddington Larchmont-Kent-Smythe, your tantric pupil is a bastard," Bea is saying into her phone. "I want you to take his laptop and run it over with your car and then call me immediately."

Then she takes a pencil from the gold-plated cup on Richard's desk and jabs it through a hasty chignon, ready for war. Cilla leans over the back of the sofa and hands me a scotch.

"Drink up," she tells me. "It will bring you the strength of my forebears."

"You're from Yorkshire," I say, taking the glass from her.

"I have distant family in Inverness," she says. "It's quite dramatic, actually—"

"Enough." Bea stops her. "You can lie about Scotland after we vanquish Clive."

"I don't know if I think we *can* vanquish Clive," I say.

Bea slams her hand on the desk and then lifts it up to reveal the fly, crushed. "I can vanquish anything."

Nick tugs at his hair. "Let's assume you can't, and that this is running tomorrow no matter what," he said. "What's next?" He turns to Freddie. "What do you think?"

Freddie is surprised. He didn't expect to be consulted.

"Er, well. Let's see." Freddie pushes off from the wall and starts wearing his own groove in the floor. "I'm not sure what good Marj could do at this point. It's not like Clive works for the *Mail.* There's no one above him to call and turn the screws."

"Should we give her and Barnes a heads-up that this is coming?" I ask. Through a cracked window, I can still hear murmurs from the party. There are going to be some hungover dignitaries at the wedding. Maybe they'll be throwing up too much to check the Internet.

"We could," Freddie says. "But if we tell Barnes, he'll tell Father, who'll call Gran, and she'll probably scare up Agatha, who will call Edwin, because if she has to get dragged into this then she'll think he should, too." He shakes his head. "Then we'll all look peaky tomorrow."

"Unless they call it off," I say. "I mean, to me, that's the other issue."

The room gets quiet. Everyone, I can tell, is wondering which would be considered the greater ignominy: canceling the wedding, or going through it knowing the people gathering under the Buckingham Palace balcony will have read or heard my sister's testimony and think they're bearing witness to a sham. I wish Lacey were here, because as much as she was the architect of some of this, it doesn't feel right trying to solve it without her.

"If they cancel, then I think you're done, Bex," Bea finally says.

Gemma nods. So does Freddie.

"Bea's right," Nick says. "It's hard to come back from that in a month's time and say, 'Er, sorry about that, big misunderstanding, let's do it all again, shall we?' "

"Maybe we call Xandra Deane and give her a counter-scoop," says Cilla.

"About what?" Bea asks. "What could possibly overshadow this?"

"Quick, somebody plant drugs on Nigel," Gemma jokes.

"Plant them? More like find them," Freddie says. Then his eyes widen. "Maybe Lacey and I should elope."

This suggestion is met with chuckles, until we see he's not kidding.

"It's not actually the worst suggestion," Bea says slowly.

"Yes it is," Nick and I say, almost in unison.

"Think about it, though," Freddie says, coming around and sitting in front of us on the coffee table. "We can claim we were having a lovers' tiff and so she made up all that stuff to Clive. And if we're married, legally married, it mucks up his entire thesis that I'm snogging Bex and Lacey is furious about it, because if we were, why would she then go off and marry me?"

Bea opens her mouth and Gemma whacks her in the leg, shaking her head sternly. Freddie has turned pale, as if saying the words *I'm snogging Bex* was a step too close to revisiting the inciting incident in front of everyone.

Nick ponders this, then shakes his head.

"No," he says. "We've got a bit to work out, Fred, but that's a sacrifice you can't make. I won't allow you and Lacey to be stuck like that."

"I'm sure she'd muddle through," mutters Bea.

"It might be the only thing she and I can do, though," Freddie says helplessly, spreading his hands. "We owe you. We've got to do something." He is emotional. "*Please.*"

"I appreciate it. I do," Nick says. "But even discounting all that, we just cannot use the press," he says. "I think... I think Mum would hate it, if she knew. Don't you?"

Freddie nods slowly.

"So we batten down the hatches and ride it out," I say.

"I do think we probably have to tell Marj," Nick says. "I don't know if I can countenance giving her a heart attack tomorrow."

"Giving her one tonight isn't much nicer," Freddie points out.

"Maybe not, but I don't want it to look like she napped on the job," Nick says. "She might be of help. You never know. She's got a crafty streak, that one." He stands up. "But I do have one thing I'd like to do first."

He takes my hand and scoots down on one knee. "Gran is perfectly welcome to cancel the wedding tomorrow if she'd like," he says. "But she can't cancel our marriage. Not if we do it now." He kisses my palm. "Marry me tonight."

The words give me a thrill—and, apparently, have the same effect on Gaz, who gasps and clasps his hands together. His mushroom tart falls to the floor.

"Eleanor can have it annulled," Cilla points out.

"Not if neither one of us signs the papers," Nick says.

"She can make you abdicate your position," Bea says.

"I'll call her bluff. She'd *never*," Nick says. "It would turn a house fire into an inferno."

"Plus she'd have to bump me up a notch, which she wouldn't, because it's all my bloody fault to begin with," Freddie said. "And she can't dock us both and put Edwin two heartbeats closer to the throne. She'd rather marry Bex herself."

Nick turns to me. "Can I get up now, love?" he asks.

"Oh, shit! Yes," I say. "I'm sorry. And I just swore during this romantic moment."

Nick pulls me up to standing position with him. "Wouldn't be the first time," he says lovingly. "I seem to recall you using that word when I gave you the ring in the first place."

"Can we really do this?" I ask.

"Why not?" he says. "We've got the marriage license, right?"

He looks at Freddie, who nods.

"And the rings," Nick says.

"Safe as houses back at ours," Freddie confirms.

"And we've got a whole room full of witnesses," Nick says. "We can sneak into the chapel at St. James's from Clarence House. We just need a minister."

"You can get ordained in five minutes on the Internet, though, right?" I ask. "Gaz would kill it."

Gaz heaves a disappointed sigh. "As correct as that is, it is my great displeasure to inform you that, in the UK, we need a proper vicar for it to be legal."

"This reminds me of my cousin," Cilla begins.

"Now is not the time," Bea snaps.

"My cousin, the *vicar*," Cilla finishes, giving Lady Bollocks a piercing look. "He's actually my mum's cousin. He would've done our wedding, except he isn't speaking to her."

"Can he keep his mouth shut?" Bea asks.

"He has with Cilla's mum," Gaz pointed out.

"Might be a tough secret to keep anyway." Nick says. He looks at me. "Bex. My love. Once and for all, are you in?"

I smile up at him. "I always wanted a small wedding."

# CHAPTER FIVE

I can't breathe under here," I cough. "I don't know how I did this so often."

"Well," Cilla says from above me, "you were pretty stonking drunk most times."

We'd gotten the green light from Nick an hour after our summit. PPO Twiggy was off on his motorbike fetching the vicar, the rest of the gang was gathering the license and rings, and Lacey responded to my all-caps text with a message saying not to do anything else drastic until she got to me. Cilla and I passed the time reverting me from Rebecca into Bex, and dissecting every conversation we'd ever had with Clive for hints at the cunning we'd clearly missed. We came up empty. Other than veiled remarks about Paris, which seemed self-pitying then and now look designed to inspire a servile pity in *us*, there was nothing. Clive's poker face was expert, and we'd quite simply been had.

"I feel almost sorry for Joss," I'd said, pulling back on my jeans. "And sorry *about* her. I feel responsible. She really was so angry at me, Cil. Maybe I could've done more."

"That one was born under an irrational star," Cilla had said as she zipped my Jenny Packham back into its hanging bag. "You can't worry about her if she's not worried about you. Let's get you and Nick sorted instead."

And thus, I am sneaking into Clarence House in the back of PPO

Popeye's car—or, more accurately, on the floor in the back, under a very familiar, itchy afghan.

"Like old times," Cilla had laughed when Popeye threw open the Mercedes door to reveal my old nemesis. He'd grinned mischievously, his telltale piece of spinach clinging to his left upper bicuspid. Like old times indeed.

"I can't believe I agreed to this. Clarence House is basically down the street. I should've just walked," I say, lifting up the blanket. A wisp of cool air comes in and I inhale it hungrily.

Cilla, sitting in an actual seat as Nick used to do, giggles. "Can you imagine? All of these people lined up to see you and you just stroll past, merry as you please?"

"They wouldn't even look twice," I say. "Freddie used to pull that in Piccadilly Circus. I don't know if I'd have the guts."

"That boy always was reckless," Cilla says.

A question, still unanswered, bubbles to the fore. "Cil, is this crazy? Can Nick really forgive and forget?" I ask. "Can anyone?"

The sound of Cilla breathing out through her nose tells me she's considering this very seriously.

"I think he has already forgiven," she says. "As for the other, I don't know, Bex, but maybe it's better if people don't forget. Because history only repeats itself when they do." She nudges me with her foot. "We're here."

I feel the car turn into the drive, and think how apt it is that we're taking our next steps at a place built and christened for another important Duke of Clarence: the eventual William IV. As Popeye comes to a smooth halt, my phone buzzes. I give a Pavlovian shudder, but it's just Lacey: Good news. Almost there.

Nick is bouncing with anticipation as he opens the door. Then a look that's of unutterable comfort to me washes over his face; a mixture of love and awe and nostalgia.

"That's the same thing you were wearing the day we met," he says, his voice thick.

I glance down. I am in *better* jeans, and a *cleaner* navy-and-white-striped tee, and the Botox in my armpits prevents me from ever getting that sweaty anymore. But thematically he is correct.

"Full circle," I tell him. "You did just open the door for me."

Nick leads us through Clarence House, and out to a pass-through into the courtyard of St. James's Palace, the most senior of them all and the official seat of the monarchy. Portions of St. James's were destroyed in a fire, but among the bits that still stand is the rectangular Chapel Royal. When Nick pushes open its doors, I see a ceiling fresco done by my old friend Hans Holbein—it feels right that he's here somehow—and Gemma and Bea lighting tall white tapers at the altar. Nick and I face each other with the hugest smiles. Then he takes my hand and runs a finger over the Lyons Emerald.

"N and B," he says. "A nice, normal wedding, just for them."

"I think we need to let N and B out of the house more often. And not just for the Navy, or Paint Britain," I say. "Our lives can't always be Marj's show to run, or Eleanor's. I want to be what's expected of me, but there has to be a way to do that while also making sure we don't lose ourselves again. Don't you think?"

Nick nods. "I can't promise it will be easy, but I swear to you, Bex, I will always fight for you. For *us*. We're a team."

"We're a team."

I squeeze Nick's hand. I am jittery with basically everything: nerves, anticipation, love, and a lurking fear that Richard will come bursting through the doors to put a stop to this.

The doors do, in fact, burst open, but it's just PPO Twiggy and a small, balding man in a crooked clerical collar.

"Oof, sorry if I bumped into you there, Officer Thingy," he slurs. "I'm a wee drunky, in point of fact. Usually off duty by now." He hiccups. "Lovely to see you all. Which one of you is my cousin?"

Cilla rolls her eyes. "Right here, Cousin Bernard," she says.

Bernard eyes the flame-haired Gemma. "You sure it's not her?"

"Reasonably," Cilla says, steering her cousin over to a nearby pew, and sitting him down with a pat on the shoulders. "Bernard, I know you're half in the bag right now, but do you think you could toss together a quick wedding for my friends?"

Bernard squints over at us. "Crikey, they're a bit tall."

"Does that affect things, do you think?" Cilla asks patiently.

Bernard considers it. "Shouldn't think so," he says. "It's mildly frowned upon to marry people when you're as bladdered as I am, but..." He puts his fingers to his lips. "I won't tell if you won't."

Freddie tries to stifle a laugh, the first sign of real lightness I've seen from him all day. "Is it too late to book Bernie for tomorrow?" he wonders. "The look on Gran's face would be worth more than the entire Abbey."

Next to him, Bea huffs, "I suppose I should not be shocked that there is not a more elegant solution to this muddle."

"You wanted discreet," Cilla says impatiently. "There's nothing better than a man who might wake up tomorrow and think it was all a dream. Besides, this is the only vicar we've got. You want to keep faffing around or can we get on with it?"

Cousin Bernard has scooted toward Gemma. "Shall I take your confession?" he slurs, with a suggestive nudge.

"It'd make your ears bleed, Father," Gemma says cheerfully. "And we need to get this sorted. We're running out of time."

"But Lacey isn't here yet." I feel a twinge of panic. Our relationship is still bent, but I can't meet this milestone without her.

"Bex!" I hear, and there she is, like magic, breaking away from PPO Stout. We hug each other tightly, the most enthusiastic one I've gotten from Lacey in years, before I notice that she's also trailed by my mother and Aunt Kitty (who has gone from jet-lagged to looking like she thinks she's hallucinating). Both are wearing pajamas under their matching trenches, as if Lacey has dragged them out of bed at the last minute—which is probably exactly what she's done.

"Hi, Nancy," Nick says, coming down the aisle to meet her. "Sorry about the hour."

Mom rubs her eyes. "Lacey said something about the wedding? Is it on?" she asks, yawning. "She's a bit too keyed up to give good details."

"It is happening right now, in fact," Nick says, glancing over at me. "Once we tell Marj, tomorrow's show might not go on, so...just in case."

"Well," Mom says after a beat. "That seems sensible."

"I think I've missed something," I hear Aunt Kitty whisper.

"Just a spot of blackmail," Gaz tells her soothingly.

"Yeah, about that," Lacey says. "Good news! I kind of did something."

There is a collective groan. Even Bernard groans.

"That's what got us here in the first place," complains Bea.

"No, no, it's good. I think," Lacey says, flushing. "I saw Nick leave the party, and Clive wasn't even that subtle about sneaking after him, and I just got so mad. I couldn't believe he had the balls to show up acting like we're still friends, and then *stalk* you, right there at Buckingham freaking Palace. So I followed him. When I got to Stout and Twiggy, they were more than happy to tell me where the three of you were." She snickers. "Stout even slipped me a Taser."

Stout suddenly seems very busy with a button on his coat.

"I was tempted to barge in and use it, too," she says. "But then I got to the door and I could hear Clive talking. And I got a better idea."

She pulls her phone out of her pocket, swipes at it, and pushes play. It's a little quiet, and crackly, but it's there: "*I did the digging, I manipulated the sources, I got the story, all by myself. The Royal Flush is going to be bigger than Xandra Deane. And you're at* my *mercy now.*"

"I believe this is what they call being hoisted on your own petard," Gaz says.

"How did you even get this?" Nick is clearly impressed, and frankly, so am I. Whatever I thought Lacey had been up to all evening, gathering evidence wasn't on the list.

Lacey blushes. "It's a little ridiculous," she says, "and I didn't even know if it would work. But I figured, why not borrow from the Douchebag Playbook that got us here? So I used the voice memo on my phone, and kind of jammed the end of it under the door. I spent that entire fight on my stomach in the hallway of Buckingham Palace, praying nobody would go to bed early." She wrinkles her nose. "The Queen Mum did walk by, but she just poked me with her cane and told me a curtsy would have sufficed."

"You're lucky she didn't crack you on the head with it," Freddie noted.

"Anyway, I got almost everything," Lacey finishes proudly. "I stopped just before the very end because I was afraid Clive would catch me when he left, and he would have stepped on me. Plus, I had to get to Pudge."

"Pudge?" Bea asks sharply. "You've talked to her?"

"She was still at the party," Lacey says. "I remembered you saying she hates this stuff, so I played it for her." Lacey takes a breath. She is enjoying having the group in the palm of her hand. "She was fuming. Said she was going to go do unmentionable stuff to his chakras. And then she had me email it to her."

Gaz takes the phone. "Let me hear this," he says, walking off past Bernard, who is now fully snoozing, his mouth wide open.

"I mean, I don't know if this fixes anything. His piece can still run," Lacey says. "But at least we have counter-proof that he's a disgusting scumbag, and it's entirely possible Pudge beat him home and put his laptop in the dishwasher. I may have undone the effects of all that time she spent in the ashram, but..."

She trails off. There is a moment of silence in the candlelit Chapel Royal while everyone processes this. Nick and I exchange dumbfounded looks. Then I wrap my sister in my arms.

"Even if it doesn't work," I whisper, "you are my hero. Thank you, Lacey."

Lacey squeezes me back. Over her shoulder, I see Nick watching us. He looks pensive, and I know he's thinking about his brother, standing alone across the aisle.

Gaz wanders back over to us. "It might not stand up in court, but it's jolly gripping," he says. "If it ever needs to fall into Xandra Deane's hands, a transcript wouldn't make you two look tremendous, but it would make him look like a sociopath. Hearing it might be enough to shut him up, at least temporarily."

"Well done, Lacey," Freddie says admiringly. "And to think, I almost had to rope you into eloping with me to create a diversion."

Lacey looks alarmed.

"Don't worry, I never would've pimped you out," I tell her.

"Thank God," Lacey says. "I think one Porter is all that family can handle."

We hug again, bringing in Mom and a bleary Aunt Kitty, as Freddie walks over to Nick and extends his hand.

"Thank you for letting me be here," I hear him say. "I meant what I said tonight. I respect you, and I love you, and—"

Nick cuts him off by grabbing his proffered hand, which turns into one of those guy embraces where they first slap each other on the back, and then give in to it.

Cilla clears her throat. "So, are we actually going to have a wedding, or do you lot just plan to spend all night slobbering all over each other?" But her tone is kind.

She leans over and pokes Cousin Bernard, who jolts awake.

"Did I miss my cue?" He peers at Nick as he clambers to his feet. "Don't I know you?"

"No," Cilla says, steering him to the altar.

Watching her wrangle everyone into their places, I pull Lacey to the side.

"Walk me up the aisle. Please," I say. "You should be up there with me tomorrow, too, but since it's too late for that, maybe this is our second chance to do it right." I pause. "Or... our first chance, technically. You get the gist."

Lacey beams and blots at her eyes. "I do," she says meaningfully, through a sniffle. Then she processes my jeans and striped shirt and bursts out laughing. "Only you would change out of a designer gown and into jeans for your own wedding."

I look down at myself and laugh, too.

"I can be a duchess tomorrow," I tell her. "Right now I just want to be *me*."

Lacey and my mother and I loop arms, me in my jeans, my mother in her pajamas, my sister still in her ball gown—and, I like to think, my father watching closely from somewhere blissful, in his Cubs cap. Together we walk the comparatively compact thirty feet to my groom, still in half of his tux, the hair on his head agitated from a night of tugging at it. We look at each other with enormous smiles, tears rolling freely down our cheeks, the two of us doing all the sloppy emoting that we cannot tomorrow even if I am allowed up that aisle.

My mother takes Nick's hand and places it on top of ours.

"We're not giving her away, sweetie," Mom tells him lovingly. "We're bringing you in. Welcome to our family."

Nick's lip quivers. They release us and step back, sniffling, as Bernard clears his throat.

"Dearly beloved," he begins, hiccupping again and swaying slightly. "In the presence of God, and those other chaps in his gang, we have come together to witness the marriage of..." He peeks down at the cheat sheet Cilla wisely provided and then looks back up at us and blanches. "My liege," he sputters, bumbling into a kneel.

"Discretion, Bernard," Cilla prods, tapping her nose.

"Of course, but I'm just so honored to...oh, hellcrackers, I should probably start again," he says, returning to his feet. "Don't suppose anyone has any coffee? No? Right." He smacks himself on both cheeks, like an angry man applying aftershave, then takes a meditative breath. "Get cracking, Bernard, bring your A-game."

Nick nudges me with a grin. "Well, there goes that nice, normal wedding."

I smile back through tear-filled eyes. "That's okay. Normal has never been our strong suit, right?"

"Dearly beloved," Bernard begins anew, with fresh command. "In the presence of God, the Father, the Son, and Holy Spirit, we have come together today to witness the wedding of Nicholas and Rebecca, to pray for God's blessing on them, to share their joy and to celebrate their love..."

His words melt into me as Nick and I look into each other's joyful faces. I don't know if we will wake up tomorrow to blistering scandal or blessed silence. I don't know if we will live blissfully, or go blind from looking for trouble in our periphery every day until we are old. And yet, as the vicar performs the familiar ceremony, I do not float above myself. There is no fear of what lies in wait for us, no nostalgia for where I've been or who I was, no temptation to stop and say good-bye to a version of myself I'm leaving behind. I am fully in the moment when Nick and I say the words that have united millions of couples across hundreds of years, because they are the culmination of eight years of friendship and longing and love that began on a rainy Oxford night and survived in the face of every other element. So it no longer matters whether we're allowed to make these vows again, in front of the Queen or the country or the world. Here, in this hallowed place, I have made them to the only person who counts, and he to me. The kiss that blesses these promises forges the only certainty I need: that even if we are never a duke and a duchess, we will forever be Nick and Bex. An unbreakable we, at last.

*The End*

# ACKNOWLEDGMENTS

Our first and most fervent thank-you doubles as an apology to everyone in our lives whom we accidentally neglected in the process of writing this book. For nearly a year, we were down the rabbit hole of royals and research and world-building, writing and revising and cutting. We must have said the words "I can't, I have to work" a thousand times, and we're infinitely grateful that our friends and family heard them so patiently, and stuck with us, never taking our reclusive behavior personally. Special thanks in this regard goes to Carrie Weiner, who frequently put out our hair when it was on fire. We will be repaying her with infinite Diet Cokes and snacks.

We owe the world to our impeccable and indispensable agent, Brettne Bloom, whom we're also lucky to call a beloved friend. Thank you to Elizabeth Bewley for the gift of Brettne when we needed her most; you are as sunny as your *Royal We* namesake but exponentially smarter. Thank you to Hachette for its support of us as authors, and for keeping us in the family by bringing *The Royal We* to Grand Central. We are grateful to the entire GCP team for all its hard work and enthusiasm, especially our brave editor, Sara Weiss, who stared down a first draft that was...well, let's just say "longer." Our copy editor Angelina Krahn was tireless in keeping our draft clean and our semicolons in check (no small feat there). Thanks to Mari Okuda for not killing us after we turned in our notes on our page proofs. And cover designers Elizabeth Turner and Anne Twomey worked themselves to the bone, and their design—using brilliantly funky artwork from Noma Bar—makes us as proud and excited as the words we put inside it. Thank you so much, all of you, for your collective genius.

We're intensely grateful to Eliza Hindmarch for giving our manuscript a tireless and thorough "Britishisms" pass (any errors on that front are ours, for what we decided to call "artistic license"); to Annalisa, The Madam Editor, for helping us make sense of Britain's approximately eighty-two million daily newspapers; to The Royal Order of Sartorial Splendor website and Ella Kay from the Court Jeweller for being indispensable resources about monarchial tiaras and other sparkly regalia; and to Julie O'Sullivan for helping craft the alternate history that enabled our Lyons dynasty to come to pass. Nick's cryptic crossword clues originated in the Sunday *Times* cryptic 4561 by Tim Moorey, originally published on October 27, 2013. And we wouldn't have any of our favorite details about the interior of Buckingham Palace if not for the hugely sympathetic and kind guides and guards there, who took pity on the two sad American women who idiotically showed up at the wrong time for their tour. Tickets are available on an extremely limited basis and we nearly missed what was our only window; thank you, everyone at Buck House, for accepting our tragic apologies and finagling us into the last tour of the day. We had the most wonderful experience there and no, we're not just saying that because the tour ends with Champagne. Although that didn't exactly hurt.

We also probably ought to acknowledge the Duke and Duchess of Cambridge. It was November 2013 when we first suggested those two should have another baby right around the time *our* baby would be published, for optimal synergy. Apparently they took that to heart. Thanks, you two. You're extremely thoughtful.

And last, but never least, we need to thank our own families (royally, if you will): Jim and Susan Morgan; Elizabeth Morgan; the Hamiltons and the O'Sullivans; Maria Huezo, without whom no deadlines would be met; Gail Mock; and Kathie Cocks (plus, we believe, a dose of extra luck from the Great Beyond, courtesy of Alan Cocks). We thank Dylan and Liam Mock for the cuddles and their indomitable cheer when we were too stressed to see straight, and Kevin Mock, for picking up way more than his fair share of slack. You are, collectively, the most sterling support system, and we love you like Gaz loves curry.